THE
TOKEN

Also by Sharon Bolton

Sacrifice
Awakening
Blood Harvest
Little Black Lies
Daisy in Chains
Dead Woman Walking
The Split
The Night Train
The Pact
The Fake Wife
The Neighbour's Secret

The Craftsmen series
The Craftsman
The Buried

The Lacey Flint series
Now You See Me
If Snow Hadn't Fallen
Dead Scared
Like This, For Ever
A Dark and Twisted Tide
Here Be Dragons
The Dark

Sharon (formerly S J) **Bolton** lives in Buckinghamshire with her husband and, occasionally, her grown-up son and is working on her nineteenth novel – her ninth with Orion. Her first book, *Sacrifice*, was voted Best New Read by Amazon UK, while her second, *Awakening*, won the 2010 Mary Higgins Clark Award (part of the prestigious Edgars) in the US. In 2014, she won the CWA Dagger in the Library. She has been shortlisted for the CWA Gold Dagger, the CWA Steel Dagger, the Theakston's Prize for Best Thriller, the International Thriller Writers' Best First Novel award, the Prix du Polar (France) and the Martin Beck Award (Sweden).

THE TOKEN

SHARON BOLTON

ORION

First published in Great Britain in 2025 by Orion Fiction,
an imprint of The Orion Publishing Group Ltd.
Carmelite House, 50 Victoria Embankment
London EC4Y 0DZ

An Hachette UK Company

The authorised representative in the EEA is Hachette Ireland,
8 Castlecourt Centre, Dublin 15, D15 XTP3, Ireland (email: info@hbgi.ie)

1 3 5 7 9 10 8 6 4 2

Copyright © Sharon Bolton 2025

The moral right of Sharon Bolton to be identified as
the author of this work has been asserted in accordance
with the Copyright, Designs and Patents Act of 1988.

All rights reserved. No part of this publication may be
reproduced, stored in a retrieval system, or transmitted
in any form or by any means, electronic, mechanical,
photocopying, recording, or otherwise, without the
prior permission of both the copyright owner and the
above publisher of this book.

All the characters in this book are fictitious, and any resemblance
to actual persons, living or dead, is purely coincidental.

A CIP catalogue record for this book is
available from the British Library.

ISBN (Hardback) 9781 3987 2310 8
ISBN (Export Trade Paperback) 9781 3987 2311 5
ISBN (eBook) 9781 3987 2313 9
ISBN (Audio) 9781 3987 2314 6

Typeset by Input Data Services Ltd, Bridgwater, Somerset

Printed in Great Britain by Clays Ltd, Elcograf, S.p.A.

www.orionbooks.co.uk

For Finnley David Cooper, our 'fair-haired warrior'.

DAY FOURTEEN

Tuesday, 16 October

Prologue

The bow of the boat reared like an angry horse; a second later it plunged deep beneath the surface. As a great wave surged towards her, Holly Baker realised she might have made the worst mistake of her life. She could die out here. And never see her son again.

The water hit her full in the face, a foretaste of what drowning would feel like.

Gasping, Holly struggled to keep upright on the drenched seat. Beyond the sails, she saw the swell of the ocean, mustering its strength, getting ready to throw them into the night again. Each time they slammed down into water that felt solid as rock, she felt sure the hull would shatter.

She clenched her eyes shut and tried to picture her son's face. Pale skin, big dark eyes, curly hair that he hated getting cut.

Closing her eyes didn't help. With her eyes closed the sounds of the Atlantic at night amplified. The sea sucked at the boat, as though trying to eat it whole, and the wind was a constant presence: racing through sails, dancing around the mast, tormenting the numerous ropes until they rattled like old bones.

'Big one,' muttered the skipper. He was a man in his mid-fifties called Thomas, with fading red hair and a faint Cornish accent. Holly had met him hours earlier, had handed him her life with a brief shake of the hand. He'd promised them his boat, a forty-foot sailing yacht called *Gemini*, which was more than capable of taking eight people to St Helen's on the Isles of Scilly. The night crossing would be dull, a bit cold, but he had to be back in Plymouth by midweek.

They'd set out on water still as a mill pond, gleaming gold in the setting sun; the storm had come from nowhere. An experienced sailor might have spotted the cumulonimbus clouds on the western horizon and known that severe weather was imminent. Holly had not. Which rather begged the question – why hadn't the skipper?

From Plymouth Sound, Thomas had aimed for Lizard Point, the most southerly tip of Cornwall, informing his crew that the wind was a steady northwesterly, sixteen knots, perfect sailing conditions. Tug, one of the other passengers, who didn't seem affected by the rolling, rocking motion, had cooked supper. All had been well. But then the wind had strengthened, tipping the boat over at what felt like an impossible angle and most of their small group had been unable to keep their food down. A relentless darkness had fallen, and the land became a series of distant lights. Rain fell and the wind started to gust. Those not required on deck had gone below.

And now, somewhere between two and three o'clock in the morning, three people were on watch: Holly, the skipper and a man called Craig who'd spoken little since the storm broke. He sat beside Holly on the starboard cockpit seat, his gaze fixed on the ocean.

The two-metre wave, the promised 'big one', rolled beneath the hull and then they were roller-coasting down the other side. Almost immediately, the next wave broke over the bow, surging up the side decks, cascading over the cabin roof. Holly turned her head to avoid taking it full in the face.

Some way behind the boat – impossible to judge distances at night – she caught sight of two tiny lights, one red, one white. Thomas had told her to keep a look-out for other vessels; the big ships moved fast. She was on the point of mentioning it when both lights vanished.

'It's pushing thirty-five knots,' Thomas said. Craig answered with a grunt.

There was something up with these two. Hours earlier, Holly had begun to suspect they didn't get along, and that made no sense, because if it hadn't been for Craig's old friend Thomas, who owned a boat, the trip wouldn't have been possible. But she'd seen none of the ease in each other's company, heard none of the banter, that signified old mates. They'd spoken together rarely and only then in hushed voices.

'Where are we?' she asked, finding her voice.

Thomas didn't look her way. 'About five miles further west than when you last asked.'

He hadn't struck Holly as being a talkative man, but he'd grown increasingly silent, even sullen, as the night passed. She wondered, and it wasn't a comforting thought, whether he too was alarmed by the turn the weather had taken.

'Holly.' Thomas turned her way. 'I'm getting odd readings from the chart plotter. Could you go below and check what position the instruments are giving you? You'll find paper on the chart table. Write it down.'

Below was the last place Holly wanted to be. Going below made the nausea twice as bad. But she did need the loo. She got to her feet, bracing herself against the tilt of the boat.

'You can put the kettle on if you want,' Craig said.

He was joking. She hoped. There was no way she was handling boiling water.

'Close the hatch behind you,' Thomas warned.

The cabin was even darker than the last time Holly had been below. In fact, pitch black. It smelt of sweat and vomit, of diesel and the remains of supper that only Tug, Craig and the skipper had been able to keep down. Two indistinct forms lay on the two bunks: Tug would be one, Robin the other. One of them was snoring in a steady, rhythmic fashion. Tara and Sabri, two of the other women on board, were in the starboard stern cabin, while Cheryl, too large to share, was in the bow cabin by herself. When the current watch ended, Tug and Robin would go up top with Sabri and Tara. Cheryl had been excused watch duty.

Using memory alone, Holly found the door of the toilet, or the heads, as she'd been taught to call it. The tiny cabin stank like the public lavatories in Exeter city centre. The light switch didn't work for some reason, but she could hear liquid sloshing about on the floor. Refusing to speculate about its nature, she tugged off her lifejacket and coat. The boat bounced, throwing her against the fibreglass wall. Bracing herself, she pulled down her jeans and managed to land on the tiny toilet.

Back in the main cabin, a figure made her jump, but it was only Tara, in fleece pyjamas, fluffy socks on her feet, which she'd regret if she was heading for the loo. She carried a tiny torch that shone a beam of bright light in the gloom. A loud snore rang out.

'I can't believe they can sleep in this.' Tara kept her voice low. 'I heard Tug say the wind was a force six gusting seven.'

'Is that bad?' Holly asked.

Tara shrugged; she didn't know either.

'How's it going up there?' Tara glanced at the hatch. 'Still raining?'

'Hard to tell where the water's coming from.' Holly groped her way towards where she remembered the chart table being. There'd been a series of tiny lights on it earlier, but they all seemed to have gone out. As though the boat had lost all power. Tara's next words stopped her. 'I hope we're doing the right thing.'

Holly opened her mouth to reply and found herself flying through the air. She crashed into the chart table and for a moment was conscious of nothing but pain. A deafening crashing sounded from above, followed by the scraping of running lines. In the cabin, crockery rattled in one of the cupboards and the cutlery tray flew open, scattering utensils across the floor. As the boat righted itself, Tug sat upright.

'What the hell?' He seemed fully awake. 'Who's on deck? And what happened to the frigging lights?'

'I'm on deck.' Holly had no memory of getting to her feet, but she was clutching the companionway rail, heaving herself up the steps, pushing aside the hatch as the boat tipped again.

Chaos. A sea-soaked, bewildering scene of chaos.

Water was surging over the port deck. The boom, the huge, reinforced tube of aluminium that held the main sail in place, was swinging from one side of the cockpit to the other. There was no sign of either the skipper or Craig. Ignoring the pain in her ribs,

Holly stretched up to look over the cabin roof towards the bow. Both men had vanished.

The boat swung again, tipped again, and a torrent of water came racing along the starboard deck.

'Skipper!' she yelled. 'Craig!'

The guard rail was under water. They were going over this time, and there was nothing she could do to prevent it. She clung hard, could feel herself falling.

Holly slid along the cockpit floor, could see the ocean beyond the stern, a great, gaping maw, greedy to claim her, and came up hard against the wheel. As she clung on, thinking of nothing but survival, the boat straightened and veered round, bringing the boom crashing across the cockpit again.

'What's happening?'

She twisted round to see Tug, his coat unfastened, no life jacket, yelling at her from the cabin steps.

'Craig and Thomas are gone.' Holly had to shout to be heard. 'They're not on the boat.'

Muttering a curse, Tug pulled himself into the cockpit, ducking low to avoid the swinging boom.

'Hold her steady,' he called. 'Put the engine on.'

As Holly fought her way round the wheel to the engine controls, she saw Tug grab the main sheet, the rope that controlled the huge sail, and haul it in. She pressed the *On* button. Nothing happened. There was a *Start* button too, so she pressed that. Nothing. The buttons seemed dead. She noticed, then, that the electronic instrument panels had gone dark.

Tug, behind her now, pulled her to her feet.

'See if you can see them,' he yelled into her ear. 'Keep hold of something. Robin, get up here!'

The other man, Robin, appeared on the cabin steps.

'We've got a man overboard.' Tug was still bent over the engine switches as he yelled at the new arrival. 'Get to the radio. Press that red button, the one with the plastic cover. Hold it down for five seconds then release. Holly, can you see them?'

Holly had both arms wrapped tight around the back rail. 'Nothing,' she shouted back.

'The life jackets have lights,' Tug yelled. 'You'll see them. What the fuck is wrong with this engine?'

So much black water. Holly blinked. Was that . . .?

She felt Tug grab her hand, then close it around a rope. 'Hold this,' he told her. 'Let it go when I say so. I need to reduce the jib.'

There was something in the ocean, but it was so hard to judge distances at night.

'OK, release it slowly,' Tug was saying. 'Keep your eyes on the water.'

The rope burned through Holly's hand as Tug wound half the big sail away. Behind her, in the cockpit, she heard Tara's voice.

'Tug, Robin says he doesn't think the radio is working. Can you come and look at it?'

Something that could have been a light. There it was again. Gone in an instant, but this time, she was sure. 'I saw a light. Tug, I saw a light.'

She glanced up at the tall man by her side. In the darkness, his face seemed frozen in terror.

'Tug!'

He seemed to pull himself together. 'Point to it,' he told her. 'Don't take your eyes off it. Not for a second.' To Tara he called, 'Get Robin up here. I need someone on the helm.'

Holly turned back to face the stern. The light was gone.

'I've told Cheryl to stay in her cabin!' Minutes later, Tug was at the helm, the only one capable of stopping the boat from being swamped by waves. His fingers clutched the wheel like claws. Even with his strength, every gust, every rogue wave, threatened to spin them out of control again. 'She's not mobile enough to move around the boat right now.'

Holly, Tara, Robin and Sabri were squeezed together on the starboard cockpit seat, holding on for dear life and staring down into churning black water. The relentless pounding of the waves against the hull seemed to have intensified.

Tug wiped salt water from his face. 'OK, it looks like something happened, maybe a freak wave, maybe the boat hit something in the water, and both Craig and Thomas went overboard. They're both wearing life jackets, so should still be alive, and our first responsibility is to find them.'

Holly glanced sideways, from Robin to Tara to Sabri. Three faces, all looking as terrified as she felt.

'On top of that we've no electrics,' Tug went on. 'I can't begin to explain how that happened, but there we are. I've switched batteries, but it makes no difference. We can't put the engine on or radio for help. We're out of phone range and will be for hours yet. With this cloud cover I can't even use what little astral navigation I once knew. On the plus side, the boat looks sound, the conditions are challenging but manageable and we can use the sails. And we know roughly what heading we were following. We have to retrace our course and look for our two lost crew members.'

A shock of fear rippled through Holly. Go back? They couldn't go back. They had to press on, as fast as they could.

'Shouldn't we launch the life raft?' Tara called.

'Not while the boat is safe,' Tug replied. 'And let's all pray it stays that way. Right, that's your job, Tar. I need you to poke your head below every five minutes. Any sign of water on the cabin floor and we rethink. The rest of the time, both you and Sabri look out for anything in the water. You too, Holly.'

There had been water on the floor. In the heads.

'How could they both go overboard?' Sabri looked as though she suspected Holly of sabotaging the boat. 'Did neither of them say something? Call for help?'

'Not that I heard.'

'Likely one of them slipped and grabbed the other,' Tug replied. 'Either way there's a good chance we'll spot them.'

'What if we don't?' Sabri asked.

'We'll find them,' Tara said.

'And if we don't?' Sabri insisted.

For a second, no one replied. Then Robin spoke up.

'I guess we split the money six ways.'

DAY ONE

Wednesday, 3 October

Chapter 1

I'm doing it, texted Holly. *Today. I'm burning this place to the ground.*

The conditions were perfect for arson. It hadn't rained for a fortnight and the wind was light but constant. The building, with lots of old timber, would go up like a torch. In the bag at her feet were a box of Cook's matches and a bottle of nail varnish remover. Down the corridor was a room that wouldn't be used for the next hour, and she knew from experience that she'd find in it a lot of flammable material.

An emoji came back: a man's cartoon face holding a hand against his forehead. At the same time, the woman across the desk put the phone receiver down.

'Sorry about that.' She gave Holly a tight smile. 'Where were we?'

'You were about to explain why that bitch in human form thinks it's OK to read my son's worry book out to the entire class. He's embarrassed, humiliated and feels completely betrayed. Do you have any idea how hard it was for me to get him in the car this morning?'

'Miss Baker.' Lines appeared around the headteacher's mouth like the rays on a child's drawing of the sun. 'Either you moderate your language, or this interview is at an end. I won't tell you again.'

'OK, she's an insensitive, unprofessional bully who thinks embarrassing and humiliating a ten-year-old is acceptable behaviour. That worry book is private. My son has it for a reason. This has all—'

'I understand he was writing in it while the class was engaged in a task.'

Holly clenched her fists. 'That's literally what it's there for. He needs an outlet for his negative feelings. You've been told this several times. His counsellor has written to you.'

A line of boys, some of whom Holly recognised as her son's classmates, ran past the window in the tail end of a noisy game. Charlie would not be among them. Charlie stayed in the car until the first bell of the day had stopped ringing. Charlie was always the last child to enter the school building. Apart from those who were late.

Charlie was never late. On the few occasions that Holly hadn't been organised enough to get to the school gates on time, he'd refused to go in.

Mrs Milton sighed. 'Miss Baker, we do our best. But there are twenty-eight children in Charlie's class. We simply can't give him the attention and the specialist care that you, clearly, think he needs.'

'I was promised last term that all staff would undertake autism awareness training. Ofsted now recommends it as best practice.'

'In ideal circumstances,' the headteacher countered. 'It's something we hope to get round to in the next year or so.'

'He leaves this shithole in less than nine months.'

With an exaggerated sigh Mrs Milton pushed her chair back a couple of inches, as though needing to distance herself from the contamination that was Holly. She said, 'Charlie's father phoned me last week.'

Holly told herself to stay very still. 'He did what?'

'I found his approach constructive. He thinks, and I agree, that—'

'I have custody of Charlie. You shouldn't be discussing him with anyone but me.'

'We think it best to include both parents in our conversations about a child's welfare. Mr Collingwood feels Charlie would thrive in a smaller environment, one more tailored to his particular needs. I understand there is a very good independent school in Weybridge that have offered him a place.'

The bell rang, loud and insistent, making further conversation impossible. Milton got to her feet.

'You'll be wanting to get to work,' she said. 'Let's talk again when you've had time to think through what I've said.'

After crossing the room, she held the door open for Holly, giving her no choice but to walk through it. The corridor outside was busy, as staff made their way to classrooms for morning registration. Children poured through the main door and streamed up the stairs. The younger boys' changing room, the place she'd identified as the ideal ignition point for the fire, was a short distance away. The bins were always full of old paper towels; discarded PE kit and sundry lost clothes littered the floor and benches.

Well, obviously not while the place was full of kids. She wasn't a monster.

A school bus pulled up alongside Holly's car before she had the chance to drive off. Unable to complain – she'd parked illegally when all was said and done – she resigned herself to at least a five-minute wait. The bus was always full, and the kids never seemed to leave it quickly or even willingly.

Pulling the morning's post from her briefcase, she started to sort through it. A couple of subscriptions that she really should cancel because she never got round to reading them and an underwear catalogue that she pushed back into its envelope. Not something Charlie needed to see. There was an A5-size envelope with the stamp of an estate agent in the top-right corner. And it was a posh-looking envelope: good-quality paper in a colour between ivory and cream, a first-class stamp, her name and address in a calligraphic script. When she picked it up, it was heavy.

Curious, and because the bus had by no means finished offloading its cargo, Holly opened it. A coin of sorts fell out, enclosed within a small plastic square. It was a little like the commemorative coins that Charlie received occasionally from her parents to mark important national occasions – royal weddings or jubilees. This coin, though, showed no financial value, nor did it display the sovereign's head. About an inch and a half in diameter, it appeared to be bronze but probably wasn't, and at its centre was carved a star inside a circle. Around the edge ran a line of text that wasn't English.

It was accompanied by a very short letter; curiously, from a firm of solicitors that she knew, which she'd had several dealings with.

This is your token. Keep it safe. Tell no one. On the event of my death, it entitles you to an equal share of my wealth. Good luck.

Logan Quick

Christ, thought Holly. Logan Quick was one of the richest men in the UK.

Chapter 2

Cheryl Young's alarm went off, as usual, at eight thirty, vibrating away beneath her pillow. She woke with a start.

She didn't always dream, but earlier that morning she had, and it had been a good one. A young man she remembered from years ago, who'd smiled at her more than once as they'd cleared the glasses in the beer tent. He'd been tall, handsome and dashing, a little like a buccaneer of old. She'd never spoken to the man, didn't even know his name. He might not even be alive any more for all she knew, but he came back into her head from time to time. The man, whom Cheryl had named to herself Nicholas, because that had always been her favourite boy's name, belonged in the realm of what might have been. In the dream, she and the man – Nick – had been behind the tent, he'd stepped closer until she could feel his arms around her, his lips pressing closer to hers, the bubble of excitement in her stomach. She didn't care what anyone said, she knew what romance felt like.

But the dream was slipping away, as most dreams do, and so she got up, pulling on a dressing gown and stepping into slippers. The heating never came on until nine thirty when her mother woke. For the next hour the house would be cold, and it had to be silent, but the hour was hers.

Cheryl stepped carefully downstairs, knowing from long practice which stairs creaked. As the years and the pounds had accumulated, more of them made more of a noise, but her mother slept more deeply these days. The house smelled of stale smoke, as it always did in the mornings, but opening windows would make it too cold. In the kitchen, she boiled water on the hob, because it made less noise than the whistling kettle, and took her tea through to the sitting room. She didn't risk lighting a fire – Mum would know – but she wrapped herself in the throw from the back of the sofa and was cosy enough. She switched on the TV, using the subtitles app, until the post arrived at nine. As the hour drew near, her heartbeat began to build.

It was rare for the post to be late. When their usual postman was away and his replacement wasn't familiar with the route, it happened; also, sometimes when the weather was bad, but Cheryl had a plan for those times. Anything she didn't want her mother to see went straight into the meter box by the front door. Her mother checked the meters every day, but not usually until the evening.

The brochure from Saga was due. At fifty-one, Cheryl wasn't sure she was quite old enough for Saga holidays, but she loved the photographs of people who, although older, were still so glamorous, with their beautiful hairstyles and clothes. The men always had hair – silver, true, but perfectly styled – and no one was ever fat in the Saga brochure.

The Saga brochure wasn't about what might have been; the Saga brochure was about what could still be.

Today was going to be a late-post day. She wouldn't have time to look at it before she had to see to Mum. Her morning would be tied up doing chores and then there was the solicitor's appointment in the afternoon. Her mother, it seemed, was finally getting round to making her will. For some reason, the thought made Cheryl nervous.

Back in the kitchen she filled the kettle and had just switched it on when the alarm, loud and demanding, went off in her mother's room.

Footsteps on the path outside. She heard the letter box opening and post dropping onto the floor. Cheryl dashed out and gathered it up. The brochure had arrived, plus a gas bill that her mum would want to see and grumble over. And an envelope, a posh one, addressed to her, not her mum.

The envelope was cream and textured, and her name and address on the front seemed to have been handwritten, until you looked closely. And it was heavy. There was something inside other than a letter.

'Cheryl!' Right on time.

'Coming, Mum.'

Cheryl gathered the post up and pushed everything but the phone bill into the meter cupboard.

Chapter 3

Lauren was still asleep when he came out of the bathroom. She lay in the centre of the bed, where she'd rolled as he'd left it. Her butterscotch hair was spread over the pillow and what he could see of her face was plump and pink, slightly creased from being pressed against the bedding all night. There was a thin sheen of sweat at her temples and her entire body was on full view. Lauren was never cold, and she slept like a newborn baby. Increasingly, these days, there were times when he envied her; others when it annoyed the hell out of him.

Still damp from the shower, he found the chillier air of the bedroom cooled him quickly and he checked to see if any windows were open. Lauren would air the room when she got up and change the sheets, putting them quickly into the laundry. Soon there'd be no trace of the night they'd spent together.

Feeling a moment of regret that he couldn't climb back into bed, wrap himself around the furnace that was Lauren's plump body and sink back into oblivion, he walked to the table beneath the window where his laptop sat. Pain was forming around his nose and forehead, and he'd woken feeling stiffer and more cumbersome than usual. Both were sure signs that the barometric pressure was dropping and a storm was coming in.

Sure enough, the clouds out west were moving fast.

He sat and tapped a key to wake up the laptop. His new website, one he'd created himself with no assistance from tech support, was ready to launch. He'd been through it many times but knew it wouldn't hurt to run one last check.

His photograph dominated the home page. Photoshop had erased the fine lines around his eyes, forehead and jawline, offering a hint of the man he'd been ten years earlier. He'd been tempted to lower his hairline, darken the hints of grey at his temples, but knew it wouldn't do to look too handsome. He wasn't entirely sure about the font: Bradley Hand suggested he was trying too hard to be hip. He tried it in a lower size. That was better: *craig lewis: fire safety consultant*; it made the lower casing look less pretentious.

The menu bar running along the top of the home page invited the user to check out his CV, his contact details including his address in Newquay, client recommendations and the various services he offered.

A sound in the corridor outside made him jump but it was only his German Shepherd, Cobalt, looking for company. The dog gave a low-pitched whine.

'Good boy,' he called softly. 'Back to bed.'

The dog, obedient as ever, pattered away down the corridor. One by one, he proofread the sub-pages. It was good to go. He'd launch it at noon.

Opening his main email account, he checked for urgent messages, followed by WhatsApp, Messenger and his various social media accounts. Nothing needing immediate attention. Next, he checked the Find My Friends app. He followed several people with their knowledge, including his two kids, and a few without, including his ex-wife. All were where he'd have expected them to be. Last of all he checked the person he probably should have looked at first.

Shit!

Leaning back over the bed, he pulled the duvet away from Lauren and slapped her arse. Solid as a newly peeled boiled egg. He was on the point of doing it again when she grunted in annoyance and rolled away from him.

'He's thirty minutes away,' he told her. 'You need to hustle.'

Pulling a face, Lauren swung her long, tanned limbs from the bed. As she stood, she caught sight of one of the magazines on the bedside table. 'Going shopping?' she asked.

He'd been looking at helicopters, a guilty pleasure.

'A man can dream.'

They both knew a helicopter was the last thing he'd be buying. 'And it's now twenty-five minutes. Get out of here.'

She sashayed to the door, bending to collect her clothes on the way, turning to blow him one last kiss.

He wondered if he might have married her had circumstances been different, and thought perhaps that he would. Assuming, of course, that she hadn't already been married to his best friend.

Chapter 4

Faster than was wise, Tara Webb turned off the main Trebetherick road and onto Daymer Lane. This close to the coast, it was inevitable that many of Tara's callouts would involve near drownings, even actual drownings. She should be used to them by now. And knew she never would be. She hated the wet ones.

Two hundred metres from the car park her phone rang; she pressed answer without thinking.

'Tar, it's me.' The voice dripped with forced patience. 'I need an answer on Friday's meeting.'

'Can't talk now,' she told her estranged husband. 'I'm on a callout.'

Tara wished she had the nerve to finish the call, to press the *end* button before he could, but old habits . . .

She glanced down at the passenger seat. With no time even to open the post before she'd hurried from the house, she'd brought it with her. On the top of the pile was a letter from Justin's solicitor. She'd started to have a visceral, physical reaction when they arrived, which they did with increasing regularity these days.

'Ten o'clock,' Justin said, as though speaking to an unruly child. 'Bodmin offices. She's making a special trip, so I want you there, Tara.'

The car park was in sight, a woman with an expectant air standing at its entrance.

The morning's post had also brought a very fancy-looking envelope that Tara was hoping was an invitation to something nice. A gallery opening or an exhibition would be lovely; even a new dress shop would be something to look forward to.

'I'll get back to you,' Tara said. 'I have to go.'

'Be there, or I'm sending you the bill. And, Tara, I'll make sure you pay it.'

Justin ended the call, as he always did. In nearly thirty years of marriage, Tara didn't think she'd ever once put the phone down on her husband.

Turning into the car park, she pulled into the space nearest the beach path. The woman on look-out duty was wearing the long, padded coat favoured by open-water swimmers, a knitted bobble hat covering her damp hair. She was a Merry Mermaid, one of two groups of swimmers who regularly met here. Tara had been a Merry Mermaid herself once, before she'd fallen out with the group. She would know several of the women on the beach below and none would be pleased to see her. Tara's own swim group were meeting here this morning too but wouldn't arrive for another half-hour yet. She'd face the enemy alone.

'I'm the community first responder,' Tara called over as she locked the car. Deliberately, she kept her face turned away from the ocean. 'Did you call the ambulance?'

'Are they coming?' the woman demanded.

'On their way,' Tara replied. 'Where's the casualty?'

'How long will they be?'

'Is she still on the beach?' Tara asked.

The woman gestured towards the rocks at the north end of the bay. 'She's down there. There are people with her. She needs an ambulance.'

'Please stay here and tell the paramedics where to come when they arrive.'

Daymer Bay on the Camel Estuary was popular all year round with swimmers. From recent experience, Tara knew the water temperature had slipped into single figures and the gauge in her car had indicated the air temperature to be eleven degrees. On top of the wind-chill factor, it would make for a cold day for swimming. Plus, there was a storm coming in.

On her way down, Tara could no longer keep her eyes from the water. The waves were building, and cloud cover had turned the sea a threatening grey. White horses were starting to break some distance from the shore. She felt the shudder building and knew she'd never hold it back. With a bit of luck, anyone noticing would put it down to the cold.

The group came into view as Tara reached the bottom of the path. Predominantly women, mostly middle-aged, definitely the Merry Mermaids. She called out while she was still several metres away.

'Good morning! I'm Tara Webb!' At least half would know her name already but establishing any sort of authority with this lot would be tricky. 'Where's the casualty, please?'

The group watched her approach. She didn't have a uniform as such, but the high-vis jacket, with Community First Responder embossed on the rear, and two medical bags helped a lot. Usually. Oh great, there was Madge. And Caroline. Both giving her hard stares.

'When will the ambulance get here?' That, unsurprisingly, was Madge.

The casualty – female, early forties, thin – lay on a towel on the sand, partly covered by a coat. All colour had drained from her face and she was shaking. Her eyes were dull and unfocused, and her long hair was dripping onto the sand.

Tara pulled a dry towel from her bag and, on her knees, wound it around the woman's head, turban style. Before setting off, she'd wrapped it around a hot-water bottle, and it would provide some immediate warmth. A second towel went around the casualty's neck. Normally, Tara would ask the crowd to back off, give her space. Today, they were providing shelter from the wind.

'Are you medically trained?' someone behind her asked.

'She's a retired nurse,' replied a voice Tara thought she recognised. 'She swims here a lot. She knows what she's doing.'

'She's a bossy cow,' Caroline muttered.

'What happened?' Tara raised her voice to cut above the mutterings around her.

'She seemed fine in the water,' the familiar voice informed her. 'We noticed a problem when she came out. She stopped talking and slumped on the sand. Wouldn't get changed.'

Classic hypothermia.

Tara reached out and held the woman's face. 'Can you tell me your name, love?'

'It's Alison.' Caroline gave a heavy, impatient sigh.

'I need to hear her speak. How old are you, Alison?'

The woman's eyes met Tara's with no apparent intelligence behind them; the lights were on, but no one was home.

Someone said, 'It was her first time swimming. I think she stayed in too long.'

A classic rooky error. After the initial shock, the body grew used to the cold water, kidding the swimmer into thinking she was fine. The inexperienced always stayed in too long.

'If there's any men here, you should turn your backs,' Tara announced. 'I'm cutting her swimsuit off. The rest of you, I need her clothes and some more dry towels, dry robes if you can spare them and any hot-water bottles. Quick as you can, please.'

She glanced back over her shoulder to find a less-than-hostile face. 'Julie, I thought it was you. Get behind her, hold her upright and use your body to warm her up. Open your dry robe and wrap it round her as far as it will go. Does anyone have a hot drink?'

'Anything else we can do for you?' Caroline muttered.

As Tara pulled scissors from her bag, Julie did what she'd been told.

'I need a couple of you to lift her while I take her suit off.' Tara cut through the shoulder straps of Alison's swimsuit. The woman's flesh was cold and clammy. Most worryingly, there seemed to be a thin blue line running around the outside of her lips.

Other women knelt around Alison and together they pulled the wet swimsuit away.

'Clothes!' Tara called.

The women, most of them sensible, had organised themselves. They passed Tara items of clothing and helped her dress the patient. Tracksuit bottoms, socks, T-shirt, sweater, scarf, then a dry robe, properly fastened. Cold-water swimmers usually came equipped with hot-water bottles and several were produced. As Tara was arranging them around Alison's chest and groin, and one of the other women was offering sips of hot tea, she heard the siren of the ambulance at last.

'Thank goodness.' Caroline didn't bother to lower her voice this time. 'The professionals are here.'

'You should repeat that post of yours about hypothermia and tag the Mermaids into it,' said Becca, an hour and a half later, as the Sea Swimmers, still damp and salty, settled themselves at their usual window table in the nearby café. 'That'll really piss 'em off.'

Tara, opening her post, was only half listening. The letter from Justin's solicitor was simply confirming the appointment on Friday morning but was a harsh reminder all the same that everything was about to change. She put it on top of the credit card statement and the newsletter from the local MP. Hoping the fancy invitation was something that might cheer her up, she'd saved it for last. The envelope was made from heavy, hallmarked paper and her name and address had been written on the front in an elaborate italic script. Something was sliding around inside it.

Pulling it open, Tara found a folded sheet of paper of the same quality as the envelope and a small coin-like object encased in plastic.

Puzzled, and slightly disappointed – a gallery opening would have been nice – Tara unfolded the letter. It had been typed on headed notepaper, sent from a firm of Exeter solicitors, and was very short.

This is your token. Keep it safe. Tell no one. On the event of my death, it entitles you to an equal share of my wealth. Good luck.

Logan Quick

Chapter 5

The phone rang as Holly reached the road where her parents lived. Coffie.

'Tell me you didn't do it. I have other plans for my morning than getting you out of prison.'

'Tim called her,' Holly replied. 'That shitbag thinks he can go behind my back and get her on his side.'

'And is she?'

'Of course she is. If Charlie switches schools, she never has to see either of us again. Where's the downside for her?'

Coffie said, 'Holls, I know you don't want to hear this, but—'

'No.' She swung over and parked.

'OK, what about a private school closer to you?'

'There's no way I can afford a private school right now. And Shit-For-Brains will only cough up if I agree to him getting custody. Which means I lose Charlie.'

Coffie said, 'But what if it's only for his last year at primary school? He could come back when he goes to secondary.'

Holly leaned over to reach her bag from the passenger footwell. 'You really think Tim will give him up once he's got him?'

'He might. From what you've told me, he doesn't strike me as a devoted dad. He might find the reality of dealing with a child with additional needs . . .'

'Don't.' She opened the car door.

'Don't what?'

'Don't call Charlie a retard.'

'Holly, you know I'm not doing that. But he's not thriving at that school. He needs to be somewhere that will make him happy.'

'He needs to be with someone who loves him.'

'And his dad doesn't?'

'Botox Brenda doesn't. She never will. He'll be miserable there.'

'He's miserable now.'

Holly ended the call and locked the car. She'd phone Coffie later, apologise, say she passed through a stretch with no signal. Her friend wouldn't be fooled, but he'd go along with it.

'Only me,' she called, letting herself in.

No immediate answer came back, but she could hear someone moving around upstairs. She aimed for the back of the house, where a small dining room looked out over the garden.

'Morning, Dad.'

As usual her father was sitting in a winged armchair, staring out at the bird feeder, where a cluster of sparrows were quarrelling over the seed. Holly walked round the chair until she was sure he could see her. She had no idea how reliable his hearing was these days.

'Hi, Dad.' She crouched and forced a smile. Reaching out to touch his hand, she noticed that his dressing gown gaped open, revealing crêpey, veined skin. He looked so much older than his fifty-seven years. And he smelled of urine. 'Mum upstairs?'

Her father's eyes met hers for a second. It was weeks since Holly had heard him speak. He tried, occasionally, to articulate a thought, but rarely had the muscle strength or control to finish a sentence.

His hand, the one she'd touched, seemed to clutch at hers. She let him hold it for a second, ready to give him a reassuring smile when he looked at her again. His eyes, though, were fixed on a point behind her. She glanced round to see a framed picture leaning against the floor-to-ceiling window.

'That's pretty,' she said, taking in the watercolour of an English seaside village. Tall pink flowers dominated the foreground. The water – a tidal river, judging by moored sailing yachts – took up the middle ground and rising above it, climbing a steep, green hill, was a sprawl of old cottages.

'Is it new?'

Her father's grip tightened. Sounds came out of his mouth, none of which came close to forming actual words. She glanced to one side, to the dresser where they'd kept paper and pencils for some time now, but her dad had long since lost the ability to hold a pencil and write his thoughts. He was trapped inside a body that no longer felt any connection with his brain. It was the cruellest of diseases.

Dropping a kiss on her father's head, Holly got up. 'I'll go ask Mum,' she said. 'She'll tell me.'

Holly squeezed past the stair lift, the rental on which she paid, and found her mother changing the sheets in the main bedroom. She stepped over a heavily soaked pair of incontinence pads.

'Again?' she asked.

'Practically every night.' Her mother pulled the bottom sheet from the bed and dropped it onto a pile.

'Can't the carers do this?'

Her mother hung the plastic mattress protector over the door. 'They only have time to wash, dress and feed him. Mary says we need an hour in the morning.'

Mary was her father's sister.

'And is Mary offering to pay the bill?' Holly muttered, knowing she was being unfair. Her aunt's part-time teaching salary couldn't possibly stretch to chipping in with her brother's care. She bent to pick up the damp sheets. 'I'll stick these in the machine,' she said.

'It's playing up,' her mother replied. 'It's nearly ten years old, Holly. And I can't get the dryer to work.'

It would be the filter again, Holly thought. At least she hoped it was. The filter was easily fixed. Replacing both washing machine and dryer was beyond her.

'I'll take them with me,' she said, resigning herself to a car that smelled of her father's piss for the next few days. 'Dad seems upset. Is something bothering him?'

'That man's been again.' Her mother gave a heavy sigh. 'Yesterday. He means well, and God knows we don't get many visitors these days, but I'm going to have to tell him to stop.'

'What man?' Holly watched her mother sink onto the unmade bed.

'An old friend. He's been a few times now. Knew your dad years ago, long before I met him. He knows all about you and Charlie, though, so they've obviously been in touch over the years.'

'And that's a problem?'

'He brought your dad a picture of the village where they both grew up. It's a nice gesture, Holly, but he struggles with things that remind him . . .'

Holly joined her mother on the bed and slipped an arm around her waist. 'Of the man he used to be?'

'Drives a big black Volvo,' her mother went on. 'One of those with tinted windows.'

'I'd better run, I've got a lot on this morning. Speak to you later, Mum.'

Holly left, keeping all four windows cranked open on the thirty-minute drive to chambers.

Chapter 6

Sabri Carter didn't think she'd ever understand people who voluntarily entered the English sea from mid-September through to late June. Personally, she wouldn't go in the water off the Cornish coast at any time of year – had these people never read a sewage report? – but when the temperature was less than twenty degrees?

'Is it an ethnic thing?' She turned onto the main road that would take them back to the Royal Cornwall.

Steph, the paramedic at Sabri's side, had been scrolling through her phone. 'Come again?'

'Swimming in winter,' Sabri said. 'They were all white, those women, did you notice? I've never seen anyone with my ethnicity in cold water. Anyone of colour, for that matter. Too much bloody sense.'

'None of them had a BMI below thirty. I'd say that was more of an issue.' Steph kept her voice low, although the communicating window was closed. 'You need body fat to go into cold water. Probably why it's mainly women who do it. More fat than men. As a rule.'

Steph, a native Cornish woman, had a BMI that was dangerously high, but Sabri didn't mention it.

'Except our friend in the back,' she said instead. 'She's skin and bone. No wonder she got cold.'

The lights ahead changed, forcing Sabri to stop abruptly. 'Have you come across that CFR before?'

She was thinking back to the tall blonde woman who'd met them on the beach. The second Sabri had laid eyes on her, she'd felt uneasy.

'Don't think so, why?' Steph was scrolling again.

'I thought she looked familiar. But not in a good way.'

Steph glanced up. 'She's a recently retired nurse. At least I think that's what she said. You'll have come across her at some point.'

Steph was probably right. But there was something about the woman, about her no-nonsense practicality, her subtle bossiness, her poise, even crouched on damp sand, that was – no, not just familiar – deeply unsettling.

'Tara Webb.' Steph was glancing down at notes now. 'That's her name. Ring any bells?'

'None at all,' Sabri answered truthfully. The name meant nothing. The woman herself, though? There was something there. She was sure of it.

Sabri's phone rang as she pulled in to the ambulance bay. Knowing she'd have to wait to be unloaded, she answered it. 'Hey, babes. Where are you?'

The sixth-form college her eldest attended reserved Wednesday afternoons for sport. Seventeen-year-old Maddy, who didn't have a sporting bone in her body, usually went home to pretend to study.

'There's a letter for you,' Maddy said. 'I thought it might be about that job.'

The job had been a long shot. A first-aid instructor with a big multi-national firm. It would mean more travel than Sabri was used to, but the kids were all older now. Importantly, it would bring an end to shift work, and a ten-grand increase in salary.

'Go on, you can open it.' Sabri glanced sideways at Steph. She hadn't mentioned applying for jobs to any of her colleagues. While they all moaned regularly and frequently about the work, taking active steps to leave might be seen as something of a betrayal. Steph, unsurprisingly, was scrolling through TikTok.

Not waiting to be told twice, Maddy was tearing open the envelope.

'Oh,' she said, sounding disappointed, and Sabri felt an answering tug in her own insides.

'Mum, listen to this. It says, "This is your token. Keep it safe. Tell no one. On the event of my death, it entitles you to an equal share of my wealth. Good luck." I mean, what the actual?'

Sabri had only been half listening. She made her daughter read it again.

'Signed by a Logan Quick,' Maddy concluded. 'Do you know him? Is he a long-lost relative? An Indian prince? Have we got rich relations?'

An Indian prince called Logan Quick? Bless that daughter of hers.

'Sweetie, it's a scam.'

'No, it looks really official. It's from a firm of solicitors. Can I call them? Oh, there's no phone number.'

'Scam.'

'And there's an actual token. It's got some sort of weird writing on it.'

'Put it in the bin and get on with some work. I'll be home by four. Love you.'

'But, Mum—'

'Bye, love.' Sabri ended the call with a heavy sigh. Maddy would get no work done that afternoon.

Chapter 7

'Glad that's settled.' Robin marked First Dance Song as done. 'Right,' he went on. 'Got something else to show you.' From the briefcase at his side, he pulled out a small paper-wrapped parcel. Putting it on the table in front of Jax, he watched her face melt into a puzzled frown.

Her hair, silver at the front, the rest a colour Robin had only ever been able to describe as mink, fell around her face as she looked down. Jax's hair always looked as though she'd walked through a windstorm. It had been her hair that Robin had noticed first, all those years ago; that and her eyes, now the exact same colour as the silvery grey strands that framed her face.

'What is it?' she said.

'Open it.'

Without waiting to be told twice, she ripped the paper away to reveal a tiny rectangular box in the shape of a coffin. Her eyes opened wider and her mouth made that tiny movement he knew meant she was biting her bottom lip. He watched her lift the lid and read the Gothic script on the inside.

I have love in me the likes of which you can scarcely imagine.

Jax had broached her plans for a Gothic Steampunk wedding months ago, had drawn together a Pinterest board of images that matched her vision. Since then, the two of them had planned every detail together. The black, red and gold colour scheme, the specially dyed black flowers for the arrangements and bouquets, the masks, feathers, mock skulls, clocks, keys and trails of lace that would decorate the tables.

'What's the text?' she asked. 'It's beautiful but I don't recognise it.'

'It's from Mary Shelley's *Frankenstein*.'

Tears filled her eyes and she reached out a hand to grasp his. 'God, I adore you.'

He swallowed. 'I wasn't sure they'd arrive on time, so I didn't say anything. We can fill them with anything you like but I'd suggest cherry liqueurs with dark chocolate might work best. Right, have you written your vows yet?'

'I have them in my bag.'

'Want to run through them?'

Suddenly, he wanted nothing more than to hear Jax pledging a lifetime of devotion to him, right here and now.

'No, they're a surprise. How about you? You all set?'

'Always.'

A text message alert sounded on Jax's phone. She looked down. 'I've got to go. Thanks so much, Robin.'

Every time she said goodbye something inside him died a little. He stood up when she did, so that she could kiss him.

She leaned in and kissed him on first one cheek then the other. 'See you in church, gorgeous man. Love you.'

'Love you too,' he replied, knowing that he, at least, was speaking the absolute truth. Jax was his first love and his last. Love began and ended with her. It was that simple.

He watched her walk out of the restaurant. She moved with such unconscious grace, drawing eyes as she went. Outside in the street a blue BMW had pulled over, hazard lights flashing, holding up traffic. The driver, a great-looking guy in his late forties, climbed out of his seat and met Jax as she strode across the pavement. They kissed for long seconds before he turned and opened the passenger door for her. As she disappeared inside, Jax's fiancé, Neil, caught sight of Robin watching and gave him a mock salute.

In just a couple of weeks, Robin would officiate at their wedding. In over twenty years as a wedding planner and marriage celebrant, it would be the first time he'd do so while his heart was being ripped in two.

As he waited for the bill, he went through the post that had arrived that morning. His heart stopped when he saw the classy-looking cream envelope with embossed italic script and the postmark indicating it had come from a firm of solicitors. What fresh hell was this? He almost didn't open it, but inside was something small but heavy that was sliding around. Curious, Robin pulled it open.

This is your token. Keep it safe. Tell no one. On the event of my death, it entitles you to an equal share of my wealth. Good luck.

Logan Quick

Chapter 8

Craig finally escaped the Wadebridge WI a little after two. His talk on the importance of fire safety in the home had gone as well as he could have hoped and each of the thirty women in attendance had taken a business card promoting his services as a fire safety consultant. He'd been asked to stay to lunch of course and while he wouldn't normally turn down free food and female company, something had urged him to make his excuses and leave.

In the car, he didn't immediately turn on the engine, even though he could sense some of the women hovering. He pulled out the letter that had arrived that morning, the one from the firm of solicitors in Exeter, accompanied by a strange round token.

He felt the now-familiar surge of excitement, indistinguishable from the nervous anxiety that had kept his stomach churning for the last several hours. And for what was probably the dozenth time that morning, he read the short paragraph that promised him an imminent share of an immense fortune.

Chapter 9

The solicitor's office was on the first floor of an old Tudor building. No lift. It took nearly ten minutes for Cheryl to heave her mother up the stairs, and of course she got the blame for making them late. Once they'd been greeted by a woman who seemed far too young to be a solicitor, but who was perfectly polite and pleasant, as much to Cheryl as to Sheila, they sat around a small wooden table and the solicitor ran her eyes down a sheet of handwritten notes that Sheila had handed over.

'No mortgage on the house, that's much easier, estimated value of around five hundred thousand,' the young solicitor read. 'Savings of some twenty thousand, around ten thousand in premium bonds. We're looking at an estate in the region of half a million pounds. So, what are your intentions, Mrs Young?'

Sheila's hands were clasped on the strap of her handbag. She took a breath and spoke up clearly. 'I plan to leave my entire estate to the Royal National Lifeboat Institute.'

For several seconds, silence filled the room.

Then, 'Your entire estate?' the solicitor queried.

'That's right.'

'To be clear, everything you own, once any taxes and sales expenses have been paid? All to the RNLI?'

'That's what I said.'

As Sheila sat back on her chair, her expression a mixture of defiant and smug, Cheryl found her voice. 'Mum, you can't be serious.'

Her mother's head snapped round to make eye contact. 'Why can't I?'

'What about me?'

Thin eyebrows lifted. 'What about you?'

Feeling a moment of shame that they were having this conversation in front of someone else, Cheryl forced herself to go on. 'What will I do? How will I live?'

Sheila's stare hardened. 'You'll get the state pension like every other scrounger out there.'

'I'm not sure I will. And not for years yet. How will I live till then?'

'Meadowcroft are always looking for staff. Especially on the night shift.'

Meadowcroft was the local care home. Her mother was expecting Cheryl to spend the rest of her working life doing almost exactly what she'd spent the last twenty doing: caring for elderly people, bringing them food, cleaning their rooms, helping them get washed and dressed, wiping their arses when they could no longer do it themselves. And all this for minimum wage. She thought of the travel brochures tucked away on the highest shelf of her wardrobe and wanted to weep.

'I'll have no home,' she managed.

'You'll find a room somewhere. Nice bedsit. Be easier than keeping my house clean. I'm doing you a favour if you could see it.'

It was the casual cruelty that hurt the most, the totally unfeeling way in which Sheila had stripped away her daughter's hope and her future.

'At least now I won't have to worry about you slipping me something in my tea.' Sheila chortled to herself. 'It's in your interests to keep me alive as long as possible.'

Cheryl looked to the young solicitor for help. The other woman seemed uncomfortable, even upset, but said nothing.

Sensing an advantage, Sheila pressed it home. 'What? You thought you'd be a kept woman all your life? You haven't even had to put out for it.'

The unexpected coarseness shocked Cheryl more than her mother's plans to disinherit her. She turned to the solicitor again.

'She's not in her right mind. You can see that, can't you? She doesn't know what she's doing.'

A hand slapped down on the tabletop. 'I know exactly what I'm doing. I know my worth and I know yours. I'm leaving my money to the lifeboats. I can't think of a more worthy charity. Can you, Cheryl?'

Cheryl felt the blow like a physical pain. Her mother hadn't moved again, hadn't touched her. But it felt like she'd been gut-punched.

Sheila wasn't done. 'Well, can you?'

This was a battle she could never win. Cheryl felt her whole body deflating. 'No,' she said. 'I can't.'

Sheila turned back to the solicitor. 'So, you can draw something up?'

The young woman stood up, clearly wanting to bring the meeting to an end. 'Of course. I'll get a draft to you in the post.'

Cheryl got to her feet and followed her mother towards the door.

'Miss Young.'

The solicitor was standing in front of her desk when Cheryl turned back. It was the first time the young woman had spoken directly to her and not to her mother.

'I'm your mother's solicitor so I can't advise you,' the girl said. 'But I strongly suggest you get some legal advice of your own as soon as possible.' She gave Cheryl a half-smile.

'Good luck with that,' Sheila said as she reached the top of the stairs. 'You've no money and legal aid isn't what it was.'

How had she reached such a state, Cheryl wondered, as they made their laborious way down the stairs, when a few kindly meant words of a stranger were all that stopped her sinking to the floor in despair?

Chapter 10

Trevor Winter, who'd be known to his friends, if he had any, as Tug, lived a ten-minute walk from the garden centre where he'd worked as a security guard/jack of all trades for the last three years, and the first thing he did when he got in was to sort the mail.

The post, masses of it, because the building held thirty flats on four flours, was pushed through the communal letter box once a day. Early commuters stepped over it and often on it. Up until three months ago, the old lady in flat seven had sorted it into piles, but she didn't leave her home till nearly nine thirty and by that time much of it had been trampled; some, particularly birthday cards that might contain cash, was nicked. But the old lady had done her best and her altruism had created an order of sorts. And then she'd inconveniently had a stroke and died. It had been the build-up of post, rather than the smell coming from her flat, that had prompted Tug to investigate. Borrowing a spare key from the letting agent, he'd discovered her body, already liquidising in the summer heat, in the hallway. She'd been on her way to sort the post.

Since then, only Tug had made an effort to throw away the obvious junk and sort the rest but by the time he got home, it was usually a scattered mess; today, a scattered wet mess. Sighing, he got to work.

There was something for him.

Tug never got post. He made a point of removing himself from mailing lists. His old unit had moved to e-communications years ago and no one alive, so far as he was aware, knew when his birthday was. He couldn't remember the last time he'd received actual post.

And this looked classy. A cream-coloured envelope, his name and address written in some sort of fancy script. And there was something inside. He tucked it into his bag.

Heads up, lads.

The words, in the voice of one of his old service mates, sprang into Tug's head, putting him on instant alert. He could feel blood flowing into his muscles, his heart flexing, getting ready to accelerate. Moving nothing but his eyes, he took a slow, careful look around outside. He took in the kids shooting into a basketball hoop on the court across the way, the handful of parked cars, the overflowing bins, the cat sitting like a statue on the wall opposite.

Tug felt sweat breaking out between his shoulder blades and made himself take a long, deep breath. All was well.

As he turned towards the stairs, he caught movement in the corner of his eye. The car was back. A black Volvo, its windows darkened, was pulling out of the car park. It had obviously been waiting in the spot by the bins or he'd have seen it as he approached the building. He'd noticed it more than once over the past few weeks, registered that it was far too new and too fancy to belong to any of the residents who weren't involved in criminal activity and had braced himself for some sort of drug-related gang war breaking out on his doorstep.

As he climbed the stairs, he wondered if a subliminal anxiety about the appearance of the Volvo – definitely real, he'd seen it several times – was feeding into an almost certainly imagined sensation of being watched. But whatever was causing these mild panic attacks, he had to get a grip.

In his flat, he stood the unopened envelope on the mantelpiece above the gas fire, before changing into shorts, T-shirt and training shoes and crossing from his bedroom to the room where he kept his gym equipment.

Tug hadn't bothered with pictures or even mirrors in his flat; they gathered too much dust. But on the wall of the gym was a framed photograph that showed eight men in a high-speed boat. Next to it hung another framed image: a black shield featuring an upturned sword with the motto *By Strength and Guile*.

Tug worked out for ten minutes longer than his schedule, all the while conscious of the waiting envelope. When the time was up, he fixed himself a pint glass of squash with a sprinkling of salt and downed it in one. He needed a pee, so he went for that first and then, as he was already in the bathroom, he had a shower.

Finally, when his usual schedule would have had him in the kitchen preparing dinner, he carried the envelope to the window. He'd needed reading glasses for a couple of years now and he polished them carefully before opening the envelope.

This is your token. Keep it safe. Tell no one. On the event of my death, it entitles you to an equal share of my wealth. Good luck.

Logan Quick

For several seconds, Tug stared at it in wonder. Then, for fuck's sake! He was going to kill that twat, Nolly.

Chapter 11

Holly got home a little after five, later than usual because Wednesday was cross-country club at Charlie's school. He hated team sports – the noise, the physical jostling and the need for coordination were especially triggering – but he excelled at track and field. At ten years old he showed signs of being an exceptional endurance runner and the popularity he earned through his cross-country medals went some way to balancing out his peculiarities.

Holly still had work to do, but it would wait till Charlie had gone to bed. Wednesday was always a good evening. The physical exercise helped calm him, and Wednesday was pizza night.

Her first task, and an urgent one, was to get her father's stinking sheets into a hot wash. With a bit of luck, the smell would have dissipated by the time Charlie got back. He'd been known to refuse to enter a place that smelled bad, and he had an uncannily keen nose. That done, she pulled the morning's post from her case.

Busy all day, she'd quite forgotten about the strange solicitors' note, with the odd round coin. Barker, Momen and Dodds was an Exeter firm. The note had been signed, rather elaborately, in blue ink, but wasn't addressed to her specifically. Or to anyone. She double-checked the name and address on the envelope. Yes, definitely meant for her.

It was a scam, of course; they got ever more sophisticated. She couldn't see any number she was supposed to call, but sooner or later they'd be in touch. The first contact was always the most important.

She took a photograph quickly with her phone. She'd send it to one of her contacts in the firm the next day; they had a right to know about nefarious activity being done in their name. In the meantime, better that Charlie didn't see it. Charlie, like many people with his condition, had problems recognising dishonesty. Charlie would instinctively take it seriously.

The sound of a car pulling up outside told her that he was home. She gathered up the post she didn't need to keep, including the solicitors' letter and its accompanying token. On her way to open the front door, she dropped everything in the bin.

Chapter 12

'Logan Quick married Amanda Holt,' Jason announced. 'I'm sure I remember her in the Olympics. Horse rider.'

Sabri was staring down at the left-over chicken, wondering whether, if she cut it into smaller chunks, the family might not notice how little there was. What they were all going to eat tomorrow night, she had no idea.

'I want a pony,' thirteen-year-old Bethany told her father.

They wouldn't starve; there was plenty of bread in the freezer; she always stocked up when she saw it on offer. But beans on toast for dinner? It wasn't the frigging 1940s.

'Can we move house?' Darren asked. 'If it's real. Can we have our own pool?'

There had been a time when coming home from work had caused the knots inside Sabri to loosen. She could forget the drug-crazed morons who'd punched or slapped her, the drunken twats who pissed inside her ambulance. In the warmth of the family room, making dinner while the kids and Jason chatted and laughed and watched TV around her, it was as though none of it had happened, not really.

'She was in that cross-country event thing at Greenwich, along with Zara Phillips,' Jason said. 'Back in 2012. Do you remember, Sab?'

Something had changed these last few years, and the cosy feeling of plenty had slipped away. Money didn't stretch the way it once did. The kids, older now and social-media savvy, always wanted better and more of what was better, blaming her if it wasn't provided. Even Jason seemed to have handed over to his wife responsibility for steering the family ship. She sometimes wondered if *Ask your mother* was the single most frequent phrase to come out of his mouth. Because if she was in charge, then when it all went wrong, it was her fault.

'We could go away for Christmas,' Maddy said. 'Sadie's family are spending Christmas in the British Virgin Islands.'

Sabri divided the chopped chicken between four bowls, leaving her own empty.

'Where are the British Virgin Islands?' Maddy asked.

Jason, who should know better, was intent on his laptop. Maddy had commandeered Sabri's iPad, while Darren, the middle child, sat at the family computer. Bethany was leaning over her older sister's shoulder.

'He was forty-one at the time.' Jason seemed fixated on Logan Quick's private life. 'She was twenty-six. A real babe too. That's money for you. No wedding pics.'

Sabri gave the onions a stir before adding diced sweet potato and red lentils. The curry was a mid-week staple and she'd already had to face down requests that they eat out for once, or at least order in pizza, because they could afford it now, couldn't they?

'He divorced her,' Maddy chipped in. 'Five years later. So, he wouldn't leave her his money, would he? She'd have had – what do you call it? – a divorce settlement.'

'Two kids,' Darren added. 'Ludo Quick, born in 2013, so he'll be twelve, and Coco Quick, born in 2015. Which makes her ten. Why would he leave his money to a total stranger and not to his kids?'

'He wouldn't,' Sabri answered, knowing no one was listening. They were all entirely caught up in the dream of unexpected riches.

'So, can I have riding lessons?' Bethany asked. It was something she begged for regularly. Not usually twice in one evening, though.

'Who calls their kids Ludo and Coco?' Jason said.

'It says a share of his money.' Bethany had current possession of the letter.

'Net worth, five billion,' Jason said, in a much more subdued tone. He gave a low whistle.

Jason had commandeered the token itself, sparking a family row about where the safest place to keep it would be.

'Maybe he's left some to them and some to us,' Bethany suggested.

'Why would he leave it to us, though?' Darren had spun round on his stool to face his sisters. 'We don't know him. Dad, I don't think you should keep the token in your wallet. It's the same size as a ten-pence piece. You might spend it by accident.'

'We need a safe,' Bethany agreed. 'We can keep our jewellery in it.'

'You want jewellery now?' Her father reached out and wound his hand around his youngest daughter's long, black hair.

'Maybe Mum saved his life one day.' Maddy looked like she'd discovered a new element. 'That has to be it. Think back, Mum. Have you ever saved anyone?'

'I like to think so.'

Jason accidentally spending the so-called token could be the best thing to happen; bring this nonsense to an end once and for all. Why couldn't the letter have been an invitation to a new job? That would have been a realistic dream, one they could all sensibly get behind.

A picture came into Sabri's head, too quickly for her to erect any sort of mental block against it: the five of them on a Caribbean beach, dazzling colours and a scented breeze, surf tickling their bare feet, warm hands clasping her own.

'Your mother's been a paramedic since she was twenty-five,' the children's dad reminded them. 'She'll have saved countless people. The question is, did anyone announce themselves as eccentric billionaires when you restarted their stopped heart?'

'Is anyone planning to eat tonight apart from me?' Sabri asked. 'Because I don't see a cleared table, never mind cutlery.'

'Maybe you saved one of his children.' Maddy wasn't letting it go. 'If one of his children was dying, say if they'd accidentally swallowed something really poisonous, like . . . what's really poisonous, Dad?'

'Red Bull,' Jason replied.

Maddy rolled her eyes.

'Bleach,' Darren told his sister, as Sabri spooned the curry over the chopped chicken in four of the bowls and into her own empty one.

'Say his little girl drank a bottle of bleach and she was dying and you saved her, Mum,' Bethany chipped in. 'And then he said to himself, one day, I'm going to leave that lovely woman all my money.'

'I'm not sure I could save a child who'd drunk a bottle of bleach, sweetheart. OK, dinner's ready. Jace, will you get that laptop off the table and find some knives and forks because I think our children have collectively lost their brains.'

'I know what we can do, if it's real,' Darren said.

'It's not real.' Sabri put the last bowl on the table. 'Sit down, everyone.'

'New car would be nice,' Jason said, as he moved his laptop to the counter. It was still open on Logan Quick's Wikipedia page. 'Nothing fancy. Maybe one of the small Teslas.'

'No, Dad, a Ferrari,' said Darren.

'We can go to India,' Maddy said. 'Find out where we came from.'

'You come from Devon,' Sabri told her. 'The Royal Devon and Exeter Hospital. All of you.'

'You know what I mean,' Maddy argued.

'Can I please have a pony?' Bethany asked.

Another unbidden vision came into Sabri's head: her bowl with its scant portion of food being hurled across the room, striking the window and falling with a broken clunk to the floor, because nothing short of that dramatic would convey to these idiots that she really, really wasn't in the mood for this crap, tonight of all nights. Only the sure and certain knowledge that only she would clean it up stayed her hand.

'No, come on, guys, I know what we can do.' Darren grabbed the rice bowl and started spooning it onto his plate. He'd take all of it if he wasn't careful.

'What, Darren?' Sabri hadn't meant to snap, but enough was enough. 'What will we do in the entirely impossible event that a billionaire we've never heard of before today has left us some money?'

Darren's eyes opened wider; his face took on a pinched look, the one his mother recognised from when he was much younger. When he was about to cry.

'I only meant . . .'

'What?' she snapped again, too angry to back down.

'You could go back to medical school,' he finished. 'Be a doctor, like you always wanted.'

Chapter 13

When he got home that evening, Robin put the letter from Barker, Momen and Dodds, along with its mysterious token, in his tiny study, alongside the other letters he'd received from solicitors over the course of the past twelve months. At least this one, on the face of it, wasn't going to cost him anything. It was a scam, of course, but it was hard to see how he could be charged money simply for receiving it through the post.

The others, though? The others got more demanding by the week. The emails were worse; the emails were harder to ignore. And then there were the phone calls.

A little over a year ago, desperate for business, still crippled by loans he'd taken out during and following the Covid pandemic, Robin had ignored all his misgivings and agreed to organise and officiate at an outdoor wedding by a waterfall near Tintagel. Not remotely suitable for events, the site was a mile walk from the nearest car park and offered neither toilets nor shelter. Had the weather held, it might have worked.

That August, though, had seen unprecedented thunderstorms throughout the southwest. The heavens had opened as the bride set out to walk down the impromptu aisle. He'd kept the service as brief as possible, but by the time they all got back to the car park, the guests were soaked and the couple's parents furious.

Spirits had largely been restored by the reception in a nearby tithe barn; Robin had even persuaded a hairdresser to turn up and repair some of the damage to the bride and bridesmaids. All's well that ends well, he'd told himself, as he'd finally arrived home.

All was not well. His bill for nearly twenty thousand pounds was ignored for three months. After he'd sent the third reminder, he made a claim through the county court. He had no choice. He'd paid the venue, the florist, the band directly. He couldn't afford not to recoup the money. The groom's father had counter-sued for twenty-five thousand pounds' worth of damages including emotional distress. Robin couldn't even begin to find twenty-five thousand pounds, never mind the legal costs on top. Thanks to the remortgage, even selling his house wouldn't raise enough. On top of that, the fees for servicing his various loans were mounting daily.

His court date was set for 14 December. On the 15th, he could be bankrupt, unemployed and homeless. And that was only the beginning.

It was getting difficult to move around in the small room. Robin's study was piled high with boxes and packages, wedding paraphernalia of various themes and vibes: fairy lights, nets of sugared almonds, rustic place settings, Jax's miniature coffins, wedding directional signs that mimicked official AA signage; all of it contributing to his mounting debt, none of it likely to be recouped for weeks yet. One box sat unopened. Absent-mindedly, he ran a paper knife around the seal to find that the leprechaun's gold had arrived. Minty and Toby, due to tie the knot in three weeks, had never lived in Ireland, but both claimed Irish ancestry and wanted to go to town with Irish theming. A massive rainbow of multi-coloured fairy lights would stretch from one end of the hall to the other, culminating in a black cauldron of fake gold coins. The couple had refused to go for chocolate coins, which would at least have doubled up as wedding favours, opting instead for a metal coin of bright gold edged with concentric circles and delicate beading. An image of a bearded, long-haired man, no doubt some Irish hero of old, sat in the centre. Together with unrelieved green décor and shamrock place-settings, the venue was going to look like a down-market Irish pub.

Coincidentally, the coins looked the exact same size as the token that had arrived that morning.

Chapter 14

Tara had a commission to finish: a burst of gleaming, silver fish leaping from the ocean. Each of the fifteen glass pieces, and they were all unique, would be individually fastened to her client's bathroom wall. It was no good, though, her mind simply wasn't on the job. She gave up, switching off the kiln and closing down her studio.

Night had fallen while she'd been trying to work and the house was in darkness, apart from the gentle swirl of the screensaver on her laptop. She wandered over to the dining table and pressed a key to waken it.

Outside, the solar-powered lights around the dell were glowing, lighting the gentle curves of the ferns and the soaring reach of the trees. A soft wind kept the garden in constant movement. Directly below where she stood, a solitary spotlight picked out the bronze statue of the impossibly thin girl diving into one of the pools. Tara had named her Hope, for no other reason than the word came into her head every time she looked at her.

Justin and the boys had nagged her many times about closing the drapes when she was alone at night, reminding her that someone could easily make their way across country and onto the house's land. Anyone, they'd warned, could watch her while she wandered the length of her huge living room at night; they could see her cooking, eating, curling up under a throw to watch TV. They would know she was alone and unprotected. The male campaign to unsettle her, she realised, to instil a creeping sense of unease, had begun long before Justin had moved out and started divorce proceedings.

Leaving the drapes as they were, Tara typed *Logan Quick* into the search engine.

He was a Cornish man. Born the youngest of two children to Sandra Quick, now deceased, he'd grown up with a single mother and a succession of foster families. The identity of his father was unknown. He attended Redruth Comprehensive, leaving at age sixteen with no qualifications and thereafter holding a number of unskilled jobs, including bricklayer's assistant, cleaner in a strip club, and shop assistant in a number of retail establishments. An accident in his early twenties had resulted in spinal damage and, it was rumoured, mild cognitive impairment. He spent three years unemployed, but a relatively modest National Lottery win in 1995, some five hundred thousand pounds, changed his life forever.

His current fortune was estimated to be in the region of five billion.

Tara's phone, never far from her side since the boys had started school, began to ring. Lawrence.

'Hey, baby.' She put the phone onto loudspeaker.

'Mum, Dad's worried about you. He's been calling you all day. He thought you might have had an accident in the garden.'

Tara stifled the sigh. An accident in the garden would suit Justin just fine.

'I'm sound of limb, thank you. You had a good day?'

'He asked me to remind you about Friday.'

'Babes, you ever heard of Logan Quick?' No sooner had the words left her mouth than Tara regretted them.

'Who?'

'Nothing. Just something I saw on X.'

'Hang on.' Lawrence fell silent. He was looking the man up on his phone. 'Oh, the porno billionaire. Why you asking about him?'

'Porno?' Wikipedia had said nothing about porn, just that Quick's early business dealings weren't entirely reputable.

'Made his money from sex shops and porn websites. Nice guy.'

'He's leaving me his fortune.' Oh, why had she said that?

Lawrence gave a soft laugh. 'He's what?'

She was committed now. 'I got a letter this morning. From a firm of solicitors. Apparently, I'm going to inherit a share of Logan Quick's vast fortune.'

'Yeah right.'

'Exactly.'

'Can you send me a picture?'

'Of who? Logan Quick? No, there's no photo attached to his Wikipedia page.'

'Of the letter.'

'If I must. It came with some sort of fancy coin.'

Tara positioned the token on the letter and took a photograph with her phone. She sent it via text message to Lawrence.

'Funny sort of scam,' he said, after a few seconds. 'I mean, what's in it for the scammers?'

'Good question. I guess I contact the firm of solicitors and at some point I'll be asked for my account details.'

'Fair play, it's a bit more original than the Nigerian prince. What's written on the coin? I can't make it out.'

'Looks like Latin. So, anybody's guess.'

'You won't do anything daft, will you, Mum?'

'No, darling, I won't do anything daft. And tell your father I'm trying to rearrange my schedule so I can make Friday's meeting. He does not need to phone me through the night.'

'He worries about you, Mum. We all do.'

'I know,' she lied. The boys, possibly, when they spared her a thought. Justin, not at all. Justin would love to get her out of the way.

Getting up, after she'd wished Lawrence a good night, Tara tucked the envelope away in the kitchen drawer beneath a pile of tea towels. And then she remembered where she'd heard the name Logan Quick. Grabbing the phone again, scrolling through her contact list, she found the number she was looking for.

'Miranda?' she said, when the call was answered. 'It's Tara Webb. I'm so sorry to bother you.'

A heavy sigh, then, 'No worries. What can I do you for.'

The other woman's voice sounded slurred; a TV was playing loudly in the background. A reality TV programme, judging by the language Tara could hear.

'There was a woman I met at your drinks last Christmas. Lovely woman. Really interested in having one of my sculptures for her new place. I couldn't get onto it straight away because I had a massive backlog but I've done some sketches and—'

'Peregrine, get down!' Miranda snapped. 'No, leave that. Bad boy.'

'Well, the thing is, I've lost her business card. I should have saved her number in my contacts, but things have been a bit hectic since Justin and I, well, you know—'

'Is this going anywhere, Tara?'

'You couldn't give me her number, could you? I can call back, if you don't have it to hand. Or pop round? How's that lovely husband of yours? Arthur, isn't it?'

Miranda's husband, Arthur, fancied Tara rotten.

'Maybe tomorrow night?' she added, reaching for a pen.

'Whose bloody number?'

'God, I'm stupid. Amanda, she was called. Amanda Quick. Used to be a show jumper. Lovely woman.'

Amanda Quick née Holt was Logan Quick's ex-wife.

'Can't stand her myself. Frightful slag. Hold on.'

Several seconds of silence followed. Then a number was read out. Tara scribbled it down.

'Thanks so much,' she began, but didn't get to finish. The call had been ended.

Chapter 15

Seeking solace over his impending destitution, Robin opened a bottle of Peroni and watched – not for the first time – *Seven Brides for Seven Brothers*. He had a passionate, albeit secret, love of musicals. When he'd been married, briefly and unsuccessfully in his late twenties, he'd been able to kid himself that he bought tickets as a treat for his wife. On the day she declared that musicals bored her to tears and she'd only gone along with it the last four years because she hadn't wanted to rock the boat and upset him, he'd wondered if he'd ever really loved her at all.

Jax adored musicals. *Phantom* was her favourite. Of course it was.

His phone was ringing. A number he didn't recognise, but prospective new clients were always to be welcomed. Without thinking, he answered.

'Mr Knight, my name's Shireen from Assurance Debt Management Services. I'm calling about the outstanding balance on your account.'

Robin's stomach churned. Two years earlier, he'd bought a car on credit. It had cost far more than he could afford, but he could hardly turn up to client meetings in a rust bucket. The monthly repayments had been eye-watering and, one month, distracted about the Tintagel wedding furore, he'd missed a payment. It had been a simple mistake, but having the money in his account for a change had felt like a breath of fresh air and when nothing bad happened, he skipped the following month as well. He'd planned to put it right when things improved, but nothing improved as quickly as it should have done, and his credit card company had passed the loan on to a debt collection service. The people at Assurance were relentless.

They'd phoned him daily, sometimes more than once, badgering him about how and when he was going to pay the money back. Unable to bear it any longer, he'd bought a new phone, giving the number only to trusted clients, but somehow Assurance had got hold of it.

Seven Brides wasn't doing it for him anymore. Robin got up and crossed the hall to his study. The letter from Barker, Momen and Dodds still sat on top of the pile. Edging his way around boxes, he upended it and let the token fall onto his desk.

Was there any possible way?

Chapter 16

Tired after the trip to the solicitors, Sheila went to bed earlier than usual. Cheryl settled her mother and then ran her own bath. Along with the food treats she occasionally managed to sneak, sinking into hot water was perhaps the only sensual pleasure she had. Only when she knew the sound of the water tank refilling would mask any noise she made did she let herself cry.

That morning, she'd had a future, could look forward to a time when she could live for herself, replace servitude with comfort, see something of the world and surround herself with nice things. Now, nothing lay ahead but years of ever more laborious and disgusting tasks as Sheila became increasingly elderly and infirm. And when her mother finally died, something worse.

Meadowcroft was the place the elderly went when they hadn't the funds for anything better. It had a terrible reputation. It was never properly clean, the food was inedible, the staff lazy and unreliable, management uncaring. The only reason the local authority didn't close it down was the knowledge that they'd have to find somewhere else to house the fifty or so residents.

Cheryl was shivering when she pulled herself out of the bath but couldn't have said for certain whether it was with cold or anxiety. Only when she was downstairs in the kitchen did she remember the envelope from that morning.

Retrieving the post from the meter cupboard, Cheryl dropped the travel brochure into the kitchen bin. She didn't think she'd ever be able to look at one again. As she carried the fancy envelope with the embossed writing back to the table she wondered if she'd have the nerve to kill herself, to slit her wrists in the bath, let her mother find her daughter's corpse when she finally dragged herself out of bed. Cheryl felt an unfamiliar stab of pleasure at the thought of her mother spending the rest of her own days in Meadowcroft, being taken care of by zero-hours strangers with unfamiliar accents and dark skin tones. Her mother was shockingly racist; she'd hate being dependent upon people of colour for her intimate care.

Distracted by the thought of her mother's discomfort, Cheryl was careless opening the letter and gave herself a small paper cut. Tears sprang into her eyes, as though they'd been waiting for the excuse. Attempting to suck the pain away, she pulled the headed letter out with her other hand.

As she blinked away tears the words came into focus.

This is your token. Keep it safe. Tell no one. On the event of my death, it entitles you to an equal share of my wealth. Good luck.

Logan Quick

Cheryl sat at the kitchen table for a long time. On the same day that her mother had announced plans to disinherit her, someone else was leaving her money. And the word wealth was mentioned. It was a joke, another cruel trick of Sheila's. There was no way she was going to fall for it.

Nevertheless, before she went to bed that night, Cheryl retrieved the travel brochure from the kitchen bin.

Chapter 17

Shortly before ten o'clock, a new email pinged into the inbox of Craig's laptop. Knowing it would be another of the WI ladies, thanking him for his enjoyable and informative talk and hoping he wouldn't mind if they asked him just one last question about fire safety in the home, he ignored it. He'd respond to them all tomorrow, politely but briefly.

One more time, he typed the name *Logan Quick* into the search engine and the same menu sprang up: *Logan Quick, CEO of Quick Holdings* followed by *Logan Quick net worth*, then *Logan Quick children, Logan Quick wife, Logan Quick Island*.

Craig clicked on the top item. He already knew he'd find very little, especially compared to better-known British businessmen like James Dyson, Richard Branson or Jim Ratcliffe. Not that Logan Quick's net worth could stand up to any of theirs. As expected, it was the same as the last time he'd looked, but all sorts of people could access these pages and they were updated frequently, if not always accurately.

The Wikipedia page, too, remained the same: some information about Quick's various companies, of which he was chairman, not CEO; a bit of personal stuff; still no photographs. Logan Quick, it seemed, had made a point of staying out of the public eye. His CEO, a man called Clayton, had been the public face of the businesses for a long time now. Quick himself had no X account, no blog, no social media presence at all. He was something of a ghost.

Craig closed the site down. There was nothing here he didn't already know. And nothing to explain why a man he'd never met was leaving him a fortune.

In his pocket was the coin that had arrived with the letter. It was warm from being close to his body for most of the day and felt smooth and comforting beneath his fingers. Google Translate had helped with the Latin motto.

Cuique meritum. To each his deserts.

Craig was startled from his daydream by the sound of metal clanging onto concrete in the adjoining garage. Annoyed, he got up. He was sure he'd closed and locked the heavy swing door behind him when he'd arrived back, but it wasn't unheard of for one of the neighbourhood cats to find its way inside in the seconds it took him to get his car in and out. Even a bird could cause a small measure of havoc.

He unlocked the door between the house and garage and found the light switch. Nothing happened; the bulb had blown again. Using the torch on his phone, Craig turned to the garage door. Shut tight, as he'd thought. Uneasy now, he shone the thin light around. A half-empty paint can lay on its side, cream-coloured emulsion leaking from it. He bent to pick it up, listening for the tell-tale scrabbling that would direct him to the animal intruder. Cat, he hoped; they were easier to deal with than birds. Except, when had a cat ever been so clumsy as to knock over a paint can?

'Puss puss,' he said. Before he had a chance to feel stupid, he noticed the lid was open on his chest freezer.

'Anyone here?' OK now he did feel daft. There were no hiding places in the garage, other than the other side of his car and the freezer itself. He made himself walk all the way around the vehicle, even hunkered down to check beneath it, before gingerly approaching the freezer. Still at a distance, he stood on tiptoe to peer over the rim. As he took a step closer to check all the way in, he realised that he should have looked inside his car. He never locked it when it was parked in the garage. And the windows were tinted. The vehicle's interior would make the perfect hiding place. His heartbeat, already painful against his chest wall, seemed to accelerate. Freezer or car? Which to check first? He made a decision.

The freezer was empty. Breathing a sigh of relief, Craig reached up to close it.

Chapter 18

After Charlie had gone to bed, Holly checked her messages. A couple were from school, reminding parents of expected pupil behaviour. While they'd been copied to all parents, Holly couldn't help feeling they were aimed at her. And one from Coroline – her actual name, not a misspelling – who was Holly's other employer. Kind of.

Booking tomorrow evening. Gwynorth Manor. Dinner in hotel restaurant then company. 7 p.m. arrival, five hours total. Mr Jameson. Please confirm.

Derek Jameson was a regular. An estate agent who owned a chain of shops in the Southwest, he lived in Bristol but visited Cornwall every other month to meet with his local staff, and enjoy the sort of activities his middle-aged wife probably wouldn't believe two people in their right minds would want to do to each other.

Holly switched to the babysitting app. Charlie hated babysitters as a rule but got on surprisingly well with Sandra Morrison, a local lady in her early sixties who ran a boat repair business with her husband. Charlie adored boats. He knew every major manufacturer of sail boats, motorboats, cruise ships and high-speed RIBs. He knew their specifications and their expected performance. He knew which multihulls were expected to win the next America's Cup and the names of every Cornish Crabber moored in the nearest harbour.

For Charlie, the opportunity to talk about boats and look at photographs for a whole evening more than made up for the inconvenience of having a stranger in the house. Sandra was free – she usually was – and quickly replied to Holly's request that she be at the house by 6.30 p.m.

Holly messaged back to say she'd be delighted to meet Derek Jameson the following night and was getting undressed when the phone rang. Caroline.

'Tamara, I'm so sorry to bother you.' Caroline always addressed her ladies by their professional names; she claimed it cut the risk of making mistakes in front of the clients. 'But I saw you were up, and it reminded me I've been meaning to talk to you for a while now.'

'Everything OK?' Holly asked, unsure whether she wanted it to be or not. Her 'other work', as she liked to think of it, paid well, but in her darker moods she couldn't help feeling that it, more than being a barrister, more than being a mother, defined who she was.

'Fine, fine,' Caroline replied quickly. 'To be honest, we get more requests for you than we can fulfil. Any time you want to give up the day job . . .'

It wasn't the first time she'd dropped the same hint.

'The thing is, I think it's time to get you a professional portfolio,' Caroline went on. 'Half a dozen shots, couple of changes of underwear, maybe a swimsuit or a strategically draped bed sheet, I leave all that up to you and the photographer.'

'Is it necessary?' Caroline's agency, Cornish Courtesans, obscured all the girls' faces on the website, but it never felt enough. There were times when she broke into an ice-cold sweat at how exposed she was, how fragile her reputation. And Charlie's.

'It is.' Caroline stood for no dissent. 'You'll be expected to pay fifty per cent of the cost, so that'll be three hundred pounds. We cover the rest, and the hotel booking. I'll get Pam to ring you in the morning with the details.'

Three hundred pounds was more than Holly herself would make from her evening with Derek Jameson. Once she added in the cost of the babysitter, she'd lose money.

After wishing Caroline a good night, Holly flicked back through the photos on her phone to find the ones she'd been using in the three years since she'd joined the agency. A friend had been the photographer – selfies didn't really work – and they weren't bad at all. Still, she had to admit, they were a long way from the professional shots used by some of the other women. The one that worked best, according to the agency, showed Holly naked on a crumpled bed, face down. She held what purported to be a martini in one hand (it was actually watered-down apple juice) and was reaching for a pair of leopard-skin-covered handcuffs. The accompanying copy described her as playful, affectionate and adventurous.

She got up and crossed the landing to the bathroom. It was several days since her last client and she knew from bitter experience that when it came to shaving pubic hair, it didn't do to rush.

DAY TWO

Thursday, 4 October

Chapter 19

Sabri woke in the night with a feeling of deep sadness. It had been a long time since she'd seen her family so animated, so caught up in an idea, so together as they'd been earlier. And Darren's comment about medical school had touched her to the heart. She could never admit to the children how disappointed she was with her life, how she fought every day with a sense of wasted potential. And yes, downright jealousy of those who had what should have been hers.

A chance encounter, a momentary failure of judgement, and the bright, shining path ahead of her had turned into a dead end. She'd have been a great doctor. A consultant by now. Their lives would have been so different.

A familiar voice at the back of Sabri's head reminded her that, had she finished medical school, she probably wouldn't have met and married Jason. The kids, in the form they existed now, would never have been born. As usual, Sabri told herself that she wouldn't change a thing. That nothing was worth giving up the children she had now, the family she and Jason had created.

She never asked herself whether, deep down, she truly believed it.

There was a faint, artificial glow in the room and Jason's side of the bed was cold. Rousing herself, Sabri saw her husband at the dressing table, the laptop open in front of him.

'What are you doing?' she asked.

He started, shutting down the screen, but not before she'd spotted the website he'd been looking at. *Watches of Switzerland*.

'Couldn't sleep.' Jason closed the laptop and got up. In the dim light from the street she watched him cross the room in his boxers. He'd been so taut when she'd met him, so full and defined and solid, as though he carried more blood around than most. Such a big, raw, physical presence. In the beginning, she'd told herself it didn't matter that he wasn't her intellectual equal, that good principles, a strong moral core and innate kindness counted for so much more. Plus, he'd been gorgeous in the early days, way out of her league.

Now, when he moved, his flesh danced around his frame. 'Are you going to contact those solicitors tomorrow?' he asked.

'I'll try. If you promise not to spend any money we don't have.'

'Yet.'

He pulled down his boxers before he slipped back into bed and she felt her heart sinking. But they had sex so rarely now and he always took it personally if she turned him down. *How can I not take it personally?* he'd protested once. *I can't think of anything more personal.*

He moved close, pressing his body against hers. He was cool from the night air and she felt her skin goose-pimpling. He nuzzled the side of her face, breathing into her ear. 'What shall we do now?'

'If you order a Swiss watch I'll cut your cock off,' she replied, as she felt it press into her.

Chapter 20

Tug dropped flat behind the remnants of a low stone wall. The impact took the breath clean out of his body. Not dead yet.

The relentless hammering of machine-gun fire drilled into his head, grenades were being tossed about like sweets at a kid's party and a shower of rubble threatened to bury him alive. Still breathing.

He lay in the dirt, sweat pouring off his already dehydrated body. Six hours they'd been at it, and the old fort was awash with blood, spent munitions and body parts. An Afghan kid barely out of his teens was lying face up not ten metres away, screaming. His legs had been blown clean off and a mass of gore was spilling from his guts. The sick fuckers had mined the open courtyard.

Fast air on its way. Estimated five minutes to first strike.

Any second now a five-hundred-pound laser-guided bomb would land on the north tower of the fort, where a good portion of the enemy were holed up. And where Tug was lying face down in blood-soaked sand. He had half a mind to stay where he was. An air strike would be quick. A million times better than the torture he faced were he to be captured alive. Better than dying slowly, minus his arms and legs, after a mine had got him.

The Afghan lad missing half his body – Zain, that was his name – was looking at him, pleading with him. He'd been a nice kid, brave. His lips moved, formed something that could have been *brother?*

Tug rolled onto his side, freed his pistol from the holster, aimed and fired. He didn't wait to see the boy's head explode. He was up, running, cutting a path through the mines instinctively, expecting any moment to go flying through the air in a mist of blood and pain.

He heard the bomb land, saw the air thick with flying masonry and body parts.

And woke to find himself covered in sweat. It took him several seconds to realise that he was home, that Afghanistan was thousands of miles away and the battle of Qala-i-Jangi had been over twenty years ago. He leaned over to switch on the bedside light.

At least this time he'd woken in bed. Not so long ago he'd come out of the flashback to find himself crawling along one of the block's internal corridors, kitchen knife in his hand. He'd fixed child locks on all his kitchen cupboards and drawers after that, but in the hands of a man like Tug, anything could be a weapon. Even worse were the flashbacks that happened in the daytime. In the day, a lot more people could get hurt.

Knowing he wouldn't sleep again any time soon, Tug got up. He opened Rightmove on his laptop and went to a search he'd saved a few days earlier. The cottage in Dittisham was still on the market. Stone built, with walls over two feet thick, it sat on the very edge of the River Dart in the tiny Devonshire village. Two bedrooms, one big enough to take his gym equipment, a small kitchen and a living room with wood-burning stove. No room to park a car, but he wouldn't need a car, he'd only leave the village for a monthly trip to the supermarket.

The cottage was on the market for nearly three quarters of a million. Two days ago, it might as well have been ten million for all the chance Tug had of owning it. Now, though, he was heir to Logan Quick's billions.

Exhausted, his pulse still far too fast, he couldn't help laughing at himself. Hours earlier, he'd called every one of his old service mates he was still in touch with. All had denied all knowledge of any sort of practical joke, but one of them was lying. One of them had to be.

All the same, he'd buy a sailboat, when he lived in Dittisham. Something under twenty feet long; he had no need of a cabin, this was for day sailing only, but he might keep a tent on board, so that he could pitch up on quiet beaches on summer nights. He would call it *Redemption*.

Chapter 21

'Good morning, Barker, Momen and Dodds. How can I help you?'

Robin took a breath, telling himself he'd done his homework. He'd checked that Barker, Momen and Dodds was a real firm of solicitors. He'd done an online search with the Solicitors Regulatory Authority to make sure they were properly licensed to operate in the UK. He'd accessed their website, which had told him very little other than that the firm operated in the fields of dispute resolution, real estate, employment and trusts and estates. They had offices in Singapore, Exeter and not far from Holborn station in London. They were contactable by email, telephone, a crisis hotline and even the good old-fashioned postal service. Until they'd answered the phone, though, he hadn't really believed in them.

'I got a letter from you,' he began. 'There wasn't a contact name. It mentioned someone called Logan Quick.'

'May I take your name, sir?' the young man asked after a moment. Then, 'Ah, yes, Mr Knight. Can you confirm that the token is in your possession as we speak?'

Odd question. Robin looked down at the letter on the kitchen table. The token lay on the envelope.

'Yes, I'm looking at it now.'

'Keep it safe, Mr Knight. It's very important that you keep it safe. We'll be in touch when the time comes. Good morning to you.'

'No, wait. I need to talk to someone. I mean, who is Logan Quick? And why would he be leaving me money? I'd never even heard of Logan Quick before yesterday. I've certainly never met him. Is this for real?'

'It's certainly real, sir. But I can't discuss this case over the telephone.'

'So, what do I have to do? Make an appointment?'

'Nothing is required of you at this stage. If you wanted to make an appointment with Mr Caiger, I can do that for you now. Mr Caiger is the partner dealing with this case. An initial consultation costs one hundred and fifty pounds, with future consultations billed at three hundred pounds per hour.'

'You want me to make an appointment that will cost me one hundred and fifty pounds, not to mention my travel costs, before you'll tell me anything?'

'Making an appointment, or not, is entirely your choice, Mr Knight. Nothing is required of you at this stage.'

'Can you tell me how many tokens you sent out?'

'I can't discuss this case over the telephone.'

'Is this even legal?'

'Sir, we're one of the country's leading law firms. We never knowingly involve ourselves in illegal activity.'

'What happens if I lose it? This token thing? What if I lose it?'

'Try to avoid that eventuality, sir. I'm sorry. I have another call coming in. Good morning.'

The call was ended.

Ten minutes later Robin called back and made an appointment for the following Tuesday. In between calls, he'd made the token safe. He hoped.

Chapter 22

Thursday was delivery day at the garden centre. By the time Tug had emptied the nursery wagons of chrysanthemums, dahlias, asters and pansies, the hellebores and cyclamens had arrived. They all needed wheeling in, stacking on the pallets and tables, then watering. The other staff in the centre all seemed to find something else to do when the deliveries came in and so Tug worked alone. It didn't usually bother him. He didn't like to talk much, and the heavy physical work was like an extra gym session. For three hours, he didn't stop working, barely looked up, which is why he missed the arrival of the van that only delivered once a year, in early October. Had he seen it, he would have made sure to be the one to meet it, to take charge of the delivery; had he seen it, what followed might never have happened.

One second, Tug was winding away the hose pipe after watering the new arrivals; the next he was back in Afghanistan, racing through the minefield of Qala-i-Jangi, desperate to be as far away from the north tower as possible, because the laser-guided bomb was already falling. Amid the whistling of shells, the rattle of gunfire, the screaming of injured men, he was aware that he wasn't running alone. Behind him, men from his unit, and lads from the Northern Alliance were following him through. He was the canary in the coal mine, his footsteps showing the safe route through, until one misstep sent his fragmented mass to spray the fort.

When he came back to reality, he was lying amid the chaos of an overturned table. Plastic pots, earthenware, foliage and compost littered the floor. Faces stared down at him. A short distance away, a woman was crying out in pain. Sirens were getting closer.

'It was the fireworks, mate,' said Alf, one of the other garden centre staff. He and Tug were sitting in the staff room. Someone had made Tug a brew, but his hands were shaking too much to hold it steady. 'Some twat stacked them next to the storage heater. Left them there for over an hour. They all went up at once. Ten grand's worth of pyrotechnics up in smoke. We all thought World War III had broken out.'

'Who did I hurt?' Tug asked.

'Ah, she'll be fine. Lot of fuss about nothing.'

'What happened?'

Alf gave Tug an odd look. He knew about the PTSD of course, they all did. But none of them had actually witnessed it before.

'You came charging out the warehouse like the hounds of bleedin' hell were after you. Knocked a couple of old dears over before you dived under the perennials.'

'Suspected broken hip.'

Tug and Alf turned to see the manager in the doorway of the staff room.

'Her husband's already talking about suing us,' he went on. 'I'm going to have to let you go, Tug. I can't risk you running amok every time someone lights up a sparkler.'

'You can't do that.' Alf looked shocked. 'It's a disability, is PTSD. You can't sack someone for being disabled.'

The manager ignored Alf. 'Go to the office. You can collect your money in lieu of a month's notice.'

'He'll sue you,' Alf said. 'It's not like it was his fault the fireworks went up.'

Tug said nothing. They all knew he'd never get legal aid to sue, even if he could be arsed.

He collected his things from the staff room and left via the main entrance. He made a point of knocking one of the garden gnomes off its shelf as he passed. It made a very satisfying cracking sound as it broke on the tiled floor.

He stepped outside, into a day that was darkening as clouds rolled in. At the very back of the car park sat a Volvo with tinted windows. Black.

Chapter 23

'Sabs, is this true? You're the heiress to Logan Quick's fortune?'

It was Mel Poulter on the phone, the mother of one of Darren's best friends.

'No, of course not. Who told you that?' Half a day. They hadn't made it through half a bloody day.

'It's all over the school. Everyone's talking about it according to Stuart.'

Sabri sighed, making sure it was audible. 'It's a scam, Mel. I'll bet loads of people got the same letter we did.'

'Well, if they have, I haven't heard about it. And the solicitors have confirmed its real. Well, that's what Stuart said, anyway.'

'What solicitors? And how would Stuart know anything about it?'

'The kids are saying the letter you received came from a firm of solicitors and that Jason phoned them on the way to school this morning.'

Sabri leaned back against the kitchen wall.

'Didn't you know?' Mel sounded gleeful.

None of them had been in touch. 'I've had my phone switched off. Sorry, Mel, I'm getting another call.'

'Could be the solicitors. How very exciting. Don't forget your old friends when you're billionaires.'

'Bye, Mel.'

What the hell? She couldn't phone Jason until lunchtime because the print shop where he worked didn't allow personal phone calls.

He'd spoken to the solicitors? And they'd confirmed it was real? It wasn't possible. Chinese Whispers had gone into overdrive.

But what if it was real? What if they were to become the people you occasionally heard about on the news; those to whom wonderful, unexpected things happened? Would she go back to medical school? Would she even get a place now with, at best, twelve working years left in her before retirement?

Her phone was ringing again, this time a number she didn't recognise. Tentatively, Sabri pressed accept.

'Mrs Carter, this is BBC Cornwall. I'm calling about a report we've received this morning that you've been named as the heir to Logan Quick's fortune. We'd love to interview you on the show later.'

Sabri ended the call, realising as she did so that her world had shifted, irrevocably.

Chapter 24

Justin's car was parked outside the house when Tara got home. Tempted to pull up behind him and block his exit, she thought better of it and parked alongside.

He might have brought the analyst with him. What was her name, something like Tilly? Tara had once had a family dog called Tilly and while she'd never met Justin's girlfriend, the photographs she'd seen showed a thin, nervy-looking woman, with curly, mousy hair like the Bedlington Terrier that the canine Tilly had been.

'What're you doing here, dickhead?' she called as she let herself in.

Justin didn't reply, but she hadn't really expected him to. Tara carried her wet gear through to the laundry room and stuffed her swimsuit, gloves, socks and towels into the washing machine. She turned it onto the rinse cycle and hung up her bag. The smell of coffee drifted in. Bastard was helping himself.

He was in the living room, staring out across the garden.

'Good swim?' he said, when he saw her reflection in the glass.

Bite me, she thought. She said, 'What do you want?'

Justin gave a heavy sigh, the picture of the ever-reasonable man dealing with a difficult wife. 'We can be civilised, surely? You're low on milk.'

'So, keep your thieving mitts out of my fridge.'

She braced herself for a snarky comment about how it wasn't her fridge, it wasn't even her milk, because he paid for everything. Justin never tired of reminding her that she'd taken early retirement aged fifty and her glass sculptures barely paid for her hair appointments. To be fair, she took every opportunity to remind him that he'd pressured her to take retirement, because her shift work wasn't all that convenient; also, an NHS nurse, not even one in management, didn't really fit the corporate wife profile.

He walked over, putting his mug down on the kitchen counter. 'Do I get a kiss?' he asked, when he was close enough to slap.

'No, you fucking don't. What do you want?'

He shrugged. 'Thought we could chat. Lawrence told me about your letter from Logan Quick.'

'From his solicitors. Allegedly.'

Justin made a pretence of glancing around the room. 'So come on, let's see it.'

'I know Lawrence showed you already.'

'The letter, yeah. I want to see the token.'

'Well, you can't.'

He raised both hands in a despairing gesture. He was still, she realised, annoyingly, intimidatingly close. 'Come on, what do you think I'm going to do, steal it? Where is it?'

'In my fanny.' She turned away and made for the stairs. 'And I'm covered in salt. I'm going for a shower. Let yourself out.'

Justin didn't let himself out. She'd known he wouldn't. He followed her upstairs and was waiting when she emerged, dripping, from the shower. The towel she'd chosen was small, little more than a hand towel.

She'd washed the sea water from her hair, and it streamed down her back. In her early fifties, Tara's hair was still as long and blonde and soft as when she and Justin had met. He'd always loved her hair. And he'd never been able to resist her straight from the shower.

He unzipped his pants, pulled the towel from her grasp, and pushed her up against the window. Tara's face fell against the cool glass, and she wondered what the cleaning lady might make of it when she arrived the next day. It wouldn't be the first time her face cream had been smeared over exactly that spot.

Justin clasped one hand around her breast and began fingering her nipple as his other hand entered her from behind. He moaned at how wet she was, thinking her more than ready for him. He was an idiot. Knowing what was coming, she'd doused herself liberally with KY jelly after the shower.

She felt his dick pushing against her and tilted her arse so he could get it straight in.

It was probably one of the biggest ironies of Tara's life that sex with her husband had got better since he'd left her.

Chapter 25

'And he broke his back?' Chris finished his second glass of Merlot and reached for the bottle. Holly, who couldn't remember the last time someone had ordered a bottle of wine for only two people at lunchtime, was still working through her first glass. The restaurant was fancier than she'd have chosen, but Chris had made the booking without consulting her.

'So what?' Chris went on. 'Is he crippled?'

A droplet of red wine, like blood spatter from a wound, landed on the sleeve of Chris's collarless shirt. Hissing with annoyance, he reached for the water jug. Holly thought, but didn't say, that he was lucky it had hit his shirt and not the full-length, cashmere coat slung over the back of his chair.

Chris invariably made Holly feel ten years older than she was and a total frump. She made a point of always wearing black, functional clothes to work, a size too big, teamed with low heels. Her hair was pulled back into a tight bun, and she avoided make-up. At home, she wore jeans and plus-sized sweaters. She knew perfectly well why she did so. Holly had two wardrobes, and never the twain could meet.

'Thankfully no,' she said, watching Chris use his fingers to scoop water from the jug and splash it on his sleeve. 'He was in a lot of pain for weeks and even now can't do half of what he used to, but he won't be permanently disabled.'

Chris held his arm up to the light before dabbing at his shirt fabric with the edge of the tablecloth. 'And the company are saying what? No harm, no foul? Even though the accident was on company premises and was a result of, allegedly, their negligence?'

'Pretty much,' she agreed. 'They paid him his full salary for the first six weeks and only when they were talking about putting him on statutory sick pay did he and his wife think to consult a solicitor. Even now, they're nervous about taking his employers to court.'

'Understandable.' Chris's eyes were wandering. His specialism was commercial disputes, where the big money could be found. Little people and their problems held no interest for him.

'Shockingly exploitative on the part of the company.' Holly was starting to find her old friend annoying. 'If they'd made him a decent offer of compensation, without needing to be asked, as anyone with a shred of moral fibre would have done, he'd probably have been loyal and hardworking for the rest of his life.'

Conscious she was starting to rant, Holly shovelled up a forkful of quinoa and wild rice. The vegan salad had been the cheapest thing on the menu. Chris had ordered fillet steak with several side orders. And he'd be drinking most of the wine.

'He has a son with severe autism, which means his wife can't work,' she added.

Chris nodded, as though he understood everything now. 'Like Charlie,' he said, and it wasn't even a goddamned question.

'Not remotely like Charlie. Charlie is very high functioning. This lad needs a special school.'

He gave a mock scared look. 'My mistake.'

Holly glanced at her watch and didn't even try to hide that she'd done so.

Chris put his knife and fork down. 'Thing is, Holls, I need a favour.'

Holly's appetite vanished. 'Oh?'

Chris picked up his glass and took a huge glug, as though bracing himself. Holly wasn't fooled; her old friend had no shame. 'Yeah,' he said. 'So, I've been asked to leave chambers.'

Fair play, that was a big deal. 'What happened?'

He gave his classic naughty-boy face. 'I shagged a junior clerk.'

'Is that a sackable offence now?'

'It is if you do it in the managing partner's office and he accuses you of sexual misconduct.'

'The managing partner accused you?'

'No, the clerk. Claims I've been pressuring him for weeks, threatening to make life difficult for him if he doesn't put out. And he's Black, so obviously everyone takes his word for it.'

Holly put her knife and fork down, closing them carefully to indicate that she was finished. And waited.

'I need a loan,' Chris went on. 'Something to tide me over. I've got rent due next week and I need to appoint my own solicitor. A couple of grand should cover it. Let's say three.'

He wanted her to give him three thousand pounds.

'Chris, I don't have that kind of money.'

That wasn't strictly true; she had a healthy enough savings account. But that money was for Charlie's secondary school. There was no way he could go to the local comprehensive. They'd eat him alive. She needed twenty grand a year to send him to a private school and his dad wouldn't chip in unless she agreed to share custody.

Chris leaned back in his chair and raised one eyebrow.

'I'd like to help, but . . .' Holly began.

Her old friend's face became sullen. 'You don't want to?'

'Three thousand pounds? That's so much money.'

'My rent's two grand a month. And a man's got to live.'

And if he didn't find another job soon, would he expect her to pay next month's rent too? She said, 'Can no one else help?' Chris's family weren't exactly working class.

'No one else who owes me.'

'I don't owe . . .' Oh.

'I still have the pictures on my hard drive, Holls.'

Chris, a man she'd known for twelve years, had been the friend who'd taken the photographs when she'd applied to join Cornish Courtesans. She'd dismissed asking her female friends, knowing they'd be too judgemental, and she certainly wasn't about to strip off in front of her heterosexual male friends. Chris, totally uninterested in the female form, had been the ideal choice. And he was a decent photographer. He'd done a good job, and to this day hadn't asked for anything in return.

On Chris's versions, her face would be plainly visible.

'I called the agency,' he went on. 'Cornish Courtesans, nice name. I enquired how much it might cost to hire you for the night. What percentage of that do you get, Holly? You probably earn three grand in a week.'

Oh God, he was serious.

'Not nearly that much. I can't get out all that often. I have a young son.'

He shrugged. 'Hope he's broad-minded about what his mother gets up to.'

'Are you blackmailing me?'

He looked genuinely hurt. 'Holly, that's an ugly word between friends. I just need a bit of help, that's all. For a month or two.' He smiled. 'Maybe three.'

Holly swallowed hard, but the lump in her throat seemed to get bigger if anything. 'I need some time,' she said. 'I can't put my hands on that much cash right away.'

Chris leaned back in his chair. 'No worries,' he said. 'I'll call you later in the week.' He glanced around. 'I'll get the bill.' He smiled at her. 'Shall we split it?'

Chapter 26

'Only me,' Cheryl called, as she opened the front door. She stretched her visits to the public library for as long as she could. There was a table where she could make herself coffee, and the librarians, all kind ladies, often brought in cakes or biscuits. They were aware she never put much in the donation tin, but she sensed they knew and understood her circumstances.

It occurred to her, as she pulled off her coat and gloves, that Sheila had set her free. If she no longer had to wait around for her inheritance, there was nothing to stop her leaving now. Finding a job would be easier now than in ten years. She could move out. Let Sheila know how it felt to be abandoned.

But what if the solicitors' letter was real? What if she really was going to inherit money? Wealth? How satisfying would it be, after all this time, to be the one with power?

She carried her bag through to the kitchen and thought her heart might stop.

Her mother stood behind the kitchen table, an odd look of triumph on her face. On the table were an old Christmas biscuit tin that Cheryl kept on the very top shelf of the dry goods cupboard, her collection of travel brochures from the top of her wardrobe and the letter from the solicitors that had arrived the day before.

'Well, well, aren't we the one with secrets?' Sheila said as, one by one, she removed Cheryl's secret treats from the biscuit tin.

It wasn't easy to get one over on Sheila. Every time she went to the shops, Cheryl was expected to stick rigidly to the list, keep the receipts and hand over the exact change. But the greengrocer's stall on the weekly market didn't give itemised receipts and every week she'd been able to hold back a tiny amount of cash without rousing Sheila's suspicions. And that cash was hers to spend as she wanted.

Cadbury's Fruit & Nut was Cheryl's favourite, but she also loved Jelly Babies, Club Orange biscuits and chocolate marshmallows. Mainly, though, she bought anything on special offer.

'No wonder you're the size of a house.' Sheila looked her up and down. 'Pigging out on this rubbish every time my back's turned.'

That was mean and untrue. She rationed herself to one treat a night, after her mother was in bed. Chocolate and romantic fiction. Sometimes Cheryl thought it was all that got her through the days.

'It's only a bit of chocolate, Mum.' How could her mother make her feel dirty over chocolate? Worse, though, was to come.

'And are you going somewhere?'

As Sheila moved on to the travel brochures a tiny voice inside Cheryl told her to be angry. She'd had no idea her mother was capable of climbing onto a chair to reach the top shelf of the kitchen cupboard, let alone the top of her wardrobe.

'I mean, please tell me what this lot is all about.'

'They're just brochures, Mum. They don't cost anything.'

'Ecuador and the Galapagos Islands? Tanzania?' What did I miss, Cheryl? When did you win the lottery?'

'I didn't mean anything.'

'And this?' Sheila had pulled the letter from its envelope. 'What the bloody hell is this?'

Well, at least she knew now the letter wasn't a prank of Sheila's. Her mother looked furious.

'It just arrived. It wasn't my fault.'

'You think, what? You're going to inherit a fortune and go swanning around the world while I'm left here to manage by myself?'

Cheryl registered the fear behind her mother's aggression; she was genuinely afraid of being left alone.

Sheila gave a wail of fury. 'Don't just stand there like a big-eyed cow. Say something. I don't know who put you up to this, but I know you'd never have thought of it for yourself. What did you think you were going to do? Frighten me into changing my mind?'

Her mother thought she'd sent that letter to herself.

'It arrived yesterday, Mum. Before I knew anything about your will. You can check the postmark. And I have no idea where it came from or who this man is.'

For several seconds, Sheila neither spoke nor moved. Then she pushed the letter back into its envelope and stalked past Cheryl and into the sitting room. The fire was still burning brightly in the hearth. Sheila pulled the fireguard away and glanced back.

'Last chance,' she said. 'Admit it was you.'

'I had nothing to do with it, Mum. Use your brain. Where would I get the paper from? Or a typewriter?'

'Don't you speak to me in that tone.' At last, Sheila looked uncertain.

'Let me put the kettle on. I got you two books about the lifeboat service. And some good stories. One by that author you like. Milly something. We can start it tonight.'

'Well, if it's nothing to do with you, you won't mind then.' Sheila opened her hand and the envelope dropped into the flames.

Cheryl ran forward. Pushing her mother out of the way – something she'd never done before – she dropped to her knees. The envelope was properly alight, the flames eating up the crisp paper. There was less than half of it left, and that half was a charred mess.

'How dare you push me?' Her mother had landed in the nearest armchair. 'Have you forgotten everything I've done for you?'

Cheryl felt a stabbing pain in her ribs; her mum had kicked her.

'There are worse places to end up than Meadowcroft, you know?' Sheila's foot connected once again with Cheryl's ribs.

'Why would you do that?' Cheryl felt despair creeping over her. The letter had brought her hope. Of course she didn't think it was real – how could it possibly be real? – but it had put a dream into her head. It would have been nice to keep the dream for a while longer.

'Hitting an old lady,' Sheila went on. Cheryl said nothing. She hadn't hit her mother, she'd never hit her mother; she'd pushed her out of the way as she'd rushed to save the letter and she shouldn't have done that, but there was no harm done. 'They put you away for that, you know?' Sheila went on. 'Grievous bodily harm. Not that I need anything new on you.'

This again. As the last blackened curl of the letter shrank to nothing, the despair in Cheryl turned to a rage she couldn't remember ever feeling before. She stood up and stepped out of range of Sheila's feet.

'I'd be very careful if I were you, Mum. If I'm going to prison – and you're probably wrong, it won't be much worse than working at Meadowcroft – then I might as well go for something worthwhile.'

She reached out and picked up the poker, gripping it firmly in her right hand, before looking her mother full in the face. She saw, with immense satisfaction, the gleam of terror in Sheila's eyes.

Chapter 27

'So, I'll see you Friday,' Justin said, as he zipped up his pants.

'And will you be needing a blow job in the car park?' Tara gave her best icy smile as she reached for her bathrobe and wrapped it around herself.

'I've asked a couple of estate agents to call round,' he said, after a second. 'They'll check with you first to make sure it's convenient.'

Tara's stomach clenched. 'It won't be. Call them back and tell them you've changed your mind. Because it will be very embarrassing – for you – when I don't let them in.'

He gave a heavy sigh. 'Tar—'

'No, don't Tar, me. You can't put this house on the market unless I agree. And I don't.'

'Where's the harm in finding out what it's worth?'

'No.'

Tara glanced back, over her shoulder, over the steep dell that was the property's surrounding land. The garden was all hers. She'd done everything, other than the heavy landscaping, and it had taken years of planning and hard physical labour. Built on the crest of a wooded valley, the house overlooked a paved path that wound its way through birch, rowan and hazel trees. Ferns, huge and luscious, lined the way while great swathes of flowers appeared like wonderful surprises. She'd made the most of a natural spring, coaxing it into tiny pools, rushing streams and waterfalls. In her heart of hearts, Tara sometimes wondered if she loved this house as much as she loved her children. And now, having done nothing wrong, she was expected to give it up.

'You can't stay here, Tara. You know that. You can't afford it and it's far too big for you.'

'It was too big for four of us, but I don't remember you having a problem then.'

Justin was fully dressed now, ready to go back to his new life. She wondered if he'd even bother to wash his cock before putting it in the analyst that night.

'You're putting off the inevitable,' he told her.

'Then I'll put it off as long as I can. You set this whole process in motion, Justin, so you'll have to see it through. You can't sell this house until the finances are settled and that's months away. Maybe the court will give it to me outright, who knows?'

Small chance of that, but even the possibility would piss Justin off no end.

He gave a short, unpleasant laugh as he left the room. 'You're not taking this Logan Quick bollocks seriously, are you?' He shook his head, before turning to leave the room. 'Oh, Tara.'

Forcing a house sale would be understandable if Justin needed the money, but he didn't. He had a flat in Notting Hill that he shared with the Bedlington Terrier. The two of them had just returned from a two-week holiday in Barbados. He couldn't even argue that he'd give the money to the children; he'd made it perfectly clear they'd be expected to make their own fortunes, just as he had. Justin had a perfectly nice, well-funded lifestyle with a woman fifteen years his junior and was probably seeing more of his children than he had when they were younger. He was happier than he'd been in decades. Which meant that selling the house was about taking it away from her.

'I mean it about the estate agents,' she called to her husband's retreating feet on the stairs. 'Don't you dare send them round here.'

There was a pause when he reached the bottom. Then, 'I'm stopping your allowance,' he called up. 'There's enough in the joint account for this month. After that, you're on your own.'

Tara crossed quickly to the top of the stairs. 'You can't do that,' she said, as fear grabbed a tight hold of her stomach.

He looked up. 'Watch me.'

She had no savings that she could access. All their money was held jointly, but she had no idea of the details, let alone the passwords that would enable her to access funds.

'Of course, if you decide to be reasonable, we can come to a financial arrangement very quickly.' He gave a nasty smile, a second before retrieving his keys from the table by the front door. 'I'll let the estate agents contact you directly, shall I?'

A cold wind rushed through the house as Justin left. Trembling, Tara returned to the bedroom. She sat by the window and picked up her phone. Dialled a number. It was answered on the fourth ring.

'Am I speaking to Amanda Holt?' Tara said. 'Logan Quick's former wife?'

Chapter 28

It was only a matter of time.

The story was out, faster than he'd have expected. A couple of hours earlier, on the drive-time news, the local radio station had run a story about a woman from Truro who'd received a mysterious token in the post the previous day; a token that promised her a future of untold wealth; a token that sounded identical to the one currently on Craig Lewis's kitchen table. The woman had refused to comment, and details were scant, but he knew a thing or two about how the media worked. The story was too good to let go. BBC Cornwall would pursue it and before long, probably the next day, the national networks would pick it up. The woman and her family wouldn't know what had hit them.

She'd been a fool. The *tell no one* clause in the letter had been good advice.

And now, it was only a matter of time before the other recipients were found and outed. The solicitors' letter had referred to 'a share' of Quick's wealth, so of course everyone assumed there were others, and the British media liked nothing more than a challenge.

His phone was ringing. His ex-wife. He ignored it.

Through the dimpled glass of the front door he saw the hired Transit van with his mate at the wheel pull up outside. He moved back through the hallway to access the garage and open the swing door. They'd wait till after dark before packing everything up. After dark, he could avoid any awkward questions or difficult encounters with the neighbours.

By the time the name Craig Lewis leaked – and it would, he'd put money on it – the man himself would be whereabouts unknown.

DAY THREE

Friday, 5 October

Chapter 29

BBC Cornwall were five minutes into the midnight show as Sabri got into her car, and the first voice she heard as she pulled out of the car park was her husband's.

'Yeah, so I spoke to the solicitors this morning when I was driving the kids to school,' Jason was saying. 'You know what kids are like, they were giving me no peace. I'm not allowed to give out any details, confidential and all that, but it's all very exciting.'

Sabri's body began to squeeze in on itself. So, he had made the phone call. She'd been hoping Mel had got it wrong. Well, now she knew why her husband had been refusing to take her calls all day. He'd known she'd go ape shit.

'I can imagine,' the reporter replied. 'So, tell me, Jason, what did you think when you first saw the letter? What was going through your head?'

'Well, we were all pretty floored, I can tell you. I mean, we don't know Logan Quick. The wife thought it was a scam. She'd have put it in the bin if I'd let her. And then where would we be?'

'Where indeed? And what are your plans to spend the money?'

Jason laughed. 'Blimey, give us a chance, mate. The bloke's not dead yet.'

'That was Jason Carter, speaking to our reporter earlier today. A very lucky man, if it turns out to be genuine. What do I think? I think we should wait and see.'

Travelling at nearly fifty miles an hour, Sabri closed her eyes. Did Jason realise what a dick he'd sounded? And how could he? He'd known she would hate it.

She switched off the radio and drove home far too fast, jumping more than one amber light. To find a Tesla parked in their driveway.

Something inside her, something that felt like a tightly strung wire, snapped.

She couldn't bring herself to park behind it – what the hell had he done with his own car? – and so she pulled over in the street. How was it possible? What idiot would sell Jason a car that expensive? He didn't even have enough for a deposit and God only knew what the monthly repayments would be.

She got out and walked towards the house on legs that didn't feel like her own.

It was a grey saloon, quite modest-looking, given how expensive it must be. It was a classy car, a beautiful car, and she wanted to take a brick to the windscreen, to kick dents in the paintwork, to run her keys down its length, because nothing else right now would give an outlet to the rage she was feeling. With an effort, she controlled herself, walking quickly past it to the front door.

A decade and a half of controlling her fury so as not to scare the kids helped her hold it together as she let herself in and made her way upstairs. Jason was pretending to be asleep; there was no fucking way he was really asleep, not with a Tesla in the driveway. She closed the bedroom door softly and stayed by it.

'Have you lost your fucking mind?'

Her voice seemed to have dropped an octave. It always did when she was trying not to scream.

He let a couple of seconds go by, then, 'What? You back? What time is it?'

'Cut the crap, Jase, I can tell when you're asleep. It was bad enough hearing you be a complete dickhead on the radio. And now a Tesla? I ask again, have you lost your fucking mind?'

He sat up and reached for the bedside light. 'It's on test drive. Chill out, babe. I've got to take it back tomorrow.'

Oh, thank God. Thank God for that. Even so.

'What the hell are you doing taking a Tesla for a test drive? We can't begin to afford one. We can barely afford to get mine through its MOT next month. And you phoned those solicitors. What the actual fuck, Jase?'

'Keep your voice down, you'll wake the kids.'

'The kids are going to be broken-hearted when they find out this is all a scam. And you'll have done it to them. Not that stupid con trick of a letter. You. Their dad.'

'Sab, it's real. It's not a con. It's real. I spoke to them.'

There was a wall inside Sabri's head, she realised. Stone built. Dense, solid, impenetrable; one that refused to let through the possibility of good news. No, he was not doing this to her. He was not going to let her hope.

'They said they couldn't talk to me, that they can only talk to the recipient of the letter. That's you. But they said it's absolutely genuine and that you could make an appointment to see them at any time.'

'They're not real solicitors, Jason. They're a bunch of con artists. Probably somewhere in Taiwan.'

'They're registered with the Law Society. I checked.'

'It's not possible.'

'It'll cost us one hundred and fifty pounds for a half-hour appointment and they'll explain everything.'

Exhaustion washed through Sabri. For a moment there . . .

'And there it is,' she spat at him. 'They've sent out thousands of the things. We pay our one hundred and fifty pounds and when we get there, it's an empty flat about a pizza shop.'

'We don't have to hand any money over in advance. We pay the one hundred and fifty pounds at the appointment. I checked that too. I'm not an idiot, Sab.'

'We don't have a one hundred and fifty pounds, Jason. We have exactly forty-six pounds in the account to last to the end of the month. How can you not know this?'

The bedroom door nudged Sabri's back. She stepped forward and turned to watch the door opening slowly, tentatively. In the light from the landing she saw her three children, in night clothes, standing in the doorway.

'It's OK, Mum.' Maddy reached out a hand towards Sabri's arm. 'We've sorted it. You can take the money from our bank accounts. All three of us.'

'Fifty quid each,' Darren added.

'Then pay us back later,' Bethany chipped in. 'You have to pay us back when we have the man's money. Obviously, we want it back.'

Knowing she had to get her children back to bed, that they'd barely be able to function in the morning, Sabri crossed the room and climbed into her own bed, still wearing the jeans and sweater she'd driven home in. She had nothing left. Exhaustion was sweeping through her.

As though acting on instinct, all three children followed her, the girls climbing into the bed on Sabri's side, forcing her up against Jason. Darren squeezed in beside his dad. For several seconds no one spoke. Then:

'Things are going to be very different from now on, aren't they?' said Maddy.

Chapter 30

Holly always allowed herself thirty minutes to say goodbye to Derek Jameson. Unlike some of her clients, he never slept during their encounters. He liked to talk after sex, to drink the miniature bottles of Scotch from the mini bar. He liked her to massage his shoulders and back. He liked a long kiss goodbye. Above all, he liked to watch her dress.

'You in court tomorrow?' he asked, as she rolled up her stockings. She was wearing peach-coloured underwear. Some of her clients liked her in red, black or animal print but Derek preferred a classier approach. He wanted the girlfriend experience.

'Not till next week.' She unhooked her bra from the chair arm and slid the straps onto her arms. People always imagined a barrister spent her life in court. In reality, most of the job was prep work. She bent over to retrieve her pants, giving him a full view of her bottom. His gasp was audible from across the room.

'Do you have to wear a wig and gown?'

Holly stiffened. Please let this not be going where she thought it was. She stepped into her pants and pulled them up.

'Them's the rules.' She smiled at him over her shoulder. He was still in bed, only one hand, his left, visible on top of the covers.

'I'd like to see them. Can you bring them next time?'

Jesus wept, he wanted to fuck her in her gown and wig. She found her dress and stepped into it, then her shoes and coat. She forced herself to smile as she approached the bed and bent over him. He smelled of Scotch and garlic. His right hand was still somewhere in the crotch region.

'We could, you know, pretend I'm in the dock. That I've been a naughty boy.'

Oh, for the love of God.

'I'm sure that can be arranged. Good night, Derek. Take very good care of yourself.'

She collected her bag on the way to the door and blew him a kiss. It was the little things, not the sex, that kept them coming back.

Outside, in the corridor, she came face to face with the head-teacher of her son's primary school.

Chapter 31

In the early hours of Friday morning, Cheryl woke suddenly; the alarm clock beneath her pillow told her it was nearly four o'clock in the morning. She eased herself out of bed and made her way through the dark and chilly house.

The fire had gone out, of course. They never added coal after nine o'clock at night and it had always burned down to embers before she took Sheila up to bed at half past ten. At four in the morning, she couldn't even feel a residual warmth coming from the grate.

Cheryl lifted the poker and began to move the ashes around. After several minutes, she found what she was looking for. The token, that funny round coin that had arrived with the letter, had survived.

Chapter 32

Tara woke on Friday morning to the sound of her phone ringing. It wasn't by the side of her bed, which meant she'd had more to drink last night than she'd realised. She found it in the bathroom, but only because she'd given up looking and needed a pee. Several missed calls from Esther, the swim friend, which was odd, because of the whole group, Esther was probably the one Tara knew the least. It began ringing again as she settled herself down on the loo.

'Hi,' she said, hoping Esther wouldn't correctly interpret the waterfall sound in the background. God, her head hurt.

'Tara, I'm really sorry to be bothering you, but I'm about to go into meetings and I thought this was something you'd want to know.'

'No problem, lovely,' she said. 'What's up.'

'Have you seen Facebook this morning?'

'No, I've been in the garden since it got light.' God, she was going to hell. 'What about Facebook?'

'Well, I hate to be a sneak, but I really don't think it's on. Maybe you can ask her to take it down.'

Suddenly, it was no longer just last night's booze that was churning around inside Tara.

'What?' she said.

'Becca put that photograph on her page. You know, the one she took of that solicitors' letter. She doesn't mention you by name, but she's tagged you in it, so most people will probably work out it was you who received it.'

Tara had shared the solicitors' letter and its accompanying token with her swimming buddies. She'd seen no reason not to. They'd written it off as a hoax, but not before Becca had taken a picture with her phone.

'You are kidding me.' Finally, she stopped peeing.

'Sorry, I'm really not. And it's attracting a lot of attention. A few people have shared it.'

At that moment, the doorbell rang.

'There's someone at the door, Esther. Thanks for letting me know.'

Ending the call, Tara grabbed an old dressing gown of Justin's from the back of the bathroom door. It still smelled of him and she made a mental note to burn it.

The doorbell rang again.

Tara opened up Facebook as she made her way downstairs. Becca's post with the photograph of the solicitors' letter popped up right away. Sixty-three frigging comments. And four shares.

The bell again.

Through the glass surround Tara could see the outline of a woman. For a moment, she thought it might be Becca come to apologise, and then realised she couldn't access the property without the code.

So, who the hell was it? And how had they got onto the drive?

Tara pulled open the door ready to yell and was surprised by the sight of an attractive young woman who looked familiar. Wearing a red raincoat, buckled at the waist, and boots that Tara would have priced at somewhere between four and five hundred pounds, the woman had brown skin and a blow-dried black bob. The perfect polish of her black boots was marred by scuffing.

Further down the drive a man carrying a huge camera was heading to the house.

'Mrs Webb? I'm Jasmin Basri from BBC Cornwall. We'd love to talk to you about the letter you received from Logan Quick's solicitors. Can we come inside for a moment?'

The woman's self-assurance was close to intimidating; Tara had to stop herself from stepping back and allowing her in. She said, 'How did you get onto my property?'

'We rang the bell at the bottom of the drive several times. We thought perhaps it wasn't working.'

Tara hadn't heard the drive bell. Mind you, she'd also missed several calls from Esther. In the meantime, these two had climbed over her gates.

'It's working.' She raised her voice to reach the bloke with the camera. 'Point that at me and I'm calling the police.'

'We'd love to get your side of the story,' the journalist went on. 'A set-the-record-straight piece. How did you feel when you opened the letter?'

'I've nothing to say to you and I want you off my property.'

'Do you know Logan Quick? Why do you think he'd leave you his money?'

'I'm closing the door now. Leave.'

'Do you know a Sabri Carter? She's received one of these letters too? We interviewed her husband last night. Is she a friend of yours?'

Having closed the door on the news crew, Tara made tea and took it back to bed. As she passed the landing window, she saw the tail end of a red coat disappearing over the top of the property's huge entrance gates and remembered that saved somewhere on the house computer were the instructions that would allow her to change the code. Maybe having to climb over the gate would put an end to Justin's habit of dropping in unannounced.

Tucked up under the duvet, feeling her pounding heart finally starting to settle down, she soon found Sabri Carter on Facebook. A brown-skinned woman, thin and horsey-looking, of about Tara's age, she was married to a very good-looking white bloke and was a paramedic. She wasn't a prolific poster, just the odd family occasion, and had made no mention of receiving a token.

She did know Sabri Carter, she realised. She'd been driving the ambulance that had taken the hypothermic swimmer to hospital two days ago.

After several false starts, she typed out a message.

Hi. A journalist told me this morning that you'd received a letter from Barker, Momen and Dodds. I got one too. Do you want to talk?

She waited several minutes before getting up to find paracetamol. When she got back to bed, a message had appeared.

How do I know you're not a journalist?

Fair enough. Tara found her photograph of the solicitors' letter and messaged it back.

Why don't you show me yours? She added to the pic. And waited. An image appeared. The same letter.

Want to talk? Tara texted. A second later, her phone rang. Someone calling her on Messenger. It was Sabri. Her heartbeat escalating, she pressed answer.

'Hi,' she said. 'This is Tara.'

Chapter 33

Leaving chambers early, Holly approached her son's school with trepidation. The headteacher's office window directly overlooked the playground where parents waited to collect their children. Of course, there was no reason why she shouldn't have been in the hotel the previous evening, it was a public building after all, but leaving a bedroom not long after midnight, with tousled hair and smudged make up, wearing clothes very different to her normal school pick-up wear. Well, it didn't take a genius to work out that she'd met someone for sex.

The teacher on door duty appeared. The infants always left the school first. A second teacher joined the first and both looked in Holly's direction.

She was being paranoid. No way could Mrs Milton have made the leap to Holly being a paid escort, but if Chris was as good as his word, if he followed through on his threat to expose her, then having been spotted in a compromising situation would be seen as cast-iron proof. Especially for people who didn't like her anyway.

Holly felt panic rising. No one would want a publicly disgraced barrister representing them in court. She'd never work again. Tim would sue for custody and win. She'd lose Charlie.

As usual, the other mums were keeping their distance. God, they'd love it when they found out. Holly the Whore. The pictures would be passed round at coffee mornings, and it would only be a matter of time before the kids found out. Charlie would be tormented with pictures of his mother's naked tits and ass for the rest of his school life. Children killed themselves for less.

Holly knew at that moment that she'd give Chris his money; she had no choice. But the amount he wanted was eye-watering and she had no illusions that it was a one-off request. She'd be working for him from now on. Her old friend had become her pimp.

Her son came through the doors and set off at a run towards her. He never normally did that. He was usually the last to leave, hanging around till the other kids were safely away.

Knowing she would pay Chris was one thing; finding the money another. Holly had spent much of the previous night awake, going through her finances. She had nearly fifty grand in her savings account but that was for Charlie's secondary school. Fees would be a little over fifteen grand a year. With another five or so on top for extras, she only had enough to fund three years out of the seven he'd need. And then university. It already wasn't enough and Chris, demanding three grand a month, would go through it like a swarm of genetically engineered locusts.

Nor could she fund Chris out of her income. What was left over after she'd met her own and Charlie's needs went to pay for her father's care and to top up her savings. Her dad cost her eighteen grand a year and he was still in his late fifties. He could live for years yet, and his needs would only escalate.

Charlie dropped his bag at her feet and beamed up at her. 'Mum, guess what?'

Holly bent to pick the bag up. 'I never will so you'll have to tell me.' It was their standard response to a question they'd long ago agreed was impossible to answer. She even risked putting a hand on his shoulder as they walked to the car. Normally, Charlie didn't like to be touched, but he seemed in such a good mood, and she so badly needed to feel her son right now.

'*Charlie and the Chocolate Factory* has come true.'

The Roald Dahl book had been his favourite since he'd been tiny. Aged four, he'd found it impossible to believe there were other little boys in the world called Charlie. So, obviously, the book was about him.

Holly opened the car and held the door for her son to climb into the passenger seat. She joined him, turned on the ignition and indicated to pull out.

'You and five friends are going on a VIP tour of the local chocolate factory?'

'No, silly. And it would be four friends. Five kids get the golden tickets, not six. I don't mean it lit – lit . . .'

'Literally?' she suggested, proud as punch that even at ten years old, Charlie was starting to grasp the concept of literal versus figurative. So many autistic kids never came close.

'No, not literally. But almost the same. This very rich man, like Willy Wonka only real, has sent out some golden tickets. Nobody knows how many. But whoever gets one will get a share of his money when he dies. And he's really, really rich.'

The lights changed as Holly reached the end of the road and the traffic came to a stop. She glanced sideways.

'Well, that sounds fun. Hold on, how do you get hold of these tickets? Is this a ruse to get me to buy endless supplies of chocolate?'

He took her seriously, as usual. 'You don't have to buy anything. They come in the post. A girl's mum at St Barnabus's got one. She got a letter from some solicitors.'

'And a golden ticket?'

'No, a token.'

Her mind still on the Chris problem, Holly took a moment to register what her son had just said. 'A what?'

'A token. Like a coin, only gold. Actually, it might not be gold. Someone else said it was silver. With some odd writing on it.'

Somewhere behind them, a car horn sounded.

'Bronze,' Holly said. 'They're bronze, or they seem to be. And the writing is Latin.'

Charlie looked at her curiously. He was rarely sensitive to her moods but even he could hear the tone of her voice had changed.

'So, you did know about it?' he accused.

The horn sounded again. Holly glanced up to see the lights had changed. She drove forward.

'Sweetheart, I don't think it can be real. I think it's probably a joke. A mean one, I agree, but a joke all the same.'

Charlie understood the concept of jokes; he just couldn't spot them for himself. 'No, it's real. It's been on the radio and everything. And the man is a real man. A real billionaire.'

'Wow.'

'What? What is it, Mum?'

Holly took a deep breath and made a decision. 'When we get home, I need you to help me search through the bins.'

Chapter 34

'See you in church,' she'd said. Of course, for Jax, who'd been married before and who would never marry in conventional style, it was a deconsecrated church that she'd had in mind.

Jax and Robin had met years ago in London; she'd been a third-year medical student, he a set builder at the National Theatre. He thought he'd found the one, the woman he'd grow old with; he'd fallen helplessly, hopelessly in love. She'd loved him too, at least she'd said so and he'd never known her lie. But then she'd been transferred to a hospital in the North. He'd been willing to go with her, leave his job and start again. He'd have done anything to be with Jax. She'd told him no, said all the right things about not wanting him to sacrifice his own career for hers; she'd insisted she'd be working around the clock, would have no time for him. Eventually, even he got the message: Jax was actually glad of the excuse to leave him behind. Maybe she'd even requested the transfer in the first place.

Jax had gone out of his life.

And then, some five months ago, she'd called him out of the blue to say she was in discussion with several wedding planners and was he interested in being one of them. Robin had been awash with misgivings. Jax wasn't someone you forgot, or got over completely, but in the two decades since he'd last seen her, he'd managed to push her firmly to the back of his mind. And now she wanted him to organise her wedding? Knowing it could lead to disaster, he simply hadn't been able to resist. Besides, a deconsecrated church? – well, he knew the perfect place.

The former church of St Michael the Evangelist overlooked the ocean not far from St Agnes. Run by the National Trust, it wasn't a huge space but would be perfect for the sixty guests Jax and her fiancé were planning. It had pointed arches, flying buttresses, ribbed vaults, stained-glass windows, ornamented stonework and more leering gargoyles than you could shake a stick at.

Robin had arranged to meet her one evening in early May. The car park was empty when he arrived, apart from the Nissan Leaf that the manager drove and a motorbike. Knowing he was ten minutes early, he'd walked towards the clifftop.

Below him, on the beach, light and colour had fled, leaving an expanse of black, dappled sand and rock pools gleaming like oil slicks. The ocean, though! The ocean was a churning, bouncing mass of colour.

A storm had blown in overnight, leaving a turbulent sea in its wake. Giant waves were rolling in and the 'white horses', the name given to the spray that topped those about to break, had turned a deep shade of pink. From the sun, now low and huge on the western horizon, shone a path of gold.

'It's perfect,' came a voice from near his feet, and Robin looked down to see a woman on the cliff path. She was as tall as he remembered and still slender; her silvery hair flew across her face and at the sight of her he felt hands twisting his heart like damp washing. 'I want to get married at sunset,' she went on. 'Whatever time it happens to be in October.'

She walked towards him with her arms held out. 'Hey, stranger,' she said. 'How dare you get even better looking?'

'Well, I could say the same about you,' he had the presence of mind to reply as she stepped into his arms and his head reeled with the scent of her. Inside he was thinking, *Oh, God, please no.*

She was back – in his life and in his gut – and this time, there was no getting her out again.

Robin arrived at the church ten minutes early, by design this time. Once again, Jax's motorbike was waiting in the car park. No sunset this time. The sky was overcast, the beach in darkness. In the poor light, the sea looked millpond flat. Jax was standing on the clifftop, her back to him. Knowing she'd hear the crunch of his feet on the gravel, he approached slowly and stood by her side.

He said, 'The luckiest man who walks on this earth is the one who finds true love.'

'And that one I know,' she replied. 'Bram Stoker's *Dracula*.'

She'd turned her head to smile at him, but he didn't let himself look directly at her. As he'd crossed the car park, he'd known what he was going to do, and if he met her eyes, he might chicken out.

'It isn't true,' he went on. 'Because I love you. I never stopped. And that makes me the least lucky man in the world.'

He waited for her to laugh, to tell him he was a jerk, that this was completely inappropriate, to ask him what the hell he thought he was about. She did none of those things.

'I love the darkness in your soul because it cries out to mine,' he said. 'I love the sadness I see in your heart because I know I can chase it away.'

His eyes fixed on the dark sea, Robin found the words came easily. 'I love your bitchy sense of humour and your absurd sentimentality when it comes to animals. I love that you care passionately about the planet and that you still dream of living on the moon. You're the weirdest, most wonderful human being ever born and every hour I spend without you hurts.'

Still nothing. He let his eyes drift sideways. She was still there.

'If you're a hundred per cent sure of what you're doing, if you love Neil as much as I love you, then say the word. You'll never hear this again and your wedding in a couple of weeks will go without a hitch. You may even wonder if you dreamed it. But you didn't dream it, Jax, it's real and I had to say it.'

'I think I knew.'

He turned to face her then. She was looking directly into his eyes. Robin took a step closer and gave her a second to move away. She stayed where she was. Jesus, was this actually happening?

'I think that's why I got in touch with you again.'

Her jacket was cold and unwieldy, but her breath was warm against his face. Her lips were soft and slick with lip gloss and her hair wrapped itself around both their faces. She pressed against him and he thought perhaps he might lose his balance and that the two of them would tumble over the edge and die together on the rocks below.

He had no problem with that.

Abruptly, she stiffened and pulled back. At that moment, he heard what she must have. Maybe she'd been listening out for it, whereas he'd never been so totally and completely wrapped up in a moment before. A car was approaching the church.

They both turned and a second later Neil's blue BMW appeared round a bend in the road.

'Now what?' she said.

Chapter 35

The phone rang when Tara was pulling off her gardening boots at the back door.

Amanda Holt. Logan Quick's ex-wife.

'Tara Webb,' she answered, conscious of her heart starting to beat uncomfortably fast.

'Oh, yes, hello. I got a message you called yesterday. Something about a drinks party?'

'We met last Christmas.' Tara walked through the house to where she'd left the solicitors' letter on the dining table. 'At Miranda Overbright's house.'

'So, what can I do for you?' The woman's voice sounded cold, disinterested.

'Probably nothing, and I apologise for troubling you. But I had a letter this week, supposedly from your ex-husband's solicitors. It said that I would receive a share of his wealth when he dies.' She'd reached the table. 'An obvious scam, but I thought that you, and he, should know someone is doing this.'

Silence.

'I've since heard of another woman who received the same letter. And of course, it's been on the local news, so you probably know all about it already.'

'I don't listen to the news. What exactly does this letter say?'

Tara read the letter aloud.

'Again. Read it again, please.'

Tara obliged.

'I will fucking kill him.'

'Are you saying—'

She got no further. The line had gone dead.

Tara glanced at her watch. Almost half past four. The solicitors' office would still be open. She dialled the number of Barker, Momen and Dodds.

Chapter 36

The local evening news was coming to an end.

'And finally,' the anchorman read from the autocue, 'the story of the mysterious tokens that residents of Cornwall have been finding on their doormats. Supposedly advising recipients that they are due to inherit a vast fortune, the tokens appear to have been sent on behalf of reclusive local billionaire, Logan Quick. Jasmin Basri has more.'

Sheila sat upright in her armchair. 'What's she saying? Turn it up.'

Cheryl's mother often dozed during the news; meals made her soporific and the two always ate at five thirty. Not this time, worse luck. Cheryl found the remote just as a young Asian woman wearing a red coat and a multi-coloured scarf appeared on the screen. Behind her were a pair of wooden gates.

Cheryl increased the volume on the TV, as much to drown out the sound of her heartbeat going into overdrive as to allow her mother to hear what was being said.

'I'm standing here in front of the stylish, multi-million-pound home of local woman Tara Webb,' the reporter said to the camera. 'Not someone you'd think would need a sudden windfall in the post. Yet that, it seems, is exactly what happened. Because two days ago, Mrs Webb received a solicitors' letter telling her she was due to inherit a share of the fortune of entrepreneur Logan Quick.'

'That's it,' Sheila said to the TV. 'That's what we got. We got one too.'

'Ssshh,' Cheryl hissed, before she could stop herself.

'And she's not the only one,' the reporter was saying. 'Ambulance driver Sabri Carter, who lives just fifteen miles from here in Truro, received a token in the post too. In an interview with our sister radio channel, Mrs Carter's husband told us that his wife has never met Mr Quick and has no idea why she's been singled out in this way.'

The reporter was no longer in front of the gates. Instead, she walked slowly up a wooded lane, her colourful scarf blowing in the wind. The Webb property gates were visible some way back.

'No one knows how many of these tokens have been sent out,' she went on, as she brushed the floaty scarf from her face. 'And the firm of solicitors acting for Mr Quick refused to comment when we contacted them earlier today. Similarly, we've been unable to get any reaction from Mr Quick himself through any of his registered companies. Significantly, though, neither the solicitors nor Mr Quick's representatives have denied his involvement in the unusual case, leading many commentators to conclude that this is all for real.'

The screen switched back to the studio.

'Very exciting,' the man at the desk said. 'Let's hope more becomes clear in the coming days. In the meantime, people are advised to check their post very carefully.' He smiled, a big cheesy grin that showed huge white teeth. 'After all, it could be you.'

Sheila's head snapped round to face Cheryl. 'What did you do with that letter? Where did you put it?'

Cheryl felt as though she'd been waiting for this moment for a very long time. 'It burned, Mum. You threw it on the fire. Remember?'

'Why didn't you stop me?'

'You were too fast.' She got up, out of the chair, because she didn't trust herself to keep a straight face. Her mum looked like an angry chipmunk. 'Nice cup of tea?' she offered.

'You heard what they said. It's real. That man has left us some money.'

Me some money. Not us. Me. 'He's not dead yet. Wills don't work until someone dies. I thought you'd know that, Mum. Seeing as how you've spent so much time thinking about yours lately.'

As Cheryl left the room, she thought it might not even matter if the letter did turn out to be fake, if the token (carefully hidden upstairs beneath a loose piece of carpet) was nothing more than worthless junk. She couldn't imagine anything more satisfying than the expression on her mother's face just now.

Before the kettle started whistling Cheryl heard Sheila's voice again. Coming from the hall this time.

'Hello? I want the number for BBC Cornwall. News desk.'

Chapter 37

'Mum, I want to see Coffie too.'

'And I want you to go to bed. It's nine o'clock.'

'I won't sleep. There's too much stuff in my head. I might as well stay up.'

Charlie was bluffing. It didn't matter how much was going round in his head; once that head hit the pillow, it was as though a light had gone out. He was the best sleeper Holly had ever known.

A knock sounded at the door and the enormous outline of Holly's colleague in chambers and possibly only friend appeared behind the glass. Charlie shot forward. 'I'll get it.'

A rush of cold air shot through the house and, on the doorstep, Coffie bent to look her son in the eyes.

'Step aside,' he drawled in his low, rich Caribbean accent. Coffie was from Guyana.

Charlie raised both arms and shimmied. He actually shimmied. 'Let the man come through,' he growled, in a passable imitation of the huge man on the doorstep.

The two fist-bumped and Coffie entered the house. He was in gym clothes but smelled of lemon and rosemary. His hair, short and tightly curled, was damp from the shower or possibly from rain. As always, he seemed far too big for Holly's tiny hallway. As always, he was the most beautiful man she'd ever laid eyes on.

And, as she invariably did, she gave a silent sigh. Couldn't happen.

'We saved you some lasagne.' Charlie had taken Coffie's hand and was dragging him through, past Holly, towards the kitchen. She pushed down a wave of jealousy – Charlie hardly ever held her hand – and told herself her son would do anything to avoid going to bed.

'This is it,' he was saying as she followed them into the kitchen. She couldn't see round Coffie but guessed he was being shown the letter and its accompanying token that she and Charlie, after a deeply unpleasant hour, had found in the recycling bin.

'Have you been eating off it?' Coffie was staring down at the letter as Holly took up her place at the third edge of the kitchen table.

'Mum put it in the bin. Can you believe it? She didn't even tell me about it. Imagine if I hadn't heard about it at school today. The bin men come on Monday. It would have been lost forever. How much do you think we'll get?'

'Easy, tiger.' Coffie held up a hand to calm Charlie's outburst. Another man, a less sensitive one, might have patted him on the head but Coffie never touched Charlie unless invited to do so. 'Let me read and inwardly digest.'

'You're funny,' Charlie said. Holly rolled her eyes. Now, he got a sense of humour? Leaving them to it, she took the remains of the lasagne from the oven.

'"This is your token," Charlie was saying, as she found salad in the fridge. "Keep it safe. Tell no one. On the event of my death, it entitles you to an equal share of my wealth. Good luck." I know it off by heart.'

Holly piled a plate high. 'Charlie, give Coffie room to eat. If you're staying up, you need to sit down and calm down.'

Her son ignored her, of course. 'Mum says you know about wills and stuff. What do you think? Is it real?'

Coffie ate slowly, his eyes only leaving the letter to glance at the token itself. Once, he picked the coin up and turned it over. He'd know some Latin, all barristers did. Giving him time, Holly focused on tidying the kitchen. Trying to curb Charlie's excitement had taken all her emotional energy that evening; she'd had no space in her head even to start processing her own feelings.

Money. A lot of money. She didn't need to worry about her parents anymore. She could sort Chris out once and for all. She could give up the other work.

It could not be that easy.

After what felt like an age, when she could sense Charlie on the verge of exploding, Coffie put his knife down. He looked up at her.

'Have you spoken to the firm directly?' he asked.

'I meant to. I took a picture. I was going to send it over. But I've had so much going on the last couple of days I never got round to it.'

'Is it real?' Charlie demanded.

'Barker, Momen and Dodds not issuing any sort of denial suggests it might be,' Coffie said, in that slow, easy way he had. 'They're a big firm, major players, and there's been enough publicity for it to have appeared on their radar. If it was a scam, I'd expect them to be all over it.'

'Why?' Holly whispered. Why would a man she'd never met leave her money?

'That said, it's early days,' Coffie went on. 'When did this arrive? Wednesday? We could see something from them over the weekend, or early next week.' He smiled down at Charlie. 'I wouldn't order the Axopar just yet, youngster.'

The Axopar was a high-speed motorboat, Charlie's current favourite.

'Let's say for the sake of argument that the letter is genuine,' Holly said. 'That Barker, Momen and Dodds are acting in good faith. What then?'

'According to social media, so this might be incorrect, recipients can make a half-hour appointment with the firm to find out more information,' Coffie told her. 'Nothing will be given out over the phone. And the appointment will cost one hundred and fifty pounds.'

'Can we do it? Mum, we have to do it.'

'Hold your horses, youngster, the lawyers are speaking. Even if the firm is genuine, it's still fraught with problems. How many tokens have been sent out? If half the population of Cornwall have received one, there might not be much to go around. What happens if this Logan Quick character changes his mind? There could be a whole lot of disappointed beneficiaries out there. Would they have a case to challenge the new will?'

'We know there's at least two,' Charlie piped up. 'A girl's mum at St Barnabus's got one.'

'It says tell no one,' Holly pointed out. 'Have we violated the terms simply by telling you?'

Coffie thought for a second. 'Hard to say. We could argue that was advice, rather than a condition. More to the point, it says keep it safe. That's the bit that worries me.'

'Why?' Charlie asked.

Coffie took his time, glancing down at Charlie before meeting Holly's eyes. 'Are you the named beneficiary or just the token holder? What happens if this token is lost or stolen? Do all the benefits of the will pass with it?'

'She threw it in the bin,' Charlie told him. 'I can't believe she threw it in the bin.'

'Do you have a safe?' Coffie asked Holly. She shook her head. At the same time, she felt an urge to get up and lock the front door.

'You mean someone could steal it?' Charlie looked from one grown-up to the other. Damn, she'd known it was a mistake to let him stay up. Now he'd be anxious about losing the wretched thing.

And she was too, she realised. She was suddenly conscious of how vulnerable she and Charlie were. A woman alone with a young kid. A woman who would do anything, give up anything, to keep that kid safe. Was anything in the world more vulnerable than a mother?

'You should keep it,' Charlie told Coffie. 'Keep it safe for us. No one will mess with you.'

When Coffie met Holly's glance she couldn't read what she saw. She watched his eyes drop to the token. Did his hand, then, give a tiny, involuntary start towards it?

Charlie grabbed it and pushed it in front of the man at her table. 'Mum, we should give it to Coffie. He'll keep it safe for us.'

Coffie stared down at the token. Catching the light, it seemed to gleam up at them.

Holly realised she was holding her breath. Was she about to lose her second friend in two days? And this time one she cared about?

After what seemed an age, Coffie picked up his knife and resumed eating.

'Charlie, I would not touch that thing if you begged me. But I advise you and your mum,' he glanced at Holly again, 'to put it somewhere very safe and tell no one, absolutely no one, that you have it.'

'I won't.' Without questioning, Charlie made the promise that Holly didn't think she'd ever have been able to wring out of him. 'I won't tell anyone. I swear.'

An hour later, when Charlie had been persuaded – by Coffie of course – to go to bed, Holly showed her friend out.

'Guess I can't ask you out anymore now you're an heiress,' he said, as they stood by the front door. 'You'll be second-guessing my motives.'

'Yeah, yeah.' Pretending not to take him seriously had become the way they dealt with Coffie's refusal to hide his interest. One day, she knew, they'd have a serious conversation about why she wouldn't go out with him. He'd already refused to accept that she didn't find him attractive. *You can't hide chemistry*, he'd said. *And you and I have it in spades. And don't give me any malarky about being a single mum. Charlie loves me.*

Malarky about being a high-class whore would probably do it. And then the man whose opinion she valued most would despise her.

'Do you think I should make that appointment?' she asked, reluctant to let him leave.

'I don't think you have a choice,' he replied. 'But be careful, Holly.'

'Charlie won't tell anyone. And neither will I.'

'I didn't mean that. Something about this whole business feels wrong. I think someone's messing with you.'

'It's working,' she replied.

He shook his head and reached for the door. 'No, love. It's only just begun.'

DAY FOUR

Saturday, 6 October

Chapter 38

His new website was getting more attention than he'd anticipated, although judging by the contact emails coming in, most of the traffic was from ladies of the Wadebridge WI. *Dear Mr Lewis,* one woman wrote, *(or can I call you Craig???), I'm afraid your talk, while super informative in itself, has made me rather anxious about fire safety in my home. Do you by any chance do home visits?*

At his feet, Cobalt was dreaming. His eyes were half open, showing only the whites, and his whole body was trembling as he made puppy-like whimpering sounds. He reached out with his bare foot, running it soothingly along the dog's flank.

Closing the site, he ran another *Logan Quick* search. In the two days since the story had broken, as he'd anticipated, the national print and news media had picked up on it. With relatively little in the way of concrete content to work with, because both Tara Webb and Sabri Carter were staying tight-lipped, they'd focused their attention on Barker, Momen and Dodds, the Exeter-based firm of solicitors that were handling Quick's will, and the London offices of Quick Holdings.

Both establishments had been well prepared for the media shitstorm. They'd brought in extra security to prevent unauthorised persons accessing their premises and the media relations rooms were operating on voicemail only. A brief, almost identical statement appeared on both websites to the effect that no further comment would be made, at this time, on the subject of Mr Quick's inheritance plans.

Jasmin Basri of BBC Cornwall had done a piece-to-camera appeal for other token recipients to get in touch, offering in return advice on financial and personal security matters and an opportunity to *tell your side of the story.*

One of the news agencies had sent a team to the Isles of Scilly, even chartering a helicopter to fly to the private island of St Helen's where Logan Quick lived most of the time. They'd been refused permission to land on the helipad but managed to get extensive footage of the luxury home that Quick had built only a few years earlier. Quick appeared to be something of a mariner. A yacht was moored in the bay and tied up to a pontoon not far from the house were a high-speed RIB and a flash-looking motor cruiser.

The online version of BBC Cornwall was featuring a breaking story about a possible third token having surfaced, this time in St Austell, but carrying the proviso that the reports were, as yet, unconfirmed.

Social media, on the other hand, was awash with speculation and several enterprising souls had modelled up their own version of what the tokens might look like. Some were genuinely claiming to be recipients, others, brandishing gigantic chocolate coins, were taking the piss. Logan Quick and tokens were both trending on X; some of the memes were actually quite funny.

'Hey!' A warm hand dropped onto his bare shoulder.

He hadn't heard Lauren getting up. She leaned closer until her breasts brushed against his back. At the same time, he moved the mouse to wake it up and fought the instinct to close down the screen. No secrets, that's what he'd promised her. No secrets between the two of us.

'You OK?' she asked.

'I'm good,' he told her. 'Cobalt woke me barking at something. Couldn't get back to sleep.'

She glanced down at the dog, now snoring contentedly. 'Watcha doing?' she asked.

She leaned closer, gave a heavy, disapproving sigh, then stood up abruptly and walked to the adjoining bathroom.

He checked his phone. It was instinctive whenever he was with her. Her husband – his best friend – was many miles away.

She reappeared, leaning against the bathroom doorframe. 'I think he's suspicious,' she said.

Something sharp tugged at his insides. Not now. Not when they were so close.

'I caught him with my phone the other day. He said he'd heard an alert and was bringing it to me, but he looked shifty.'

'He can't access it, though, can he?'

'He can if he holds it in front of my face while I'm asleep.'

'We'll be careful,' he told her. 'It won't be much longer. Go back to bed. I'll be there in a minute.'

Lauren climbed back into the bed and turned on her side with a heavy sigh. He wouldn't have been surprised if she'd fallen asleep again. Sleeping was practically her superpower.

Opening up Facebook, he saw that both Webb and Carter had set their accounts to private and so he typed Sabri Carter and tokens into Google. The first image that flashed up was one taken of Carter getting into her ambulance. She'd turned, possibly at a tap on the shoulder, and her face showed a mixture of anguish and fury.

He had a feeling she'd be the first to break.

Chapter 39

'All three of us are from the southwest.' Holly pressed closer to Coffie and his phone as they watched the clip of the previous night's news coverage.

'So is Logan Quick,' he replied. 'Not sure you can read too much into that. They're both quite a bit older than you.'

'Mum and Dad's age,' Holly agreed, glancing around to make sure none of the other parents were within earshot. 'Three women. Wonder if that means anything.'

It was close to noon on Saturday and she and Coffie were in the grounds of Lanhydrock House waiting for Charlie's cross-country race to come past. The three-kilometre course wound a figure of eight, starting at the house, curving down towards the river and then back up an impossibly steep hill before a fast, downhill sprint to the finish. The runners would appear any time now.

'I'm thinking of getting in touch with them,' Holly said. 'I found contact details for them both last night.'

'Not a good idea,' he replied, predictably. 'They've neither of them proved good at keeping secrets. Why should they keep yours?'

It was a fair point. Late on Friday night, at a loss to where she could hide the token, she'd eventually put it in the pocket of the holdall she kept in a lockable cupboard at the back of the wardrobe. Along with all the other stuff she kept carefully hidden from Charlie.

Her phone rang. Wanting to ignore it, she couldn't resist glancing down. Her mother.

'Hey, Mum, I'm at Charlie's race, can't really talk.'

'Holly, I need you to get an injunction.'

To the sound of bells jangling and people cheering, the runners appeared at the top of the hill. In the lead was a dark-haired boy in a yellow and blue sports strip, too far away for her to be sure it was Charlie.

'A what?' she said, as spectators started to shout encouragement.

'An injunction. Against that so-called friend of your dad's. You have to stop him coming round here. He's causing too many problems.'

It was definitely Charlie in the lead. But a bigger boy was close on his heels. Around her, noise levels increased and she took a step back from the crowd.

'I don't care how far back the two of them go, he's upsetting Dad,' her mother said. 'You can do that, can't you? Get an injunction taken out.'

The runners were getting closer.

Holly cupped her hand around the phone in an attempt to shield out the noise. 'Seems a bit extreme. Why don't I have a word with him? Explain the situation. When's he due back?'

'He never says, he just appears. Holly, I can't hear you! Can you go somewhere quieter?'

Charlie shot past. He always finished a race strongly and there were only a hundred metres to go. He'd win for sure now. Coffie left her side to join the parents running with the boys towards the finish line. She could no longer see her son.

'Mum, I have to go. I'll come round on the way back. See you in a bit.'

She ended the call before her mother could argue. Ahead, the race had finished but other parents were blocking her view. She couldn't see Charlie cross the line. Nor would she be at the finish to congratulate him.

Only as she jogged forward did the last thing her mother had said register.

'I don't even know his name, Holly. He's never told me his name.'

'Bloke in a black Volvo?' Coffie turned into the road where Holly's parents lived. 'The police can trace him through that, if he's still being coy about his identity. Get your mum to take a picture of the registration next time and we'll take it from there.'

Holly slipped her phone into her bag. She'd just taken another irate call from her mother, this time informing her that the watercolour of Newton Ferrers, the gift from her father's new friend, was being consigned to the bin.

'Newton Ferrers is where Grandad was born,' Charlie announced from the back seat. He was sitting on old towels to protect Coffie's upholstery from the mud, his winner's medal gleaming proudly on his chest. 'It's on the River Yealm. Mooring for nearly three hundred boats, but some areas dry out at low tide. Can I have the picture, if Grandad doesn't want it?'

'We'll ask,' Holly said. 'Maybe this friend of his will want it back.'

Ping. She retrieved her phone. A text from Chris.

Wishing she could ignore the message, knowing it would be impossible even to try, Holly made sure neither Coffie nor Charlie could see the screen before opening it to be confronted with a photograph of herself, lolling in an armchair, naked. Both legs hung over one arm while she leaned back against the other. Her left arm was clutched across her chest to hide her nipples, but her left thigh and butt cheek were on show to the world. She was pouting at the camera, completely recognisable.

Chris had added a caption: *One of my favourites!*

Chapter 40

Tara walked into the Blue Anchor near Fraddon to find it empty apart from Sabri Carter. Sitting at a corner table, she was wearing what looked like a man's puffer jacket over jeans and had a beanie cap pulled down over shoulder-length dark hair. A pint glass of lime and soda sat on the table in front of her. She looked up as Tara approached and gave a shy smile.

'Are you in disguise?' Tara had meant it as a joke, but the other woman's face creased in confusion.

'Sorry, I mean – I am.' Tara's raincoat was turned up at the collar, her hair tucked inside a beret. She'd kept her sunglasses on, even though the pub interior was so dim she was in danger of falling over the furniture. 'Ignore me. Childish sense of humour. Let's start again. Can I get you a glass of wine? I know we're both driving but we can have one, can't we? I feel we probably need one. Gosh, it's dark in here.'

She was talking too much. She always did when she was nervous.

In a single, graceful movement, Sabri got to her feet. She might dress from House of Primark but she had a natural poise. 'Wine would be great, thank you. And we can sit in the window if you like. I've got into the habit of avoiding windows the last few days. There always seems to be people staring in at me.'

Tara had seen footage of Sabri's home on the news bulletins. A semi-detached house on the outskirts of Truro, with a tiny front garden that offered no protection from the news crews.

'Been bad, huh?' Tara asked.

'I'm learning what it's like to be an A-list celebrity,' Sabri replied. 'Only without their bodyguards. Work are already seriously pissed off. We found an Italian photographer wandering round A&E cubicles last night and I can't pull out of the ambulance bay without at least two motorcycles following me.'

'Someone was taking pictures of our swim group this morning,' Tara said, as she and Sabri settled themselves in the window seat with two glasses of Chablis. 'We get the odd perv doing it, but the camera looked professional. Even when we were changing. I'll probably see my bare arse on the evening news tonight.'

Sabri's face twitched in what might have been a smile but was probably a grimace and Tara told herself to rein it in. Women from Sabri's culture probably didn't talk about body parts. Don't ask her where she's from, she told herself. Just don't.

'You look so familiar,' Sabri said. 'I don't mean from the bay last week. I thought then I'd seen you before, that I knew you.'

'I was a district nurse for thirty years,' Tara said. 'I often had patients in and out of the Royal Cornwall. We probably came across each other a lot.'

Sabri nodded as though it made perfect sense, then said, 'How are you?'

Where would she start? 'It's mental, isn't it?' she replied. 'Even my swim buddies are looking at me like I've done something wrong. They think I'm not telling them everything. And no one will believe I've never met Logan Quick.'

'And you haven't?'

'No. Not that I can remember anyway.' She paused. Why come if she wasn't going to be completely honest? 'I have met his ex-wife, though. And I spoke to her last night.'

Sabri's brown eyes widened in surprise. 'And . . .' she prompted.

'Well, I may have set the cat among the pigeons,' she admitted. 'She seemed surprised, to say the least.'

Sabri nodded but didn't pursue the idea. She said, 'Have you made an appointment?'

Tara picked up her glass. 'I'm going on Monday. I was surprised to get an appointment so soon to be honest, so I think they must have cleared the week for us. I asked if I could bring you, but they said no. Has to be one at once.'

'Thanks for trying.'

'I'll tell you all about it. They're not putting a gagging order on me. They can fuck off.'

'I should go myself,' Sabri said. 'Jason and the kids won't give me any peace until I do. But using the kids' savings. That really does feel like scraping the barrel.'

Tears were glinting in Sabri's eyes. Without thinking, Tara reached out and put her own hand over the other woman's, wondering whether she should offer to pay Sabri's fee herself. One hundred and fifty pounds was nothing to her. But they hardly knew each other and all this was awkward enough.

'This will shatter them if it's not true,' Sabri said.

Us too, Tara thought, as she released Sabri's hand. We might say we don't believe it but deep down we're starting to hope. It was on the tip of her tongue to ask Sabri what she'd do with the money, but something held her back.

'But it might be worse if it is true,' Sabri went on. 'We're regular people. We've no idea how to deal with that level of wealth.'

'People manage,' Tara said, at the same time conscious of how much easier it would be for her. Not remotely in Logan Quick's league, she'd become accustomed, the last couple of decades, to having money. 'People win the lottery all the time. They don't all go into meltdown.'

'I wonder how many others there are,' Sabri said.

Silence for a moment. They had no way of knowing.

Tara asked, 'Did you bring it?'

'I've sewn it into my bra,' Sabri replied. 'Hold on.' She turned her back and began to wriggle, her elbows out at right angles. Tara reached into her bag and pulled out her own token. She placed it on the tabletop as Sabri did the same.

'They look the same.' Sabri reached out. 'May I?'

Tara nodded, although her insides clenched at the sight of someone else handling her token.

'Yours is in my right hand.' Sabri smiled as she raised both to the light. She twisted them so she could compare the other sides.

'They're not identical,' she said. 'Almost, but not quite. There's a tiny number in one point of the star. Yours is five, mine is two. Look.'

She passed them back and Tara took her turn. Unlike Sabri, she needed to fish her reading glasses from her bag, but she soon saw the other woman was right. The tokens did have the tiniest of numbers. It was the only thing that differentiated them.

'Does this mean there's at least five of us?' Sabri asked.

Tara put both tokens down on the table and used her forefinger to push the one with the number two a little closer to Sabri. 'Maybe,' she said. 'The Latin means *to each his deserts.*'

Sabri made no move to reclaim her token and, for a second, Tara half expected her to get up and walk away, leaving it behind. 'I know,' she said, eventually. 'I was a medical student for three years. Knowing some Latin was inevitable.'

'So, the question we really should be asking ourselves,' Tara said, 'is why the hell does this Logan Quick think he knows what we deserve?'

Chapter 41

On Saturday, Cheryl arrived home to what appeared to be an empty house. Closing the front door, she eased the shopping bags down and rubbed her hands to release the soreness caused by heavy plastic carrier bags. She'd given up asking if she could buy a wheeled trolley.

'Mum?' she called. No answer.

Her mother's coat and hat were hanging in the cupboard under the stairs. Not that she ever went out alone; she wasn't steady enough on her feet. As Cheryl carried the bags through to the kitchen, she couldn't help wondering what the chances were of Sheila having had a heart attack, maybe a stroke, while she'd been out. It was a cruel thought, and she didn't mean it, not really, but Sheila, never an easy person to live with, had become close to impossible in the days since she'd heard about Logan Quick's legacy.

Sheila wasn't in the sitting room, the dining room they hadn't used in years or the kitchen. No sign of her in the back garden either, but that was another place she largely avoided. Which meant she was on another of her treasure hunts.

'It has to be somewhere,' she kept repeating. 'Metal coins don't vanish. Are you sure you haven't got it?'

Movement sounded from upstairs. Leaving the shopping on the kitchen counter, Cheryl moved silently up. She couldn't avoid the odd creak, but Sheila's hearing wasn't what it used to be. Another sound. Then a grunt from Sheila. Cheryl reached the top of the steps and turned towards her own bedroom door.

All her clothes had been thrown onto the bed. Her three pairs of shoes lay scattered on the floor. Her mother was balanced on the bedroom chair, reaching up to the top shelf.

'What are you doing, Mum?' Cheryl asked, knowing exactly what Sheila was doing. She was looking for the token. But to find it, she'd have to lie full length on the carpet, reach under the bed to where the carpet was joined and slide her fingers beneath it.

Sheila twisted round and the chair wobbled. Cheryl strode – not as quickly as she could have done – and caught her mother round the waist.

'Get down, Mum. What do you think you're doing?'

To her surprise, her mother slapped her hand away. 'Don't touch me. I know you have it. You're trying to steal it from me. After all I've done for you.'

Not even trying to hide the sigh, Cheryl held up both hands to take her mother's. Sheila grabbed them, squeezing hard, and dropped to the floor with a thump.

'Where is it?' She leaned close to Cheryl, her small, grey eyes glinting with spite.

'You burned it, Mum. You threw it on the fire. Surely you remember?'

'Don't think you can leave me here by myself, lady.'

'Mum, you're hurting me.'

'It's not too late, you know. I can still go to the police.'

Cheryl tugged her hands free and stepped away. 'I'm going to unpack the shopping,' she said. 'It seems you can get yourself up and down stairs after all, so I'll leave you to it.'

'Murderer!'

Cheryl looked back at her mother and saw something of the rage, frustration and helplessness simmering away inside her. Her mother was suffering.

Well, who would have thought it? It felt good.

Chapter 42

Late on Saturday, three days after the solicitors' letter had arrived on his doorstep, and two days into the most spectacular bender he'd been on in decades, Tug realised that the tokens were making the news.

He'd started drinking within hours of being fired, kicking off with beer and whisky chasers and moving on to cheap, supermarket vodka when the pubs refused to serve him. He'd stopped only to pass out and to piss. He woke in darkness, and realised that if he didn't get to the bathroom in the next sixty seconds, he'd have a whole heap of nasty laundry to deal with.

The flat looked like the aftermath of a police raid. The remains of food he couldn't remember eating littered the floor; a jumbo packet of crisps was open on the armchair and take-away cartons sat on the lid of the pedal bin. A packet of cereal had spilled across the counter and the sink was piled high with bottles. On the carpet between the coffee table and the TV was a pile of congealed food that could, at a stretch, be vegetable soup.

Tug had never bought a can of vegetable soup in his life.

The TV was on, and he had a vague memory of watching a Steven Seagal movie sometime during the day. Currently, it was showing the six o'clock news and had reached the section on local issues. A young woman on the seafront was talking about untreated sewerage being discharged directly into the sea following the recent heavy rain; the sea swimmers, as usual, were kicking up a fuss about it.

Tug, meanwhile, had his own sewerage problem to deal with.

He got his trousers down in the nick of time – since when had he slept fully dressed? – and sat waiting for the noisome evacuation.

His head felt like it was trapped between a pair of frigates moored in a choppy sea and his stomach, like his bowel, was on the edge of emptying out. He couldn't remember having to shit and vomit simultaneously before but hey, what was life without new adventures?

'And finally, this evening, another of the mysterious tokens has emerged in Cornwall, although this time it seems to have vanished as quickly as it appeared.'

Tug raised his head.

'Mrs Sheila Young, of Armitage Road in St Austell, claims she received a token, along with a letter from Barker, Momen and Dodds, in the post last week,' the familiar voice of the anchor went on. 'Unfortunately, it seems her daughter, Cheryl, threw the letter on the fire. Our reporter, Jasmin Basri, went to meet her.'

Grabbing a fistful of toilet paper and clutching it to his arse, Tug staggered to the bathroom doorway. On the screen was a young, brown-skinned reporter wearing a bright blue coat and yellow scarf, perched on the sofa in an old-fashioned sitting room. Sitting at an angle, glancing nervously at the camera, was a large woman in her late seventies.

'It came last Wednesday,' the woman was saying. 'My daughter opened it. I don't get about as much as I did, I'm registered disabled, so she opens all the post for me, and it said, you know – what you said earlier.'

'That you would inherit an equal share of Logan Quick's wealth when he passes away?' the reporter prompted.

The woman's chins wobbled as she nodded. 'That's it, that's right. That's what it said.'

'And it came with a token? What did it look like?'

'Small and round, like a two-pence piece, but not a coin. It was shiny too, like new coins are.'

'And you don't have it anymore?'

'Cheryl, that's my daughter, threw it on the fire.' The old woman rolled her eyes. 'But that shouldn't matter, should it? These solicitors will have records.'

The Basri woman looked doubtful. 'Well,' she began, 'there is some doubt about whether the beneficiaries have to be in possession of the tokens to inherit. How will you feel if it has been lost? If you miss out on your inheritance?'

The older woman's eyes widened. 'They can't do that. It was sent to us. Ask the solicitors, they'll know it was sent to us. Cheryl didn't know what she was doing when she threw it on the fire.'

Tug glanced at the mantelpiece where his own letter and token sat. No way would that thing melt in a domestic fire. It looked like solid bronze.

On the TV the scene switched back to the studio. The anchor had been joined by Jasmin Basri, the reporter, this time wearing a tight-fitting purple dress.

'So, that's three of these so-called tokens that we've been able to track down, Jasmin,' the anchor said. 'And we still haven't managed to get a glimpse of one.'

Basri held up a newly minted two-pence coin. 'From Mrs Young's description the token she might have burned looked a bit like this. She says she's planning to make an appointment with the solicitors later this week and has promised to let us know what happens. But the other two recipients we know of are being very tight-lipped about the whole business.'

'I think the letter advised them to keep the existence of the tokens a secret, is that right?' the anchor said.

'It seems that way. So maybe it's not surprising.'

The anchor glanced down. 'And these would be Sabri Carter and Tara Webb?'

The reporter nodded. 'We caught up with Mrs Webb earlier today, but she seemed very reluctant to talk to us.'

'I think we have that footage,' the anchor said. 'Let's have a look, shall we?'

The scene switched again, and Tug saw the same reporter standing in front of some wide, wooden gates at the bottom of a tree-lined lane. He watched a small electric car approach as the gates began to open. The camera zoomed in to show the woman in the driving seat. She was around fifty with blonde hair and a long face with a perfect profile. A classy-looking girl. She kept her eyes facing forwards.

Basri leaned in and tapped on the glass. 'Mrs Webb, have you decided what to do about your token? Have you made an appointment with the solicitors?'

The blonde gave no sign of having heard. The gates opened and the car moved forward.

'Why do you think Logan Quick is leaving you his money, Tara?'

The gates began to close, but not before Tug caught a glimpse of a massive place with huge glass walls.

'Well, there you have it.' The scene cut back to the studio. 'It seems the mystery of the tokens has only deepened.'

DAY FIVE

Sunday, 7 October

Chapter 43

'OK, so are we good?'

While he waited for his daughter's response, Cobalt came racing up the beach towards him, dropping the piece of driftwood at his master's feet. He bent to pick it up. He couldn't throw nearly so well with his left arm but his right hand was clamping the phone to his ear. It was a windy day, sixteen knots gusting twenty according to the shipping forecast, and he was struggling to hear everything his daughter said.

As the silence stretched on, he threw the stick and Cobalt raced after it. The beach was deserted apart from the two of them, but it was rare to find it otherwise. The odd visiting yacht anchored in the bay, but not normally once summer was over. The white sand, edged in marram grass and unbroken by rocks, stretched ahead of him, lifting like low clouds as the wind caught it.

'Sweetheart?' he said, wondering if the signal had gone.

'I guess.'

It was all he was going to get. 'Great. So can I talk to your brother?'

'He's out.'

Really out, or signalling for his sister to say he was out? Either way made no real difference; he could hardly call his daughter a liar.

Sand spattered over his boots as a panting Cobalt dropped the driftwood. Big brown eyes gazed up at him and drool dripped onto the sand.

'When is he back?'

Another pause, then a heavy sigh. He suspected the girl was multitasking, messaging her mates on whatever platform was currently in vogue, probably about her loser of a dad. Mind you, he was doing the same; the late-afternoon dog walk was usually the time he called his kids. He threw the driftwood again, into the sea this time. It was calm after a peaceful night but would move from slight to moderate later.

He listened to the shipping forecast religiously; he wasn't entirely sure why, because he hadn't been on a pleasure boat in years. The sea unnerved him, if he was honest with himself, and he often wondered why he chose to live so close. His dog, on the other hand, adored the beach and the water. He'd raced straight in after the stick and now his big, fluffy head was bobbing in the gentle waves.

'He doesn't tell me anything,' his daughter said after several seconds. 'Later, maybe.'

'OK, I'll try him later. So, what else is new with you?'

Wrong question. Or rather, right question, wrong timing. He should have asked her that first. Now, she'd think he was only talking to her because her brother wasn't around.

'Not much.'

'School OK?'

'I guess.'

Jesus, it was like pulling teeth.

Give them time. His ex-wife's words rang in his head. *This is a lot for them to deal with.*

'Mum said we could come over and see you at half term.'

Just once, it would be nice if the woman checked with him first.

'Not half term, sweetheart, I've got too much on. Maybe later. For a weekend?'

Another pause, while he watched Cobalt reach the driftwood and turn back towards shore. 'Not worth it,' she said. We can't leave school till after matches on Saturday.'

He'd forgotten that. Bloody silly school. And stupidly expensive.

'Christmas then. You can both come for a nice long stay at Christmas. Bring some friends. It'll be fun.'

He felt a pang of guilt. Was he promising something he'd be unable to deliver?

'Maybe,' she said. 'How's Cobalt?'

His kids had been visiting when the puppy arrived. He sometimes thought the dog, rather than the dad, was what kept them coming back.

'Is that your father?' His ex-wife's voice was shrill in his ear, even before she reached the other end of the line.

'Mum wants to talk to you.' His daughter sounded smug now, the way she did when she knew her brother was about to catch it. He took a deep breath. *Here it comes* . . .

She didn't disappoint.

Chapter 44

High tide at Daymer Bay on Sunday was at one thirty in the afternoon, plenty of time for Tug to travel from Falmouth to Wadebridge. At the bus station, he liberated a bike by cutting through its padlock and cycled the seven miles to the bay. He arrived as the small hatchbacks in the car park were offloading numerous middle-aged women wearing long padded coats and carrying over-stuffed kit bags.

As the women made their way down the short path to the beach, Tug pretended to be locking his bike while keeping a close eye on new arrivals. Tara Webb was one of the last, pulling up in a small electric Fiat that he recognised from the TV.

Keeping his eyes well away from the women disrobing, Tug walked a short way down the beach before setting down his rucksack and pulling his own clothes off. It was a hell of a long time since he'd swum in the sea.

He set off at a run and was first to enter the water. Fuck a duck, it was cold. He forced himself to keep going, diving forward when he figured it was deep enough, feeling the cold rush over his head. He set off from the beach in a slow front crawl, feeling the burn cover every inch of his skin. The cold took his breath away, gripping a tight hold around his chest and giving him an instant freeze headache. He was getting cold-water shock. On a mild Cornish October day. His old mates would never let him hear the end of it.

A babble of sound – shrieks and giggles – told him the women had entered the water.

Tug stopped swimming and hung upright, judging that he was too far away from them to be intimidating. Tara Webb wore a blue and turquoise suit that looked like a mermaid's tail. She wore thermal boots and gloves and had wound her long, fair hair onto the top of her head. She seemed to be encouraging a woman who'd hung back, who was stepping cautiously through the ankle-deep waves. As Tug watched, the two women joined hands and the water crept to their knees.

She was looking his way. She dropped the woman's hand, letting her walk on alone, and stood, staring across the waves at him, as though she knew he'd come to the beach in search of her.

Tug broke eye contact first, twisting in the water and setting off for the far end of the bay in a fast front crawl. Fifty-five years old and only now had he become fanciful? But the connection he'd sensed across the water had been real, he was sure of it.

Well, that was a twist he hadn't seen coming.

Chapter 45

Sheila, who'd been charged with a brittle, nervous energy since she'd learned that the letter she'd thrown in the fire could have value after all, had been smoking twice as much as usual. At seven o'clock on Sunday, several hours after the lady from BBC Cornwall and her team had left, she sent Cheryl for a new packet.

Cheryl went willingly enough. Being away from her mother for a whole half-hour was more than worth the effort of walking up the hill. Even in the drizzle that had started sometime during the afternoon.

She pulled on a raincoat and found an umbrella, waited patiently while Sheila handed over the required amount of cash. There was nothing wrong with her mother's brain, she reflected. She knew, to the penny, how much everything cost.

Movement caught her eye as she stepped out onto the street. Lesley, the woman next door, was standing in her front window. Had she actually banged on the glass? Shifting the umbrella over to her other shoulder, giving herself an excuse not to have seen, Cheryl set off. She'd barely gone ten paces when she heard a door opening.

'Cheryl!'

Lesley was on her doorstep, her arms folded over her chest. 'Is it true?' she called. 'I saw your mum on the news.'

'I've got to catch the shop,' Cheryl called back. The shop didn't close until ten, but it was all she could think of. 'Can't stop.'

A nasty thought occurred to Cheryl as she pressed on: Lesley had three teenage sons. She really didn't need a small army of young people offering to search the house. A youngster would probably find the token in a jiffy. She'd have to drop some subtle hints to her mother about not being able to trust anyone. In the meantime, she'd better get a move on.

Cheryl was close to breathless by the time she reached the top of the hill and was dismayed to see a gang of lads outside the shop.

They'd seen her, were watching her approach.

'Hey, fattie, buy us some cans.'

Cheryl let the umbrella drop lower, so that it was almost completely covering her face.

'I'm telling you, it's her. Number seventy-three.'

A pair of grubby trainers appeared in front of her. The umbrella blocked everything else from view.

'Excuse me,' she tried. The trainers didn't move.

'Excuse me,' her words were echoed back at her. 'Can I ask you something?'

She lifted the umbrella.

'Is it your mum who's got that token thing? The one who was on the telly earlier?'

'That was my mum,' she admitted. 'But we burned the letter. By accident.'

'Harsh.'

The group backed off, leaving Cheryl to enter the shop and buy her mum's cigarettes. To her relief, there was no sign of them when she came out. Light had all but left the sky by this time but the streetlights – those that hadn't succumbed to vandalism – were reflected in the puddles and the rain-streaked road, casting a golden gleam over the street. The road was quiet, not a single moving car in sight, and the curtains of the houses she passed were all drawn against the darkness. Cheryl felt a rare moment of peace, all the more welcome for the turmoil of the past few days. She had no idea how she was going to handle the meeting with the solicitors. They'd almost certainly demand to see the token; sooner or later she'd have to admit the truth. And then she'd be exposed as a liar on television. She'd probably be accused of trying to cheat her elderly mother.

The blow came totally out of the blue. One second, she was making her way down the shining gold street; the next she was spinning towards the road. She caught the rear bumper of a parked car with her hip, registered the flash of pain as her foot slipped off the kerb and she slammed down, hard, onto the wet road.

Dark-clad figures, at least four of them, were surrounding her. One of them had leapt out from behind the thick hedge outside number forty-three, had swung his fist into her stomach as a second had grabbed hold of her handbag. If it hadn't been hanging from the crook of her elbow, he would have made off with it immediately. Instead, it had become tangled in the umbrella and the resulting tussle had sent her flying.

Lying in the road, conscious of puddle water seeping into her clothes, she watched the boys kick the umbrella away, grab her handbag and run off down the street. Only when she realised that no one was coming to help her did she get painfully to her feet.

The boys, the same ones who'd been outside the shop earlier, would be disappointed in their haul. They'd no doubt make use of Sheila's cigarettes, but the loose change in Cheryl's tatty old purse didn't even add up to a pound. Apart from that, they'd find a packet of tissues, opened, a comb and hairbrush, a set of door keys and a lip-salve. They hadn't been looking for money or cigarettes, though. They'd been after the token.

They'd try again. They knew where she lived. And now they had keys to the house.

DAY SIX

Monday, 8 October

Chapter 46

Monday was Cheryl's worst day since the token had arrived. She hadn't slept the night before. Every creak of the house had sounded like the first attempt to burgle it. The locksmith Sheila had reluctantly agreed to engage was due first thing the following day so the house would be safe after that, but there was still one more night to get through and the only way she could secure the back door was by dragging the kitchen table up against it and piling it high with saucepans that would topple over and make a hell of a racket if disturbed.

And now she'd lied to the police. Sheila had insisted on calling them, and Cheryl had been forced to repeat her lie that she had no idea where the token was. Lying to the police was probably a criminal offence in itself. She'd felt genuinely ill by the time she'd managed to get Sheila upstairs and into bed.

Seriously into nicotine withdrawal, her mother had woken in a foul mood.

And then the broadcaster had arrived, complete with a full news crew. The house had felt like it was bursting at the seams with camera men, lighting men, sound men, make-up girls. Her mother had loved it. Jasmin had insisted on interviewing Cheryl about her attack of the night before, had dwelled for what felt like an unreasonable time on the fear the two women were living in, with the token still unaccounted for. And then worse was to come.

Sheila had made the phone call to Barker, Momen and Dodds, who'd refused to speak to her, insisting that only Cheryl herself could make the appointment. Spitting feathers, Sheila had had no choice but to hand over the phone. The camera had been inches from Cheryl's face, the big microphone hovering close, waiting to hear every stammer, every slip-up.

She'd made an appointment for the Wednesday afternoon, nothing earlier had been available, and Sheila was refusing to accept that she wouldn't be allowed into the meeting with her daughter. She'd pressed close to Cheryl all the time she was speaking and still made her repeat every word of the conversation once it was over. The cameras had caught all of it.

By the end of Monday, Cheryl was beginning to wish the token really had been destroyed in the fire.

DAY SEVEN

Tuesday, 9 October

Chapter 47

Holly walked from her own chambers to the offices of Barker, Momen and Dodds on the edge of the cathedral yard. Not due in court that day, she'd nevertheless changed into court attire, figuring the black suit and white, band-collared shirt stood a good chance of fooling the media.

As she drew close, she clutched her black case and fixed her eyes on her phone. Ignoring the news crews, she walked straight inside. Her appearance created a little confusion at reception – they understandably thought she was there on a case – but after paying her bill, she was directed to a waiting area on the first floor, close to a door with *Joseph Caiger* inscribed in gold. It had been a quick matter of looking him up to learn that he was one of the firm's partners and that his speciality was wills and probate.

She had a choice of three armchairs, two of which were white. Holly, who'd started her period that morning, and who didn't feel easy on white furniture at the best of times, opted for the brown chair facing a huge print of orange poppies. To her left a frosted glass wall screened off the solicitors working in the communal area; on a low coffee table were a bowl of fresh flowers, still in bud, and a box of tissues.

Holly took out her phone, set it to record, and placed it in her inside jacket pocket, as Caiger's door opened to reveal a tall man with the look of a pirate. Curly black hair fell in long ringlets around his ears; his face was tanned and smooth and his eyes looked dark. His clothes, though, were extraordinary. He wore a black shirt and tie, black Dr. Martens and trousers that were patterned in a bright pink paisley. A scarf in similar colours hung around his neck and he carried a heavy corduroy coat in a dark shade of rust. As he drew closer, she saw that he was older than she'd first thought. Their eyes met. He gave her the tiniest nod, just as a man Holly assumed was Caiger appeared in the doorway.

A coin landed on the carpet, making no sound. The dark-haired man had reached the stairs.

'Excuse me!' Holly was on her feet. The pirate turned.

'Miss Baker? Come through, please.'

'I think you dropped something.' Holly bent to pick up the coin. Not a coin. A token. She felt an urge to check her purse, make sure hers was still in it.

'Miss Baker, come inside, please. Can I get you some coffee?'

The pirate had drawn close, was reaching out to take the token back. As Holly dropped it in his hand, his own tightened around it.

'I got one too,' she said. 'How can I get in touch with you?'

'Maybe a glass of water?' Caiger had rested his fingers lightly on Holly's arm.

The other man stared for a second. Then he pulled a wallet from his trouser pocket and fished a card from it. He handed it over before turning on his heels and walking out.

Holly glanced down. *Robin Knight, wedding planner and celebrant.*

Feeling a strange sense of triumph, Holly turned to face Caiger. 'Was that against the rules?' she asked.

Caiger was younger than Holly had expected, maybe early forties, slim but not tall and with thick, dark hair. He looked like he needed a shave, but some men always did. His suit was well cut, and he smelled of bergamot. Holly declined the offer of anything to drink and was waved towards a conference table.

She didn't think she'd ever been in a lawyer's office with less clutter; there wasn't even any paperwork on his desk. Everything in the room, from the pictures on the walls, to the vase on the filing cabinet, looked stylish, corporate and totally unpersonal. It couldn't have been more different to her own workspace. At work, with no Charlie to stress out over mess, Holly gave her untidy nature free rein.

'We haven't come across each other, have we?' Caiger pulled a chair back for her. 'But I don't get involved in personal injury much.'

Well, she'd have been disappointed if he hadn't known exactly who she was.

Holly took a moment before allowing herself to be seated. The floor-to-ceiling windows looked out over the cathedral yard where the trees had started to turn in earnest. The scarlet and apricot colours of foreign specimens stood out among the dark tan of the English oaks.

'Beautiful room,' she said.

'Modern offices have a lot to recommend them.' Caiger gave her a tight smile. 'Our last place went back to Tudor times. We were glad to get out of it.' He inclined his head to the table. 'Please.'

As Holly took a seat and pulled out her legal pad, she wondered if her clothes were as much about sending a message to Caiger as avoiding the press outside. She wasn't going to make this easy for him.

Several seconds went by.

'I expect you have some questions,' he said. 'Fire away. I'll tell you what I can.'

Caiger had neither legal pad nor device, which meant he too was probably recording the meeting.

'Is this for real?' She started with the first of the fourteen questions that she and Coffie had brainstormed. 'Are you really acting on behalf of Logan Quick and is he really leaving me money in his will?'

She saw a slight bristling on the solicitor's face.

'Mr Quick has been a client of this firm for nearly fifteen years. We handle much of his business and personal affairs. I myself drew up his most recent will and I can assure you it is entirely genuine. And that you are, currently, one of the beneficiaries.'

'Can I see it?'

'Regrettably not.'

Holly made a note. That had been a long shot, but worth a try.

'Why me?' she said, when she looked up. 'Why would Logan Quick leave me money?'

'I'm afraid I can't answer that. Mr Quick didn't share his motivation with me.'

'Have he and I ever met?'

Caiger shook his head. 'I couldn't say one way or the other. If you have, he didn't share the information.'

'You said, currently, just now,' she went on. 'That I'm currently one of the beneficiaries. What did you mean by that?'

'You're a lawyer yourself, Miss Baker. You must be aware that wills can be changed at any time.'

And Logan Quick wasn't an old man. He was younger than her parents. Damn it, she was not going to let herself feel disappointed. Disappointment meant she was starting to hope.

'How many other beneficiaries are there?'

'I'm not at liberty to disclose that.'

'More than a thousand?'

No reply. Instead, Caiger gave a surreptitious look at his watch.

'The man who left your offices just now.' She thought back to the card. Robin Knight. 'Is he a beneficiary too?'

'You saw the token he dropped. You can draw your own conclusions. I'm not at liberty to say.'

'Do any of the other beneficiaries and I know each other?'

'Again, I couldn't say. But not to my knowledge.'

'Did Mr Quick share with you his reasons for leaving money to me?'

A slight pause. 'He did not.'

Holly took a moment to make sure her notes were comprehensive. Ten minutes of the thirty-minute appointment had passed. When she looked up again, she said, 'Am I the beneficiary or the token holder?'

Caiger breathed out audibly. 'A tricky one, to be honest with you. And one that may be subject to legal challenge in the fullness of time.' He leaned forward and placed his hands in the prayer position beneath his chin. 'Mr Quick was very clear about who should receive the letters. But the will refers to the current holders of the tokens. To be clear, you are not directly named in the will itself.'

Holly thought about the token in her purse and where she could keep it safe for what might be years.

Caiger said, 'The clause in the letter about keeping it safe was my idea. It took a little persuasion before Mr Quick agreed.'

'So, if I lose the token, I can't claim my inheritance?'

'Correct, you cannot. Or rather, almost certainly not without considerable legal shenanigans and probably not even then. I advise you to put it somewhere very safe.'

'If it's stolen from me, will the new holder be able to claim?'

Caiger leaned back in his chair. 'Another tricky one, and something I was very aware of while I was drawing up the will. The law doesn't like to benefit criminals. On the other hand, our first duty is to our clients. For what it's worth, I think the wording is watertight, and that the person who has possession of the token when the inheritance is claimed, will be the one who benefits, howsoever it was obtained.'

Holly held his stare.

'But I guess I would say that, wouldn't I?' he concluded.

Caiger had no real skin in the game, Holly acknowledged. A long, drawn-out legal battle over the will would bring in thousands of pounds of fees. Maybe hundreds of thousands with an estate the size of Quick's. Caiger didn't care if Holly inherited or someone else did.

Which rather begged the question, did Quick?

'Are there any conditions to inheriting? Other than being in possession of the token.'

'There are not.'

'The letter said I should tell no one that I was a recipient,' Holly said. 'Does that mean I've already broken the terms of the will? I told that man outside, for a start.'

'An act I didn't think was wise, if I may say so. But the advice to keep the existence of the token secret was merely that. Advice. Again, included at my instigation. There is no mention in the will itself of secrecy.'

Holly made a note.

'I do strongly advise, though, Miss Baker, that you exercise discretion. These offices have been besieged for a week now because one recipient was foolish enough to talk to the media. I understand she is experiencing the same annoyance at her home, and she has a family.'

Sabri Carter. The ambulance driver.

'I think you too have a young son,' Caiger said.

Alarm shot through Holly before she reminded herself that, of course, Caiger knew her circumstances. 'Are you saying I need to be afraid?' she asked.

'I'd say having the media on the doorstep of the Carter home, while a nuisance, is probably what's keeping the family safe right now,' he replied. 'But I'm not sure that can be relied on. It really would have been much better if they'd been discreet.'

Another glance at his watch. Holly wondered if he was expecting another token holder, if he was trying to bring this meeting to an end ahead of time so she wouldn't run into whoever it was.

'One last question,' she said. 'What happens when Logan Quick dies?'

'There will be the usual legalities and formalities to go through. It will take some time, of course. But I advise making a claim through these offices at the earliest opportunity.'

Holly got to her feet. Caiger did likewise and held out a hand for her to shake.

'Good luck, Miss Baker. I do hope it works out for you. In the meantime, take very good care of yourself. And your young son.'

Chapter 48

The recent storms had brought down most of the leaves in Tara's garden and she was raking them when the call from an unknown number came in. Heart sinking – it would be another journalist at best, an estate agent at worst – she knew there was nothing to be gained from sticking her head in the sand. Or a pile of autumn leaves. And so, she answered it.

'My name's Holly,' a young female voice said. 'I'm sitting on a bench outside Barker, Momen and Dodds in Exeter.'

A sudden gust sent a flurry of fresh leaf fall skimming around Tara. She said, 'How did you get my number?'

'It wasn't hard. It said on the news that you're a glass artist. I googled all the glass artists in Cornwall until I found a Tara.'

It was windy in Exeter too, judging by the whistling in the background. If Exeter was indeed where this Holly was calling from.

'I didn't think of that,' Tara admitted. 'What can I do for you, Holly?'

A moment's silence, then, 'I got one too.' Holly's voice had dropped. 'I've just had my appointment with Joe Caiger.'

Suppressing the jolt of excitement, Tara told herself to take nothing on face value.

'I'm surprised you're not surrounded by journalists,' she said. 'Maybe you are.'

A soft laugh. 'No, I'm kind of in disguise.'

'What's your second name?'

Another moment of silence and then, 'Do you mind if I don't say for now? It's just, I've seen the way you and the other lady, Sabri

Carter, are being hounded and I have a young son. He wouldn't cope with that very well. He wouldn't cope at all.'

'How are you coping?' Something in the young woman's tone as she spoke about her son was inclining Tara to trust her.

A heavy sigh, then, 'Tara, I wouldn't know where to start. I mean, it's all completely bonkers. Logan Quick's fortune? Fuck!'

Tara walked to a nearby bench and sat down. It felt damp, even through her jeans. She said, 'Tell me about it.'

'My son's so excited. It will kill him if it's not real.'

'Oh, it's real all right,' Tara said, hearing her voice sounding almost angry. If she tried to pin-point the moment she'd started believing it, it would probably be when she heard the raw fury in Amanda Holt's voice. 'What I'm not sure about is whether it's a good thing or the exact opposite.'

Amanda Holt hadn't sounded like the sort of woman who'd let her former husband's fortune go to strangers without a fight.

'I know,' Holly replied. 'There are times this last week when I've been terrified. I keep thinking, what if someone breaks into the house and tries to hurt Charlie.'

Well, the girl sounded genuine. All the same . . .

'Holly, your token has a number on it. A number in triple figures. Can you tell me what it is?'

'Hold on.'

Tara waited. It would be the easiest thing in the world to make a number up. Somehow, though, she doubted the number of tokens ran to triple figures.

'I can't see three digits,' Holly said after several seconds. 'There's what appears to be a number seven, but it's very small. Is that significant?'

'Possibly,' Tara replied, thinking, so, at least seven of us.

'I met a man who had one too,' Holly was saying. 'His appointment finished as I was going in. I didn't see a number on his token, I didn't have time, but it looked exactly the same as mine. He lives in Bodmin.'

A man? Not all women then. 'Do you have his details?'

'He gave me a business card.'

Tara made up her mind. 'I'm glad you phoned me, Holly. I've been in touch with the woman in St Austell who you may have seen on the news. She's called Cheryl. Got a dragon of a mother.'

'I've seen her,' Holly admitted. 'Is she for real? They're claiming their token was lost.'

'Hard to say. But she sounded credible on the phone. Nervous, though. I'm meeting her tomorrow in her local library. I think she suggested it to get away from her mother. So, with your chap in Bodmin, that makes five of us. Although the number on your token suggests seven.'

'I guess.'

'We should stay in touch. What about a WhatsApp group? Would you be up for that? And I've started work on a spreadsheet.'

'A spreadsheet?'

'I've been trying to identify things that Sabri and I have in common. We're both roughly the same age, mid-fifties, and we both have an NHS background. We've both got children, as do you. Mind you, she's happily married and I'm in the process of a divorce.'

'The man I met, Robin, he looked to be that sort of age. I'm only thirty, though.'

'Well, that's the sort of thing we need to know.'

Silence on the line for several seconds, then, 'That's actually a good idea.'

Tara found herself smiling. 'I've been known to have one or two. Holly, if we all put our heads together, maybe we can figure this out.'

Chapter 49

Robin was distracted. Otherwise, there was no way he'd have allowed the token to fall out of his coat pocket. He probably wouldn't have handed over his business card to the perfect stranger in the solicitors' waiting room, but he wasn't thinking straight. Seconds before thanking Joe Caiger for his time, Robin had received a text from Jax.

We need to talk. Can you meet me lunchtime? Around 1 p.m.? I'll be at Wheal Glynn.

It said something about his priorities, he reflected, as he hurried from the offices, narrowly avoiding bumping into a big bloke with a neatly trimmed beard, that the question uppermost in his mind was not the impact that inheriting a share of Logan Quick's fortune would have on his life, but whether he could drive from Exeter to Bodmin in time to make the meeting with Jax.

He'd heard nothing from her since the kiss on the clifftop. In fact, as the three of them, plus the two witnesses, had gone through the motions of the wedding ceremony, he'd come close to thinking he'd imagined it. When the rehearsal was over, she'd kissed Neil, climbed onto her Honda, and roared away, leaving her fiancé to thank Robin and the manager for their time.

Every day since, he'd waited for the phone call telling him his services were no longer required, that she and Neil had found a new celebrant; one who didn't try to abscond with the bride.

In his car, having pushed his way past several aggressive journalists and photographers, Robin was on the point of texting that he might be a few minutes late, when another message came in.

Don't respond. I'm with Neil all morning. He looks at my messages.

Well, that presented questions all by itself. For now, though, he had to get going. The drive would take him over an hour if the roads were clear and, in Cornwall, they rarely were. And then he had to walk to the remote derelict tin mine that was Wheal Glynn.

Only Jax would choose such a spot for a rendezvous. Wheal Glynn lay in a forested valley outside Bodmin called Cardinham Woods. He'd have to park, then follow a steep trail along the river for over a mile to reach the mine. It made sense, though. Not long after they'd met, Jax had told him that Wheal Glynn was one of her favourite places in the world.

A small, squat, square stone tower, topped with an ornate chimney, the old silver and lead mine sat on a steep bank of ferns and bracken, and was largely overgrown with moss, lichen and ivy. There was a fairytale quality about it, and Robin had used it more than once for wedding photographs.

He pulled into the car park at Cardinham Woods a little after one o'clock. Her Honda was parked at the far end, closest to the trail, but there was no sign of its rider. She'd gone on ahead.

Pulling on his coat, Robin started to jog down the trail. Very quickly, the woods closed up around him. Tall fir trees reached to the sky and the light danced around on the forest floor as though living things were scattering at his approach. The thick, scented air of the forest seemed to stick to his lungs, constricting his air supply. He slowed his pace, trying to catch the clean, citrus scent of the evergreens, but the dense aroma of wet soil and rotting fungi only intensified. It seemed to Robin that the air was thick with spores and that if he were to linger here they'd steal into his throat and the forest would colonise him, from the inside out.

For all that, there was a lightness in his heart, something he hadn't felt for a very long time. With the promise of Logan Quick's millions, he could rearrange his debt to make it more manageable. And Jax wouldn't ask him to meet her here, in a place they both loved, to give him the brush-off. He was on the brink of something amazing.

A cacophonous honking above the treeline told him an arrowhead of geese was passing overhead. The river bounced over rocks and stones as it rushed ahead of him. He rounded the last bend and saw the abandoned mine.

No sign of Jax.

Robin stepped a slow, lazy circle, partly to get his breath back, partly because Jax would have found a discreet spot to wait and watch him approach. Still no sign of her.

'Do I close my eyes and count to ten?' he called, after a few moments.

'Up to you,' a voice replied. 'You seem to like games.'

Jax's fiancé, Neil, stepped out from the shelter of the mine building.

'I'm guessing I'm fired.' Robin tried not to sound nervous as Neil stepped closer. The other man was younger and bigger, almost certainly stronger. It was unlikely a man in his position would resort to physical violence, but he'd be wise not to rule it out.

'Oh hell, yes, you're fired.' Robin was a tall man, but Neil was on higher ground and seemed to loom over him. 'We've found another celebrant who's free on the twenty-eighth. I expect you to send over all your contacts for the other suppliers before the end of the day and don't even think about sending us a bill.'

Well, he couldn't argue with any of that. 'Are we done?' he said.

Neil seemed to draw himself up. He too was breathing heavily. 'No, we're not fucking done,' he said. 'We're a very long way from being done. You're lucky I'm not beating you to a pulp, you treacherous motherfucker.'

He was bluffing, he had to be. A surgeon couldn't risk damaging his hands.

'I know about the Bellingham wedding,' Neil went on. 'I know you're being sued. If you contact my fiancée again, if you so much as like something she posts on Instagram, I'll add my own case. I'll make sure you're ruined. I'll drag your name through the mud. Not only will you never work again in this business, you'll be such a laughing stock your own mother will disown you.'

'Now, are we done?' Robin asked. 'Or do you still need to punch me in the face for good measure?'

He took a step closer to the other man, at the same time wondering what the hell he was doing. Did he really need a broken nose on top of everything else?

'Oh, I wouldn't sully myself.' Neil didn't back away. If anything, he leaned closer. 'I don't need to. You see, I know people. So, if you want to be out of work, out of a home, facing several bankruptcy charges, a social pariah and needing a new kneecap, go ahead. There's every chance you'd end up on my operating table. And I'll make sure you never walk again without a limp.'

At last, Neil stepped back. 'Now, we're done.' He turned and started to walk away up the path.

Shaking, Robin let himself relax. All things considered it could have been worse. He could have been lying on the forest floor now, bleeding and in pain. Although he wasn't sure he could hurt much more than he did right now.

Directly opposite the mine building was a fallen tree. He walked over to it and collapsed down. He'd stay here for a while, until he could be sure Neil had left the car park. He couldn't exactly blame the man for being a dick. If the tables had been turned, he wouldn't have ruled out murder. At least he'd only risked one of his legs. One had to look on the bright side.

Tears filled Robin's eyes. He didn't care about the token, he realised, or Logan Quick's ridiculous, manipulative will. He'd give it up in a heartbeat for a life with Jax. Hell, he'd give it up for the chance of seeing her one last time.

The blow took Robin completely by surprise. Lost in his own self-pity, he didn't hear Neil's returning footsteps. He didn't hear him bend to pick up one of the broken branches. He didn't even feel the rush of air as it came hurtling towards his head.

He felt the massive shock of pain and saw the forest floor rushing up to meet him. He landed face first in a pile of leaves.

'Changed my mind,' said the voice directly above him. 'I'm sullying myself.'

Neil was wearing biker's boots. Robin felt the fine bones of his nose break when they made contact.

DAY EIGHT

Wednesday, 10 October

Chapter 50

Three people were sitting on the mezzanine level of St Austell public library when Tara reached the top of the stairs, but only one of them looked up: a large woman in her early fifties. Her hair was short and dark blonde and was either damp from the rain or in need of a wash. She wore a scarlet cardigan over enormous breasts. Her round, shiny face had a hint of a bruise on the right cheekbone, but she broke into a smile as Tara approached and got to her feet. Her hand felt podgy and damp.

'You must be Cheryl.' Tara kept her voice low, although the other two people, both of whom looked like students, were some distance away.

'I am. Are you Tara? I like your coat.'

'It's nice to meet you. Shall we sit down?'

The two women pulled out chairs at the closest table and sat. Tara said, 'Would you like to see my token? So you know I'm for real?' She reached into her purse and held it in the palm of her hand. Cheryl leaned close. She smelled of cheap perfume and cooking fat.

'I didn't bring mine.'

Tara tucked the token back into her purse and put it in her handbag. She'd deliberately chosen one with a buckle fastening and a long strap that she could wear across her chest. 'I wanted to ask you about that,' she said. 'It said on the news that you'd lost it. That you threw it away.'

Cheryl glanced around. 'My mum threw it on the fire,' she confessed. 'But I got up in the night and rooted through the ashes till I found it. I only found the token, though, not the letter. Does that matter?'

'So, you have it somewhere safe?'

'Yes, it's—'

Tara held up a hand. 'No, don't tell me. Don't tell anyone. To be honest, I think it's best for you and your mother if everyone believes it's lost. If only the two of you know where it is. Especially given what happened to you on Sunday. Are you OK now?'

Cheryl nodded. 'I've got some nasty bruises but that's all. And we've had the locks changed. So, no one should be able to get in. It's worrying, though.'

'It is,' Tara agreed.

A cloud passed over Cheryl's face. 'What about the solicitors? We're going this afternoon. Will they need to see the token?'

'I wasn't asked to show mine. I'd leave it where it's safe if I were you.'

'The woman I spoke to, the secretary, she said they would only see me and not my mum. That they would only meet with the person who'd been sent the token. And that was me.'

Tara was beginning to regret sitting quite so close to Cheryl. There was a stale smell coming from the other woman, of sweat and clothes not washed often enough. And of farts too, as though she had a nervous stomach.

'Sounds right,' she agreed. 'They said that to me too.'

'Mum went nuts when I told her. She says no one will keep her out.'

The woman had eczema patches on the backs of her hands and more than one scabbed-over sore.

'Do you want your mum to go in with you?' Tara asked. 'Will you feel more comfortable if she's there?'

'No, I want to see him by myself.' The frown lines between Cheryl's brows deepened. 'Can I ask you something?'

'Of course.'

'The press conference said that whoever has the token gets the inheritance,' Cheryl said. 'So, if my mum takes it off me, will she inherit the man's money?

Tara gave herself a moment to process the unusual question. 'I suppose so. But she wouldn't do that to you, would she?'

Cheryl's silence spoke volumes.

'Does she know you still have it?'

'Not for certain. I told her it must have been destroyed by the fire. I keep finding her looking for it, though. She thinks I'm hiding it from her. Which I am, I suppose. Do you think I'm awful? Trying to cheat my mum?'

There was no way on earth this woman would cope with inheriting millions. What the hell was Logan Quick playing at?

'I think only you can really understand your personal circumstances,' Tara replied. 'And I'm the last person to judge anyone.'

Cheryl nodded as though she understood. 'You said on the phone that you were trying to get a – some sort of group together.'

'A WhatsApp group,' Tara said. 'Of people we know for certain have got a token. There's five of us so far. I can add you if you like. But you need a smartphone.'

'I don't have a smartphone,' Cheryl reminded her.

'Don't worry, we can cope. And I'm working on a spreadsheet of us all. I'll show you.'

Pulling her laptop from her bag, Tara opened it and found the Excel file she'd been working on.

'I'm trying to work out what we might have in common,' she explained. 'The year we were born, where we were born, where we went to school, what we do for a living, that sort of thing. If we can find a connection, we might be able to work out how we connect to Logan Quick. And why he's doing this.'

'But . . .'

'What is it?'

Cheryl's face was creased with worry. 'We don't want to do anything to annoy him, do we? What if he changes his mind?'

Tara sat back in her chair.

'Well, that's a fair challenge. And you must decide for yourself what to do. But I've spoken to some of the others and, to be honest with you, Cheryl, we're all worried. Sabri can barely leave her house without being leapt on by journalists and photographers and she's terrified for her children's safety. I'm experiencing much the same thing and my estranged husband has cancelled his financial support on the grounds I don't need it anymore. That may eventually be the case but in the short term, I'm probably going to have to sell my house. Holly and Robin have managed to stay under the radar so far, but Holly is a single mum with a young son and Robin . . .'

She paused for a moment. Well, she'd come this far. 'Robin insists he's fine, but he doesn't sound it. I think something's happened to him and he doesn't want to worry me.'

Cheryl looked down. Tara could see confusion, even distrust, on her face.

'And you were set upon in the street,' Tara reminded her. 'People were prepared to hurt you to get your token.'

'In my head,' Cheryl said, her eyes still fixed on her lap, 'there's a voice telling me to give the token up, that I haven't done anything to deserve someone giving me a lot of money, and that I'll only regret being greedy.'

Tara said nothing. What Cheryl was saying rang all too true.

'But, for the first time in my life, people are taking notice of me. All my life, they've ignored me. Now, suddenly, I matter.'

A light had crept into Cheryl's eyes; it quite transformed the woman, turning her into someone to be wary of.

'And you know what, Tara?' she went on. 'I like it.'

Chapter 51

Holly finished programming the dishwasher. Electricity was cheaper after eleven o'clock at night and so all her household appliances were scheduled to run through the early hours of the morning. Every little helped.

Glancing around the kitchen, she made sure nothing out of place would upset Charlie when he came down in the morning and went to collect her briefcase from the hallway. Tomorrow's client – she couldn't even remember the poor man's name – was suing his local convenience store for negligence and she wasn't anywhere close to being on top of her brief.

The man – what the hell was his name? – in his early seventies, was registered blind and hadn't seen the yellow, *Caution Wet Floor* cones positioned either side of a wine spillage. He'd slid in a puddle of Sauvignon Blanc and cut himself on broken glass. Timing, recorded on CCTV, strengthened Holly's case; the spillage had occurred over an hour before the fall. On the other hand, the store was family owned, it had been after ten o'clock at night, and the only staff member on the premises claimed he'd been too busy at the till to see to it. The store was insured but if Holly won her case, the insurers would almost certainly dispute the claim. Either way, it would be a bad outcome for someone.

A sudden loud knocking startled her. Coffie? Except, he never came round without calling first and would never bang on the door after Charlie had gone to bed. The media? Surely Tara hadn't given her away.

A second knock. Even Charlie would wake up if this carried on. Holly left the kitchen and, through the opaque glass in the front door, saw the outline of a man. Nerves building, she attached the chain before she opened it. Not the media. She almost wished it had been. Chris, cashmere coat around his shoulders, stood on her doorstep.

'I wasn't sure I'd find you in.' Chris slung his coat over the banister and followed Holly through to the kitchen. 'I thought you might be . . . working.'

He pulled out a stool and sat at the central table, running his eyes over her papers. Holly gathered them all together.

'Thank you,' he said, with a nasty smile. 'I'll have a glass of red. Merlot if you have it.'

'Why are you here, Chris?'

He held eye contact as he pushed the cuffs of his sweater back over his wrists. If she hadn't known better – Chris was a physical coward – she'd have thought him gearing up for a fist fight. 'I came to give you my bank details,' he said. 'I could have texted them, but I thought it might be nice to have a catch-up.' In an instant, the pretence at a smile was gone. 'Give me your phone, Holly.'

'What?'

'I want your phone. I want to make sure you're not recording this.'

'Because you know you're breaking the law?'

Her phone was on charge, directly behind where he was sitting. Fair play, had she known who was on her doorstep, she probably would have set it to record.

When she didn't move, he spun round on his seat and spotted her phone. A second later, he had it.

'Fourteen years maximum,' Holly told him. 'Don't tell me you didn't check.'

The glint in his eyes was pure wicked; how had she never seen that in him before?

'In ninety-nine cases out of a hundred, a victim of blackmail will use any means to avoid appearing in public,' he replied. 'They will avoid publicity to the best of their ability and will go so far as to spend their last penny rather than allow their name to appear in the public press or become known in the law courts of this country.'

The bastard was quoting Hansard at her.

'It's not a loan, is it?' she said. 'I'm never going to get this money back.'

He looked hurt. 'Holly, where's the trust?'

Taking her by surprise, his hand, still holding her phone, darted out towards her, quick as a snake. She flinched away before it could recognise her face. He gave a heavy sigh, as though she were the one at fault.

'A thousand,' she said, hating herself. 'It's the best I can do.'

He shook his head. 'Won't touch the sides.'

She felt her throat constricting, a stinging in the back of her nose. 'Don't do this. I have a little boy.'

He held the phone out again. This time, she didn't move away.

Chapter 52

Cheryl was exhausted. She'd never have believed that a car ride from St Austell to Exeter, with her mother and Jasmin, the journalist, behind her in the back seats could have left her longing for the peace of her early-morning alone time but it had. The questions had been non-stop, and Sheila's attempts to answer them on Cheryl's behalf had made matters worse. The two women had continually talked over each other, as Jasmin had tried to get information from Cheryl and Sheila had insisted on being the only one who could respond. Constantly having to twist round to face them had given her a sore neck.

Then that dreadful meeting with Mr Caiger, when she'd been too nervous to speak and couldn't remember any of the questions she and Tara had agreed that she would ask. He'd thought she was a half-wit and had cut the meeting short after only fifteen minutes. In the car on the way home, her mother had barely been able to contain her fury at how little Cheryl seemed able to relate.

'He couldn't tell me anything really,' she'd kept insisting. 'Only that they'll be in touch when the time comes.'

'Did you tell him you'd lost the token? Don't tell me you were that stupid,' Sheila had demanded, more than once.

'No,' answered Cheryl, truthfully. 'I didn't tell him that.'

'I think a forensic search of the house might be a good idea, Mrs Young,' Jasmin had said. 'I can organise that. Then, perhaps the station can keep it safe for you?'

The two had exchanged a look then, a look that told Cheryl they both knew she'd hidden it somewhere.

There was no way Sheila would let the token out of her hands once she'd found it, but she'd agreed to Jasmin bringing what she called a 'crew' over the following afternoon. There was nowhere in the house, or the garden, where Cheryl could hide the token. Not from a group of people determined to find it. In twenty-four hours, it would be in her mother's possession.

The fire was dying down. They never put coal on it after nine o'clock and the room was getting chilly. The heating was programmed to switch off when Sheila went to bed at ten o'clock. Cheryl made sure the fireguard was in place and turned to leave the room.

The scrapbook was on the small coffee table by Sheila's armchair.

Cheryl's mouth dried in an instant. She hadn't seen the scrapbook in years. She'd even managed, for the most part, to push its existence to the very back of her mind. It was a cheap thing, bought years ago for a quid in WHSmith's. From memory, only the first five or six pages had been filled. After that, the source material had run out.

Without thinking what she was doing, Cheryl picked up the book and carried it to the window. Drawing back the curtain a fraction to let in light from outside, her eyes filled with tears, and it was several seconds before the headlines of the first page came into focus.

Search for missing girl continues.
Appeal for witnesses unsuccessful.
And then . . .
Body found.

Cheryl's eyes fixed on the last of them as the opening lines of the story came into focus. *The body of a young woman was recovered from the water today by the coastguard. While formal identification has yet to take place, the sad discovery is likely to bring to an end the seven-day search for nineteen-year-old . . .*

Cheryl closed the book.

Burn it!

No sooner had the thought appeared in her head than she was back at the fire, staring down into the dying embers. She'd never have to see it again. She moved the guard aside and held the book directly above the coals, feeling the heat of them starting to eat into her skin. Greedy for fresh, easy fuel, a flame leapt up and caught the bottom corner of the book. It ignited quickly. After only a couple of seconds Cheryl was forced to drop it, to use the poker to make sure it didn't fall out onto the hearth. Only when she saw the book charred beyond recognition did she realise her mistake. The scrapbook wasn't proof, just a record of proof. She'd gained nothing. All she'd done was provoke her mother, who wouldn't let the destruction of the book go unpunished.

Careless of the scrapbook still burning in the hearth, not even bothering to replace the guard, Cheryl left the room and climbed upstairs. Her mother was gently snoring. Without turning on lights, Cheryl went into her own room and lowered herself until she lay flat on the carpet. It was hard to breath like this, but she stretched out until her hand could reach beneath the loose fold of carpet. For a second, she could feel nothing, and thought her heart might stop beating, but then her fingers touched the cool metal of the token.

Back on her feet, Cheryl collected the half-empty glass of water from her bedside table and carried both it and the token into the bathroom. She filled the glass then, treading carefully, went to stand at the foot of her mother's bed.

Sheila grunted in her sleep, a spasm of what looked like pain crossing her face.

'Cheers, Mum,' said Cheryl. She took a gulp of water first, to refresh her dry mouth. Then she swallowed the token.

DAY NINE

Thursday, 11 October

Chapter 53

On the day of the press conference, when news of the tokens spread the world over, high tide at Daymer Bay occurred at ten minutes past nine o'clock in the morning. Tara pulled into the car park at three minutes past.

'And we've got some breaking news,' the BBC presenter was saying, as Tara tucked her purse and phone into the glove compartment. 'Barker, Momen and Dodds, the Cornish firm of solicitors at the centre of the story about Logan Quick's eccentric last will and testament, have announced a press conference at eleven thirty this morning. I think our reporter, David Lyme, is on the line now. David, what's happening in Exeter?'

Tara turned up the volume.

'Well, Jeremy, there's been a lot of activity around the offices of Barker, Momen and Dodds since news of Logan Quick's will broke,' replied the new voice. 'Earlier this week we saw increased levels of security around the firm as, presumably, the recipients of the mysterious tokens were dropping in to find out more. Nothing official has been announced as yet but, maybe this morning, that will all change.'

'And I've just heard from the producer that we will be covering the press conference live, so stay tuned, folks. More on Logan Quick and his intriguing legacy as we get it.'

The station moved on to another story and Tara turned off the radio. Almost immediately, her phone began to ring.

Holly was reading case notes when Coffie opened her office door. 'You need to see this.' He put a notepad computer on her desk. 'It's going out live now.'

'Mate, I'm on a deadline,' Holly argued.

The screen showed a YouTube channel and two bearded young men in T-shirts sitting side by side at a desk. Both wore headphones and were speaking into enormous microphones. Each had a laptop. The background looked like a giant, purple egg box.

'These two have nearly four million subscribers,' Coffie told her. 'And they're talking about you.'

'So, that's Intense Bulk Protein Shakes,' the boy on the left was saying. His hair had a ginger tinge, otherwise he was practically indistinguishable from the one on the right. 'Perfect for that protein hit directly after the gym or in between meals. Toby uses it all the time, don't you, Tobes?'

Tobes, the darker-haired kid in a yellow T-shirt, smirked as he flexed his very unimpressive muscles.

'And now back to the main story,' Ginger Hair went on. 'And that's treasure hunts. We do love a treasure hunt, don't we now? We might dream of winning the lottery but given the choice between having millions handed to us on a plate and seeking it out for ourselves on a swashbuckling adventure of derring-do? Well, what would you do, Tobes?'

'I'd take the plate,' Tobes replied.

Ginger laughed. 'And yet from the dawn of time, we've yearned for treasure, the harder to find the better. Take the hunt for the golden hare in the seventies. The book that started the whole thing off sold over a million copies. People were looking for the thing all over the world. And where was it found?'

'I don't know, Ben, tell me where it was found.'

'Berkshire.'

Both men laughed.

'Course, that was before we were born,' Ben went on. 'So, how about this one. Back in 2010, an art dealer called Forrest Fenn announced that he'd buried a bronze chest full of gold, jewellery and artefacts somewhere in the Rocky Mountains. It took a decade, and hundreds of thousands of seekers, before it was finally found in 2020.'

'Seriously?' Holly sighed. She really did have a hell of a lot to get through.

'Give it a minute,' Coffie told her.

'My favourite is the Lake Toplitz Nazi treasure,' Tobes said. 'This lake, somewhere in the wilds of Austria, was used by the Nazis as a naval testing station in the 1940s. Towards the end of the war, they began sinking containers into the water. It's believed they dumped billions of dollars of gold down there, meaning to come back and get it when all the, you know, the fuss about the Holocaust had died down. But that didn't happen. And the lake is three hundred feet deep. At least five divers have died trying to recover the lost Nazi gold. But tell me, Ben, why are we talking about treasure hunts?'

'Because we have one of our own here in Cornwall,' Ben replied. 'And we're about to find out a whole lot more about it at a press conference this morning given by Cornish solicitors Barker, Momen and Dodds.'

Holly looked up at Coffie, saw the *I told you so* look on his face.

On the screen, Tobes said, 'When we say treasure, in this case we're talking cold hard cash, aren't we?'

'Possibly,' replied Ben. 'But it all depends upon the possession of a mysterious token, a small bronze coin covered in ancient writing. We know an undisclosed number have been sent out, and three have come to light, in the hands of some ordinary local women, prompting many to speculate what these three have done to be singled out like this.'

'Intriguing.'

The two young men shared smiles and knowing looks.

'Just the sort of mystery we love,' Ben went on. 'The press conference starts at eleven thirty, folks, and we'll be covering it live, so stay tuned.'

The pair moved on to another story. Without speaking, Coffie cut the volume and scrolled down so Holly could see some of the comments appearing.

I've heard whoever has the token gets the money. We need to find these bad boys.

It's a scam. I can't believe people are falling for this.
Anyone know where these bitches live?
We could snatch one of her kids. She'll soon hand it over then.
Holly had seen enough. She turned the laptop away.

'You cannot go public,' Coffie told her. 'Put that bloody thing in a bank safe deposit box and forget all about it till you hear Logan Quick has died. I tell you, Holls, that man has handed you a poisoned chalice.'

'Cheryl! Get your lazy arse in here.'

More than once over the last couple of weeks, Cheryl had wondered if her mother was in the early stages of dementia. Sheila had never been a mild-mannered woman, but her spite had been subtle. She'd never made a habit of swearing. Since the arrival of the token, though, her language had deteriorated and all too often her manner stretched from irritated to abusive.

Or maybe she just couldn't cope with her daughter having the upper hand.

Cheryl straightened up from the washing machine and joined Sheila in the sitting room. The TV was on, uncomfortably loud.

'There's a big announcement today.' Sheila didn't take her eyes from the screen. 'I've forgotten what they called it. It's happening at eleven thirty. That's in ten minutes. You need to get on the phone to those solicitors. They can't spring surprises on us like this.'

'What sort of announcement? Mum, please turn that down, I can't hear myself think.'

'I told you, about the will. He must have died already. Get on the phone. You know the buggers won't talk to me.'

Cheryl left the sitting room and picked up the phone. If nothing else, the chance to eavesdrop would make her mum turn the TV volume down. As she waited to be connected, she felt a churning in her stomach that was beginning to be all too familiar. There were times when she honestly couldn't say whether she was glad the letter with the token had been sent to her or not. Life had been a lot easier before.

On the other hand, Sheila planned to make her homeless. Even a modest inheritance would make a massive difference.

'I'm afraid Mr Caiger isn't available, Miss Young,' a woman with a crisp accent told her, as Sheila appeared in the hallway. The arrival of the token had worked wonders for her mother's mobility. 'May I take a message?'

'I've just heard about today's announcement,' Cheryl said. 'Has Mr Quick changed his mind?'

'Has he died?' Sheila hissed.

'Mr Caiger anticipated that some of the token recipients would be in touch,' the woman told Cheryl. 'In fact, you're the second lady I've spoken to this morning. Mr Caiger has authorised me to tell you the press conference is being held at Mr Quick's instigation but does not affect your position at all.'

'Thank you,' Cheryl said, before putting the phone down.

'What?' Sheila demanded. 'What's happening?'

'I think we'd better watch the TV, Mum,' Cheryl said.

Tug watched the press conference on repeat. Twice. He'd seen it live on the BBC's twenty-four-hour news channel but wasn't sure he'd taken everything in.

The bloke called Joseph Caiger entered the room and walked towards a podium, for all the world like he was president of the USA. Two other men stepped in after him and vanished from view. After wishing the assembled group a good morning, Caiger introduced himself as the partner responsible for wills and probate.

Tug thought he could hear a tremble in the man's voice, as though he wasn't entirely comfortable with what was going on.

'A little over a week ago,' Caiger said, 'a number of letters were sent out from this office, informing the recipients that, in certain circumstances, they were due to inherit an equal share of the wealth of Cornish businessman Mr Logan Quick.'

Glancing down, the man cleared his throat before continuing.

'I can confirm that Mr Quick has been a client of this firm for several years and that we issued those letters on his instructions and in good faith.'

Tug felt his insides tightening, although he knew already what came next.

Another glance down, then, 'This firm has acted responsibly throughout and in accordance both with the law and with our client's instructions.'

Slimy git, thought Tug.

'I can further confirm that Mr Quick's will does indeed currently reflect the contents of the letters sent out.'

'You mean it's for real?' someone called out from the audience.

'What do you mean by currently?' another asked.

'Questions at the end, please.' Caiger ran the tip of his tongue over his bottom lip. 'I am now in a position to confirm that seven letters were sent out, all to people living in the Southwest. No further information will be issued about the token recipients at this time.'

A murmur ran around the room; several people bent to make notes.

'I can also confirm, because this is very important, that it is the token, and not the letter, which indicates the beneficiary,' Caiger went on.

'You mean whoever has the token gets the cash?'

Caiger fixed the reporter with a hard stare before replying. 'Precisely.'

Tug reached out for the token that lay on a small table to one side of his armchair. He closed his fist around it.

In the press conference, there was a flurry of noise as those assembled absorbed the implications of what they were hearing. Caiger held his hand in the air.

'I'm almost done, ladies and gentlemen. This next part is important, so I ask your patience. Mr Quick has authorised us to tell you that he has recently been diagnosed with pancreatic cancer and that, despite the best medical care available, his doctors are not optimistic about his life expectancy. He is not expected to live beyond the next twelve months.'

*

Robin watched the press conference that evening. He'd spent most of the day in bed. His head hurt too much to work and so he'd cancelled the meetings he'd had planned for the next few days. More than once, in the forty-eight hours since Neil had beaten him up, he'd wondered if he'd sustained internal damage, if maybe there was an unseen bleed that would, over the course of the next few days, bring his life to an end. On balance, he'd decided, he'd prefer it if it did.

He couldn't breathe too well either; he should really go to hospital. But a fear of bumping into either Neil or Jax in the corridors held him back. And so, he stayed home and licked his wounds.

When the press conference was over, he switched the TV off. So, it really was legit after all. He was going to inherit a fortune in the foreseeable future. The disgruntled clients could do their worst. He'd survive.

He wished he could care.

The doorbell rang. Robin pushed himself to his feet and made his slow, unsteady way to the front door. Bracing himself to answer well-intentioned questions about his injuries, he pulled it open.

Jax.

Clad in her usual black leathers, clutching her helmet under one arm. Her eyes opened wide with shock at the sight of him.

It was a dream. He'd slipped into a coma in front of the TV and his subconscious, for once, had picked exactly the right direction to go in. Well, who was he to argue?

He said, 'I'd say you should see the other guy, but I guess you already have.'

'I will kill him,' she said.

'No argument from me. Do you want to come in?'

Without waiting for an answer, he turned and led the way into his sitting room. He had a moment of wishing that the empty bottle of red wine and the glass with its tell-tale purple stain weren't still on the coffee table, and that he'd cleaned his teeth and showered in the last twenty-four hours but decided it would hardly make any difference.

Jax dropped her helmet and jacket on the sofa. 'Sit down and keep still,' she told him. 'I need to have a look at you.'

She knelt in front of him. He winced when she took his head in her hands.

'Shit,' she said, when she saw the wound at the back of his head. 'Robin, this needs stitches. And an X-ray. Your nose looks broken. If it's not properly set, you'll spend the rest of your life looking like an unsuccessful rugby player.'

'I've developed a recent but acute distrust of the medical profession,' he replied.

She tilted his head so that he was forced to look at her. 'If part of that is directed at me, I didn't tell Neil what happened on Friday. He heard me telling my sister over the phone.'

'That text came from you.'

She leaned back on her heels. 'No, it came from my phone. It was sent by Neil. I was in theatre all day yesterday. He knows my locker combination. I think he must have seen us when he arrived on Saturday. Or enough to rouse his suspicions.'

Robin had a moment of feeling glad that Jax, at least, had not given him away. 'Yeah, well, I can't exactly blame the man. I'd have done the same in his shoes.'

She ran her fingers lightly down his cheek. 'No, you wouldn't.'

How little she knew him.

'I'm taking you to hospital,' she said. 'Can I drive your car? I don't think you should be on the back of a bike in your condition. If not, I'll call an Uber.' She saw his raised eyebrows and added, 'I'll stay with you. Nothing else will happen, I promise.'

'Give me a minute.' Robin took a deep breath. He didn't want to throw up in front of her, but his nausea had got worse since he'd answered the door.

'I'll get you some water.'

Robin closed his eyes until he heard her come back. The water was cold from the fridge.

'Why are you here, Jax?' he said, when the nausea had receded a little.

'Neil forgot that messages sent from my phone also appear on my iPad,' she replied, which didn't answer his question, but possibly explained how she knew what had happened. 'He deleted the ones he'd sent to you from my phone, but they were still on the iPad until I synced it up. I'm so sorry, Robin.'

Jax being nice to him really wasn't helping right now.

'It's for the best,' he said. 'I'll take myself to hospital. I can drive.'

'Did you mean what you said on the clifftop?' she asked him.

Of course he'd meant it; he'd meant every word and a thousand more besides. He tried to shake his head but it hurt too much. 'What does it matter?'

'Well, I'm postponing the wedding,' she replied. 'So, I'd say it matters quite a lot.'

DAY TEN

Friday, 12 October

Chapter 54

'What's up?' Jason said.

'Nothing.'

Everything. Sabri lowered the window to let some fresh air into the car. The farting invariably began within minutes of leaving her parents' house after supper. She'd yet to determine which of the four was responsible; probably all of them. Tonight's meal had been unusually heavy on pulses and vegetables, not to mention spices. There were times when she suspected her mother of doing it deliberately.

Her husband gave an audible sigh.

They were drawing closer to the sewerage treatment works. On balance, her family's emissions were the lesser of two evils and so she closed the window.

Jason tried again. 'You upset about what your mum said?'

Instinctively, Sabri gave him the combination of glare and head jerk that meant *not in front of the kids*. Glancing behind, though, all three were intent on their phones. Darren even had headphones on. She and Jason could be planning their cold-blooded murder and they'd remain oblivious.

Sabri said, 'Since when has my mother been an authority on the scriptures? She went to time and trouble to dig that one up.'

Jason shifted in his seat, as though trying to raise one buttock and let the fart out without her knowing. 'I switch off when she starts talking about Paradise,' he admitted. 'She made it clear years ago I'm going nowhere near it.'

'According to the prophet, if anyone deprives an heir of his inheritance, Allah will deprive him of his inheritance in Paradise on the Day of Resurrection.'

Jason thought for a second. 'How does that work then? You are the heir.'

'I think she meant Quick's real heirs are his children. If I take his money, I'm depriving them.'

'You got off lightly.' Jason slowed down as they approached a speed camera. 'Your dad wanted to know if it's because of some deal I've been involved with. I think he suspects I'm head of a criminal gang.'

Sabri's dad knew perfectly well Jason didn't have the brains to head up a gang of any sort. He'd made no secret of despising his son-in-law over the years; or his daughter for the choice she'd made.

'You'd think, of the whole world, my own parents would be supportive,' she said. 'Maybe offer a bit of genuine advice. Hell, investment tips wouldn't go amiss. I mean, how do we even begin to handle millions of pounds?'

'We'll cope, love. It's a nice problem to have.'

Sometimes she wished she had Jason's uncomplicated approach to life.

'She's got so used to me being the family disappointment, she can't cope with the idea of anything going right for me,' Sabri said. 'And if we become rich, even marginally better off than we are now, if I don't have to go cap in hand to her and Dad next time there's a bill we can't pay, if we don't rely on them for the school trips and the mobile phones and the extra sports equipment . . .'

'Babe, you need to breathe.'

'They lose power over us,' she finished. 'And I don't think they can cope with that.'

Jason looked puzzled; most of her family dynamics went over his head.

'You know what she said to me when she was giving us our coats? She said, *You need to ask yourself what you've done, Sabri, to earn that level of good fortune. And if you can't answer, that will tell you something.*'

Her phone pinged.

'That your new secret thread?'

Jason could be a twat at times. She'd shown him the WhatsApp group, *The Famous Five*, the day Tara set it up, had let him read the thread several times. She'd made no attempt to keep it secret.

Or maybe she needed to calm the hell down. 'Tara's worried about Robin,' she told him. 'He's reading all the messages but not replying. She's asking him outright if he's OK.'

'Any sign of the other two?' Jason asked.

'Not so far.'

'And still none of you know each other?' Jason turned into their road and slowed down to meet the new twenty-mile-an-hour speed limit.

'It's hard to be sure from photographs and that glimpse we had of Cheryl on TV, but I could swear I've never met her, Holly or Robin. Tara looks familiar, but she would. We worked for the same NHS trust for years.'

Jason pulled into their drive behind Sabri's car. The Tesla had been returned undamaged, thank God. She'd made Jason promise not to spend any more money, but he hadn't been smart enough to hide the suspicious wrappings she'd found in the outside bin. After that, it had been the work of minutes to find the new shirt in the wardrobe and the trainers at the back of the boot cupboard.

'Sab,' Jason said.

'We home?' Bethany muttered from the back seat.

'Sab,' Jason repeated. She followed his gaze to where the front door of their house stood open.

Chapter 55

'I've known Neil since med school,' Jax said, when she and Robin were sitting side by side on his sofa. 'We started dating shortly after my first marriage fell apart and we've been living together for five years. I guess we both took it for granted we'd get married one day. We work. At least I thought we did.'

Robin had spent six hours of the previous night in A&E. The wound on the back of his head had been stitched, the bones in his nose reset and an X-ray had confirmed that his ribs were bruised, not broken. Jax had been with him the entire time, had speeded the process up for him, only saying goodbye when she'd bundled him into an Uber and sent him home.

As Robin remembered the old Chinese curse about living in interesting times, he heard the beep on his phone that told him another WhatsApp message had come into the group that Tara had set up.

'I think we're very good at keeping our thoughts away from subjects that disturb us,' Jax was saying. 'Or maybe that's just me.'

Robin thought, but didn't say, that he'd never had any success keeping his thoughts away from Jax.

She frowned. 'So, I think I've been having doubts about marrying Neil for some time, I just didn't let myself dwell on it.'

'You always seemed very animated about the wedding,' Robin said. 'I'd have classed you as one of my more enthusiastic brides.'

It had been more than that. Joy had shone out of her.

'Yeah, that fooled me for a while.' She gave a tight smile. 'But then I realised, the only time I got excited about the wedding was when I was talking about it to you.'

Another ping on Robin's phone. Jeez, not now, Tara. He glanced down. Not Tara, Holly.

'After that, it didn't take long for me to realise. It wasn't the wedding that was doing it for me. It was you.'

She glanced down, as though embarrassed by her confession. Eyes fixed on the sofa, she said, 'I was too young when we met. I wasn't ready. You were exactly the right man, just at the wrong time.'

Robin took a deep breath. 'You'll be better off with Neil. He's younger than me, fitter than me, definitely a hell of a lot more successful. I'm on the verge of bankruptcy and I never earned that much when things were going well. Frankly, I could be homeless before the year's out.'

Her face fell. 'You said you loved me. Were you lying? Was it a game?'

If he were even halfway decent, he'd lie now, send her back to a better life with her posh thug of a fiancé.

'I love you so much it's killing me,' he told her truthfully. 'You're all I can think about. And if I'm pushing back now, it's because I daren't let myself hope.'

His phone pinged again. 'Oh, for God's sake, Holly.'

'Who's Holly?' Jax asked, an edge to her voice.

The phone started ringing. Holly, of course.

'I'm sorry,' he told Jax. 'I've got to take this. I won't be a minute, I promise.' He pressed receive. 'Yes?'

'Robin?' Holly didn't bother introducing herself. 'You need to switch your TV on. The Peter Morgan show on Talk TV. His X account has been trailing a big announcement for the past ten minutes. He's going to name the seven beneficiaries of the will. We're going to be named on TV, Robin.'

Fair play, this was big. Robin took a deep breath that hurt. 'Thanks for the heads up.' He gave Jax an apologetic look. 'You're the most important thing in my life right now, Jax, but something is a bit more urgent.'

Getting to his feet, he found the remote. It took several seconds to find Talk TV but then the familiar face of the controversial journalist and show host filled the screen.

'And now, as promised, I can exclusively reveal the names of the seven people who are due, before the end of the year, to inherit Logan Quick's millions. They are . . .

Holly Baker, a junior barrister from Exeter,
Sabri Carter, an ambulance driver living in Truro,
Craig Lewis, a fire safety consultant from Newquay,
Tara Webb, a retired nurse living in Wadebridge,
Trevor Winter of Falmouth,
Cheryl Young of St Austell and
Robin Knight, a wedding planner in Bodmin.'

Robin turned off the TV when it was clear that Morgan had moved on to another story. Jax hadn't said a word since he'd taken the call from Holly.

'Well,' she said, when the two of them made eye contact once more. 'That feels like something you should have mentioned.'

Chapter 56

'The only other people with keys to our house are the two we just left,' Jason said as he switched off the car engine.

Sabri had yet to move. She was staring, rather stupidly, at the open front door of their house.

'Slide over as soon as I'm out,' Jason told her in a low voice. 'Keep the doors locked. Don't let the kids move. Anything happens, reverse the hell out of here and call the police.'

Sabri watched the door of her house inch open further in the wind as something cold clamped around her heart. She said, 'You can't go in there.'

'We could have left it unlocked,' Jason countered. 'We left in a rush. It's probably fine.'

This was bad. This was the start of her life falling apart. Somehow, she knew it.

'Nobody move,' Jason announced, in a deceptively cheerful voice, as he opened the car door. 'We may have left something at Grandma's. We might have to go back.'

Maddy gave a heavy sigh, but her eyes remained on her phone. Neither of the other two appeared to have heard their father.

'Where is it?' Jason's voice was so low Sabri barely heard it.

She let her hand slip under her jacket to the side of her breast, feeling the small, round coin sewn into her bra.

'It's safe,' she said. 'I promise you, it's perfectly safe. Jason, don't go in.'

He frowned and closed the car door, before mouthing, 'Lock it!' at her.

Sabri did what she was told but stayed in the passenger seat. There was no way she was driving away and leaving Jason. She opened the phone app and let her eyes dart down to the '9' digit as her husband approached the front door. She held her breath as he stepped inside.

'Mum, what's going on? What's Dad doing?'

Great. Her eldest chose that moment to re-engage with the world.

'Just checking something. We're staying here for a minute.'

'Why are we—'

'Maddy, be quiet!'

Bethany looked up at her tone and nudged her brother. Darren took his headphones off. Any second now, they'd be out of the car, and she couldn't stop all three of them. She braced herself to leap into the driver's seat, to get her precious children away from the house that wasn't their own anymore.

Oh, thank God, Jason was back. He left the house, talking to someone on the phone. Sabri jumped out of the car. He shook his head, gesturing that she stay where she was, but the kids were hot on her tail.

Chapter 57

Tara's first thought, when the Peter Morgan show ended, was that maybe the media pressure on her and Sabri would lessen now that all seven recipients had been named. And then she was ashamed of her selfishness. Sabri and her family had it far worse than she did. Her second was that she should make contact with the two new guys as soon as possible.

Easier said than done. Trevor Winter, the security guard, had no online presence that she could pin down. The name was simply too common. She had more luck with Craig Lewis, the fire safety consultant. A website popped up almost immediately and seemed highly probable. She left a quick message, even risking her phone number. Then she lowered the lights in the main room and left it for her studio. She was raking tonight, a task that required full concentration.

The piece, one she'd been planning and prepping for weeks, was a wall-mounted representation of an ocean sunset, intended for her eldest son's birthday. Earlier that week, she'd finished most of the groundwork and now the glass panel, with colours already fused to show the blue and green ocean, the multi-hued sky and the bright orange glow of the sun, was sitting inside the kiln, surrounded by a cordierite dam, getting hotter by the second.

Outside, the rain that had been threatening all day was thundering down, clattering on the deck outside and on the roof above her head.

Tara shivered, realising for the first time how exposed the studio was. Since the media had started hanging around the house, she'd made a habit of closing all the blinds once the light faded. She rarely worked in the evening, though, and so she and Justin had never bothered putting blinds in this room. Through the rain-smeared windows and the relentless downpour she could barely make out the glow of the solar lights in the dell. Beyond them, nothing but blackness for miles.

Anyone out there would have a perfect view of her.

Enough. Turning her back on the wild night, she checked the temperature of the kiln. It was close to the required nine hundred degrees centigrade; time to get tooled up. From a cupboard she pulled her protective clothes: steel-capped boots, an all-encompassing leather apron, foundry gloves and a full headshield. Dressed like a welder, she locked the door of the studio, a habit she'd got into when the boys were still at home, and one she'd never managed to break. She took a moment to steady herself. Raking without full concentration risked burning the house down.

The kiln temperature gauge now showed nine hundred degrees centigrade. She was good to go. With the raker, a long, poker-like tool, in one hand, she lifted the kiln lid and braced herself against the wall of heat. Raking had to be done fast. She had forty-five seconds before the glass cooled too much to make further work possible.

She started with the sea, dragging the raking tool from one side of the blue glass to the other, creating undulating horizontal lines that would resemble waves on the finished piece. She drew three lines, then a fourth, but already the glass was getting claggier. Closing the lid, she put the raker safely in its holder and pulled off her headshield and gloves, ready to wait the hour needed for the kiln to get back up to temperature. Pulling out a stool, she stared out at the night.

A sudden flash. One of the garden's security lights had been activated. Getting up and approaching the window, she peered out through the rain streaks. Making his way along the gravel path through the trees, climbing up towards the house, now a few metres below the statue of the diving girl, was the tall figure of a well-built man.

Chapter 58

An hour after they'd been called out, the police wished the Carter family a good evening. They'd dusted for fingerprints and talked about checking the neighbours for CCTV coverage, but it was clear they weren't hopeful. Had it not been for the family's recent notoriety, they probably wouldn't have bothered coming out at all.

On the plus side, nothing of value had been taken. The TV was untouched, and they hadn't even bothered with Jason's laptop, although in all fairness it was a very old model. Sabri's jewellery, such as it was, was still in its box. On the other hand, the house was wrecked. Every cupboard, every wardrobe, every drawer had been emptied, its contents strewn around so that barely a square foot of carpet remained to stand upon.

The burglars had been looking for the token.

After her shower, Sabri wrapped a dressing gown over her pyjamas and crept along the corridor. She wasn't surprised to find Darren's room empty. Pushing open the girls' door, she saw him curled up in his duvet on the floor between the two beds. Maddy, the only one still awake, raised her eyes to look at her mother. Sabri blew a kiss and softly closed the door.

She crept downstairs through the darkened house and found Jason sitting in the dark living room by the window, staring out at the street. Across his knees was something long and thin, shining metallic in the light from the street. A shotgun.

Sabri kept her voice low; the kids had been upset enough for one night. 'Where the hell did that come from?'

'Mitch lent it me. No one is coming through that door without my say-so.'

So gallant, this man of hers. And so stupid.

'Put it away, please. What if one of the kids comes down and startles you?'

For a second he didn't move; then he lifted the shotgun, broke it and leaned to tuck it beneath the chair.

'Better?' he asked.

'Not really.' She took a seat on the sofa. 'We can't live like this, Jace.'

Chapter 59

Tara's heart was thumping. The man outside was too tall, too broad, to be either her husband or one of her sons, who would have no reason to be in the garden on a night like this in any case. Was he a journalist, braving the weather, not to mention committing trespass, to get some footage of her at home?

He was coming towards her, looking straight at her. He carried no camera or sound equipment that she could see, and he seemed to be alone. Somehow, she didn't think this man was part of a TV crew.

He was carrying something, though. In his right hand. Something that gleamed in the moonlight.

Telling herself he couldn't get in, that the glass was triple glazed and unbreakable, that all the doors and windows were locked and the burglar alarm, connected to the local police station, was activated, Tara nevertheless moved away from the outside window. She saw him reach the end of the path and step into the shadow of the house, vanishing from view.

Then his head reappeared, followed by his torso. He was climbing the front wall of the one-storey guest wing and was about to scale the surrounding railing to reach the patio and outdoor kitchen. From there he could walk right up to the studio window.

Tara watched him swing first one leg then the other over the wooden rail and land on the decking. He paused, maybe to get his breath. Maybe to give her time. Either way, he still appeared to be looking right at her and with the studio lights on full she couldn't be anything but totally visible.

Tara's phone was feet away and the signal was good in the house. The police could be here in minutes and calling them was the only sensible thing to do right now. But something held her back.

The man started walking again, slowly this time, as the deck lights were activated, illuminating the scene. He looked to be in his mid- to late fifties and was around six foot two, solidly built. His hair was dark, swept back from his forehead, but his close-cropped beard was grey. He wore jeans, walking boots and a woollen scarf tucked into the neck of his black leather jacket. He was not dressed for the weather.

And there was definitely something shining in his right hand. Not a knife, though, which had been her first thought, but the silver tip of a walking cane. He carried it tucked against his body, and there was no hint of a limp in the way he walked.

When he was only a few metres from the house, she realised she'd seen him before. He'd been on the beach the previous weekend, had run into the waves ahead of the regular swimmers. All the girls had noticed him; he'd been the subject of considerable conversation, not all of it ladylike.

This was bonkers, the way he was coming right at her, as though he had every right in the world.

Practically at the window now, he reached one hand into his jacket pocket. Thinking *gun*, Tara braced herself to duck. The hand withdrew. He was holding something, too small to make out. He stopped a foot from the glass and maintained eye contact as he held a small coin up for her to see.

Not a coin. A token.

Chapter 60

For several seconds Sabri and Jason faced each other in the darkened room. Outside the house, traffic went past; they heard a neighbour calling out goodnight to someone. Jason said, 'I wish you'd tell me where it is.'

'I wear it,' Sabri confessed. 'It's sewn into my bra.'

He gave a hollow laugh.

'If someone threatens one of the kids, I'll give it to them,' she admitted. 'I won't hesitate.'

He gave a long, audible sigh. 'I guess I won't either.'

Tears were a second away. 'What are we going to do?' she asked.

'We could sell it.'

The last thing she'd expected. 'What?'

'Sell it,' he repeated. 'Auction it.'

'Are you serious?'

'Yep. We're too – what's the word? – vulnerable. I can't protect you and the kids, not all day every day. What if someone snatches one of them? We need money now, for a safer house. Better schools.'

She said, 'Logan Quick has less than a year to live.'

'I can't keep you safe for a year, Sab. If we hold on to that thing, something really bad's going to happen.'

Exactly what Sabri had been telling herself for the last hour.

'Then we get rid of it,' she said. No amount of money could make up for something happening to her family. 'We chuck it in the sea.'

'No, we sell it. The whole bloody world knows about Logan Quick and his ruddy tokens. We can put it on eBay or, I don't know, hold one of those press conferences. We can agree a minimum price we sell it for. Say ten million. Someone offers us that, someone legit, and we hand it over.'

Jason got up and joined Sabri on the sofa, taking both her hands in his. 'Ten million will change our lives, Sab. Ten million will make all the difference. Ten million is enough. Sod it, I'll take five. Even one. Nothing matters more than you and the kids.'

This. This was why she loved this dumb, reckless man of hers. Sabri felt tears well up and let them fall without even trying to stop them.

She said, 'No one will pay ten million for a coin that might be worthless.'

'A coin that might be worth billions. Even hundreds of millions. Isn't it worth a try?'

'And if it turns out we could have inherited billions?'

He got up, reached for her hand and pulled her up from the sofa. 'Babe, what will we do with billions? Let's quit while we're ahead.'

Chapter 61

The man outside was not the man called Robin; Tara had found photographs of Robin Knight on his wedding planning website. This wasn't him. He didn't look like Craig Lewis, either, if the Craig she'd found online had been the right one.

Seconds went by, with neither of them moving. He seemed to be waiting for her to do something.

Tara took a step forward and leaned closer to the glass. The token looked real. She watched him tuck it back in his pocket and pull out a phone with a Post-it note stuck to the leather cover. On it were eleven digits. His phone number. He cocked his head to one side before pointing to his phone and raising his hands in a question. He wanted her to call him. It couldn't hurt, could it? *Could it?* Reaching back, Tara picked up her own phone from the worktop. She misdialled on her first attempt and then he answered on the first ring.

'I'm Trevor,' he told her, before she had the chance to speak. 'Trevor Winter. Also known as Tug.' He had a West Country accent, a man born and bred in this part of the world.

'You were on the beach at the weekend,' she said.

He let his head fall and rise in acknowledgement. 'I hope I haven't scared you.'

Seriously? He thought a huge male approaching the home of a lone female at night could be anything other than scary?

'Sorry,' he added, correctly interpreting the look on her face. 'Wasn't sure what else to do.'

'How do you know where I live?'

With his free hand he wiped rainwater from his eyes. 'I followed you home on Saturday.'

And again, he didn't think that could be construed as threatening?

She said, 'I'd have noticed. There were no cars behind me.'

He gave a small, silent laugh. 'I was on a bike. I left before you, waited at the end of the road. I kept up until you turned into your lane, which was obviously a dead end.'

There were more than a dozen houses along the lane.

'I'd seen your place on TV.' He answered her unspoken question. 'I figured I could work it out from that. The reporters outside made it easy.'

'They're still out there?'

He nodded. 'Half an hour ago they were. It took me that long to skirt round the edge of your property and make my way up through the garden.'

'Why are you here?'

He didn't reply immediately. Then, 'I needed to talk to someone. To be honest, it's been doing my head in.'

Well, she knew that feeling.

'My token isn't in the house. It's in a safety deposit box a long way from here.'

She was lying. The token was in the garden, buried beneath the feet of the diving girl statue. Tara had waited until nighttime to bury it, had gone out in black clothes, worked entirely in the dark. No one could have seen her do it.

It took him seconds to work out what she meant.

'One's more than enough for me, love.'

So, now what? Tell him to get lost? Call the police? Continue talking through the glass as he got wetter and wetter? Tara had the strangest feeling then. She'd been alarmed by his sudden appearance in her garden, even scared. But not surprised. It was almost as though she'd been expecting him.

She said, 'Do you want to come in?'

A flicker of surprise crossed his face. 'If you're OK with that.'

Was she? Honestly, she didn't know. But the whole business had been doing her head in too. Pointing left, she directed him to one of the back doors of the house and left the room. Out of sight, she quickly tapped out a message to the WhatsApp group.

Man claiming to be Trevor Winter has arrived at my house. Has what appears to be a token. I'm letting him in. Wish me luck.

It was the only safeguard she had time to put in place.

Winter brought the cold air inside when he stepped through the door. He bent to take off boots that were caked in mud before pulling off his jacket and scarf. He smelled of rain, damp earth and, oddly, coconuts. Inside the house, he was bigger even than he'd seemed through the glass.

'Can I hang this?' He held his jacket up as he unwound the scarf from his neck.

Tara took the sodden clothes and told him to wait where he was while she dealt with them. In the laundry room, she hung both jacket and scarf over the sink. Then, indicating the way to the kitchen, and staying several paces behind, she followed him through the house. His socks left damp footprints on the polished oak floor. He'd left his cane behind, seemed to have no need of it.

'Nice place,' he said, as he took in the enormous living area. 'Been here long?'

'Ten years or so,' she replied. 'Can you show me some ID? I realise I should have asked before I let you in. And people know you're here, by the way. I texted some friends just now, with your name and everything.'

He smiled at her, showing even teeth that were surprisingly white for a man of his age. Pulling a wallet from his pocket, he opened it to show a driving licence. Yep, the headshot on the card was definitely the man standing in front of her. For good or bad, he was Trevor Winter.

Who, even without the boots, jacket and scarf, was dripping water onto her floors. She pulled a couple of towels from a drawer and handed them over. He took them with thanks, wrapping one around his neck and standing on the other.

'Would you like a glass of wine?' she offered. 'Or I've some Scotch somewhere.'

He looked like a man who drank Scotch.

She saw him brace and his jaw tense. 'I'm a recovering alcoholic,' he told her. 'Is coffee possible? Stronger the better.'

Tara was suddenly conscious of a half-finished glass of red on the kitchen counter. She had a rule about not drinking when she was raking. What had she been thinking?

'How many days sober?' she asked, as she reached into the cupboard for the coffee and the filter jug.

'Two.' He was keeping a decent distance between the two of them, she realised, hovering at the edge of the kitchen area. 'I've some way to go.'

'Are you here because of the public outing?' She released boiling water from the tap at the sink.

'The what?' He looked genuinely puzzled, but if he'd been on his way here while the show had been broadcast, he might not know.

'We were all named on the Peter Morgan show this evening. All seven of us. Social media's going batshit. I thought that's why you'd come to find me.'

He was silent for a moment. Then he shook his head. 'No, I found your details on Facebook. Yours and Sabri Carter's. And I know about Cheryl Young from the TV. Of the three, you seemed most able to handle a strange bloke showing up on your doorstep.'

Wondering what that said about her, Tara heard her phone ping. A WhatsApp message – from Holly, of course. *What the hell! Tara, be careful!!!*

Bit late for that, Holly.

'Five of us have a WhatsApp group.' She held out her phone so he could read the message. 'I can add you, if you like?'

He nodded his permission, and she added him to the group while the coffee brewed.

'I wasn't sure you were home,' he said, when she'd finished. 'No cars in the driveway.'

'I've started leaving mine on a neighbour's drive,' she told him. 'Trying to fool the media.'

'I guess that's something I have to look forward to now.'

At that moment, Tara's phone rang. 'Holly,' she said, after glancing down. 'Video call. Shall I get it? She might want to check you out.'

Trevor nodded his agreement, and Holly's face, her long, dark hair pulled back into a ponytail, appeared on the screen. She was on the move, wandering around a small, modern kitchen. Fridge magnets suggested a child lived in the house. Tara beckoned Tug closer so they could both see and be seen.

'Well, now we're seven,' Holly announced after she and Tug had exchanged greetings. 'Craig has shown up too. Maybe you should rename the group the Magnificent Seven.'

'Cue stirring music,' Tug muttered.

'How?' Tara asked. 'How did Craig find you?'

Holly pulled open the fridge door and reached for something inside. 'He saw the Peter Morgan show and found Sabri's number. Sabri gave him mine. She's in a bit of a state, by all accounts. Her family home was broken into earlier this evening.'

'Are they OK?' Tug asked, before Tara had the chance.

'They're fine, they weren't in. And the token is safe. She told me to tell you, Tara, that she's still keeping it in the same place.'

Tara let herself smile.

'They're pretty shaken up, though.' Holly glanced away, towards the kitchen door. 'Me too, to be honest.'

'You can move in here,' Tara offered. 'I've got more security than Fort Knox. Hell, Sabri and her family can too. God knows there's enough room.'

And it would piss Justin off big time.

Holly stopped moving and gave the camera a hard stare. 'Yeah, state-of-the-art security only works when you don't admit strange men in the middle of the night.'

'I like you already, Holly,' Tug said.

Holly glanced back over her shoulder to the kitchen door. 'Thanks, Tara, but I don't think my son could cope with living in a strange place. And this could go on for another year, if that press conference was telling us the truth. Anyway, I'm calling to tell you that Craig wants us to meet up. All seven of us, as soon as possible.'

'Can't hurt,' Tug said.

Behind Holly, the door opened and a boy of around ten appeared. He had dark curly hair and big dark eyes like his mother.

'I've got to go,' Holly said. 'Keep your eye on WhatsApp.'

As the call disconnected, an alarm went off on Tara's phone.

'Somewhere you need to be?' Tug had already finished his coffee.

'Yeah, the studio. I have a piece that will ruin if I don't attend to it now. For my son's birthday next week. Is that OK?'

He shrugged. 'It's your house. Can I watch?'

Tara led the way back to the studio. It felt good, she realised, not being alone in the house for a change. She was actually glad this odd and slightly disturbing bloke was here.

'You an artist?' he asked, looking round at the pieces, in varying stages of completion, in the room.

'Strictly amateur. Now, sit down and don't come anywhere near me while I'm working. If it all goes to pot, call an ambulance. Possibly Fire and Rescue too.'

He settled himself on the stool. 'I'm excited for what's coming.'

Kitted up again, Tara set her phone alarm for forty-five seconds, opened the kiln and began raking the sky. Horizonal lines across the top of the piece created a gleaming mass of indigo, purple, black, grey and orange. She moved carefully around the outline of the giant sun. In no time at all her alarm went off.

'That was amazing,' Tug said, when she'd closed the kiln and pulled off her headpiece. 'And slightly terrifying. Do you ever get burned?'

Tara pulled off one glove, then the other. 'I have been. I've learned to be careful. Would you like some dinner? I have an hour before I can finish this off.'

He took a moment, as though not used to, or expectant of, kindness.

'That would be amazing too. Thank you.'

Chapter 62

'You're always going to wonder now, aren't you?' Jax said. 'Whether I'm with you for the money.'

It was on the tip of Robin's tongue to say he didn't care, that he'd take her on any terms. Besides, she hadn't known anything about the money when she'd called the wedding off.

She was standing with her back to him, looking out over the darkening garden. Glad that it was night, that she couldn't see the mess he'd let it get into, he put knives and forks onto his small kitchen table and switched on the oven to warm plates.

'I don't have any money,' he said. 'I have an absence of money. I owe money. And this bonkers will can't be relied on. As far as financial security goes, Neil's a far better bet than I am.'

Jax didn't turn round, but he could see her face reflected in the glass. She looked deadly serious, almost angry. 'I guess so,' she said. 'Wow, I did not see this coming.'

'No one did.'

She turned at the sound of the doorbell. 'That'll be the food.' She glanced down at the table. 'Not feeling as hungry as I was. Maybe I should—'

'I'll get it,' he jumped in, knowing she was about to say she should leave. The doorbell sounded again. He left the room quickly, before she could reply. Wondering if he had any cash to tip the delivery driver, Robin reached for the latch. There were two men on his doorstep. He could see their outlines through the opaque glass panel. Two men and no sign of take-away boxes.

Delivery companies didn't send two men to drop off Chinese food.

He slipped the chain in place and turned round. 'Jax,' he called softly. 'Lock the—' He heard the unmistakable sound of the back door opening. And then Jax's cry of alarm.

Chapter 63

The telephone rang as Cheryl was putting the empty milk bottle outside the front door and she rushed to answer it. Phone calls were unusual enough in the Young household to get Sheila out of bed; a call right now she'd inevitably assume was something to do with the tokens and insist on dealing with it herself.

'Hello?'

'Hi.' The voice was male. Deep. Not young but far from old. A nice voice, with a hint of a West Country accent. 'Is that Miss Young? Cheryl Young?'

'Speaking.' It would be a journalist. She'd ask him to call again in the morning, tell him that her mother was dealing with all calls from the press.

'My name's Craig Lewis,' the man said. 'I'm one of the token recipients. Like you.'

Cheryl recognised the name instantly. She'd written all of them down after they'd been announced on the Peter Morgan show. Her mother had insisted, screeching at her to find a pen and paper. Craig Lewis and Trevor Winter were the missing two. Holly, Tara, Sabri, Robin, Cheryl, Trevor and Craig.

'Hello,' she replied.

'I hope it's not too late to call,' he went on. 'I've been speaking to the others – well, texting the others. We've got a WhatsApp group, I don't know if you know that.'

'Yes, I know. Tara told me. I met her in the library the other day. I can't join it, though. I don't have a smartphone.'

'Cheryl, I wanted to make sure you're OK,' Craig said. 'This whole business, well, it's been a big shock for all of us. I don't want you feeling isolated.'

No one, not even Tara, had asked her how she was dealing with the shock of it all.

'So, are you?' he repeated.

The question threw her. 'Am I what?'

He laughed. 'Are you OK? You and your mother have been on TV a lot. Those people can be very intrusive. You must be feeling the pressure.'

Cheryl glanced over towards the front door.

'A bit, I suppose,' she admitted. 'There are people hanging around outside the house. We keep calling the police but all they can do is ask them to move on and then ten minutes later, they're back.'

'I know how you feel. I had to move out of my house a few days ago too. It's very unsettling.'

'It is,' she agreed. She was so glad he'd called; she was feeling better already.

'We can help each other, though, Cheryl, don't you think? We're all in the same boat. We can support each other.'

'Yes, yes, we can.'

'How would you feel about a meeting if I can talk the others into it? I think, if we all get together, we might be able to make some sense of what's going on. And at the very least, we can help each other out.'

'That's a good idea.'

She was surprised Tara hadn't suggested it. It would be nice to meet this Mr Lewis, and wouldn't it be lovely if the two of them became friends?

Cheryl's fragile bubble burst when she realised her mother would insist on coming, might even want to take Cheryl's place entirely.

'I'm glad you think so,' he said. 'I'll put it to the others, and we'll be in touch. Would you like my number? In case you need anything?'

Cheryl took down the number he gave with trembling fingers.

'Goodnight for now, Cheryl.'

'Goodnight, Mr Lewis.'

'Craig. Call me Craig.'

She took her time, framing the words in her head before she said them out loud. 'Goodnight, Craig.'

He'd gone.

Cheryl stood by the phone for a long time, until the house grew cold around her. When she slept that night, the romantic lead in her dreams was no longer called Nick. Craig was her new favourite name.

Chapter 64

'He's shacked up with a Bedlington Terrier? Isn't there a law against that sort of thing?'

The two of them had finished dinner, a shepherd's pie that Tara had expected to provide her with at least four meals. Tug, with an appetite that had surprised her, even given his size, had polished off three quarters of it and was currently on his third mug of industrial-strength coffee. It had been on the tip of Tara's tongue, more than once, to ask him whether he was planning to sleep that night. Each time, thankfully, better judgement had held her back.

Looking a lot more comfortable than when he'd first arrived, Tug was now wearing a sweatshirt, sweatpants and socks that Justin had left behind. Her husband's things were too small and tight for her new friend, but they beat the hell out of the rain-soaked clothes he'd arrived in. His own clothes were tumbling around in the dryer and Tara had already identified an expensive jacket of her husband's for him to travel home in. The rain would ruin it.

'Not an actual dog,' she replied. 'A woman who looks like one.' Glancing at her wine glass, Tara realised she'd finished it. Which meant absolutely no more. Not only had she admitted a large, unknown man into her house, but she still had to work glass at nine hundred degrees centigrade. 'I've never met her, but the boys have shown me pictures. She's thin as a bamboo pole, jumpy as a flea and her hair is this mass of mousy corkscrews that never seems to be out of her eyes. It's a wonder she can see where she is half the time.'

'Does she bite?'

'Bloody good question. You wouldn't let her lick an open wound, that's for sure.'

Tug said nothing, which probably meant he didn't approve of her bitching. She reached out, picked up his plate and stacked it on top of her own.

'On the other hand, she's fifteen years younger than me, earns more in a year than I did in ten and can talk politics and current affairs and has an informed opinion on the climate crisis, and the tensions in the Middle East and the relevance of the old silk road in modern-day commerce. In other words, way out of my league.'

Tug got to his feet and picked up the now-empty serving dish. 'Do you want him back?'

The simple question stunned Tara. 'You're the first person to ask me that.'

'Really? Seems obvious to me. Because if the answer's yes, I'd say you're in with a fair chance. She sounds exhausting and sooner or later, he'll find that out for himself.'

'And if it's no?'

'Even easier. All you have to do is – what do the young folk say? – win the break-up.'

Tara gave herself a second. She'd never considered that a possibility. Surviving the break-up, that had been the limit of her ambitions. She said, 'And that becomes an awful lot easier if Logan Quick's money is real.'

He cocked his head to one side. 'How come?'

'If I have money, I get to keep this house. I can buy Justin out, no matter how much he demands.'

Outside, the garden lights were still on, and the diving girl statue was softly illuminated. At dinner, she'd made Tug sit with his back to the view, as though if he looked too long at the statue he'd guess that she was hiding something.

Tug said, 'And that's important?'

'Yeah. I know it's too big for me, but I love it like one of my children. Almost. Definitely more than I love my husband.'

'It's a beautiful house. I don't blame you for wanting to stay.'

She smiled at him. He didn't smile back and she wondered if, in spite of what he'd said, he disapproved of how important bricks and mortar were to her.

'What will you do,' she asked, 'if the money's real?'

He answered quickly, but of course he'd already thought about it. 'Buy a small house,' he replied. 'And a small boat. Maybe a small dog.'

Carrying the plates, Tara set off for the kitchen. 'If it's a Bedlington Terrier I won't visit.'

Now he smiled. 'Duly noted.'

'And will that be enough? Small house, small boat, small dog? It sounds a bit like a . . .'

Tara stopped. It was not for her to judge the limit of someone else's ambitions.

'Small life?' Tug finished for her. 'It's all I ever wanted.'

'There'll be a lot of change left over,' she said. 'If the rumours about Quick's fortune are true.'

He thought for a moment. 'I can probably find a use for it. There's always someone who needs money. Lot of my old service mates for a start.'

Tug joined her by the dishwasher. He ran the serving dish under the tap, although he'd pretty much scraped it clean.

'Can I ask you something?' he said, handing her the dish.

'If you want dessert, I can probably find some ice cream in the fridge.'

Shit, she was flirting. What was wrong with her? She'd only just met this guy and still wasn't sure he could be trusted.

He showed no sign of responding, which was probably a good thing. 'Have you noticed anything unusual? Even before the token arrived?'

'What sort of unusual?'

He didn't reply immediately, then, 'I don't want to freak you out. God knows, this is all weird enough. Only, a few weeks ago, maybe more than that, I started noticing a black Volvo hanging round. I'd see it in the car park and outside the garden centre too.'

'The same car?'

He inclined his head. 'I can quote you the reg number. Too fancy for the estate where I live.'

'I can't say I've noticed a black car. But I wasn't exactly looking out for one.'

'How about feeling you're being watched? Before the TV crews started showing up, I mean.'

Tara felt her body tensing up. 'Now you're freaking me out.'

'Logan Quick probably didn't pull our names off the electoral roll. Someone like that would have done his homework.'

Tara couldn't help a glance round at the uncovered windows. 'You mean he's been watching us? Probably still is?'

'I'd expect him to have someone else do it, but yeah. Have any of the others said anything?'

'Not to me. But I didn't ask.'

Both of their phones pinged simultaneously. Tug found his first.

'From Craig.' He had to screw up his eyes to see the small print. 'He wants the seven of us to meet up ASAP. So we can come up with a plan.' He glanced up. 'Not sure what plan he has in mind. Or where we'd meet without the world and his wife trying to join in.'

'They could come here, I suppose,' Tara said. 'Plenty of room, and the security's good when I don't compromise it by admitting strange men.'

Trevor was still trying to read the WhatsApp conversation. 'What's a yurt?'

Momentarily puzzled by the non sequitur, she replied, 'A posh tent, I think. People stay in them at festivals. Why?'

'Robin's offering a yurt for the meet-up. It's in a field somewhere between Bodmin and St Austell.'

Tara picked up her phone and googled the yurt. 'It's a wedding venue,' she said. 'That makes sense. Robin's a wedding planner.'

'He's suggesting tomorrow night. Can you make it?'

She thought about it. 'I guess.'

Tug smiled. 'Looks like we have a date.'

Chapter 65

Three men had come for the token. None of them especially large, none that Robin would have looked twice at had he passed them in the street, but each giving off a quiet air of menace. All white, two were heavily tattooed, the third gaunt enough to be an addict, but with clear eyes, decent teeth and a steady hand. That hand had locked the back door and held a chair for Jax to sit down. He stood behind her now, one steady hand on the back of the chair. He glanced down and the tips of his fingers moved towards Jax's hair, as though he might twirl a lock around them. His eyes lingered.

Jax sat upright on the kitchen chair, her jaw tight, her eyes fixed on Robin's. She looked tense. Not terrified. He was terrified.

'Let this lady leave,' Robin said. 'She's a client. That's all. Nothing to do with . . . anything.'

The thin man's gaze left Jax to fix on the kitchen table, laid for two; on the opened bottle of wine and two glasses. Bending, he caught hold of Jax's hand. Before she could react, he'd drawn it up towards his face. Jax tried, and failed, to pull away. The thin man was looking at the huge diamond engagement ring. His eyebrows raised in a silent question.

'She's not my fiancée.' Robin tried hard to put some incredulity into his voice as he registered that she hadn't yet taken the ring off. 'I told you, she's a client. I'm a wedding planner.'

Releasing Jax's hand, the bloke gave a nod to his two companions. One moved to the line of cupboards above the worktop and began looking inside each, the other opened the door to the walk-in cupboard where Robin kept his washing machine and ironing board.

'It's not here.' Robin decided there was no point trying to bluff. 'Once I knew it was all for real, I made sure it was safe.'

Thin man's eyebrows rose again.

'I had an appointment with the solicitors on Tuesday,' Robin went on. 'I took it straight to the bank after that. It's in a box at the bank. HSBC on the high street.' He could hear his voice shaking. 'I can get it first thing in the morning.'

In the walk-in cupboard, something fell off a shelf.

'You won't find it in the bloody utility room.' He sounded angry, which was better than scared to death, he supposed. Unless it pissed them off. The thin man was still hovering over the back of Jax's chair.

'Oh, we're not looking for the – what do you call it, the token?' the thin man said, as the one in the cupboard said, 'Found it.'

He emerged, carrying Robin's steam iron. Jax gave a tiny squeal as the iron was carried to the counter and plugged in. Smiling now, the thin man brushed her hair away from the side of her face, exposing her cheek and the left side of her jaw.

'Guys, this is unnecessary.' Robin felt his stomach clench. 'First thing in the morning. You can come with me to the bank.'

The thin man ignored him. 'While we're waiting,' he said, turning to the counter where Jax had left her handbag. He grabbed and upturned it, emptying its contents onto the table. Wallet, phone, hairbrush, hair bands, tissues, a small make-up bag, and Jax's NHS ID card and lanyard. 'Jacqueline Reynolds,' he read. 'Consultant anaesthetist. Take a picture, Mike, so we can find this lady again.'

The man called Mike aimed his phone at Jax's ID card as the iron, heating rapidly, let off a burst of steam.

'For God's sake, Robin, give them the token.' Jax's composure had collapsed. She was visibly shaking.

'Only for safe-keeping,' the thin man put a wheedling note in his voice, but he was still smiling. 'Just till you pay us what you owe. Then we don't have to take your car. How's that iron coming on, Tyler?'

Tyler licked his index finger, before bouncing it off the iron's surface. 'Ouch,' he said, with a wide grin.

'Give it another couple of minutes,' the thin man said.

Jax's eyes were full of tears.

'OK, OK.' Robin held his hands up. 'I'll get it. Just don't hurt her.'

'Go with him,' the thin man instructed Tyler. 'Make sure he doesn't try anything.'

On legs that didn't feel steady, Robin left the kitchen. It was only five paces to the hall table. On reaching it, he stepped back so that Tyler could see what he was doing, and opened the single drawer. The solicitors' letter lay on top of the other contents; the token, neatly enclosed in plastic, sat on top. Robin handed both over.

Back in the kitchen, the thin man looked at the letter for long seconds, then stared at the token. Robin's heart was thumping painfully against his chest. He was calculating the leap he'd have to take to clear the table and land on the gangster if he tried to go anywhere near Jax with that iron. There were knives in the drawer under the sink. If he could reach one of them, he could go batshit crazy with it. Create enough of a distraction for Jax to get out of the house.

Thin man held the plastic casing up to the light. Robin told himself he couldn't vomit, not now. Then the man nodded.

'OK,' he said. 'I hope I don't need to say that if the police get involved, we'll be back.'

'You don't,' said Robin.

The thin man slipped the token into his jacket pocket and folded the letter. He nodded at Mike, who unlocked the back door. All three men stepped out into the night.

'How much do you owe?' Jax asked a short while later. The Chinese food was cooling rapidly in the kitchen, but neither of them could face it. The bottle of red, though, was almost empty.

He thought for a second and gave her a ballpark figure. Her eyes widened.

'You'll never see that token again,' she said. 'That business about it being surety for what you owe, it was—'

'Bollocks, I know.'

'Thank you,' she said. And shuddered.

'You need to leave,' he told her. 'Have you somewhere you can stay tonight? Somewhere they can't find you?' He stood up.

She stayed where she was. 'I'm staying with a friend,' she told him. 'But what's the point? They've got what they wanted.'

'You'll be safe enough at the hospital,' he told her. 'But you need to be careful when you arrive and leave. Probably until Logan Quick actually dies.'

He reached down, took her hand and pulled her up.

She pulled a face. 'Robin, this isn't necessary. And frankly, I'm a bit shaky to be on the bike right now.'

He took a step back, away from her. 'Jax, I can't see you again.'

She frowned. 'Are you serious?'

'Perfectly. Those three were just the first. There'll be others now. My name's out there. Others will come and they won't believe me when I say I don't have it anymore. I'm not putting you at risk again.'

Her helmet was by the front door. He left the room, pulling her with him, and found her jacket hanging at the bottom of the stairs. 'Do you need me to call a cab?' he asked.

She stared at him, a look of stunned disbelief on her face. 'That's it? We're over before we began?'

Robin's resolve broke. He stepped closer and took her face between both hands, shuddering at how close she'd come to losing that smooth, creamy skin.

'My love,' he said. 'If I survive the next few months, I'll be destitute. I'm not subjecting you to that. Now, do you need a cab?'

She shook her head. A few seconds later he heard the roar of her bike as she left his life.

Robin locked the door, checked the back door was locked too and then went back into his living room. Falling to his knees in front of the TV, he reached for the DVD case of *Seven Brides for Seven Brothers*. Inside was the token. The real token, not the gold leprechaun's coin he'd slipped into the plastic case when he'd realised that, sooner or later, someone would come looking for it.

He wondered whether he'd ever tell Jax how close he'd come to getting half her face burned away.

DAY ELEVEN

Saturday, 13 October

Chapter 66

When he woke in the night to nothing but blackness, Tug panicked. This was not his flat. Starting upright in bed – a bloody comfortable bed – he remembered. The extraordinary woman he'd met a couple of hours earlier had asked him to stay the night. He was in one of her guest rooms.

'Tug.' She'd sounded oddly hesitant as she'd followed him to the front door. 'How are you getting back to Falmouth?'

He'd wondered if she was about to offer him a lift and knew he couldn't let her. She'd had too much wine to risk being stopped by the police. Besides, he had the 'borrowed' bike to think about and no way would it fit in her tiny car. He wasn't sure he'd fit in her tiny car.

He said, 'I'll cycle to Bodmin and get a train from there.'

'On your stolen bike? Does it even have lights?'

He held out a hand for his jacket and scarf. 'I'm ex-special forces, Tara. I can get myself home.'

She glanced out through the glass that surrounded the front door. The rain hadn't stopped, it hadn't even slackened. 'You'll get soaked.'

He would; it would be miserable. 'Did I mention, Special Boat Squadron? I spent over a decade soaked to the skin.'

'You should stay.'

He felt a nervous tickle in his gut. 'Now, you're really being reckless.'

Tara had taken a step back as her face hardened. 'Actually, I'm not. Because, did I mention, this house has more security than Fort Knox? I can isolate the guest wing and my own rooms. Which I fully intend to do, by the way, in case I'm sending out any confusing signals.'

Her arms were crossed over her chest now. A very clear signal.

'You came here because you needed to be with someone who knows what you're going through.' She let her arms relax. 'It's been good, having you here. It'll be good, meeting up with the others tomorrow. We should stick together, if we can.'

He'd hummed a few bars of 'The Magnificent Seven'.

She let out an exasperated breath. 'Now, you've given me a bloody ear worm, bozo. Are you staying or not?'

Something had woken him. Movement in the house. Tug pressed the light on his watch. Zero two seventeen hours. He'd said goodnight to Tara shortly before midnight.

The room he was in, one of four in Tara's guest suite, held a king-sized bed with the softest sheets he'd ever slept in, two bedside cabinets and a built-in wardrobe along one wall. Black-out curtains hung from the floor-to-ceiling windows.

Another noise. He considered and dismissed the idea that Tara might have decided to pay a midnight visit. She really didn't seem the type. He thought back to how she'd looked in the studio, dressed like a welder, making something heart-thumpingly beautiful. Tara was special.

He swung his legs out of bed and pulled on the sweatpants she'd loaned him earlier.

The corridor was gently lit with tiny inset floor lights. The glass sculpture, a school of leaping silver fish that ran almost the entire length of the corridor wall, glowed softly. Barefoot, Tug strode towards the stairs that would take him up to the main part of the house. He paused before the last door on the right. Plant room, Tara had pointed out, when she'd shown him down here. He pushed it open and saw a heavy spanner on a shelf. He picked it up, reflecting that he might really freak Tara out if the movement was nothing more than her getting a late-night glass of water.

Halfway up the stairs he heard a man's voice, speaking low, as though not wanting to be heard; then, a woman's.

The stairs brought him to the entrance hall where damp footprints told him that someone had stood here minutes earlier. His cane stood in the umbrella stand by the door. Made of beech wood and reinforced with an internal steel pin, it was designed for users who weighed up to thirty-five stone. Tug was nowhere near that weight, but the cane had never been intended as a walking aid.

He didn't need it; the spanner would do.

Moving towards the kitchen, he saw that the huge, open-plan area was gently lit like the rest of the house and, unless someone was hiding behind one of the sofas, it was empty.

The floor creaked behind him. He spun round, spanner in hand.

Tara gasped and took a step back. Her hair was loose around her shoulders, and she wore an oversized man's T-shirt. Her legs were long, slim and tanned. He let his right arm fall.

'There's someone in the house,' he whispered.

She gave a quick, nervous nod. 'I thought it was you.'

As he shook his head, a sound made them both start.

'Was that your studio?' he said softly. She nodded again.

'Got your phone?'

She held it up to show him.

'Stay behind me, get ready to phone for help.'

He caught a whiff of her scent as she moved; it made him think of the ocean at dawn. Conscious of her closeness, he led the way through the utility part of the house, past the giant, walk-in pantry, the laundry and the downstairs cloakroom.

The intruders were in Tara's studio. He could see torch beams dancing around in the doorway. Tug closed his eyes for a second to remember the room's layout: a worktop ran around three of the walls; cupboards sat in a central square; the light switch was to the right of the door at head height.

Staying out of sight, Tug found the switch. As the light flashed on, he stepped into the doorway.

'Help you, mate?' he said.

Two people stood frozen in the bright light, a bloke of about his own age and a thin woman with curly brown hair who looked about a decade younger. Both wore dark clothes.

The bloke recovered first. 'Who the fuck are you?' he said.

Tara peered around Tug's shoulder. 'What the hell are you doing?' she demanded. 'It's the middle of the night. And why is she here?'

The bloke squared up to them both. 'Yeah, last I checked, Tara, it's still my house.'

Her husband. Possibly ex-husband; that hadn't been clear. And the Bedlington Terrier he'd left his wife for. Fair play, she did look a bit like a small, snappy dog. And was the bloke out of his mind, swapping Tara for this emaciated bint?

'You absolute shit.' Tara had pushed her way in front of Tug now. 'You're looking for the token, aren't you? You came here to steal it.'

The husband – Justin, was it? – stepped forward, hands outstretched. 'I'm not trying to steal anything, Tara, but you must have seen the news tonight. The whole world is talking about you. Besides, we thought you were out. Where's your car?'

'This is a new low, even for you.' Tara turned to the woman. 'And by the way, do you know he has sex with me, every time he comes here? What were you planning tonight, Just? A threesome?'

OK, that was information Tug could have done without.

'It's not here.' She was back on her husband now. 'It's in a safety deposit box a long way from here and, no, I am not telling you anything else.'

Tug risked putting his hand on Tara's shoulder. 'This your ex?' he said, waiting for her to pull away. She didn't. 'Well, it's your call, babe, but I'd say it's time to change the locks.'

Tara stepped back until her body was touching his. Tug felt the cool cotton of her T-shirt and the warmth of her skin through it. Her hair tickled his bare chest.

'First thing tomorrow morning,' she said, reaching for his hand.

Tug grinned.

Chapter 67

A few miles outside Bodmin, Holly pulled into the deserted, woodland-surrounded car park. For a moment, she wondered if she'd come to the wrong place, then spotted the huge yurt a couple of hundred metres away on an island in the river. Robin hadn't been kidding about it being secluded. It had taken nearly two hours to drive here.

The night stretched around her, silent apart from the rush of the wind and the rare screech of a gull. It had been some time, driving over, since Holly had seen a house, let alone a town or village. It was the perfect place for an ambush, and she'd come here to meet strangers. On the other hand, she wasn't sure anywhere would feel safe anymore. Home certainly didn't. It had taken less than five hours for the world's media to find her, once her name had been announced on the Peter Morgan show.

She picked up her phone to check on Charlie. After relentless pleading on his part, she'd agreed to him watching *In the Heart of the Sea* with Mrs Morrison the babysitter. Holly was far from sure a film about the sinking of an American whaling ship was suitable for a ten-year-old but as a bribe it had been surprisingly effective. Knowing he wouldn't thank her for interrupting, she put the phone down again.

Climbing out of the car, Holly stood for a moment at the open door, letting the wind take her hair and cool her skin. She'd been sweating, a sure sign that she was anxious, and while she understood the reasoning that had prompted Robin to suggest such a remote location, not far from Bodmin moor itself, its sheer wildness wasn't doing much to settle her nerves.

Headlights in the lane. Another car approaching. Robin. He parked beside her and climbed out.

'Holly. Sorry to be late. Good to see you again.'

'What happened to you?' she replied, before she could stop herself.

Robin looked like he'd been beaten up. His face was bruised and the bridge of his nose covered in a dressing. He'd left the car carefully too, as though in pain.

'Let's call it a domestic-related incident. Nothing to do with Logan Quick, I promise. Ah, who's this?'

Another car was heading their way, this one a small hatchback, either black or dark blue. Like Holly, the driver backed into the parking space and a tall, broad-shouldered man climbed out. He gave an awkward smile. 'Should we have agreed a password?'

It wasn't Tug, whom Holly had spoken to via FaceTime the evening before. Which left Craig Lewis. He was a good-looking man, albeit the same age as Robin and the others. It was hard to tell in the dark, but his skin looked tanned and his teeth very white. His hairline formed a widow's peak in the centre of his forehead, but the rest was dark brown, with no visible sign of grey.

'Excuse me,' he said, after shaking hands with Robin and nodding at Holly. 'Better help Cheryl.'

It took Cheryl the better part of a minute to get herself out of the passenger seat, even with Craig's help. As the two women said hello, Robin pulled a cool box from his car boot.

'Ladies.' He gestured towards the bridge.

When they reached the tent, Robin activated lights and moved aside to let the women go in ahead. Holly felt her mouth fall open and her eyes widen.

'Quite something, isn't it?' Robin said. 'I've a wedding here in a month. The owners think we're the wedding party making last-minute plans about décor and floral tributes.'

Slender bamboo poles held up a giant, circular framework which, in turn, supported the vaulted canvas roof. Thinner strips of bamboo formed a lattice around the walls. Everywhere Holly looked fairy lights hung like diamonds in the branches of real trees. It was like being in an enormous birdcage.

'It's lovely,' Cheryl said. 'I've never been in a yurt before. I expect Holly will have to be the bride, if anyone comes to ask. Not sure who the groom will be, though. Maybe you, Craig, you're handsome enough. Of course, you are too, Robin. I didn't mean . . .'

Holly glanced back to see Craig give Cheryl a fond look as Robin began unloading an assortment of soft drinks from the cool box. She left them to it and walked further into the yurt.

Circular tables surrounded a central dance floor, the chairs bamboo to match the framework of the tent. Palms and tropical plants cast green shadows everywhere and miniature birdcages holding electric candles hung over each table. A wedding had taken place recently. Traces of streamers and shrivelled balloons could be seen on the mat flooring and Holly could smell the faintest trace of beer.

It was a magical place, and Holly felt a moment of almost unbearable sadness that she'd never be a bride presiding over such a party. She and Charlie's father had talked about getting married in the early days but, as Charlie had grown older, his problems more apparent, those conversations had become fewer and fewer. Eventually, Tim had simply left.

She was still young enough to meet someone else of course. But even if she found a man who could deal with Charlie and whom Charlie could accept into his life, Holly knew she would never marry a man without telling him her full history. And then no man in his right mind would marry her.

'I'm really nervous,' Cheryl confided to Holly, as new arrivals could be heard outside.

The younger woman started, as though she hadn't known Cheryl was close.

'Sorry.' Cheryl took a step back. 'Didn't mean to scare you. My mum says I'm like a bull in a China shop.'

'I'm nervous too,' Holly said, which probably wasn't true. She was young and pretty, and a lawyer too, according to Craig. What did she have to be nervous about? But it was sweet of her to say it.

Cheryl had had no idea how nice it was to be collected by a gentleman for an evening out. To have car doors held open, be asked whether the car temperature was comfortable and whether she'd like some music. Even her mother had been on her best behaviour while Craig was in the house. It had almost felt like a date.

Cheryl glanced back at Craig who was talking to Robin by the tent entrance, and wished, not for the first time that evening, that she had something nicer to wear than the old skirt, blouse and cardigan that, nevertheless, were the best things she owned.

'I wasn't sure whether to bring my token or not,' Holly said. 'Home doesn't feel safe anymore. Not now everyone knows where I live.'

Cheryl felt a clenching in her stomach, as though her own token, making its ponderous way through her guts for the third time since Wednesday, was responding to Holly's words. Cheryl could think of nowhere safer than inside her body, but what if she was damaging herself? And what if, one of these times, the token didn't come out anymore?

'Mind you, I have a small army of reporters camped in the front garden,' Holly went on. 'Practically a bodyguard.'

'Mine's at home,' Cheryl lied.

'Was your mum OK with you coming out tonight?' Holly asked.

'Not really,' Cheryl admitted. 'But Craig told her it had to be named recipients only for legal reasons, but he would call her tomorrow and explain everything we discussed.'

Both women turned then, as the yurt flap lifted, and Tara stepped inside. She wore white jeans tucked into brown leather boots and a bold, plaid jacket in shades of bronze, orange and yellow. She was followed by a tall man with dark hair and a short, grey beard, who walked with a cane. The two of them looked like a couple.

'That's Tara,' Holly said, maybe forgetting that Cheryl and Tara had already met. 'The man's Trevor Winter. Calls himself Tug. I spoke to him on the phone last night.'

Cheryl hung back as Tara and Tug came forward to greet Holly. In the doorway another woman had appeared. Tall, brown-skinned and thin. Sabri Carter. Everyone was here.

Robin told himself to chill. This wasn't a wedding, and he wasn't in charge. He'd done his bit by finding a venue and bringing drinks but someone else had to take the lead now.

Already, he could sense alliances forming. Tara and Tug seemed like they had history although he'd been under the impression they'd met only the previous day; Sabri had joined the two of them seconds after she'd arrived. Cheryl meanwhile was clinging close to Holly but shooting surreptitious glances at Craig whenever she thought he wasn't looking.

In his pocket, his phone buzzed; Jax had called twice during the day and both times he'd ignored it.

Meanwhile, the silence was becoming uncomfortable. 'Who's going to chair?' he asked, far too loudly, but at least it was out there. 'Craig, this was your idea. Fancy taking charge?'

'What about Tara?' Holly said quickly. 'She set up the WhatsApp group. And she's been working on a spreadsheet of us all.'

'Very enterprising,' Craig said. 'And I'm sure we'd all like to hear about it, but I think there's a more pressing question to be asked first.'

'Which is?' Tug asked.

Tensions were forming too. In Tug and Craig, they had two alpha males, not usually a recipe for group harmony.

Craig took a moment before replying. He had a habit, Robin had noticed, of looking intently into people's eyes. 'Do any of us know Logan Quick?' he said. 'Have we met him, corresponded with him, had any dealings with him?'

Deliberately, it seemed, Craig looked at the security guard first; his stare seemed to be trying to spot a lie.

Tug took his time. 'Never heard of him before all this kicked off. How about you?'

Definitely tension between those two.

'I'd heard of him,' Craig replied, after a second, 'the way I'd heard of Richard Branson and James Dyson, but that's as far as it goes. Anyone else?'

Around the table, heads shook.

'No disrespect, guys,' Robin said, 'but I don't think any of us move in billionaire circles.' He'd meant it as a joke, a tension-softener. Nobody even smiled.

'Tara, maybe,' Sabri said, earning herself a sharp glance from the other woman.

'Hardly,' Tara snapped back. 'I may have a nice house, thanks to a husband who earned a decent salary for a long time, but I stand to lose that when my divorce goes through. I'm just a retired nurse.'

So much for alleviating tension.

'Do you think he knows that?' It was the first time Cheryl had spoken since the others had arrived. Robin had already labelled her a woman with zero self-worth, only comfortable being invisible. 'I mean, maybe he knows you're going to lose your house, Tara, and that's why he's leaving you the money. Because it's the same with me. My mum's leaving all her money to a charity, so I'll lose my home when she dies. It's not as grand as yours, but it's the same thing, isn't it?'

'The lady might have a point,' Tug said. 'I've just been fired. I could lose my flat if I don't find another job soon.'

Cheryl shot a nervous smile at Tug; he winked back at her.

'I'm in a mountain of debt. And facing a court case that could see me bankrupt by the end of the year,' Robin admitted, although given the events of the previous night, he'd be lucky if bankruptcy was all he faced.

'Lots of people have money problems,' Craig said.

'Do you?' Tug asked him.

Craig pulled a dismissive face. 'Not especially. I've an ex-wife and two teenage kids to support but thousands must be in my position.'

'What about you, Holly?' Cheryl asked. 'You're a barrister, so you must be doing all right.'

'I'm a junior barrister,' Holly admitted. 'We're notoriously badly paid. And I have a father who's very ill. His care is expensive. So, yes,

I have money problems too. I agree with Craig, though. How can that be enough?'

'I have another pressing question.' Craig fixed Holly with one of his penetrating looks.

'What's that?' Holly asked.

If anything, Craig's stare seemed to intensify. He said, 'Why are you here?'

Holly looked shocked. 'Sorry?'

'I'm guessing everyone around this table was born sometime in the 1970s,' Craig said. 'As was Logan Quick. But not you. You're over twenty years younger than the rest of us.'

Robin saw puzzled glances shooting around the room as Holly grew pale. He said, 'You think that's significant?'

Craig didn't back down. 'Everything's significant. She's also the only one of us educated beyond university. And a lawyer to boot. Based in Exeter, like Barker, Momen and Dodds.'

The puzzled looks were becoming nervous.

'What are you getting at?' Tug asked.

'Are you a plant, Holly?' said Craig.

Holly physically recoiled. 'What the hell is that supposed to mean?'

'I've been making enquiries.' Craig spoke with a hint of a smile, as though pleased with himself. 'The firm puts a lot of business in the way of your chambers. You'll know all the senior partners, by name if not in person. A lot of the junior associates as well.'

'Is this right, Holly?' Sabri asked.

The young woman's eyebrows shot up. 'Which part? I'm a barrister. Practically all our business comes via solicitors. That's hardly a secret.'

'If I were Logan Quick, I'd be wanting to keep an eye on us,' Craig went on. 'What better way than to place someone in the heart of the group?'

'I follow a code of conduct.' Holly seemed to be speaking through gritted teeth. 'Shenanigans like that could get me disbarred.'

'So, you'd need to be well recompensed? By someone very well resourced?'

'Oh, hold on, Craig—'
'I think that's a bit—'
'Why don't you fuck—'

'How about this idea?' Tug raised his voice above the clamour that had broken out over Craig's random bit of conjecture. He'd already decided he didn't like the bloke.

The table quietened a fraction.

'How about we trust each other till we have reason not to?' he said, before the others could start wittering again.

'Good idea,' Tara said. 'We've no reason to be suspicious of Holly. She has a young child. No half-decent mother would subject her son to what we've been through the last couple of weeks without good reason.'

'Inheriting millions sounds like a good reason to me,' Craig said.

Holly glared across the table at him.

'What I want to know is why?' Tug said. 'Of all the people in the world, why would an eccentric billionaire leave his money to us?'

'Are we good people?' Cheryl asked. 'I've been asking myself that a lot since it happened. What have I done to deserve so much money?'

'I've done nothing,' Tug admitted. 'I could use it, but I can't exactly claim I deserve it. To be honest, though, I don't think Logan Quick is doing this out of philanthropy. If it was about helping others out, he'd have picked a few charities.'

'Why then?' Craig asked.

Tug took a moment. 'I think he's playing God.'

It was a relief to finally say it. Since he learned the will was for real, Tug had been trying to suppress the uncomfortable feeling that he was a pawn in someone else's game.

'Messing with us, more like,' Sabri said. 'I'm not sure how much more my family can cope with. The kids are all over the place. Jason has his mates guarding the house for us. With shotguns. I caught one of them rooting in the kitchen cupboard this morning, though, so I trust them like I trust a Tory politician.'

'Charlie's struggling with it too.' Holly was still glaring at Craig. 'I'm not sure how he'll cope when he goes back to school.'

Tara said, 'In only a couple of weeks we've become some of the most famous people on the planet. And it's not going away.'

Holly dropped her head into her hands. From what Tug could see, she was the least OK of the whole group. No way was she a plant.

'It's the same for all of us.' Craig's tone was gentler. 'We deserve to know why.'

Unless she was a plant and struggling to manage the guilt.

'We could ask him,' Tug tried.

Silence for a second, then another.

'And how do we do that?' Sabri challenged. 'The man's a recluse. And given what we've heard the last few days, a terminally ill recluse. He's probably in a clinic in Switzerland.'

Robin said, 'If Tug's right, Quick won't be taking the euthanasia option just yet. He'll be wanting to see how this plays out.'

'What does that mean?'

'I think he's close,' Tug said. 'I think he's watching us.'

More than one person glanced around.

'Someone's been following me for weeks,' Tug went on. 'I thought I was losing it, having a breakdown. Not anymore. I think my instincts were spot on.'

He looked from one face to the next, trying to spot the flash of acknowledgement. 'Anyone seen a black Volvo hanging around?'

Alarm shone out of Holly's face. 'Seriously?' she asked.

'I'm more interested in how theatrical it all is,' Craig said. 'First the mysterious tokens arrive, like something out of *The Hobbit*. Then word gets out, as Quick knew it would, and the media circus kicks in. The solicitors are carefully briefed, denying nothing, but giving very little away. Then we have the press conference when he announces to the world he's dying.'

Robin said, 'And it all becomes a lot more real.'

Craig let his head nod in agreement. 'And immediate. The guy practically shone a countdown on the side of Big Ben.'

Tara said, 'Then all our identities are leaked to the media. Any idea how that happened?'

'That wasn't necessarily deliberate,' Tug said.

Silence.

'But probably was,' he acknowledged. 'I think you're right, Craig. It's all been very carefully managed and we're the . . . I'm not sure what we are.'

'Puppets?' Holly suggested.

'He's not in Switzerland,' Tug said. 'I'd put money on it.

'You're absolutely right,' said a new voice.

Tug's head shot round to see a woman standing at the tent entrance. She was slender, fair-haired, probably in her early forties; she was attractive too, the opposite of threatening. All the same, there was no way he should have allowed her to creep up on them.

'I work for Mr Quick,' she told the shocked group as she stepped inside.

Tara watched the woman stride towards them, detouring only to lift a chair from another table. Placing it in the gap between herself and Robin, she sat down. 'Mind if I join you?'

She smiled, showing perfect white teeth, and Tara felt something inside her recoiling. Around the table, no one spoke; no one smiled back. If the newcomer was fazed by her lack of welcome, she didn't show it.

'Who are you?' Tara asked.

The woman seemed to consider for a moment, then, 'I'm here to issue an invitation from Mr Quick. He understands you must have many questions and is more than happy to explain his thinking. He'd like you to visit him next week. If you name a date, he'll arrange for a boat to take you across.'

'Is Quick tapping our phones?' Tug asked.

'Excuse me?' Two perfectly formed eyebrows rose as the woman turned her half-smile in Tug's direction.

'How did he know we were meeting tonight? How did he know we'd be here?'

'Starting to rethink the plant idea?' Craig said.

Tara noticed more than one face turn towards Holly; the young woman took a deep and very visible breath.

'If you work for Logan Quick,' Holly said to the woman, 'perhaps you can tell the others that I don't.'

Another smile, more secretive this time.

'For real?' Holly looked on the verge of getting to her feet.

'You said something about an invitation,' Tug spoke quickly, probably to distract Holly. 'Why don't we hear the lady out?'

'Thank you, Mr Winter,' the newcomer replied. 'But there isn't much more to say. I've already texted my phone number to all of you. There's no signal here, so you probably haven't received the messages yet, but they'll come through. When you decide on the date you'd like to travel, and whether you'll be able to stay the night on St Helen's, I'll make the arrangements. Or we could make them now?'

She looked expectantly around the group.

'Mr Quick's boat, a spacious motor launch, will meet you in Falmouth,' she went on. 'The trip will take a couple of hours. He can have you back on the mainland the same day if needed.'

Instinctively, Tara turned to Tug, who raised his own brows in a silent question. Early that morning, he'd agreed quickly when she'd suggested he hang around and get a lift to the yurt. He'd helped her in the garden, making light work of all the heavy lifting, and they'd swum in the afternoon. They'd traded stories about his time in the Special Boat Squadron and hers with the NHS; they'd bought food at the local market and cooked soup in her kitchen. Tug made her feel completely safe and jumpy as a kitten at the same time. In most circumstances, she was the biggest flirt she knew, but the whole day long she'd been holding back. Tug was deeply intimidating; and yet she missed his presence when he went briefly to the bathroom. In less than twenty-four hours this odd man had become a fixture in her life, and she wasn't sure she was ready for that.

On the other hand, if he was going to St Helen's, she'd go too. For better or for worse, they were in this together.

'Hold on a second,' Holly broke the silence. 'I can't go swanning off to the Scilly Isles. I've got a job. And a son. What about a Zoom meeting?'

'I'm with Holly,' Sabri said. 'I don't like boats.'

'Mr Quick anticipated that response,' the woman replied. 'And asked me to say that he would very much like to meet you all in person, while doing so is still a possibility.'

'A dying man's request?' Robin asked.

The woman's smile faded.

'And what if we say no?' Craig asked.

The fair-haired woman got to her feet. 'Mr Quick very much hopes you won't say no.'

'I'm not going,' Sabri announced. 'The rest of you can fill me in.'

'I'm afraid the invitation is for all of you,' the woman informed them. 'Or none. I'll leave you to talk it through. You'll have my number, as soon as you reach a signal. Goodnight.'

The entrance flap of the tent closed behind her, they heard a footstep on the gravel outside, then nothing but the wind.

Silence stretched.

'What do we think?' Tara asked, eventually.

'No,' Sabri snapped. 'I'm not going.'

Craig said, 'I'd still like to know how Logan Quick knew to send her here tonight.'

Holly dropped her head into her hands.

'He has the resources to tap our phones,' Tug said. 'Or have us followed.'

'I suppose.' Craig glanced sideways at Holly.

'We're being played,' Sabri insisted. 'We shouldn't do it, guys.'

'I don't like boats either,' Cheryl said. 'And I'm scared of the sea. But if we don't go, he might change his will. We'll get nothing.'

'We could fly,' Robin suggested. 'Make our own way there. That way, we're in control.'

At that moment, a low sound broke through the rush of the wind and Tara saw Tug's head shoot around to face the tent entrance.

'What's up?' she asked him, in a low voice.

'Probably just Girl Friday leaving.' He didn't take his eyes from the yurt entrance, though. His body language suggested he was tense, even alarmed. Then he pushed his chair back several inches and leaned down to pick up his cane.

Sabri slammed her drink can down onto the table. 'Sorry,' she said, looking embarrassed. 'Didn't mean to do that quite so forcefully. But I'm not getting in any boat owned by Logan Quick, and I can't afford to fly to the Scilly Isles. I barely have enough money to pay the next phone bill, and Friday night's break-in will cost a lot to put right. You'll have to go without me.'

'I couldn't do it either,' Cheryl said. 'No matter how much it costs. Mum gives me everything I need and if I asked her, she'd say she should go instead of me.'

'So that's three of us who'll struggle to make the trip,' Holly said. 'What do you think, Craig?'

Craig was silent for a moment. Then, 'I'm happy to go, but I don't think splitting up is a good idea. I think we all go, or we don't bother.'

'I can't do it,' Sabri said.

'Me neither,' Cheryl said.

'I think that's wise,' Tara said. 'Something feels wrong to me.'

'Then we decline our new friend's kind invitation.' Tug spoke with the air of someone who'd made a big decision. 'And we wait to see what he does next.'

Craig said, 'As long as we're prepared for him to change his will again. Because I for one . . .'

Another sound outside. Loud enough for everyone to hear. More than one head turned towards the yurt entrance.

Tug got to his feet. 'Hold on to that thought, mate. We've got company.'

Before Tug could take a step away from the table, the canvas flap at the yurt entrance was pulled apart, a rush of cold air flooded through the tent, and several men stepped through.

'Fu . . . uck,' Tara heard Robin mutter.

Chapter 68

The incomers were all white men, three in their late thirties, the other two younger. One lad with ginger hair and bad skin looked barely out of his teens. Two of the older men were heavily built and tattooed, the third thin as a reed. None were smiling and a reek of trouble hovered over them like a dark cloud. Whatever this was, it was bad. Sabri had been in too many violent situations in her paramedic career not to recognise danger when it was staring her in the face.

'Help you guys?' Tug had stepped away from the table and was facing the newcomers head on.

The thin man, who seemed to be the boss, had moved furthest into the tent, the others flanking him like geese flying out for the winter. His eyes slid past Tug to fix on Robin.

'Need a word with Mr Knight here,' he said. 'He made a little mistake last night.'

'Who are these people?' Cheryl whispered. 'Do they work for Mr Quick too?'

As Robin got to his feet, Sabri realised one of the men was looking directly at her. As though he knew her.

'Anything you want to mention, Robin?' Tug spoke without turning his head.

'These guys came to my house last night.' Robin's voice was shaky but he, too, faced the gang head on. 'Threatened to hurt a friend of mine. They wanted the token. I gave them a leprechaun coin. Fool's gold.'

The man who'd been eyeing Sabri sidestepped and whispered in his boss's ear; Thin Man gave a long, slow smile. Sabri was suddenly very conscious of the token, still sewn inside her bra.

'Mrs Carter,' Thin Man said, as Sabri's insides clenched. She'd been recognised, hardly surprising given the number of unwilling TV appearances she'd made recently. 'Nice to meet you,' he went on, before looking steadily round the group, pointing to each with his forefinger and mouthing a count. One, two . . . 'Seven,' he finished. 'Isn't this a bit of luck?'

Moving slowly, Tara got to her feet. A second later, Holly followed her. Sabri did the same and felt stupidly exposed.

'OK.' Tug seemed to tighten his grip on the cane. 'I'm going to cut this short. Yes, we were all sent tokens. And no, none of us brought them with us. We're not fucking stupid.'

Well, Sabri was fucking stupid, clearly. Hers was here. And she wouldn't be at all surprised if others had brought them too.

Thin Man stepped forward, until he and Tug were only a pace apart. Tug was easily the bigger man, but he was older and would be facing five of them.

'Thing is,' Thin Man said. 'Mr Knight has proved himself very untrustworthy. So how can we trust the rest of you?'

'Not sure you need to.' Tug widened his stance and gripped the cane tighter before raising his voice. 'Is anyone on the phone to the police?'

Movement rippled around the table. Why the hell had no one thought of that? Sabri bent quickly to pull her phone from her bag. When she straightened up again, both Tara and Holly were staring at their own phones. Sabri opened hers before remembering. No signal.

'Very poor reception here,' Thin Man said. 'We checked.'

Sabri glanced a question over at Tara, who replied with a quick shake of her head.

'OK.' Thin Man was moving things along. 'I sense you're planning some heroics, big guy, so you try anything, my lads have instructions to hurt the ladies first.' He nodded back towards the table. 'I recommend you take a seat. All of you.'

Sabri dropped into her chair, followed by Robin and then Holly and Tara. Craig and Cheryl hadn't moved.

'Tug, sit down,' Tara said.

'We're going to search you one by one,' Thin Man said. 'Bags on the table, please. And jackets off.'

'No one's searching me,' Tug said.

'Tug, for heaven's sake!' Tara hissed.

'Guys, just something to consider.'

The new voice was Craig's. His hand was on top of Cheryl's on the table, as though offering comfort to the terrified woman.

'Logan Quick can change his will any number of times in the few months he has left,' Craig went on. 'Now, for some reason, he seems to want the seven of us to get his money.' He took a moment to gesture around the group. 'So, if we all lose our tokens, what's to stop him making a new will and sending out seven new ones? Without letting the world know. So, when you guys try to claim, with obviously stolen goods, you could find yourselves in a whole lot of trouble for nothing.'

Craig's words had struck home; more than one of the heavies looked doubtful. After a few seconds, though, Thin Man recovered.

'I'll take my chances,' he said. 'Besides, Mr Knight here has really pissed me off.'

He gave a quick nod at the man on his left, who strode across to Tara and wrapped his right hand around her hair, pulling her head back. Tara yelped, more in anger than pain, and Tug swung his cane, connecting with the side of Thin Man's head. As his victim staggered, Tug swung the cane again, this time into the back of the man's knees. He went down. Then, before the rest of the gang could move, Tug was on him. It had been the work of seconds.

'Hold it, fellas.' Tug was kneeling on Thin Man's chest, a knife in his hand. His own, or one he'd spotted and grabbed from the other guy? Either way, he had it poised above Thin Man's throat. 'Step away from that lady, now.'

The man holding Tara's hair took a step back, his hands in the air.

Tug was breathing heavily. 'Right, my lot, I want you out of here. Back over the bridge, into your vehicles and get the hell out of Dodge. Tara, I'd appreciate you holding on, but if anyone comes at you but me, drive like you did on the way over.'

No one moved. Tug took a deep breath. He'd hurt himself. Sabri recognised that look of suppressed pain. 'Robin, get them out of here.'

It was Craig, not Robin, who moved first, pulling Cheryl to her feet. 'Go, Robin,' he said. 'I'll bring up the rear.'

'We can't leave Tug,' Tara argued.

'I think your boyfriend can look after himself,' Craig snapped back. 'Robin, will you get a move on?'

Finally, Robin pulled himself together. He reached back for Sabri's hand; she gave it and let him hurry her towards the tent entrance. Holly followed behind with Cheryl. Tara still hadn't moved.

'Tara, I've got this.' Tug was sweating now. 'Go.'

At the doorway, Sabri glanced back to see Craig pushing Tara ahead of him. Then they were outside and running towards the bridge as though their lives depended on it. Which, she realised, might actually be the case.

Chapter 69

Out of the corner of his eye, Tug saw Craig leave the tent. It would take them a couple of minutes – no, longer, they had Cheryl with them – to get over the bridge and into their cars. In the meantime, it was five against one.

He'd faced similar odds before and lived to not tell the tale.

He kept the knife, liberated from Tara's kitchen and carried in his inside jacket pocket, pressed hard against Thin Man's throat.

'Your beef is with Robin,' he said, letting his eyes flick from one man to the other, trying to spot the one who'd move first. 'You can take it up with him. The rest of us are not fair game and if you threaten any of those ladies again, I won't be anything like as polite.'

He heard the sound of a car engine starting up. Time to move.

Swinging himself round, not nearly as smoothly or as quickly as he should have done, but he was getting too old for this shit, he pushed himself upright, dragging Thin Man up by the collar. He kept the knife tight against the man's neck.

The other four were closing in. The two older, bigger guys weren't entirely hopeless; they spread out, flanking him. At the same time, the ginger-haired kid moved out of sight, probably blocking the entrance.

'And we're moving,' he said, taking a step back, then another, dragging Thin Man along. He registered looks being traded, the three in front sending messages to the kid behind. Incoming. He threw Thin Man forward, sending him and one of the tattooed blokes flying. Two down.

Tug bent to grab his cane – no way was he leaving that behind – and missed the punch aimed from behind. He swung up, elbowing the ginger lad in the stomach and sprinting for the entrance. Three down, two on his tail.

   He was OK with that.

Chapter 70

It was nearly midnight when Holly got home. To everyone's surprise, possibly including his own, Tug's plan had worked. Holly and four of the others had piled into their cars and hurtled back along the unlit lane towards mobile phone reception and civilisation. On the outskirts of Bodmin, they'd pulled into a roadside layby to wait for Tug and Tara who, thank the lord, arrived a few minutes behind them.

They'd agreed to meet the following night, at Tara's house, to decide finally what they were going to do about Logan Quick's invitation. Holly suspected, though, the decision to decline would stand. Something about it felt wrong.

To Holly's alarm, her house was in darkness. Charlie would be asleep, of course, but she could think of no reason why the babysitter would have turned out the lights. She pulled her phone from her bag to see a text message from an unknown number – Quick's Girl Friday no doubt – and several missed calls. All from the babysitter.

Heartbeat accelerating, Holly unlocked the front door. 'Mrs M?' she called.

The sitting room was in darkness. No babysitter dozing on the sofa. No one in the kitchen either. Holly ran upstairs. Charlie wasn't in his room. Or the bathroom. Or her room. The house was empty.

As fear she'd never known before threatened to overwhelm her, a new message flashed into her phone, from the unknown number. Numb with shock, she opened it.

Don't call the police, it said. *I'll be in touch. Logan.*

DAY TWELVE

Sunday, 14 October

Chapter 71

Call the police. Everything Holly found on the internet said the same thing and the advice to those in her situation was unequivocal. If someone was missing, feared abducted, call the police immediately. The police had people trained to secure the release of kidnap victims and offer support to terrified families.

On the other hand, she found an equal number of stories about kidnap victims who were never seen alive again.

The first hour passed, and all Holly could bring herself to do was listen to the messages from the babysitter. She made a single phone call.

As the church clock struck one in the morning, she was overcome with the urge to search. She hadn't checked the house, not properly; it could all be a silly misunderstanding. She swept through it – every corner, every cupboard, even the two lofts – looking for her missing son. Then, despite the rain that had started to fall heavily, she searched both gardens, before walking up and down the street outside. Finally, soaked to the skin, unable to stop trembling, she returned to a house that felt empty and cold as a ransacked grave.

The second hour passed.

Holly didn't hear the church clock again, but when she woke with a start, on bedclothes damp with rainwater, her watch told her it was nearly ten minutes past two in the morning. Dragging herself to her feet, she lurched into the next room. Charlie's bed was the same: a dent on the pillow, the quilt pulled back. The bastards had taken him from his bed, drowsy with sleep, in nothing but pyjamas. Dropping to her knees, Holly laid her face against the sheet where her son's body had been, inhaling his scent, imagining she could still feel the warmth of his body.

The third hour passed. Holly hadn't realised it was possible to feel so alone.

At three o'clock, she almost gave in and called Coffie. But Coffie would insist on getting the police involved and she couldn't take that risk. Logan Quick was better resourced than any police force in the land. If he wanted Charlie to disappear, he could do it. And a dying man had nothing to lose.

In the days following, Holly couldn't remember the hours from three to four in the morning. She opened a bottle of red wine but didn't dare drink it. She thought she might have dozed briefly on the sofa. She forced herself to change into dry clothes only because she knew getting ill wouldn't help Charlie.

When the clock struck four, Holly, who didn't have a religious bone in her body, dropped to her knees and began to pray for the life and return of her son. At five o'clock, she climbed into her car and began the hour-and-a-half drive back along the A30.

Chapter 72

Tug woke early on Sunday morning. He opened the patio doors of his room and stepped, in bare feet, onto the cold grass outside. The morning air was sharp. Tara's garden, awash with fallen leaves, even after their marathon clean-up session of yesterday, sloped gently down towards the nearby river, its edges hazy with mist. Sometime in the night, the wind had dropped.

He hadn't slept well. His ribs hurt from the tussle with the bloke from the yurt. He'd spent most of the night conscious of Tara's drinks cabinet on the floor above and it didn't say much for the man he'd become that he'd been longing for the bottle of Scotch more than for the woman herself. He'd go home today, he decided, after the Magnificent Seven had been and gone, once they'd discussed, one last time, Logan Quick's invitation to St Helen's. Things were happening too fast. He needed some time alone, to take stock.

From the lane outside came the sound of a car engine pulling up outside the gates. A second later, Tug heard the entrance buzzer somewhere in the house. It continued. Someone was leaning on it; someone who really wanted to come in. Tug was on the point of stepping across to the gates when they began to open. A car sped through, sending gravel flying, and a second later a young woman jumped out. Holly. Tug took one look at her face and knew that events had taken a very dark turn.

Chapter 73

'We have to call the police,' Sabri said, not for the first time. Cheryl agreed but kept quiet. Nobody cared what she thought.

The seven of them were gathered again, this time at Tara's house, a mile or so outside Wadebridge. The three men stood in a huddle by the window. They'd been talking together in low voices, glancing nervously at Holly, Cheryl and Sabri on the sofas. If Cheryl hadn't known better, she'd have said they were afraid of the women, especially of Holly. Who seemed to be falling apart in front of them.

The young woman sat with her forearms on her knees as though nursing a stomach-ache. She kept her eyes fixed on the rug and Cheryl was glad of it. The poor girl no longer looked, well, normal.

'I agree.' Tara arrived from the kitchen area and knelt to place a tray of mugs on the low table. 'We can't deal with this. Not by ourselves.'

'You don't get a vote,' Holly snapped. 'None of you do. He's my child and I say we're doing exactly what they tell us to.' She looked up, briefly. 'I will kill anyone here who puts Charlie at risk.'

'How did they manage it?' Craig asked from his position near the window. 'You didn't leave him alone, did you?'

Holly's head shot up. 'Of course I didn't fucking leave him alone, you absolute—'

In an instant, Tug was across the room, kneeling in front of Holly, and had taken hold of both her hands. 'Hold it together, love,' he told her. 'Charlie can't afford for you to lose it. Now, some people here don't know the full story yet. And you might have missed something earlier. So, why don't you tell us all exactly what happened?'

Holly took a deep breath. 'He was with a sitter,' she said. 'One I've used many times before, totally reliable. Just before ten o'clock, a woman knocked on my door claiming to be a friend of mine. She said I'd be very late back, and that I'd asked her to stay with Charlie so that Mrs Morrison – my sitter – could go home to her husband.'

Sabri asked, 'And she just went? Without confirming it with you?'

'She tried to call me,' Holly replied. 'I had several missed calls. But I always put my phone in my bag when I'm driving, so I'm not tempted to look at it.'

Sabri didn't look impressed. 'Even so.'

'Did she give you a description of the woman?' Tug was still kneeling in front of Holly.

'About forty, fair-haired, attractive.'

'Like the woman who came to the tent.' Craig said what they were all thinking. 'She must have driven straight from Bodmin to Exeter. You probably weren't long behind her, Holly.'

Holly's phone started to ring; she pulled away from Tug to reach it.

'It's the same number,' she announced. 'It's them.'

Everyone seemed to take a deep breath as they drew closer. Sabri shuffled over on the sofa so that she could see Holly's phone; Robin and Craig came to stand directly behind Cheryl and Holly; Tara knelt beside Tug. Eyes fixed on the screen, they waited for the call to be connected.

The phone made rhythmic pinging sounds and then the face of a young boy appeared. He had pale skin and dark hair, and he looked a lot like Holly. There was sea and sky behind him. His face lit up at the sight of his mother.

'Hi, Mum, are you coming today?'

'Charlie? Oh my God, Charlie. Are you OK?'

The boy's smile faded. 'Yeah. I'm on Logan's island. I came in a helicopter last night. They said you're coming to get me.'

'I am. I am, sweetheart. Can I talk to Logan? Let me talk to him, please.'

The small boy looked uncertain. 'I have to give you a message.'

'What? What message?'

'The boat will bring you and the others any day you want. Who are the others, Mum?'

Holly gulped in air and swallowed hard before she could reply. 'The other people with the tokens, sweetheart. He wants us all to come to his island.'

'You'll come, won't you, Mum? Today? It's really cool. There's a dog called—'

A hand appeared, taking the phone away from the child, and Cheryl saw the same woman who'd interrupted them in the tent the previous evening. The one who worked for Logan Quick.

'Hello, Holly,' she said. 'It looks like you've got everyone together. Good, that will save time.'

Holly said, 'Where are you?'

The woman's hair blew across her face as she replied. 'On St Helen's. Charlie will have a wonderful time here. We have boats.'

'If you hurt him . . .'

The woman looked affronted. 'Mr Quick has children of his own. He wouldn't dream of hurting yours.'

Tug said, 'What do you want?'

'The invitation to visit remains open. We'd love to welcome all seven of you to the island any day this coming week. After your meeting with Mr Quick, Charlie will be free to travel home with you.'

'I'm coming today,' Holly said. 'I'll get a flight out. And I'm not leaving without my son.'

St Helen's, if that's where the woman and little Charlie were, was windy. The woman's next few words were indistinct.

'Say that again!' Holly snapped.

The woman brushed hair out of her eyes. 'I said, the invitation is for all of you. And travelling by air is not acceptable. Nor by the commercial ferries. I'll leave you to talk it through. Let me know what day suits and I'll arrange for the boat to be waiting.'

She was gone.

Holly dropped the phone with a clunk, got up, pushed Tug aside and walked to the window. She leaned against it, her head in her hands. The others gave her a moment, looking at each other, making faces, as though trying to communicate without words.

Cheryl was glad, in that moment, that she'd no children of her own. She'd never seen such raw, unbearable pain.

Then, 'I still think we should call the police,' Sabri said. 'If it was me, and one of my kids, I would.'

'You wouldn't,' Holly replied, in a low, dangerous voice. 'You wouldn't dare.'

'We have to go,' Tara said. 'We've no choice. This is a child. Call her back, Holly. Tell her we'll come today. She said Falmouth, didn't she? Last night, I'm sure she mentioned Falmouth. We can be there in a couple of hours.'

Today? Cross the sea in a boat? Cheryl felt a churning in the lower part of her stomach that usually meant she needed the loo. Not here, she prayed silently. Not in Tara's house. The token would come out and then she'd have to fish for it in someone else's toilet. Her own bathroom was one thing, when she had plenty of time to clean up after herself, but here?

'Hold on, ladies, we need to think about this.' Tug got to his feet and held out a hand to help Tara up. 'I've a few questions.'

'Me too,' Robin said. 'That woman went straight from the tent last night to Holly's house. How did she know we'd turn down Quick's invitation? Did someone call her on the way home?'

He looked around the group. One by one, heads shook.

'She knows far more than she should,' Robin insisted. 'She knew where and when we were meeting, she knew the chances were we'd refuse to go to the Scilly Isles. Someone is keeping her informed.'

'And why are we not allowed to fly out?' Tug asked. 'Why is she insisting we take Quick's boat?'

'That's a very good point,' Sabri agreed.

'You're keeping a few secrets yourself, Robin,' Craig said. 'I'm still not sure who last night's gang were. Are they anything to do with Logan Quick? Because, if not, how did they know where to find us?'

'We could get on board Quick's boat and find that lot are the crew,' Tara said.

'The gang from last night are enforcers,' Robin said. 'They work for one of the debt collection agencies I have dealings with. I don't believe they have any connection to Logan Quick, except for the fact that they quite fancy the tokens and his money. As to how they found us – following me, probably.'

'Tell us again how you got those bruises, mate,' Tug said.

Robin sighed. 'Nothing to do with Quick. Or the West Country's answer to the Kray twins.'

'Are you sure?'

'Give it a rest, Tug,' Tara said, but her voice was gentle. 'We can't turn on each other.'

'Oh, I'm with Tug. I'm far from sure I can trust everybody here,' Craig said.

'I was beaten up by a jealous boyfriend.' Robin raised his voice. 'He's a twat, but I probably deserved it. The woman in question was in my house when the Kray brothers came round on Friday night. They held a hot iron to her face, and I still didn't give up the token. That's the kind of guy I am. Now you know everything.'

'Does she know?' Tara asked, after the several seconds of silence that Robin's announcement seemed to call for.

'No, she still thinks I'm a decent person.'

'Is she OK?' Sabri asked.

'Far as I know. I don't plan to see her again.'

Something about Robin's posture, about the way he'd deliberately stepped away from the rest of them, told Cheryl he wasn't going to be pushed any further on the subject.

'Shit,' said Craig. 'Holly, I apologise for what I said last night. Tara's right. We shouldn't be fighting among ourselves. But we can't go on like this either.'

'Got any suggestions?' Tug looked exhausted.

Craig said, 'Let's talk about going to St Helen's. About how we can get there, and how soon we can do it.'

'Tug and I checked out flights while we were waiting for you all to arrive,' Tara said. 'Cheapest we can find is just short of two hundred pounds. It will be over that with taxes and baggage allowance.'

'Not possible,' Sabri said. 'I'm sorry, Holly, but I can't find that.'

'Me neither,' Cheryl said. 'I could ask Mum but—'

'I'll pay,' Holly said. 'I'll pay for everyone's flight.'

'Travelling by air is not acceptable,' Craig reminded them. 'You all heard her. Nor are the commercial ferries. It's Quick's boat or nothing.'

'What's that all about?' Robin said.

'I'd say it's about keeping our trip undocumented,' Craig replied. 'If we go by air or commercial ferry, there'll be a record. On a private boat there won't be.'

'So, when we don't come back, no one will be able to prove we ever made it to St Helen's?' Tug said.

'To hell with that,' Sabri said. 'I'm not getting on Logan Quick's boat. I've got children too. Three of them.'

Holly looked ready to pounce. 'Yeah, well, he might grab one of yours next. Then we'll see how fussy you are about the mode of transport.'

'Guys!' Craig held up a hand to get their attention. 'If we're all decided that we'll go, but we don't trust Logan Quick to get us there safely, I might know of another way.'

Everyone turned to him.

Craig said, 'What if we go on someone else's boat?'

Chapter 74

'What sort of boat?' Sabri asked. It had been years since she'd been on any sort of boat.

'Sailing yacht,' Craig replied. 'Moored at Plymouth. The skipper's a good friend of mine who owes me a favour. If he's free over the next few days, I'm sure he'd sail us over to St Helen's and back. We'd have to chip in for the diesel and sort out our own food, but that won't be expensive.'

Sabri had never been on a sailing boat. They were dangerous, weren't they? And the seas around the Scilly Isles could be rough, everyone knew that. She looked around the room to gauge reaction. She saw nervousness, suspicion, desperation in Holly's case. No one looked on the point of rejecting the idea outright.

Tug said, 'We wouldn't be at Quick's mercy that way.'

Holly said, 'What if he won't agree? What if it's his boat or nothing?'

Craig shrugged. 'We can only ask. But if I'm right about him wanting us to come privately, he should be OK with it.'

'How many berths?' Tug asked.

'Ten, I think,' Craig replied. 'He's raced with it in the past so needed to accommodate a lot of hands. We could sleep on board too. We wouldn't need a hotel.'

Sabri's every instinct was screaming at her to say no. She felt sorry for Holly, of course she did, and obviously she hoped Charlie would be OK. But she had her own kids to think about. They needed her at home, not swanning across the Atlantic.

'I'm game,' Tug said, after a moment. 'My diary's not exactly full right now.'

Robin had been checking his phone. 'I can do it,' he said. 'Nothing I can't cancel over the next couple of days.'

'And it will get you out of the way of our friends from last night,' said Craig.

If half of what Robin had told them about his circumstances were true, he'd jump at the chance to disappear for a few days.

'This coming week's half term for my kids.' Craig had turned to Sabri. 'Is it for yours too?'

The leaden feeling in Sabri's gut started to tighten. She made a show of checking her phone diary, but she already knew the answer. Jason had booked leave for the week.

'It is,' she admitted. 'But things are difficult at home right now. I'm not happy about leaving my family. They're at risk too.'

'They could move in here while we're away,' Tara suggested. 'The security's pretty good. And we're not far from the beach if they can brave going out.'

Sabri was touched – she hardly knew the woman; on the other hand, she really didn't want to sail to the middle of the bloody Atlantic. She said, 'I can't ask that of you.'

Tara shrugged. 'Why not? If I have to sell the place soon, I might as well make the most of it while I can.'

As Sabri was wondering how Jason and the kids would react to the opportunity to stay in Tara's fabulous home – who was she kidding? They'd leap at the chance – Tara had turned to Cheryl.

'How about your mum?' Tara asked. 'Would she agree to staying here? I've got a cleaning lady I can ask to help with any personal care.'

Cheryl looked uncertain; she was someone else who really didn't want to sail to the Scilly Isles.

'Why don't I pop round to ask her?' Craig suggested. 'I can pick her up, drive her over the day we set off. Explain how important it is that we do this.'

Cheryl nodded slowly. 'I think she might, if you asked her. And it's safe, this boat?'

Craig smiled. 'Of course. I've been on it loads of times.' He glanced down at his phone. 'What do you say, folks, shall I call this woman back?'

Chapter 75

'Holly, you don't know these people. And that's a fair old sail, across to those islands. Are you sure?'

'I'm not sure about anything anymore,' Holly admitted.

It was nearly twenty hours since Charlie had been taken. Another twenty or so before she and the others could set out on their journey to get him back. Craig's friend's boat simply wasn't available until early Monday evening.

Forty hours of pretending everything was normal; that she wasn't falling apart.

'Is Charlie going with you,' Coffie went on. 'I know he likes boats, but—'

'No.' Holly dropped her eyes. She couldn't look at Coffie and lie to him. 'He's staying with his dad for half-term week. And people sail to the Scilly Isles all the time, according to Craig and Tug. It's not dangerous.'

Logan Quick, thank God, had agreed to them travelling independently. Craig had been proven right. For obvious reasons, Quick wanted to keep the trip under the radar.

'And when you get there?' Coffie asked. 'When there's a posse of armed guards waiting to meet you?'

Holly forced a smile. 'He's not a drug baron.'

'We don't know what he is, Holly. Other than a bloke with nothing to lose who's messing with all your heads.'

Holly picked up the glass of wine Coffie had poured for her.

'You look ill,' he said. 'Are you really sure you want to do this?'

'I wish you could come,' she said, without thinking.

Coffie's reaction could barely be measured: a twitch of an eyebrow, a twist of the head, maybe a deepening of his stare. Tiny things. Discountable. Which made all the difference in the world.

'I should go.' She got ready to slide back her seat. If she stayed much longer, she'd break down, tell him everything. 'It's been good to get away from the media scrum.'

'Move in here,' he told her. 'There's plenty of room. Come as my flatmate, just till this wills gets sorted out one way or another.'

No, Coffie. Not now. 'I can't.'

'Why not?'

'Because you and I can't be flatmates. We both know what would happen if I moved in here.'

It was the first time any such admission had passed between them. Finally, he said, 'And why is that a problem?'

Holly got to her feet. 'I can't do this right now. I've too much to think about.'

Coffie took a deep breath. 'Yeah, that would be fine, Holly, except this thing with you and me didn't start with Logan Quick's will. You've been keeping me at a distance for as long as I've known you. And you won't tell me why.'

Holly felt her eyes filling. 'I can't.'

She turned away. But somehow Coffie was standing directly in front of her. How could he move that fast? She stood, breathing in the scent of him, feeling the warmth of his body inches from hers. It would be the easiest thing in the world to let herself lean against him, wrap her arms around his waist, let events take their inevitable course. And the worst thing she could do.

Holly made a decision.

'I need to show you something,' she said.

Coffie didn't move. 'What?'

She took a step back. 'Is your laptop handy?'

'My laptop?'

'Yes, where is it? There's something you need to see.'

Picking up on the urgency in her tone, he crossed the room and took his laptop from its case. He put it down on the dining table and opened it up.

She waited until Coffie had stepped away before typing Cornish Courtesans into the search engine. The home page came up quickly. Nine photographs appeared beneath the heading, in three rows of three. The picture headed Tamara, showing a brunette on all fours, bare arse towards the camera, was in the centre row. She clicked on it and her own page flashed up. Well, at least Coffie could say he'd seen her naked now.

She could hear him, behind her, breathing.

'I'm being blackmailed.' She made herself turn round and look him in the eye. 'By the friend who took the photographs. I've given him three grand already and as soon as he finds out about Logan Quick's will he'll bleed me dry. He won't wait for it to be finalised. I'll have to stop paying for my dad's care, which means he'll go into a home. It will break him.'

Coffie, to his credit, hadn't looked away.

'Now,' she said. 'Are you sure this is something you want to get involved with?'

No reply. She gave him seconds. Too many seconds. Then she pushed past him, picked up her bag and slung it over her shoulder.

'Thanks for the drink.' Holly avoided eye contact as she opened the front door. 'I'll see you at work.'

Coroline wasn't thrilled by the late-night phone call, even less at Holly's decision to leave the agency immediately, but when the circumstances were explained, she agreed to have all of Tamara's photographs taken off the website first thing in the morning. She went further, too, and assured Holly that the website manager could do some sort of deep clean so that the pictures wouldn't show up on any but the most vigorous of historical searches.

Holly's phone rang as she was finally getting into bed. It was Coffie.

'Hi,' she said, telling herself it meant nothing; those bridges had been well and truly burned.

'I've got a mate in CID,' he told her. 'I think I can persuade him to pay your friend a discreet visit and remind him of the UK's anti-blackmailing laws.'

Did he really think she hadn't thought of that herself?

'In the meantime, the advice is to have no further contact with the blackmailer. Block his number and don't respond to any communication you get from him.'

If only it were that easy.

'Please don't get involved,' she said. 'You'll make things worse.'

'Holly . . .'

'No, listen. I've left the agency. Those photographs should be down first thing in the morning. But Chris won't give in easily. Even if he can't harm me professionally, he'll take his photographs to Charlie's dad and Tim will believe him. He'll use it in a custody battle and then I'll be faced with having to deny it in court. Which is—'

'A criminal offence,' finished Coffie.

'I'll deal with it, Coffie. Stay out of it, please.'

She put the phone down before he could say anything else. Now that she'd left the agency, it was unlikely Chris could do anything to damage her career. The photographs, if made public, would be embarrassing but not proof in themselves that she'd ever been an escort. And sharing indecent private images without permission was an offence in itself, so it was unlikely Chris would take that risk. He could easily, though, make trouble with Tim. Tim would choose to believe him. Tim could use the accusation in a custody hearing and then the onus would be on her to prove he was lying. Which she couldn't do.

And all this was assuming that Charlie was safely returned.

For the first time since her son had been born, Holly considered the possibility that Charlie was better off without her.

DAY THIRTEEN

Monday, 15 October

Chapter 76

The robing room at Exeter Crown Court was unusually quiet and Holly had a much-needed forty-five minutes to go through her papers. Her case was due to finish today, in plenty of time to get to Plymouth for their overnight sail to St Helen's.

By evening, it would be two whole days since her son had been taken. She'd had no idea how time could stretch. Charlie had FaceTimed her again the previous night, possibly as a reward for the group's capitulating to Quick's demand that they meet him. In the two minutes they'd been allowed to talk, she'd learned he'd spent the day on various boats and watching movies. He'd been tearful, maybe starting to get a bit frightened, but OK.

Would he still be OK when he was no longer needed as a bargaining chip? She couldn't think like that. Get to St Helen's and Charlie would be fine. Get through today, and then the overnight sail, and she'd have Charlie back again.

The door opened and she glanced up. She'd already faced several barbed comments about her presence in court given the publicity over Logan Quick's will and she was half prepared for some over-officious clerk deciding to pull her case on its final day.

'Good morning, moneybags.'

Chris. He'd tracked her down and blagged his way to getting the access codes for the door. Or maybe he'd known them anyway; he'd worked at Exeter before now.

'I'm due in court,' she told him, gathering her papers.

'You've been holding out on me, Holly.' He didn't come into the room, just stood directly in front of the door. She'd have to push past him to get out. 'How long have you known?'

Holly got to her feet. She was already robed up. All she had to do was get out of the door. Even Chris wouldn't dare follow her into the courtroom. 'I've nothing to say to you. And my client's waiting.'

He didn't move.

'You know what?' she demanded. 'I'm surprised it took you this long. What have you been doing since Friday night? Wrestling with your conscience?'

'I've been in Barcelona for the weekend. Lovely this time of year. Not really paying much attention to the news.'

The bastard had been in Barcelona? On her money no doubt.

He said, 'I think we need to revisit our agreement.'

'I think you can go to hell.'

'Fifty per cent. That feels fair.'

He wanted half the money Logan Quick was planning to leave her. Oh Christ, he'd be welcome to it as long as she never had to set eyes on him again. She'd hand over all of it if it would guarantee she got Charlie back.

The door behind Chris opened. He grunted and stepped out of the way as the newcomer appeared. Coffie.

'Sorry, mate.' Coffie spoke without looking at Chris; his eyes were fixed on Holly. 'Doors open, though. It's what they're for. They told me I'd find you here. Got a sec?'

'She's due in court.' Chris turned to face Coffie. 'And she and I hadn't quite finished.'

Great. A cockfight.

'We are finished and I am due in court.' Holly picked up her briefcase. 'You can walk me to the door,' she told Coffie.

'Who was that?' Coffie asked, as he and Holly made for the room where her case was to be heard.

'University friend,' Holly replied. 'What did you want to see me about?'

'That black Volvo you asked me to look into is registered to Logan Quick's group of companies. I heard this morning. I thought you should know right away.'

Exhaustion washed through Holly. The man claiming to be an old friend of her father's, who'd been hanging around her parents' house, worked for Quick. Might even be Quick himself.

'Tug's seen the same car hanging around his place too,' she said. 'He's probably had us all under surveillance.'

She'd have to warn her mother before she set off for Plymouth, make sure he wasn't allowed in the house again.

Coffie said, 'You're not still planning to go tonight, are you?'

Holly didn't reply as they walked the last few steps of the corridor. Her client was waiting outside the courtroom. His daughter, her hand on her father's arm, spotted her and smiled.

'I think we've set something in motion,' she said. 'And now we have to see it through.'

DAY FOURTEEN

Tuesday, 16 October

Chapter 77

Holly had lost all track of time. Wet to the skin, unable to stop shivering, she might have been rooted to her seat. She had no idea how long they'd been looking for the two men who'd gone overboard. A vain hope when they'd started, with every passing minute it became less and less likely they'd pluck anyone from the water.

The inside of Holly's mouth felt, and tasted, as though it was caked with salt.

Even Tug, the only one capable of helming in the conditions, was struggling to control the boat. Each gust threatened to rip the wheel from his hands and every wave had to be met head-on lest it swamp them. And every passing minute they were heading in the wrong direction delayed her reunion with her son.

The water around them swirled with a dozen or more shades of black – the subtle gleam of jet, the dull matt of liquorice. In the sky Holly could see the deep sheen of a raven's wing against the dark grey of wet slate. Before this trip, she'd had no idea how many shades of black the world could offer; now she'd almost forgotten what colour looked like.

'Forty minutes,' Robin called.

Forty minutes was the time limit Tug had set; the search had failed.

'Are you sure you got the tides right?' Sabri shouted over her shoulder.

'Nope.' Tug didn't take his eyes from the bow. 'It should be heading east now, taking us the way we need to go. That said, tides around Land's End and the Lizard are tricky. We could have been pushed off course. And there's the wind to factor in.' He swallowed. 'Looks like I got it wrong.'

'You're not to blame,' Tara called from her seat beside Holly. 'Without you we'd all have gone overboard. We're safe, thanks to you.'

Nothing about this felt safe.

'OK, I'm calling it,' Tug said. 'I'm bringing the boat round. Robin, haul in the mainsheet. Sab, release the jib on my command, Holly and Tara, get ready to bring it in.'

'Hold on, hold on.' Sabri turned round. 'We're going to abandon them? We can't do that.'

For a second, Tug's eyes closed. 'We're heading into worse weather and I'm not risking this boat anywhere near land in a storm. We're going back into open water to ride it out.'

Sabri gave a panicked look around. 'You can't make that decision by yourself. We all have to agree.'

Tug shook his head. 'Not a democracy, Sab. I've assumed command of this vessel because I'm the only one capable and we're turning round. OK, this could get bumpy. I want everyone holding on.'

'He's right.' Robin grabbed the main sheet.

'We've done what we could,' Tara agreed.

'Everybody ready?' Tug called. 'Coming about.'

Tug began the turn. As the bow passed through the wind the vessel lurched onto its side. A wave washed over the deck and Holly felt herself sliding. The now-familiar crashing sounded from the cabin, and she hit something soft – Tara. They both fell. Landing hard on fibreglass took all the breath from her body.

'Get the jib in!'

Pulling herself up, Holly saw Robin hauling in the jib sheet.

'Jesus wept,' she heard Tara complain, then she was dragged onto the starboard seat by Sabri. Tara fell next to her and Robin joined them. They stared down at the water. It was impossible. No boat could remain at this angle and not capsize.

'Nice work,' Tug called. 'I'll make sailors of you yet.'

Things had been bad enough before; now they were worse. Heading into the wind the going was windier, wetter and bumpier. Every few seconds waves crashed over the bow. Holly found the energy to glance at her watch. Coming up for four in the morning.

'The girls should go below,' Robin yelled. 'Tug, it doesn't need all of us. You and I can take this watch.'

Tug gave a half-nod. 'Sabri and Tara, can you find every mobile phone on board? Make sure they're somewhere secure and keep an eye on them. Let me know as soon as we get a signal. Mine's in the front pocket of my bag. Holly, can you double check where the life raft is?'

More than once Tug had told them they'd only launch the life raft if the yacht was in peril.

'Just a precaution,' he added. 'There'll be a folder in the chart table. It'll tell you where everything is. Take your time.'

'Oh God, I'm going to be sick again,' Tara muttered as the three women climbed down the steps. Without lights, even the glow from the instruments, the cabin was still black as pitch. Holly found a torch directly above the steps and Tara retrieved her own from her cabin.

'This isn't right.' Sabri had opened the chart table.

'What's up?' Tara slid across the cabin floor to join her.

'Thomas took all our phones, remember?' Sabri told her. 'He said we shouldn't have them in our jackets on deck because they'd be ruined if they got wet. He put mine on charge, Robin's too. They're not here.'

'I gave him mine,' Tara agreed. 'They must be somewhere else. Look in the cupboards.'

'Tug's bag is over there.' Holly shone her torch beam towards the bunk where Tug had been sleeping. 'I'll get mine.'

Sabri began stumbling from one cupboard to the other, checking each for the missing phones. 'What about Cheryl?' she said.

'Cheryl doesn't have one,' Tara reminded her, as Holly felt her way to the cabin she'd been sleeping in earlier. Bracing herself against one wall, she felt around the space. Nothing. The phone was not where she'd left it.

Back in the main cabin, Tara was perched on Tug's bunk, her feet braced against the table to stop herself falling. 'Looks like he got Tug's as well. Any luck, Sab?'

Sabri had exhausted her search of the cupboards. She shook her head.

'Thomas took mine too,' Holly told the other two.

For several seconds, the three women stared at each other.

'They took our phones, then they vanished,' Sabri said. 'What the hell is going on here?'

Chapter 78

Nothing they could do about the phones for the moment, and she'd been asked to find the life raft. Holly wedged herself onto the chart table seat, found the folder and ran her finger down the index. There, life raft stored in the port cockpit locker.

Back on deck, she gave the news to Tug.

'We should have a look,' he told her.

He looked tired, Holly thought, the strain of the last hour was starting to tell. 'More people than me need to know how it works,' he went on. 'We might even get it out, keep it on deck.'

Pushing down the thought that if Tug wanted to ready the life raft, he was more worried than he was letting on, Holly dropped to her knees and pulled open the locker. She heard Tug hand the helm to Robin and, a second later, he dropped to his knees beside her.

The life raft was in a bag made from heavy-duty blue plastic with black straps.

'We should get it on deck,' Tug said. 'Give me some room.'

He leaned into the locker, took hold of the straps and heaved. When she could reach, Holly added her own strength to the task. Slowly, the bag emerged. When it was clear of the locker, Tug lowered it to the cockpit floor.

'I'll find somewhere to stow it,' he told her. 'If we need it, we throw it overboard, but it has to be attached to the yacht first. There should be a painter.'

Holly had no idea what a painter was. 'Is it inside?' she asked.

Tug's face was grim. 'I don't like to open it till it's needed. I don't know, though, Holly, something doesn't look right.'

Holly took a sharp breath to hold the whimper at bay; all they needed was a malfunctioning life raft.

'Better find out now,' she said.

Tug nodded and bent to the zipper. He cranked it an inch and recoiled.

'What's the matter?' Holly asked. Then she smelled it too. A stench that leapt inside her head and throat. She fought back the gag.

'Jeez,' muttered Robin, from the helm. 'What's that sme—'

Tug pulled on the zipper and the bag sprang open. What it contained was the very opposite of something designed to preserve life.

The life-raft bag held a corpse.

Chapter 79

In the dark hours before dawn, *Gemini* found a lull in the weather. The wind dropped to what Tug guessed was a little under twenty knots, the sea state settled somewhat, and the rain cleared. Stars reappeared and when he turned to face the stern, he saw the eastern sky lightening. It was possible the worst of the storm was over.

More than once, in the time since the skipper and Craig had vanished, Tug had believed himself close to death, and that his crew, the last ever under his command, would be lost on his watch. He'd never, in his life, been so afraid on water. Now, he said a silent prayer – to whom or what he couldn't have said – that the ordeal might be coming to an end.

The cockpit was quiet, drama-free, and had been for some time. Robin, still in charge of the main sail, slumped motionless on the port seat, his eyes closed; he hadn't spoken for the best part of an hour. He started upright, though, when the cabin hatch slid back, and Holly placed a steaming mug on the cockpit floor. A second followed, then a third, and Holly herself joined them.

The girl looked shocking, a far cry from the attractive young woman Tug had met only days ago. Sometime in the night she'd lost the baseball cap that had kept her hair in place. Her skin was red and there were heavy shadows beneath her eyes. Her hands were shaking as she passed him tea.

'How's things below?' Robin slid across the starboard seat so that Holly could join him.

Tug had noticed both of them avoiding looking at the seat opposite, below which lay the life-raft bag with its unexpected contents.

A dead white male, they'd ascertained, before they'd re-stowed the bag. Somewhere around five ten to six foot, slim build, between forty-five and sixty years old. It was neither Thomas, the erstwhile skipper, nor Craig Lewis.

'Cheryl poked her head out but didn't argue when I told her to stay where she was,' Holly told Robin. 'Tara and Sabri are in their cabin.'

'Still no sign of the phones?' Robin asked.

As Holly shook her head, Tug leaned against the helm to steady it while he warmed his hands on the mug. Every phone on the boat had vanished, along with the skipper and Craig. There was something major going on here that he was missing.

'Anyone know about our stowaway?' he asked.

Another head shake from Holly. 'You might want to check the cabin floor, if you're happy for me or Robin to take the helm,' she said. 'It's looking very damp.'

'Probably just rain and spray but I'll check it now.' Tug slurped down much-needed tea. 'I should have another look at the engine too.'

He climbed down and his new-found optimism vanished. The cabin floor was awash.

He checked the cupboard in the heads first, knowing damage to one of the pipes was the most likely culprit. Both wastewater and sea-water pipes were intact. Same thing with the pipes to the galley sink. Bar major damage to the hull, which he couldn't rule out, the only other place he could think of where water might be coming in was the boat speed impeller. He found it in a floor panel close to the bow cabin but, again, it looked fine.

Flummoxed, Tug decided to have another look at the engine; in better light he might spot something he'd missed the night before. Hours earlier, following standard procedure for dealing with engine problems at sea, he'd linked the engine battery with the one that powered all the domestic services on board. It had made no difference. Both batteries were flat and he had a catastrophic electrical failure on his hands.

The engine looked fine. The fanbelt was intact, oil and water levels normal. He thought for a moment, then opened the door to where Holly had been sleeping. Just inside the doorway was a panel that would allow him access to the side of the engine. He removed it and shone the torch inside. It took him seconds to see that the cable behind the alternator had been severed.

Well, that would do it. If the alternator couldn't charge the batteries, then over the course of several hours both would drain, making it impossible to start the engine. Worse was to come, though. Shining his torch around the engine, Tug spotted the source of the water inflow.

The raw-water inlet, the flexible pipe that brought in sea water to cool the engine, was leaking. The hole appeared small, because the water was trickling rather than gushing in, but during the night enough sea water had collected in the bilges to appear above the cabin floor. And the automatic bilge pump wouldn't work without the batteries. He tried to close the sea cock to shut off the water inflow. The bloody thing wouldn't budge.

The boat had been systematically and deliberately sabotaged.

Knowing there was nothing more he could do, Tug put the kettle on again and found a packet of breakfast bars in one of the cupboards. Whatever the day held, the crew would need energy. When he went up top again, a light, warm and clear, was bringing colour back into the world. The black waves had become a greenish grey and behind the boat a dull, apricot haze told him he'd lived to see another day.

Still could be his last, though.

'Do we have a problem?' Robin asked.

No point worrying them before he had to. 'Water's coming in, but it's slow. Nothing to concern us for the next couple of hours.'

Unsurprisingly, neither Robin nor Holly looked reassured.

'Tug,' Holly said, as he took the helm back from Robin. 'Can you get us to the islands? Without an engine or any instruments?'

Truthfully, Tug had no frigging idea. He'd done his best through the storm, but they'd been heading almost directly into the wind and tacking every half-hour had made holding a course close to impossible. On top of that, navigation around the Isles of

Scilly was a bastard. Not for nothing were its waters littered with shipwrecks.

'Course I can.' He said another vague and silent prayer that once the sun came up properly, land would be in sight. 'We can find somewhere to anchor and one of us can swim to shore if we have to.'

'I volunteer Tara.' Robin spoke through a mouthful of oat biscuit. 'Her Facebook page is nothing but sea swims.'

Back on the helm, Tug found himself picturing Tara, snuggled down in the port cabin, and for the first time since the skipper had gone overboard, his thoughts strayed beyond the immediate crisis.

'Is that a ship?' Robin was on his feet, looking out over the port side of the boat. 'Ten o'clock.'

It was. A bloody great container ship.

'Holly.' Tug kept his eyes fixed on the vessel. 'Can you go into the locker beneath the port side bunk? You'll find a pack of flares. Bring them up.'

The ship wasn't necessarily a good thing. If it was following one of the recognised shipping routes towards the UK, it meant *Gemini* had drifted too far south. On their present course, they could miss the islands entirely. Next stop, Newfoundland.

'Orange one,' he said, when Holly reappeared with the waterproof bag of flares.

The ship would be level with them soon. If they wanted to be seen, they had to act fast. Tug pulled the rip cord on the flare and held it high. Out of the corner of his eye he saw Tara had appeared from below. She gave him a shy smile; he risked winking in return.

'How will we know if it's seen us?' Robin asked. 'Will he set off a flare of his own?'

'The captain will try to contact us on the radio,' Tug said. 'When we don't answer he'll pass our distress message and our position on to the coast guard.'

In the cabin, the kettle began to whistle.

★

An hour later, when the ship had long since vanished from sight, when spirits on *Gemini* were sinking again, a motorboat was spotted heading their way.

Chapter 80

Cheryl woke with a feeling of dread in her heart. This was worse, far worse, than when her mother had announced her disinheritance plans. This was the reappearance of a nightmare she thought she'd left behind years ago.

In the dark hours, thrown this way and that by the bucking motion of the boat, when the crashing of the waves against the hull had been close to deafening, she'd realised why they were here. With a clarity that surprised her, because it wasn't often she could organise her thoughts so well, Cheryl knew exactly what this group had in common and when they'd met before.

Except, Holly didn't fit at all. So, maybe she was wrong. How Cheryl hoped she was wrong. But still, the tense feeling in her gut told her disaster was hovering.

And now, something was different. Above the relentless pounding of the waves she could hear the steady hum of an engine. And the boat was upright. They weren't sailing anymore.

Once the realisation had hit her, Cheryl had had a restless night, tossed from one side of the bunk to the other, her fitful dozing constantly interrupted by clattering on deck and crashing below. Only the difficulties of moving around and her constant nausea when she was upright had kept her where she was. Now, though, she desperately needed the loo.

The engine noise grew louder. Something heavy slithered across the deck. Men's voices called to each other. Something was happening and she couldn't hide down here any longer. Besides, she really had to pee. Awkwardly, she manoeuvred her body around until she could swing her legs off the bunk.

And found herself standing in water. Panic rearing, she pulled open her cabin door, causing more water to slosh over her ankles and soak the bottom of the stretch pants she'd slept in.

Paddling her way through the main cabin, Cheryl thought again about the big realisation of the night before. Of the whole group, she was the least clever, surely the last to figure out a puzzle. She had to be wrong. It was just the darkness twisting her thoughts as it so often did.

She couldn't say anything. Not yet.

Above the companionway steps she caught sight of Holly at the steering wheel. The girl didn't look to be panicking. Maybe all this water was normal.

Cheryl's feet were freezing by the time she'd squeezed into the impossibly tiny space the others called the heads. She managed to get her pants down and twist herself round so that she was poised above a toilet that looked as though it belonged in a nursery. As she lowered herself, she realised she was probably about to see the token again.

When she was done, finally, she found her shoes and coat and climbed the steps to join the others.

Holly was still at the helm, Tara on one seat, Sabri on the other. All three were pale-faced and frowning, their attention fixed on the bow. Knowing she'd fall any second, Cheryl launched herself at the seat beside Sabri, tried to suppress the grunt of pain when she landed heavily, and then she too looked towards the front.

Tug and Robin were talking to two men on another boat, this one bottle green with a big yellow cabin. Hovering a few metres away, it was noisy and sturdy and the white lettering on the side said HARBOUR MASTER.

'What's happening?' She kept her voice low, so she could be ignored if necessary. She didn't want to be a nuisance.

'Our engine's failed and we're taking on water,' Holly answered. 'This is the harbour master for the Isles of Scilly. He's going to tow us.'

'Where's Craig?' Cheryl asked. She'd already ascertained that there was no sign of the tall, handsome ex-fireman. Or the skipper come to that. Maybe they were on the other boat.

She became conscious of a stillness among the women.

'We're not sure,' Holly said, after a moment. 'But there's a search going on for them. With a bit of luck, they'll be picked up.'

It took a few minutes, of hesitant questions on her side, and incomplete and unsatisfying explanations from the others, but finally Cheryl understood. Sometime in the night, Craig and Thomas had vanished, had probably fallen overboard, and with that knowledge, all Cheryl's doubts of the night came flooding back. She looked from one face to another, as Robin and Tug returned, waiting for one of them to say what she'd spent most of the night mulling over.

This has happened before!

The harbour master fired up his engines, ropes connecting the two boats pulled tight and they began to move.

It was obvious, wasn't it? Why had no one else realised?

'I've thought of something,' she said, hesitantly.

'What's the plan now,' Sabri asked, in a much louder voice.

'The authorities at St Mary's will want to talk to us,' Tug replied. 'We have two missing crew. They'll want to know what happened.'

I want to know what happened, Cheryl thought. Two people have gone overboard, and no one told me. Am I really that unimportant?

'We can't go to St Mary's,' Holly snapped. 'We don't have time.'

'I thought they'd take us onto their boat,' Tara said. 'We've at least two inches of water below.'

No one had warned Cheryl about that either. Had they all forgotten she was onboard? Besides, she hadn't eaten in hours and was hungry. But how could she ask for food when everyone was ignoring her? They'd tell her to go back down and find it for herself, and she didn't think she could face walking through that water again.

'This is still a pretty big sea to get people from one boat to another.' Tug squeezed himself onto the seat next to Sabri, pushing Cheryl against the cabin wall. 'We're safer here as long as we're afloat.'

'We can't go to St Mary's,' Holly repeated. 'Tug, talk to them. Tell them.'

Tug had positioned himself to be directly opposite Tara, who really didn't look like she'd spent a rough night. She'd even managed to comb her hair and rebraid it into a neat plait.

'How long will they keep us?' Tara shot a sympathetic glance Holly's way. 'The authorities, I mean.'

Tug frowned. 'Hard to say.'

He hadn't even acknowledged Cheryl's arrival on deck; neither had Robin, come to that.

'I've thought of something,' she repeated.

'We have to get to St Helen's,' Holly insisted.

'Things have changed, Holly,' Sabri said. 'We lost two people last night. And this boat isn't seaworthy. It's time to talk to the police. They'll send someone to get Charlie.'

Holly gave a frantic look around the group. 'No, we can't risk it. Quick has a helicopter. And high-speed boats. He won't let the police get anywhere near him.'

Sabri said, 'You're not thinking straight, Holly. I'd be the same, in your shoes, but you're in no state to make decisions.'

'Don't you dare—'

'She's right, love,' Tug jumped in. 'I didn't want to say anything, but this boat has been sabotaged. The engine's been tampered with, and the flooding is deliberate. We might never know what happened to Craig and Thomas, but we can't rule out foul play.'

Tears filled Holly's eyes. 'He's ten years old. He's still a baby. We can't just leave him.'

Tara grabbed Holly's hand. 'We won't. I promise you we won't. But it's beyond our control now.'

Cheryl wasn't going to say anything, she decided. She'd probably got it all wrong. And if they weren't going to St Helen's now, it didn't matter anymore, did it?

Chapter 81

'Rob, got a sec?'

Robin opened his eyes. The steady hum of the harbour master's engine had been surprisingly soporific, lulling him into a state that was more asleep than awake.

Tug, who'd summoned him, was at the front of the boat, one arm wrapped around the furled sail. Around his neck hung a set of binoculars and another instrument Robin didn't recognise.

Climbing onto the side deck, he grabbed the guard rail with one hand. The boat might be upright now, thank the lord and his host of blessed angels, but it was still dancing around like a dervish.

'Harness, please, Robin.'

Tara, who he'd decided he liked a lot, might even have fancied had there been room in his head for any woman other than Jax, seemed to have appointed herself safety officer, not letting any of them leave the cockpit without being fastened to the boat. Even Tug went along with it. Humouring her, and because the last few hours had given him a new respect for personal safety, Robin wrapped his lifeline around the jackstay, the unbreakable strip of webbing that ran the length of each deck. It was another nautical term he'd learned in the last few hours. Secured, he made his way towards Tug.

'What's up, mate?' he asked.

'I don't want to worry the girls.' Tug's voice was just loud enough to carry above the harbour master's engine.

Robin glanced back. Sabri was on the helm, her face screwed up with concentration as she battled to stay directly behind the harbour master. Neither Cheryl nor Tara could be seen; both were tucked beneath the spray hood, one on each side of the boat. Holly sat next to Cheryl, staring out at the ocean.

'OK, well, you've worried me,' Robin said.

'I've been trying to attract their attention for a good fifteen minutes.' Tug indicated the vessel in front, where neither harbour master nor his first mate were visible.

'When you're towing, someone on board keeps a constant lookout to make sure nothing's going wrong,' Tug went on. 'No one has looked at us once. A harbour master should know better.'

Robin thought he'd have stayed in the cabin too, given the choice. The wind was biting and, while the storm had subsided, it had left behind some big waves. A flurry of water, droplets hard and biting as hail, flew at his face.

'Have you tried yelling?' he asked, after he'd spat the salt from his mouth.

'They won't hear us. I've got the ship's foghorn in my pocket but, like I said, I don't want to worry the girls.'

The big guy was bothered, though, it was obvious from the grim set of his face, and the way he didn't take his eyes from the vessel in front. Given what they'd been through the last few hours, and the fact that Tug's seamanship alone had prevented disaster, he should be celebrating their rescue with a bottle of naval rum and a few sea shanties. Not stressing out like this.

Knowing there was worse to come, Robin said, 'So, what's the problem? Why do you need to talk to them?'

'I've been trying to work out where we are,' Tug replied. 'Bloody difficult with no instruments and no charts, but if there was a plan to sabotage us last night, they forgot to take the binoculars and the hand-held compass. Maybe they didn't realise we had someone on board who knew how to use them.'

Tug pointed over the starboard side of the boat, to where Robin could just about make out breaking surf and something low-lying in the sea. 'I think those are the Western Rocks.' He handed over the binoculars.

'The Gilstone is distinctive,' Tug went on, as Robin didn't like to admit he couldn't see a thing. 'And the Bishop Rock lighthouse is directly ahead.'

Adjust the focus. These round twisty things might do it. Robin tried moving one and the sea became visible.

'There are six lighthouses around Scilly and no two are the same,' Tug was saying, as Robin found a cluster of low, wet rocks. 'Bishop marks the most westerly edge of the islands. They built it after a storm when nearly two thousand men were lost. This isn't a good place to be in a yacht with a deep keel.'

Great, more good news. Having found the Gilstone, Robin refocused on a white tower built onto a low-lying rock. It was maybe a half-mile away but the sea, he'd learned, was deceptive when it came to distances.

'Plus, the sun's almost directly behind us,' Tug said.

Robin lowered the binoculars, a new sense of unease creeping over him. 'So, what does all that mean?'

Tug took a moment before replying. 'It means they're not taking us to St Mary's.'

Chapter 82

It was a relief to say it out loud, Tug realised, to give voice to the insidious fear that had been niggling him almost from the moment they went under tow.

'Where then?' Robin said, after a moment. 'If you're right, which way are we heading and what's in front?'

The bloke might look and dress like an extra from *Pirates of the Caribbean*, but he didn't go in for dramatics and, for that, Tug was grateful.

'We're heading north and nothing.' Tug used his head to indicate the starboard side of the boat. 'The islands are over there. We wouldn't have come this far west if we were going to St Mary's.'

Again, that biting feeling that something was very wrong. Their present course made no sense. Come to think of it, this ill-advised trip had been wrong from the bloody start. Tug told himself to breathe, that he had four women and Captain Jack Sparrow to take care of. He had to keep his shit together.

'Did they actually say that's where they're taking us?' Robin asked.

It was a good question, and Tug had to admit they hadn't. The focus of the harbour master, once he'd come alongside, had been on checking the number of people on board *Gemini*, their state of health, the seaworthiness of the yacht and what they could remember about the events of the night. After that, they'd had the tricky task of securing a tow. They'd set off without further discussion and Tug had assumed their destination. Something else he really shouldn't have done.

There it was again, that nagging feeling that he was missing something, that if he could only see what was staring him in the face, all this might start to make some sense.

'There's no point taking us anywhere else,' he said. 'St Mary's is the administrative centre. It has the airport and the ferry terminal. Police station. Hospital. These guys will be based there.'

'I'd go with the foghorn,' Robin said. 'If they ignore that, we'll know something's up.'

A gull flew low, screeching above their heads. To Tug, it sounded like the bloody bird was telling him to do something. What, though? What was it he was supposed to do? What was he supposed to see?

'The girls will be cool,' Robin went on. 'None of them go in for hysterics.'

Tug took the foghorn out of his pocket, released the handlebar and pressed down. The deep, sonorous boom rang out across the waves.

'Just making a phone call,' Robin yelled back at the cockpit.

Tug kept his eyes on the boat ahead. Nothing. No sign of life in the harbour master's cabin and they were drawing close to the Bishop lighthouse. Ahead, if his memory served, were the Crim Rocks. Over thirty ships had been lost on those bastards.

He sounded the horn again. Again, nothing. There was no way they hadn't heard it. The heavy sigh seemed to deflate his whole body.

So, it wasn't over, after all. Somehow, he'd known it wouldn't be.

When the yacht had been under tow for over an hour, when all his attempts to attract the attention of the harbour master's boat had failed and when they'd reached the point at which there was nothing ahead, Tug realised he had to cut *Gemini* loose. He'd have done it already, but he'd made the mistake – or possibly had the good sense, he wasn't sure – of telling Robin his plans and Robin had insisted on consulting the others.

'I'm not sure we can trust these guys,' Tug explained. 'They won't respond, and we're heading into the Atlantic. The further we get from the islands, the more trouble we'll be in when the weather gets up again.'

He pointed over the port side, to where clouds were gathering in the western sky. 'That's another front coming in,' he said. 'Sometime in the next few hours, the winds will get up again. We could see another storm like the one we had to deal with last night. And that's with a severely damaged boat that's letting in water.'

The responses were exactly what he'd predicted.

That's the harbour master, he must know what he's doing. Of course they're taking us to safety, why would they not? We've no engine, no instruments, how can we manage without them?

This. This was why the navy had clear lines of command.

'We still have sails,' he argued. 'In daylight, and with calm conditions, there's a good chance I can get us to one of the islands. I'm not guaranteeing it, but I think we'd stand a better chance than we would in the Atlantic with another storm.'

'Let's take a vote,' Sabri suggested, as he'd known she would. 'Hands up those who agree with Tug.'

A moment, when no one moved, when all eyes danced from one face to the next. Then Holly's hand went up, followed a second later by Tara's. Tug looked at Robin, who wouldn't meet his eyes. So much for brotherly solidarity.

'Three against three,' Sabri said. 'So we stick with the status quo.'

Robin's hand went up. 'Sorry, ladies,' he said to Sabri and then Cheryl. 'There's something very odd going on. I think we're better off relying on ourselves.'

It was done and Tug had to hope he'd finally got something right. 'I'll untie the rope,' he announced. 'I'm not sure how they'll react, so be prepared for some evasive manoeuvres. Rob, we'll need to get the main up right away. Sabri, hold her steady. I'll take the helm as soon as we're free.'

'Tug, I think we're turning round,' Cheryl said.

Sure enough, the harbour master had come hard to starboard. Sabri, caught up in the conversation, hadn't noticed, but now the line was dragging their bow around too. Tug stepped up onto the side deck. 'Follow her round, Sabri. We've no choice but to stay behind her while we're attached. I'll see if I can find out what's happening.'

Ignoring Tara's pleas to harness on, Tug strode up to the bow. The harbour master had performed a ninety-degree turn; they were heading directly east now. Tug raised his binoculars and saw another gleaming white tower on a rounded lump of rock.

'What's happening?' Robin was right behind him.

'Round Island lighthouse directly ahead,' Tug told him.

'We're not making for the Atlantic anymore?'

'No, we're not.'

'Where then?'

'I think they're taking us to St Helen's.'

Chapter 83

Sometime in the night, Sabri had started biting her nails again, a habit she'd broken years ago. Her insides were an odd combination of achingly empty and a breath away from throwing up. Her lips were chapped, every joint in her body ached and she couldn't stop reaching into her pocket for her missing phone.

Meanwhile, land was getting closer: a small, low-lying island that might or might not be St Helen's.

'Out of interest,' said Tug, who was sitting with all the others in the cockpit. 'Did anyone bring their token along for the ride?'

Sabri, who was still on the helm, could distinguish rocks from grass on the approaching island, even see the odd stumpy, twisted tree.

'Not me,' Robin was the first to reply. 'Didn't want to risk it.'

'Me neither,' Cheryl said. 'It's under a loose floorboard in my bedroom.'

'Not sure you should have told us that,' Tug said, but Sabri could tell from the tone of his voice that he was smiling. 'Don't worry,' he went on. 'None of us has a phone. Even if we wanted to nick it, there's nothing we can do while we're all the way out here.'

'I'm not worried,' Cheryl replied. 'I trust you all.'

As the conversation in the cockpit continued, Sabri made an effort to tune it out. The urge, almost the need, to speak to her family was verging on painful. They phoned each other. It was what they did. Several times a day she heard from her kids, the girls almost every school break, even Darren texted the odd personal triumph: a goal scored, a test mark above sixty per cent. Jason called at least twice during the day, invariably when it was least convenient, but she knew she was never going to resent that again. He texted her at night too, on the rare occasions they slept apart: sweet, erotic messages about how much he was missing her.

She really should be nicer to Holly, she told herself. Charlie was all the poor girl had.

'Mine's where no one will think of looking,' Tara said. 'Especially not my tosser of an ex-husband. How about you, Sabri? Still keeping it close?'

It took Sabri a second to realise she was being spoken to. 'No, it's at home,' she lied. 'Jason's parents have a safe.'

'Holly?' Tara said. 'Tug?'

Sabri turned to see both Tug and Holly shake their heads. No one else, it seemed, had risked bringing their token with them. She ran a hand over her right breast, felt the now-familiar shape pressing and knew she'd toss it into the ocean if it meant she could miraculously be back with her family, with none of this ever having happened.

She'd never, since Maddy had first had a phone, gone so long without hearing from them and now anything could have happened: another break-in at the house, an accident with that ridiculous gun, one of the kids taken like poor Charlie. She should never have left.

On the island, a long strip of beach had come into view, topped by grassland the colour of an emerald.

'What do you think?' she asked Tug, who'd come to stand directly behind her. 'Is it St Helen's?'

'See that ruin?' he replied. 'That's the pest house.'

Sabri had seen no ruins, no buildings in any state of repair, but staring now at the patch of island Tug was pointing out, there seemed to be a regularity about some of the rocks. An assemblance that wasn't entirely natural.

'Camped in it once,' he told her. 'On an exercise. Back in my navy days. I wasn't much more than a kid.'

'You were in the navy?' Special forces, Tara had said. Sabri had assumed that meant SAS.

Tug's eyes narrowed. 'Is that a problem?'

She was on board a boat, in bad weather, with a naval man. Again.

'Sabri?' He was looking at her oddly.

'What's a pest house?' asked Cheryl.

A naval man, a blonde nurse, a fat barmaid? Was it possible?

'Long time ago, ships heading for England sometimes had the plague on board,' Tug was saying. 'They anchored here and the sick were taken ashore. The pest house was an isolation hospital.'

Sabri looked from one face to the other: Robin, Tara, Tug, Cheryl. It had been decades. Had they even exchanged names? And people changed so much.

'It wasn't the cosiest place to spend the night,' Tug went on. 'We were glad to leave it next morning.'

Sabri felt her legs give way beneath her and she landed hard on the helm's seat. One night, when her whole life had changed. Reeling in the aftermath, consumed by guilt and haunted by nightmares, she'd failed her third-year exams and there'd been no money to re-sit. All her plans had come to a crashing end that night.

'Before we came, I looked up Logan Quick's relationship with the Scillies.' The new voice came from Holly, the first time she'd spoken in ages. 'St Helen's was uninhabited for a long time, but Quick did a deal with the Duchy of Cornwall to lease the island and build his own luxury home.'

'Guys,' Sabri began. *I think I know what this is all about.*

'I can see something.' Robin, standing on the side deck, holding tight to the spray hood, was at the highest point of the boat. 'It's modern, quite fancy,' he went on. 'It could be a house.'

I know what's going on here and it's really not good.

The towed yacht passed another small headland and ahead a pontoon had become visible, stretching out across the water. It was pale, weed free, in perfect repair. Moored to it were a black, high-performance RIB and a fancy motorboat. Beyond, a familiar fair-haired woman stood on shore, watching them approach. Next to her stood a young boy.

Holly gave a high, thin cry and got to her feet. She raised her hand above her head. On the shore, the boy waved in response and set out for the pontoon. The woman grabbed his shoulder, holding him back.

The harbour master cut his engines and the sudden quiet was startling. Then the cabin door opened and the man himself emerged.

'We'll moor you up to one of the buoys here,' he called back at them. 'The bay's too shallow to get the yacht much further. We'll ferry you to the island once you're secure. Have you got another line? And a boat hook?'

For a moment, no one on *Gemini* moved.

'Give us a minute, mate,' Tug called over the water before turning to the others. 'Holly, is that Charlie?'

Without taking her eyes off her son, Holly nodded.

'Right,' Tug went on. 'In that case, I suggest we wait till we're all safely on land and Charlie is back with us before we ask these guys what the hell they think they're playing at.'

Say something, Sabri told herself. Say something now.

'Robin,' she heard Cheryl say, in that rather annoying, little-girl voice of hers that could barely carry from one side of the cockpit to the other. 'I don't have a good feeling about this.'

Sabri turned to the other woman in time to see Robin drop an arm around her shoulders.

'No one does, love,' he replied. 'But getting off this boat and reuniting Charlie with his mum feels like a priority to me.'

When Cheryl didn't look convinced, he added, 'We'll be OK if we stick together.'

'Touch to starboard,' Tug called back to Sabri. 'Bit more.'

The mooring was managed smoothly. Tug leaned over the side of the yacht and caught the loop of the buoy with the boat hook. Seconds later they were secure.

'Prepare to abandon ship,' he called back. 'Get your stuff together, folks. Try not to leave anything behind.'

It was the work of moments to get their kit on deck. Robin went below and he'd soon handed everything up. The harbour master came alongside and, when the two boats were tied together, he stepped aboard. He was a grey-haired man in his mid- to late fifties, with a beard and a beer belly.

'We thought we were going to St Mary's.' Sabri hoped she sounded annoyed and not scared. 'Where is this and why are we here?'

The official seemed to gain an inch in height. 'Mr Quick alerted us to your difficulties early this morning.' Ignoring Sabri, he addressed himself to Tug, with occasional glances at Robin. 'He explained that you are his guests, and that the yacht you're travelling on belongs to him. He asked that we bring you here.'

'Well, that's news—' Tug began.

'Charlie!' Holly called across the water. 'Are you OK?'

'Mum!' the lad yelled back. He looked fine to Sabri, and it was obvious that all Holly could think about was getting to him. All the same . . . they'd been on Quick's boat all along?

'I believe Mr Quick is waiting for you up at the house,' the harbour master went on. 'The lady by the pontoon is a member of his staff.'

No, this was all wrong.

Tara spoke up. 'Two members of our crew went overboard last night. A man called Craig Lewis and the boat's skipper, Thomas Williams.'

Tara, unlike Sabri, seemed worthy of the harbour master's attention. 'Yes, yes, you told me that already. The alert has gone out.'

'Well, that's funny, because we haven't seen any rescue helicopters,' Sabri argued. 'And I don't know about anyone else, but I want to go to St Mary's so that I can get a plane home.'

'Me too,' Holly said. 'Just as soon as my son is on board.'

'I have other business to attend to.' The harbour master climbed onto the side deck, ready to go back to his own boat. 'But I'm sure Mr Quick will see you safely to St Mary's. Now, we really need to get you off this boat. Perhaps the ladies first?'

One by one, they crossed to the harbour master's vessel. Holly went first, followed by Tara, Sabri and then, with difficulty, Cheryl. Robin and Tug practically had to lift her over the rails. Tug was last to step onto the harbour master's vessel and then the lines were slipped and the motorboat took them to the pontoon. As they all climbed down onto the unsteady platform, as Holly raced towards her son, Sabri saw another figure emerge from beyond the sand dunes.

'Tug,' she said. 'Look, it's the skipper.'

Some fifty metres or so from the end of the pontoon stood their erstwhile skipper, Thomas. As Tug set off at a run, sending the pontoon swaying dangerously beneath his weight, Sabri heard the harbour master's boat roaring away.

Chapter 84

Tug had reached the end of the pontoon when Tara caught up with him and grabbed his hand. 'I know what you're planning and it's not a good idea,' she said.

Behind them, probably a result of their sprint along it, the floating wooden platform was rocking from side to side. An alarmed squeal told Tug that Cheryl, at least, was finding it hard to stay upright. He raised his hand to shake Tara's off.

'What am I planning?' he asked, unnecessarily. He knew exactly what he was going to do.

She clung on. 'You're going to clock him one, and I don't blame you. I'd do it myself, but frankly, I'm more scared than I've ever been in my life before and we have a child to think about.'

She was wrong. He wasn't going to clock him one. He was going to throttle the bastard right here on the foreshore. Tug took a deep breath.

She was right too. He looked over at where the others, all safely on shore now, had gathered around Holly and her son. The kid had leapt onto his mother, legs around her waist, arms clinging to her like a baby monkey. She'd buried her face into his neck.

'How did he do it?' Tara was still holding his hand. 'Could someone have spotted him in the water and picked him up?'

No, that, Tug would put money on, was impossible.

'He must have had a boat following us.' Tug was thinking out loud. 'One without lights, staying far enough back that we wouldn't hear the engine. Probably that RIB. Maybe a transmitter on his life jacket that made it easier to find him in the dark. Doesn't really matter how, though, does it? Question is, why.'

'This is really weird, Tug,' Tara said. 'We need to be very careful.'

She was still right. He gave her a quick nod, turned round to share what he hoped was an encouraging smile with the others and set off again. At a measured pace this time. Still holding her hand.

'Welcome to St Helen's,' the woman who'd been waiting for them called as they approached. 'And nice to see you all again. I'm Mr Quick's housekeeper. He's been looking forward to your visit.'

As Tug stepped off the pontoon he glanced into the RIB. A ten-seater, twin engines. It would get them all back to St Mary's in no time.

The realisation hit him like a blow to the stomach, one that took every breath he had. A stolen RIB? Oh, Jesus fucking wept. Was that what this was all about?

'Tug?' Tara was looking at him strangely and he realised the others had formed a single file behind him. They were waiting for him to lead them, but for the moment he couldn't move. The gorgeous blonde nurse, the skinny brown girl, the plump one. Oh Christ, how stupid had he been? But it had all been so long ago.

'Tara,' he said. 'Did you go to a music festival in Newton Ferrers? Thirty years ago? Bad storm came in on the last day.'

Tara's eyes opened wide with horror, telling him everything he needed to know.

And it was still no excuse. No fucking excuse. He let go of Tara's hand. Striding ahead, he walked right up to Thomas and looked him straight in the face. 'Four women and a kid,' he said in a low voice. 'You must be very fucking proud of yourself.'

Thomas stiffened, as though bracing himself for a blow. Then he stepped back, out of range of Tug's fist. Smart guy.

'Follow me,' he said. It was not an invitation.

Tug took a quick look back. The others were all pale but holding it together. The woman, Quick's housekeeper, waited at the rear like a guard, making sure none of them went astray, and he wondered if she'd been the driver of the RIB the previous night.

Thomas led them across a narrow stretch of marram-grass-strewn beach, over the dunes and then through gardens in which an attempt at landscaping had largely failed; the outlook was too exposed. With every step they could see more of a huge, glass-fronted house. Built of cedar and glass panels, it was three storeys high. Most of the upper two floors had been used to create a massive living space. Internal lights revealed ceiling beams, lounge furniture and colourful works of modern art. Tug counted three balconies, a terrace, an outdoor jacuzzi.

'Bit like your place,' he said to Tara, and knew he was using a weak joke to hide how nervous he was.

She gave a low, dismissive laugh. 'I haven't got round to the landing pad yet.'

Tug followed her gaze to where an AgustaWestland, gleaming white, sat in a circle of concrete about fifty metres from the house. From memory, he thought it was a five-seater, not big enough to get them all back to the mainland. Not that he was getting in a chopper that had anything to do with Logan Quick.

Thomas, staying always a fraction too far ahead to allow for conversation, led them round the side of the house and inside.

'It's an awesome place,' Charlie whispered, when they'd all crossed the threshold, and the housekeeper had closed the door behind them. 'I'm glad you're here, though, Mum.'

He walked as though glued to his mother, one arm wrapped around her waist; Holly didn't look as though she was ever letting go of her son again.

They were in a vast, white space of marble floors, white walls and a sweeping wooden staircase. Without stopping, Thomas led them further into the house, opening the door to a sitting room in more shades of neutrals: charcoal sofas, rugs patterned in a dozen or more shades of pale grey and ash wood furniture. Tall windows overlooked the ocean. Thomas didn't enter, instead gesturing to Tug and the others to go in.

We've come this far, Tug thought. And it's only a room.

In the centre of the space, the focus of several armchairs and sofas, a circular wine cabinet had been cut into the marble floor and topped with reinforced glass. It was possible to stand on top of wine that Tug knew would be worth more than he'd ever earned in his life.

'Please sit down.' The housekeeper, like Thomas, was hovering close to the doorway. Tug was pleased that no one obeyed her. Instead, they formed a group in the centre of the room, almost a defensive circle, with Charlie and Holly in the middle. Tug fixed his eyes on Thomas.

'Are you Logan Quick?' he asked.

'No,' said a familiar voice from behind them. 'I am.'

They turned, to see that their former shipmate, Craig Lewis, had entered through another door.

Chapter 85

Holly watched the man, whom she now had to learn to call Logan Quick, walk across the room and lower himself into an armchair. He looked different. Not, like Thomas, as though nothing out of the ordinary had happened; more like the rest of them, scared and exhausted after a terrifying night.

He frowned, as though with sudden pain, and said, 'I expect you have some questions.'

Too fucking right she had questions. Charlie, though, beat her to it.

'What are you going to do to us now?'

Hearing the fear in her son's voice, knowing he was trying hard to hide it, Holly began looking around the room again, this time for possible weapons. Quick was going to die if he threatened her son again. The bastard, meanwhile, was smiling at Charlie.

'To you?' he said. 'Nothing. Why don't you go and see if Lauren will make you some hot chocolate? While I talk to your mum and the others.'

Holly glanced round to see that both the housekeeper and Thomas had quietly left the room.

'He's staying with me.' Holly put a hand on her son's shoulder, as Tug stepped in front of them both.

'This is nothing to do with Holly or the kid,' he said to Quick. 'Let me phone for a motor taxi to get them back to St Mary's.'

Holly felt as though her brain, normally so agile, was working in slow motion. Tug was in on this after all? She tried to catch his eye, but he wasn't looking away from Quick. Did the others know too? Could she trust any of them?

Quick said, 'Please sit down. You must all be tired, after a night like that.'

For a second no one moved, then Cheryl flopped onto one of the sofas as though her legs wouldn't hold her up anymore. Her plump face trembled and turned pink; she was trying hard not to cry. Robin walked round the back of the sofa and patted her shoulder.

Holly lost it.

'What the hell did you do?' It was bloody satisfying to see Quick flinch. 'You sent me below to look at some frigging instruments and when I got back on deck you'd gone. You could have killed all of us and I don't care how rich you are, you sick, twisted shit, you're going away for this. For a very long time.'

'No, he isn't.' Sabri stepped to Holly's other side, letting her hand settle gently on Holly's waist. Then she beckoned Tara forward too. 'He's dying. Come and look at him. He's got nothing to lose.'

As Tara joined them, Holly let herself look properly at Logan Quick. There was a dull sheen to his skin that she hadn't noticed before and he was breathing heavily. Also, without the smart jackets Craig had always worn, he looked very thin.

'Pancreatic cancer,' Tug said. 'So that bit was true? You've got less than a year to live?'

'Not even that.' Tara kept her voice low, as though she was back on a hospital ward; she almost sounded sympathetic. 'I've worked in oncology. And done end-of-life care. You've got weeks, haven't you, Mr Quick?'

Good. Holly was glad the bastard was dying. It would save her the trouble.

'I don't care how long you've got,' she spat at him. 'I'd kill you now myself for taking my son and not lose a second's sleep. And what the hell were you thinking last night? You could have killed us all.'

'Oh, you were supposed to die, Holly,' Quick said.

Robin was still behind Cheryl. 'That was the plan all along,' he said. 'He lured us out here on a rescue mission and left us on a crippled boat in the middle of a storm. I guess he underestimated Tug.'

Someone else who knew more than she did. Holly looked from one face to the other, from Tug to Tara, Robin to Sabri, to Cheryl. No surprise anywhere. Not a single questioning expression, except on Charlie's face. They all knew, and she was suddenly more frightened than she'd been the past two days.

'Why?' She drew Charlie even closer. The fact that he didn't object, that he was scared too, almost broke her. 'What have we ever done to this man? We'd never met him before last week.'

Silence. The only person in the room who would meet her eyes was the monster she'd have to stop thinking of as Craig. He gave her a tight smile.

'Actually,' he said, 'the others and I have met before.'

Chapter 86

So, this is what happened . . .

On the last Sunday in September, thirty years earlier, atmospheric pressure dropped sharply over the Atlantic Ocean. The resulting depression made landfall on the southwest coast of Cornwall around four o'clock in the afternoon, and heavy rain tagged along as a sort of meteorological plus one.

Folk along that stretch of the Cornish coast were used to storms, and so no one, especially in the small village of Newton Ferrers, gave it much thought. Most locals were relieved, knowing it would bring to an end, sooner than planned, the three-day music festival that none of them had wanted, and from which even fewer had benefited. Even when a tree came down, blocking the only road out of the village, they remained sanguine. It happened. It would be a nuisance for a while, but the council would have it shifted, probably before lunchtime the next day, and if a few people couldn't get to work, well, no one was going to worry too much about that. The downside, of course, because there's always a downside, is that those members of the great unwashed who hadn't yet been collected by parents or taken an early bus were stuck with nowhere to go but the local pub and nothing to do but drink.

Most of them, it seemed to the landlord of the Dolphin Inn, had done little but drink for the previous three days, and while he wasn't complaining about that, he knew he and the small village were about to have a problem. For one thing, provisions were running out; they'd stocked up for the three days of the festival and no longer. On top of that, the few hotels and B&Bs were full, meaning several dozen kids, who, let's face it, never planned for rough weather, would be facing a night outside with nowhere to shelter but their own pitiful tents and the festival marquee. Which, given the winds forecast, really needed to come down before the evening was out.

For the moment, it seemed all said youngsters were in the pub, crowded around tables, pressed up against the bar, even slumped on the floor. Their damp clothes steamed, and they smelled of body odour, stale booze and cannabis. More than one had been sick in the toilets. The landlord had been advised already to throw them all out, but it was pissing down, and he couldn't bring himself to do it. He carried on serving as the unease in his gut grew alongside the takings. The stage was set for what he always thought of as an 'unfortunate incident'.

And so, when a large bloke climbed onto a table and called for attention, the landlord exchanged nervous glances with his wife. He didn't like the look of the chap, now towering above everyone else in the room. At around six foot two and weighing a good sixteen stone, the man had an air of combat about him. Nothing about his clothes suggested the military as such, but his buzz cut, the bulk of his shoulders and his wide-legged, chest-thrust-out stance all screamed that this man, who couldn't be more than early twenties, could handle himself.

'Can I have your attention, please?' he called, in a voice that matched his stature. 'I'm a seaman in the Royal Navy and I need to get back to my barracks at Poole by zero five hundred hours tomorrow morning.'

As the landlord silently congratulated himself on being right about the man's background, the room fell silent.

'If I can get back to Plymouth tonight, I can get a late train or hitch,' the young naval man went on. 'So, if anyone is taking a boat round to Plymouth, I'd be very grateful for a lift. I can contribute towards diesel costs.'

The silence continued. The table wobbled and the seaman struggled to keep his balance. A glass fell over.

'I need you to get down, son.' The landlord found his courage. 'To be honest, I think you'll be lucky. There's a strong spring tide out there and some heavy winds in the bay. I think most boats are settled in for the night.'

Beaten, for the moment, the naval man put a hand on a convenient shoulder and climbed down.

The landlord felt someone squeezing past and looked down to see a young woman he'd been surreptitiously watching. She was blonde, her hair long and shining. Her face was classically beautiful, her body rounded but strong. She was a woman you could have a good time with without worrying she might break. She moved towards the naval man and his face softened at the sight of her. The landlord edged closer.

'I need to get back too,' she said. She was West Country, like the naval man, but what the landlord always thought of as posh Cornish. 'I'm a nurse. I'm on duty at six in the morning.'

The landlord felt a moment of regret that the roads were blocked; he might have offered to drive her round.

'I was thinking,' she went on, while the sailor was still just taking her in. 'That two of us might make it worth someone's while. Say, twenty pounds each?'

Behind them a throat cleared. 'I have an exam in the morning,' another female voice said. 'Can I tag along?'

The newcomer was a slim, brown-skinned girl of around twenty-two, tall and unusually thin. Her face was angular, her nose prominent, her black hair neither straight nor curly but falling to her shoulders in a series of kinks. She looked first at the seaman, then the blonde nurse. 'Unless the two of you want to be alone,' she added.

'Don't matter how many of you are on the early shift. You'll not find anyone to drive round Plymouth this time of night.'

The naysayer was a local, a man in his mid-sixties called Ken, who sat down at one of the pub tables once a year on his wife's birthday. Every other night he came in, which was most nights, he rested his forearm on his own spot at the bar, which the sleeve of his sweater kept polished to a shine. On his way home now, he had a big waterproof coat pulled up over his considerable girth.

'Excuse me, can I join you?' said a timid voice, female, with a strong Cornish accent. It belonged to a girl of around nineteen, at least twenty pounds overweight and with bad skin. The landlord recognised her as one of the barmaids from the beer tent. Strictly, they'd been his employees, because he'd supplied the drink for the festival, but the marquee staff had all come from a local agency. He had a feeling her name was Cheryl.

'Twenty pounds sounds like a lot but I need to get back.' She glanced at the brown-skinned girl. 'My mum's expecting me.'

'No one's going anywhere if we can't find a boat,' the blonde pointed out.

The naval man pulled up the collar of his coat. 'OK, girls. I reckon most of the yachties are at the river. I suggest we go down there, commandeer a dingy and pay a few house calls. We're offering eighty quid between us. Someone will take us round.'

'Hundred quid sounds better,' said a lad with dark, curly hair, who'd been edging closer to the group. 'There's nowhere to sleep here apart from that marquee and I don't fancy its chances if the wind gets up anymore.'

'Hundred and twenty?' offered another kid of a similar age. This one was big too, although not quite as large as the naval man. Another one who could handle himself. Possibly even another service man, judging by his tightly cropped brown hair. He held out a hand towards the blonde girl.

'Nice to meet you all,' he said, as he moved closer to her than seemed appropriate, even to the landlord. 'I'm—'

'Yeah, let's do social pleasantries at Plymouth,' the naval man snapped. 'Come on, if we're going, it'll be dark soon.'

The landlord watched the six young people make their way out into the storm and had a feeling he'd be seeing them all again before the evening was out. No one would be stupid enough to take a boat round to Plymouth tonight.

On her way back from the ladies, Shelley finally acknowledged that she was in trouble. Three days ago, the heavy sensation in her abdomen had been an ache, now it was pain, comparable to some of the worst menstrual cramps she'd ever known. She'd been fighting off nausea since they'd arrived in Newton Ferrers but that she'd put down to the food. The headache, which had grown steadily worse, she'd blamed on the music. The blood in her knickers, though. That wasn't something she could explain away. Nor the fact that she was finding it increasingly difficult to see properly.

'I'm not feeling great,' she said, when she got back to the table where her boyfriend was getting to the end of his pint. She wasn't sure how many he'd drunk that day but was pretty sure he'd reached double figures. 'I think I need to get to hospital.'

The three young men fell into step as they left the Dolphin, striding ahead of the girls. The creek was running high now, awash with waves that bounced and danced in the wind. When they rounded the first corner, a mini tornado of leaves hit them full in the face. The naval man, whose name was Trevor, but who'd been renamed Tug on account of his size, was wondering if he'd been wise letting the others tag along. None of them looked sober and he certainly wasn't. How likely was it a yachtsman would agree to take six drunk kids on his boat on a night like this? Plus, he'd already decided he didn't like the bloke with the crew cut.

'You services, mate?' he asked him.

'Fire and Rescue,' came the response.

Figured. Real services rejects who spent ninety per cent of their time with their feet up in the staff room.

'When you said, commandeer a dingy,' the curly-haired lad began, 'did you mean . . .'

'Nick one? Yeah,' Tug grunted. 'Serve the bastards right for being so bloody unhelpful.'

The fireman said, 'We'll get in trouble for stealing a dingy.'

If the weather hadn't been so appalling, Tug might have laughed. Whichever way he looked trouble was staring him in the face. Why the fuck hadn't he left earlier?

'We're not going to take it out of the harbour,' he replied. 'We're just moving it from the town pontoon to one of the floating ones. Maybe a mooring buoy. Technically it's probably not even stealing.'

'Technically, I think it is.' The brown-skinned girl, with longer legs than the other two, had caught up with the boys.

'You a lawyer?' Tug asked.

'Nope.' Both were shouting to be heard above the wind.

Tug looked her full in the face. 'Got a problem with commandeering a dingy?' If she had, she was off the team, simple as that.

'Not really,' she replied. 'I'll say you told us it was yours.'

Tug found himself grinning. 'I like you. What did you say your name was?'

She raised heavy black eyebrows. 'I didn't.'

His grin held. 'We stay anonymous as we commit a felony. I like your style.'

A few yards back, the other two girls were struggling to talk as rain lashed into their faces. 'Do you think we're doing the right thing?' the plump one asked the blonde, whose name was Tara.

'Depends how much you want to get back to Plymouth,' Tara replied. She'd been asking herself that same question since they'd left the pub. The boy who'd joined them at the last minute had been eyeing her up for most of the weekend. He was a serious lech and the drunker he'd got, the less he'd tried to hide it. She had a feeling he'd only asked to come along because of her.

The plump girl said, 'I've never been on a boat before.'

Tara turned to her in surprise. 'Really?'

'Well, there were some row boats in the park when I was growing up. My dad used to take me on them when I was little. This won't be the same, though, will it?'

Tara looked over the thin line of trees to the river. The few boats she could see were pulling at their mooring lines like tethered animals. 'No,' she said, 'this won't be the same.'

★

The pontoon rocked as the group made their way to where dozens of small dinghies and rowing boats were tied up. The fireman, whose name was Craig, glanced back at the blonde girl, but she kept her eyes on the swaying wooden platform.

'Which do you fancy, girls?' the big bloke called back.

'How about the one with a kill cord attached?' Craig snapped. If this twat thought an outboard engine would start without one, he'd been lying through his back teeth about being in the navy.

The bloke squared up to him.

'Wait up! Guys! Hold on a second.'

Craig turned round to see a small, skinny man in his late twenties heading their way at speed. He was breathing heavily when he reached them. Even in the dim light around the harbour, Craig could see that his face was gaunt and his skin bad. The guy was a user.

'I've got a RIB,' he announced, gasping for breath. 'I can take you.'

'What's a rib?' the plump girl whispered to the blonde.

'Rigid inflatable boat,' Craig told the girls.

The new arrival was looking from one face to the next. 'I'm Steve,' he told them. 'I can take you to Plymouth. That's where you all want to go, isn't it?'

Craig found himself exchanging doubtful glances with the big guy, who'd obviously seen the same tell-tale signs he had. On the other hand, the kid's eyes looked OK. No dilated pupils, and they held steady. He might not be high.

'For real?' the blonde asked.

'Fifty quid each, in advance,' the boy, Steve, went on. 'I can't risk the boat for anything less.'

Fifty quid. No girl was worth that. Craig was going back to the pub. On the other hand, did he really want to get sacked?

'No one here's got fifty quid, mate,' the navy bloke said. 'And there's no risk to the boat, not if you know what you're doing.'

If the guy actually had a boat. Especially one big enough to take all of them. He looked as though he'd struggle to fund his next meal.

'It's a tricky navigation out of the Yealm at night,' Steve argued. 'Even in a RIB. And we have to go soon. The wind's getting up and we're going to have wind over tide when we reach open water. I can do it for forty quid each. Best offer.'

'Maybe this isn't a good idea,' the blonde said.

The big guy turned to the others. 'Can you lot stretch to twenty-five?' he asked them.

They nodded, the plump girl last of all.

'I guess,' Craig admitted.

'That's a hundred and twenty-five quid for two hours' work,' the big guy told Steve. 'Now, what I want to know is, how big is this RIB of yours, what sort of engine and can you deal with big seas?'

'Ribcraft 5.85 metres, ten-seater, one hundred horsepower engine. And I've been boating since I could walk. She's this way.'

Eager now the question of money had been settled, Steve hurried them along the pontoon. Robin took up the rear, keeping a close eye on the plump girl, who didn't look too steady on her feet. He didn't need to get back to Plymouth, not really, but the tent he'd been sleeping in the last three nights had gone home with his mates, who'd caught an earlier bus, and he didn't fancy a night in the open. Besides, a sea voyage in a storm sounded fun. Robin was easily bored.

At the head of the column, Steve dropped to his knees and pulled on a thin, wet rope. Gradually, one boat out of the mass tied to the pontoon could be seen making its way towards them. One of the larger ones, it had a rigid black hull and a big outboard engine. As it came closer they could see its floor was awash. Only three seats.

'It's leaking,' the blonde said.

'That's rainwater,' said the bloke whom Robin was calling to himself the Able Seaman. 'It'll be safe enough. As long as this lad knows what he's doing. You got life jackets for the ladies?'

'Why only for us?' the brown-skinned girl snapped. 'Are we less capable than you?'

The Able Seaman held up both hands in mock surrender. 'Just trying to be a gentleman.'

'I didn't know I'd be carrying passengers,' Steve said.

Robin felt the first pang of misgiving. You were supposed to wear life jackets on a boat, weren't you? On the other hand, it was only a couple of miles to Plymouth and boats like the one at their feet crossed rough seas all the time and came to no harm. He couldn't wimp out now.

'In you get, girls.' The Able Seaman grasped the bow of the RIB. 'Two of you take the rear seats. The rest of us will have to hold on to the sides.'

One by one, the group boarded. Able Seaman, in spite of his weight, managed it easily, as did Fireman Sam. The plump girl, on the other hand, almost upturned it, before collapsing down onto one of the seats. The blonde took the other. Robin made his way to the front and sat on the hull, opposite his naval pal. Steve had taken his place at the driver's seat when they heard footsteps running along the pontoon.

'I need to come with you,' the boy called when he was still twenty yards away. 'Me and my girlfriend. She's pregnant. I need to get her to hospital.'

The boy was painfully thin, in his twenties like the rest of them. His hair had been cropped short above a widow's peak, but his thick brows suggested it would be dark brown, maybe black, when allowed to grow. His eyes looked enormous in his gaunt face. A fake diamond earring gleamed in his left ear.

'Mate, we're not the ambulance service.' Able Seaman gave the boat a gentle push, taking it away from the pontoon. 'If you need medical attention you have to wait for the proper authorities.'

'Who can't get here,' the brown-skinned girl reminded him. 'The road's blocked, remember?'

By this time, they could see the girl moving slowly along the pontoon in her boyfriend's wake. She looked young and, apart from the swollen stomach that she clutched with one hand, very thin. The look on her face suggested she was in pain.

'She might be losing the baby.' The boy looked distraught. 'I have to get her to Plymouth.'

Robin opened his mouth to offer them his place; he'd changed his mind; a night in the pub didn't feel like too bad an idea at all.

'We can fit them in,' the blonde girl said. 'Ten-seater, you said, Steve. And I'm a nurse. A student nurse, but still. We can look after her. She can have this seat.'

'I think we should take them,' Fireman Sam said.

The Able Seaman gave a heavy sigh but didn't push it. Steve pulled the boat back to the pontoon, the boy and his pregnant girlfriend climbed aboard, and they set off across the water. As the lights of the harbour faded and darkness closed around them, Robin had a sense of leaving one world behind and slipping into another.

Don't do this, a voice in his head told him. *Go back, while you still can.*

But the pontoon had already faded into the gloom and the lights of the harbour looked a million miles away. A wave washed over the bow. The Able Seaman didn't flinch and so Robin bit back the yell of disgust as the cold water soaked right through his clothes to his skin. Behind them, he heard squealing and scrambling among the girls.

'Sit still and shut up.' Able Seaman twisted round. 'This will be tricky enough as it is and, frankly, if we go in the water, I don't fancy anyone's chances but mine.'

Robin told himself he was going to sit very still until he got off the boat at Plymouth.

Shelley held tight to her boyfriend's hand and closed her eyes. An hour ago, giving birth in a tent felt like the worst thing she could imagine. Now, a tent didn't seem too bad at all. The droning of the boat's engine was making her headache worse, the continual bouncing had brought her to a breath away from throwing up and she couldn't seem to stop shaking. She figured they'd been on the water for fifteen minutes. They'd left the lights of Newton Ferrers' harbour behind and were travelling between tall cliffs.

Let it be over, let it be over, let it be over.

'Where are we?' one of the girls asked, breaking the silence that had held since they'd left the harbour. Shelley opened her eyes. Nothing. Black sea, black cliffs, black sky. Not a single light anywhere.

And the relentless thumping of the boat on the waves. She closed her eyes again. *Let it be over, let it be over.*

'River Yealm.' The boy who owned the boat had to shout above the roar of the outboard. 'It's about a mile from the harbour to open water. Then another five to Plymouth.'

Six miles. Nothing in a car.

A vice-like pain clutched at Shelley's abdomen and she couldn't help the moan slipping out. 'Can we go any faster?' she heard her boyfriend complain.

'There's a speed limit in the river,' the boat owner yelled back. 'It's there for a reason. I might risk it in daylight. Not now.'

'Breathe, sweetheart,' the dark-skinned girl said. 'Just breathe and stay calm.'

Sabri was trying to remember everything she'd learned about eclampsia, one of the most dangerous conditions facing pregnant women. She was close to certain the pregnant girl was suffering from it.

The boat took a wave head on, bouncing high into the air, and Sabri felt herself sliding along the rigid hull. It would be the easiest thing in the world to go overboard. Already her stomach muscles were aching from holding herself upright.

If she was right about the eclampsia, the pregnant girl could experience seizures any time now. She could lose consciousness, suffer a stroke, fall into a coma, even die. Too late, Sabri admitted to herself that they should have stayed in Newton Ferrers and called out the air ambulance. She should have thought of it before they'd left the harbour. If anything happened to the girl, it would be on her.

'Does anyone have a working phone?' she yelled. 'This girl needs an ambulance waiting when we get in.'

'You won't get a signal here,' Steve shouted back. 'Wait till we're round the corner.'

Sabri looked forward. No sign of a break in the dark cliffs. 'How long?'

'Wembury Bay ahead. When we clear that, we're in sight of Plymouth. You'll get a signal then.'

The pregnant girl raised her head to speak to Sabri. 'Am I going to lose the baby?'

Quite possibly. Also, no one would put bets on your own life right now.

'Not if we get you help quickly,' she said. 'How many weeks are you?'

They all clung on as the RIB hit another big wave, then her boyfriend answered. 'She's thirty-eight. We shouldn't have come this weekend, should we?'

No, you bloody well shouldn't. 'Well, you're probably going to become a dad tonight. I expect the team at Plymouth will induce labour as soon as they can. Then she'll be fine.'

Sabri turned to the rest of them. 'A phone? Does anyone have a phone?'

'I've got one,' the curly-haired boy called back. 'I kept charging it in the pub when the landlord wasn't looking. Do you want it now?'

'OK, it's worth a try.'

As the boy reached into his jacket, the naval man put a hand on his arm.

'Keep it in your pocket!' he called. 'The rest of you, hold on and keep as low as you can. We're about to hit the bay.'

'What does that mean?' Sabri asked, a second before the cliffs fell away, the boat passed into open water and she knew beyond doubt that her life was about to end.

Shit, shit, shit!

Water was streaming over the sides of the RIB but it was still afloat. God only knew how; that wave should have wiped them out. A miracle. They wouldn't get another. Steve had had no idea it would be this bad out in the bay.

For fuck's sake, you lot, stop screaming.

They had to go back. Turn round and go back. It was their only chance.

Another wave, a monstrous wall of water, hard like concrete, picking them up and spinning them around.

Which fucking way was back?

He had no control. Literally no fucking control. Something – wind, tide, hand of bloody Satan – was pushing the RIB onto the cliffs.

It wasn't even his boat. He'd nicked the keys and kill cord from a drunk in the pub. He was going to die for stealing a fucking boat.

'Hold on!' Tug yelled, for what felt like the dozenth time. 'Everyone, get down and hold on.' This was fucking insane. The kid had no idea how to deal with big seas. He had to get to the helm.

He made a quick headcount. Still nine on board, thank Christ. The lad across the bow holding on for dear life; the fat girl and the pregnant one on the rear seats; the blonde and the lad who fancied his chances with her on his side; opposite, the brown-skinned girl and the dad-to-be; and the idiot on the helm. All nine. Soaking wet, screaming with terror, but still on board.

This was a thousand times worse than he'd imagined. Bad enough in the river, even with the cliffs holding back the wind. The bay, though, the bay wasn't navigable. The southwesterly was driving straight at the shore, hitting the outgoing tide, making waves of two metres or more. An expert helmsman, who knew how to steer through big seas, would have a chance. With this kid, they were all fucking goners.

The cliffs were gut-wrenchingly close. They were being driven onto them. There'd be outlying rocks too, under the surface. Rocks that could tear the hull apart. They might be seconds from disaster. Tug took a deep breath and yelled.

'Head for open water! Steer round the waves! If you can't avoid them, take them head on.'

He wasn't sure the kid heard him; or, if he'd heard, that he understood. He looked rigid with shock, on the point of giving up; or throwing himself overboard.

Get to the helm. Stay on board and get to the helm. But if he moved, if he let go for an instant, he risked being thrown overboard.

If he didn't move, it would happen anyway.

Tug waited for a lull that would last less than a second and dived for the steering column. The cliffs were metres away.

A rogue wave caught the RIB side-on and they soared up. They were close to a hundred and eighty degrees and at that angle they'd tip. Tug hurled himself over the hull to increase the weight on the port side. The wave passed beneath them and they were level again. With seconds before the next one caught them.

He grabbed Steve by the shoulder. 'Give me the fucking helm,' he ordered.

Steve didn't move. Tug pulled him off the seat and flung him into the lap of the fat girl, before claiming the driver's seat himself. Less than a second to make the decision. *Go back or go on?* The Great Mew Stone, a bloody great hunk of rock at the mouth of the bay, was practically on them. Halfway point. If they got round the headland and past the Plymouth breakwater, the sea would calm down. They'd have phone signal. Going on made more sense.

Closing his mind to the screaming, Tug looked for the gap in the waves, for his route through. But they were coming thick and fast. He steered to starboard, but that was taking him too close to shore.

No way around the outside of the Great Mew Stone, the waves were lined up like the Great Wall of fucking China. He'd have to go inside, risk being thrown onto the rock itself or the cliffs; take his chances with the turbulence he knew would be waiting once he strayed into the lee of the rock. Washing machine on fucking spin cycle.

A fresh scream. Different. The sound of pain, not terror. The pregnant girl.

'Christ, watch it. Get the fuck off me.'

'Shelley, look at me. It's OK, Shelley.'

Something going on with the pregnant woman. Tug couldn't take his eyes off the sea. *Run with the waves, look for the gaps, take them head-on if necessary, don't be caught sideways, stay in the middle of the channel.*

A scream of horror, quickly muffled, movement to his right. A slithering sound. A splash.

'Shelley!'

Horrified faces. Hands clutching his arms, trying to grab the wheel.

'Stop! Stop! We have to go back. Shelley!'

'She's gone. She's gone overboard.'

'They both have. He pulled her over.'

The cliffs. A soaring great rock wall. Their certain death. Wave after wave coming at them. Hands clawing at Tug's own, tearing into his skin, blows landing around his head.

'Turn round. We have to go back.'

'Can anyone see them?'

'Shelley!'

The chaos was not his concern. He couldn't even spare the seconds to count how many were still on board. Tug fixed on the faintest pinprick of light, miles away. He fired up the engine and aimed for it. The boat slammed. Again. They were beneath the waves. Up again. Keep going. Ignore the panic. Ignore the screaming. Aim for the light. Look for the gaps, take the waves head-on. Hold on. Keep going. Aim for the light.

Tug didn't notice the pregnant woman's boyfriend throw himself over the side. He was conscious of nothing but the light he was following until he realised they were passing the breakwater. Calm descended.

For the rest of his life, until he died at the hands of the man who was briefly to steal his identity, Craig Lewis would never know how he managed to keep hold of the grab rope running around the RIB's hull. For the rest of his life, he couldn't honestly have said exactly what had happened seconds before that. The whole terrifying journey seemed to melt into a turbulent memory of black water, of being thrown around like a tornado had scooped them up. One second, he was clinging to something, he had no idea what, the next he felt a stab of excruciating pain as the pregnant girl tried to stand up, putting all her weight on his foot. He'd acted without thinking. He hadn't hit her deliberately; everything he'd done had been instinctive. He'd gone into survival mode, it was as simple as that. Then he was falling and of course he'd grabbed hold of anything he could. He hadn't meant to pull her overboard with him.

Another tussle, this time in the water, and she was gone. Somehow, he managed to hold on to the side of the RIB. He clung on. He was a fireman; he'd spent years building his upper-body strength. Even so, by the time they passed the breakwater and everything calmed down, he was ready to give up. He'd managed to shout. They'd heard him. It had taken four of them to get him back on board.

Cheryl watched as, one by one, the remaining passengers climbed onto the pontoon at Queen Anne's Battery in Plymouth Harbour. The nice, curly-haired boy went first, then the two girls and Steve. The boy who'd been pulled from the water went next. Cheryl wasn't sure she'd make it up the thin metal ladder; the rungs were slippery, and her wet clothes hung around her like a dead weight. Somehow, she managed to grasp the ladder. No further.

And then the nice boy bent down and reached for her; she gave him her hand and he half pulled her up. The man who was in the navy, the one who'd started all this in the first place, was last to leave the boat.

'You shouldn't take it back tonight,' he told Steve. It was the first time any of them had spoken since the pregnant girl and her boyfriend had gone overboard. 'Wait till the morning.'

'Not my boat.' Steve set off towards the town. 'Nicked it,' he called back over his shoulder.

'We should stop him,' the brown-skinned girl said. 'We need everyone. We have to report this.' She looked around the group. 'We should have called it in already, shouldn't we? We should have called the coastguard. We could have saved them. Shit, I should have thought of that.' She looked on the verge of tears and Cheryl felt her own eyes stinging.

'Not a chance,' the naval man replied. 'They were dead two minutes after they left the boat.'

'We should have looked for them.'

'If we had, we'd all be dead now,' the blonde girl said. 'It's a miracle we got back.' She half reached out towards the naval man, her hand hovering a few inches from his arm. 'And thanks to you,' she said.

'What now?' asked the curly-haired boy.

For a second, no one had an answer. Then the naval man bent down and untied the RIB. For a horrified moment, Cheryl thought he was going to suggest they all get back in it.

'What're you doing?' the boy who'd fallen in the water asked.

'The tide will take it. It'll be at the bottom before the hour's out.'

Sure enough, the boat began to slide away from the pontoon.

'I'm out of here,' the naval man replied. 'I'd say it's been nice, but . . .'

He began walking away. The others looked at each other for a moment, then the brown-skinned girl set off after him, catching him on the shoulder.

'You can't go,' she argued. 'We have to report this.'

He threw off her arm. 'You want to spend the night at the police station, be my guest. I'm due back at my barracks and that's where I'm going.'

'People died. We . . . we were a part of that. We have to report it.'

Cheryl said, 'They might still be alive.'

The big bloke shook his head. 'Impossible. Report it if you want to, guys, but you won't get where you need to be tomorrow morning. Which kind of makes the whole trip for nothing.'

He set off again. This time, no one tried to stop him.

'What's done is done,' the blonde nurse said, and she too turned towards the town, followed a few seconds later by the two boys.

Cheryl was the last to walk away. As she reached solid land, on legs that felt very unsteady, she wondered if she'd ever see any of them again.

Chapter 87

'Your friends and I shared a boat trip.' Quick seemed to be speaking only to Holly now. The others had moved away from her and Charlie, and she couldn't help the fear – stupid, probably, but she couldn't help it – that they'd joined forces with Quick.

'Thirty years ago,' Quick went on. 'We took a RIB from Newton Ferrers, bound for Plymouth. There were nine of us on board.' He let his eyes leave Holly to travel around the rest of the group. 'These five, the lad who stole the RIB, although he told us it was his, a man called Craig Lewis, and me and my pregnant girlfriend.'

'Shelley,' Holly heard Tara whisper.

Quick heard her too. 'Oh, you remember her now? Tell me something. How often have you thought of her these past thirty years? Once a year, maybe? Or did you push her to the back of your minds the minute you got off that RIB?'

Holly glanced around. Every pair of eyes was fixed on the floor.

Except Quick's. 'Because there hasn't been a day when I haven't thought about her. Not a day.' With an effort, it seemed, Quick got to his feet. 'Do you love your son, Holly?'

Holly took a step back, dragging Charlie with her. Whether through pain, medication or just years of bitterness, this man wasn't in his right mind.

'My mum loves me more than anything,' Charlie replied for her, and she loved that there was no doubt in his voice.

'I loved my son,' Quick said to Charlie. 'My baby son. He'd have been a man now. We could have worked together these last ten years.'

'What happened to him?' Charlie asked.

Quick's eyes seemed to fill. 'His mother's labour came on early. She was in so much pain. She couldn't sit still in the boat. Craig threw her overboard.' Finally, he took his eyes from Charlie to look around the room. 'Then you all left her to drown.'

I didn't, Holly thought. Why am I here? She looked at Tara, then Tug, Sabri, Robin and Cheryl. She'd liked these people, had trusted them. She said, but to no one in particular, 'Is this true?'

'Of course it's true,' Quick snapped. 'I went in the water to save her, but she'd gone. The waves were huge. I almost died myself. But I tried. This lot, this sorry bunch of cowards. They didn't do a thing.'

Robin said, 'We had no choice. And Craig, if that was the guy's name, he didn't throw her overboard. It was an accident.'

'There was nothing we could have done,' Tara added.

'You don't know that.' Quick seemed to sway on his feet. 'I went overboard, and I survived. Craig clung on to the side of the hull and he survived. You could have turned the boat round. We could have found her. You didn't even call out the bloody coastguard. You left both of us for dead.'

His voice cracked with the effort of speaking.

Holly took another step backwards, pulling Charlie with her. This fight wasn't hers. How she and her son were mixed up in it she had no idea, but if there was to be crossfire, they weren't getting caught in it.

'How?' Tug asked. 'How did you survive that sea?'

For a moment, Holly wasn't sure Quick was going to reply. Then he said, 'I got thrown onto that big rock. I clung on till it was light. A fishing boat picked me up. I'd held on to some sort of hope, until then, that the lifeboats had gone out, that Shelley had been found. But you hadn't even raised the alarm. You'd all just vanished into the night. Was it really too much trouble to call out the coastguard?'

'We should have done,' Tara said, at last. 'But you must remember how bad it was. We didn't think either of you could have survived. I'm glad you did, but you can't blame us for what happened to Shelley.'

'Yes, I can. I do.' Quick took an unsteady step towards Tug. 'You were in the navy.' He raised a trembling finger. 'Special bloody Boat Service. You knew how dangerous it was setting out that night. But you were so concerned with not getting a reprimand you were prepared to risk all of us.'

'And you!' he turned to the sofa where Sabri was perched. 'A third-year medical student who'd just finished a course in obstetrics. You should have stayed with us in Newton Ferrers, called out a helicopter. You could have helped us.'

'So could you.' Another spin on unsteady feet, another accusation. Tara's turn. 'A nurse. A bloody nurse. And you did nothing.'

Tara dropped her eyes.

'The police tried to find you all,' Quick went on. 'I told them what happened, that we'd been on a boat with seven other people. I gave them descriptions. I didn't know your names, but I told them everything I could remember. There was an appeal. It was on television, in the papers for days. Don't tell me none of you saw it!'

He broke off again as a fit of coughing took hold of him. He turned, perhaps to return to his chair, and stumbled. Tara got up, crossed to the table by his side and poured a glass of water. After glaring at her for a second, he took it.

'Sit down,' she told him. The two of them held eye contact as he did what she said.

'It was that you couldn't forgive, wasn't it?' Tara said, when his coughing had subsided. 'Not what happened in the boat. What we did afterwards.'

Quick let his head fall and rise again. 'It was as though she was nothing. A girl and her unborn baby died, and it meant nothing to you.'

'It meant everything,' Sabri snapped. 'I failed my exams because of what happened that night. I had PTSD, although I didn't know it at the time. I couldn't concentrate on a thing. I became a bloody ambulance driver.'

'I was a high-functioning alcoholic for years,' Tug said. 'Now, I'm a low-functioning one. So, don't tell me it meant nothing.'

'I'm afraid of water,' Tara said. 'I swim most days, but the sea terrifies me. I force myself to do it and I don't know why.'

'I told my mum what happened,' Cheryl said. 'She's been blackmailing me ever since.'

'Boo fucking hoo!' Quick snapped. 'I lost the woman who would have been my wife and my first-born son. You think anything compares to that?'

'That'll do, mate.' Robin looked as though he'd had enough. 'We did nothing illegal that night. Stupid, yeah, selfish almost certainly, but nothing more. And maybe we could have picked up you and Shelley but it's just as likely we'd all have drowned.'

With one last squeeze of Cheryl's shoulder, Robin came out from behind the sofa.

'What you've done, though, is very illegal.' Now Robin was the one pointing fingers and making accusations. 'Kidnapping a child, for starters. Then endangering all of us, including a woman who wasn't even involved.' He gave a quick glance at Holly. 'The whole business with the tokens is probably fraud. And that's before we get onto the contents of the fucking port locker. Sorry to swear, Charlie.'

'That's OK.' Charlie gave Robin a reassuring smile. 'What's in the fucking port locker?'

'What am I missing here?' Sabri asked. She glanced at Cheryl and then back at Robin. 'What's in the locker?'

'I haven't a clue.' Tara was looking questioningly at Tug.

'Me neither,' added Cheryl, in a voice barely meant to carry.

'What's in the locker, Quick?' repeated Sabri. 'Anyone?'

'Nothing by now,' Quick replied. 'Thomas is currently taking *Gemini* away to assess for damage. I doubt he'll find anything unusual in any of the lockers.'

Tug got to his feet. He and Robin both moved closer to Quick.

'Three of us saw what you put in the life-raft bag,' said Tug. 'I'm guessing it was the real Craig Lewis. Who'll be reported missing, if he hasn't already been.'

Quick gave a dismissive laugh. 'Craig Lewis was a loser who barely scratched out a living. Sometime in the next few weeks, maybe longer, the housing association in Newquay will enter his property and find him gone. He has no family, no one to care. He'll become a missing persons statistic.'

'No, he won't.' Holly felt a tiny surge of satisfaction at contradicting Quick. 'He's a token recipient. You've made him one of the most famous people in the country. People will look for him.'

Quick gave a heavy sigh. 'Maybe. I admit I've had to rethink my plans. I thought you'd all be at the bottom of the Celtic Sea by now. But as Sabri pointed out, I'm dying. There really isn't much the authorities can do to me.'

'You can spend your last months in prison,' Holly snapped. 'It'll be a lot less comfortable than this place. And you still haven't said why Charlie and I are here. Neither of us were born when you went on that boat trip.'

Quick sneered. 'You're a barrister, Holly, so stop talking through your arse. The CPS will never be able to incarcerate a dying man for months before his trial. Especially one with the lawyers I have at my disposal. The worst they can do is pester me with interviews and depositions. But I don't plan to be around even for those. I'm leaving St Helen's today.'

The helicopter. Holly remembered the gleaming white aircraft a stone's throw from the house.

'Why are Charlie and I here?' Holly insisted. 'We had nothing to do with what happened to your girlfriend.'

'Her name was Shelley.'

'Mum . . .' Charlie said.

'I don't give a toss what her name was,' Holly shot back at Quick. 'You're the one who put her in danger, not these guys. It was your baby she was carrying. What the hell was she doing miles from a hospital anyway? What happened to her is on you, not them.'

A hardening behind Quick's eyes told her she was hitting home.

'And this stupid revenge plan, which clearly isn't going to work, is nothing more than you trying to deflect your own blame.'

'Mum . . .' Charlie repeated.

'Tell me, Holly, how is your father?' Quick said.

'What's my dad got to do with this?'

'I think he was on the boat, Mum.'

Holly looked down at her son.

'Grandad's always talking about when he lived near the sea,' Charlie told her. 'Not that he talks anymore, but when he did, it was always about how he used to go fishing, and how he helped out with the boats in the summer.'

That was true, of course; it had been his grandad's stories that first sparked Charlie's interest in boats. But . . .

'He was in a bad storm once,' Charlie went on. 'Two of the passengers died. He said it put him off boats for a long time.'

Her dad had been born and brought up in Newton Ferrers.

Tug said, 'Holly, what's your dad's name?'

'Steven,' she replied.

'The boy who stole the dingy,' Tara said. 'He told us it was his at first, but he didn't really know how to manage it. Is he your dad, Holly?'

Quick let a satisfied smile creep over his face. 'Steve, whose criminal offence made the whole doomed enterprise possible, has been seriously ill with a degenerative disease for nearly three years. Physically he's in a bad way but his mind's as sharp as ever. I've spent a bit of time with him recently. I'd been looking forward to telling him his only child was dead.'

Holly felt sick. He couldn't touch her father, so he'd targeted her instead.

Robin said, 'You put Holly and her child at risk because of something her father did? That's messed up.'

'No.' Again Quick's voice cracked with the effort of shouting. 'Walking away at Plymouth, pretending nothing had happened, that a pregnant girl counted for nothing. That was messed up.'

'So, the tokens were all about getting us onto a boat again,' Robin said. 'You never had any intention of giving us any money. We were supposed to die last night.'

'Impossible,' Sabri said. 'He's been planning this for months. Years even. God knows how long it took him to find us all. Last night's storm couldn't have been predicted more than a few days ahead.'

'The storm was a bonus,' Tug said. 'But *Gemini* was definitely meant to sink last night. Even I couldn't have kept it afloat for ever. If we hadn't seen that cargo ship we'd all have been at the bottom of the Atlantic by nightfall.'

'The storm was the opposite of a bonus,' Quick grumbled. 'Conditions last night made it a lot harder for Lauren to pick Thomas and me up. I was in the water for a long time.'

'You really did mean to kill us all?' Holly asked.

'The same terrifying, agonising death that Shelley and my baby died,' Quick replied. 'There would have been some justice in that, don't you think?'

Robin shook his head, as though the sight of Quick disgusted him. 'Well, bad luck,' he said. 'We didn't die. So, what's Plan B? Is Thomas unlocking the gun cupboard? That housekeeper of yours making tea laced with arsenic? Because a lot of people know we set off for St Helen's yesterday. Unless that harbour master and his mate are in on it too, they know we arrived in one piece. So, if seven rotting corpses are fished out of the sea in the next few days, your two friends here will have a lot to answer for. Even if you get away with it.'

'That's true,' Quick admitted. 'And Thomas really wasn't happy about last night. I had to pay him a lot of money to go along with it. I doubt he'd be up for round two. No, looks like I'll have to rely on the tokens to finish the job off.'

'Making us all millionaires is going to punish us?' Robin said. 'Mate, I think you need to—'

'Think about it, Robin,' Quick snapped. 'Have you known a moment's peace since your token arrived?'

He let the question hang.

Holly saw the same thought process going through the minds of the others. She'd known confusion, anxiety. At the same time, though, the token had represented a wild dream threatening to become real. A future of security, when she could focus only on her career and Charlie. No more sex with flabby accountants from Wigan; Chris and his threats taken care of. The token had been a way out. And the others? Cheryl, facing disinheritance and homelessness; Robin losing his business; Sabri, her life a constant financial struggle; Tara threatened with losing her beloved home; Tug without a job or any sort of security. The tokens had given them hope.

Peace, though? That was a different matter. Once the news broke, once their identities had become public knowledge, the hounding had begun.

'I know what it's like to get a sudden influx of money you know you don't deserve,' Quick said.

His lottery win. Quick's fortune had stemmed from a lottery win in his early twenties.

'And you've only had a couple of weeks of it,' he continued. 'Trust me when I say it'll get worse. You'll lose all your friends. Some will know from the outset they can't deal with the envy, so they'll take themselves away. The rest you'll dump when guilt over the sudden inequity gets to you.'

Well, that was true. Coffie had changed the moment he'd found out about the token.

'I wouldn't put money on your marriage lasting the next few months,' Quick said to Sabri. 'You'll find someone else, of course, because there's always clever gold-diggers out there, but it won't last because the kids will hate their new stepdad and you'll never be sure he wasn't just interested in your money.'

Across the room, Sabri's face had tightened. 'Your kids will go bad,' Quick went on. 'Nothing ruins kids like money, trust me on that.'

'Good kids will deal with it,' Holly argued, because she couldn't bear to see the look of dismay on Sabri's face. 'No money in the world will corrupt Charlie.'

'No, it won't,' Charlie agreed. 'But can I still have an Axopar?'

Quick gave a nasty smile. 'Half the world will be holding out a begging bowl, from your own families to perfect strangers looking for hand-outs and loans. The other half will be suing you for some imagined slight. I've had thirty years of it. I just wish I could have done this earlier, given you more of the hell I've had to deal with.'

'OK, I'm done,' Holly announced. 'Guys, we don't need to listen to any more of this shit. Let's find a phone and call the police.'

No one moved; it was as though Quick had hypnotised them.

'Come on,' she urged. 'There's only three of them. And Charlie can take down this idiot. I'll get that cow of a housekeeper and I'm sure Tug and Robin can deal with Thomas.'

'Be careful, Holly,' Quick said, quietly.

No, she'd had enough. Quick was a delusional, dying man and his wealth didn't make him invincible. If anything, it proved how meaningless it was, because all the money in the world wasn't going to save him. She set off for the door, holding out a hand for Charlie.

'I've spent a lot of time and money learning everything I can about the six of you,' Quick called after her. 'I'd say you have more to lose than anyone.'

Something tight gripped hold of Holly. She said, 'The only thing I care about is my son, and I'll rip your throat out before I let you come anywhere near him again.'

'I won't have to. I'll just let the world know about your extra-curricular activities.'

Silence.

'What's he talking about, Holly?' Tug asked.

'Junior barristers, particularly those juggling family commitments, are notoriously short of money,' Quick said. 'I was puzzled to learn how Holly manages to live in a nice house, run a decent car, have her son's name down for a fancy private secondary school, and pay for carers coming into her parents' home three times a day. She has outgoings that far exceed her income. So, how do you imagine she meets the deficit?'

'I don't imagine it's any of our business,' Tara said.

'Maybe not, but it's a delicious piece of gossip all the same. Holly is a high-class escort. Also known as a whore. You can find her photographs on a site called Cornish Courtesans. Her face is obscured, and she calls herself Tamara, but it's definitely her.'

Holly felt the world around her slipping away. It had happened then. Somehow, she'd always known it would.

'The parents at Charlie's school are going to love it, Holly. As will the school itself, because you haven't exactly made yourself popular with the staff there.' Quick forced a smile onto his face. 'The bullying is going to be intense, I'm afraid, Charlie, when all your school friends find out that your mum has sex with men for money. So, you will lose your son, Holly. His father will apply for custody. He'll win and Charlie will be glad of it, because he won't want anything more to do with you. Ever.'

Well, at least I don't have to worry about being blackmailed anymore, Holly thought, as Charlie pulled away from her. At least, when the worst happens, you can stop dreading it. She watched her son move closer to Quick, pulling something from his jacket pocket.

'You're a cunt,' he told Quick, a second before he dropped something – the token, how the hell had he found that? – at the man's feet. 'We don't want your money. You can keep it.' Turning on his heels, he took a step towards Holly, before looking back over his shoulder. 'And everyone at school hates me already. It won't make any difference.'

He stopped inches from his mother and looked up into her face. 'I'm not going to live with Dad,' he said. 'Belinda smells of Haribos.'

'That's OK,' Holly said. 'You don't have to live with Dad.' She would die before she let anyone take her son away. 'How come you have the token?'

'I found it in that bag at the back of your wardrobe. I thought it needed to be somewhere safer and no one would think I'd have it. There's some weird stuff in there, Mum.'

Tug was walking towards Quick. He paused as he reached Holly and Charlie. 'Use that word again, son, and I'll tan your backside,' he said. 'Otherwise, you're spot on.'

Tug too had his token with him. He dropped it at Quick's feet. 'I'll manage, thanks,' he said. 'Sufficient to the day and all that.'

Tara was smiling as she joined Tug and another token hit the polished floor. There was something strangely cheering in the pinging sound they made as they landed. Over on the sofa, Sabri's hand was inside her sweater, for all the world as though she was trying to take off her bra. Then she and Cheryl exchanged a look and they both stood. A second later, two more tokens joined the growing pile by Quick's chair.

'My family don't need money,' Sabri said. 'We have each other.'

'My mum's not that bad,' Cheryl said. 'I just need to stand up to her a bit more. And you should probably give my token a good wash.'

All eyes turned to Robin, who held up both hands in mock despair. 'Guys, I was telling the truth. It's in my living room. In a DVD case. *Seven Brides for Seven Brothers*.' He winked at Quick. 'I'll FedEx it.'

Quick took his time. He pushed himself upright and turned his back on them, walking to the nearest of the floor-to-ceiling windows. Beyond them, the steel-blue ocean stretched as far as Holly could see. Lowering clouds suggested another storm was heading in.

Charlie, meanwhile, unable to bear mess of any kind, gathered up the five tokens and put them on the closest table. Then he brushed his hands down his jeans, as though to wipe off something contaminating.

'Well, that's a very noble gesture, guys.' Quick's voice came from the window. He turned back to face them, becoming a silhouette in the frame.

'Tell me something,' he said to Sabri. 'How will Jason cope with learning he's not going to buy a Tesla after all? Or a new house? Or resign from that job he hates? That his reckless spending the last couple of weeks has done nothing more than throw his family into even more debt? He has debts you don't know about, by the way. I wouldn't be surprised if you don't lose your house before the year's out. And those kids? It'll take them a long time to get over the disappointment, won't it? Maddy just coming up to her GCSEs. I doubt she'll do even as well as she was predicted to.'

Sabri looked on the verge of spitting at Quick.

'I expect that biker friend of yours will lose interest when she learns you're not going to be rich.' Robin was next in the firing line.

'And when your business goes bankrupt, as it will in the next few months, she'll go back to her surgeon boyfriend. And you, Trevor, how long before you lose your home and become just another piss-soaked ex-serviceman on the street corner?'

Holly watched Tug clench his fists. Do it, she thought. Break the bastard's jaw.

'Speaking of homeless, do you think your mother's ever going to forgive you for what you've done the last couple of weeks, Cheryl? Hiding the token from her, pretending it was lost, sneaking out to meet your new friends? She knows you intended keeping all the money for yourself, so she'll make damn sure you don't get a penny of hers. The best you can do now is get yourself a minimum-wage job and start saving.'

He came slowly back to his chair but didn't attempt to sit. 'And don't think for a moment, guys, that the hassle will go away. No one will believe you've given the tokens back. Especially when I refuse to confirm it. So, the harassment and the threats and the kidnap worries will all go on. And only you'll know for certain that there's nothing on the horizon to make it worthwhile.'

He started to walk across the room towards the door.

'I'll be leaving shortly,' he told them. 'Trevor, the key to the RIB is by the side entrance. I imagine you'll be able to get them back to St Mary's.'

He turned at the door. 'I'd hoped for more,' he said. 'But at least I can spend my last weeks knowing I've ruined your lives too.'

Chapter 88

'Come on, guys,' Tug said, as the sound of Quick's footsteps faded. 'The sooner we're off this island the better.'

He led the way back through the house, expecting an obstacle at every turn. More guards, Thomas with an automatic weapon, the doors closed against them and a poisonous gas released. Christ, he had to keep his head.

There was a boat key hanging by the back door, just as Quick had said, identifiable from the others by the attached cork float. As they hurried down the gravel path, he heard the sound of the helicopter's engines starting up.

Tara was directly behind him. 'Those clouds don't look great,' she said, gesturing out towards the west. 'I know we want to get out of here, but you know, frying pan and fire.'

'It's four miles max to St Mary's.' Tug kept up the pace. 'The RIB will do that in minutes. As long as it's seaworthy. I wouldn't put it past that creep to sabotage us again.'

The wind was definitely getting up again, splashing their faces with miniscule drops of sea water as they approached the pontoon. 'Wait here,' he told them. 'Except for Tara. I need to check it out.'

The hull of the RIB looked sound. Both engines, each a hundred horsepower, seemed pristine. No water in the bottom of the boat.

'Look in all the cupboards and lockers,' he told Tara. 'We need life jackets. Anything that seems out of place, let me know.'

Tug turned on the ignition. Tank three quarters full. More than enough to get them to St Mary's. The VHF went immediately to channel sixteen and gave out a burst of static. He checked the gear was in neutral and started the engines. A comforting, regular roar. Both props turning. All looked good.

'Life jackets here,' Tara called out. 'Ten of them. And a packet of flares. Some spare rope.'

'Get everybody in life jackets,' he told her. 'Make sure they fit. Then get them onboard.'

He fired up the engine. It responded. Looked like they were good to go.

Charlie, unsurprisingly, was first on board. 'Can I sit with you?' he asked Tug.

'Course. Help the others on first. Your mum needs to fasten her crotch strap.'

Tug glanced back at the house. From this angle, the helicopter was out of sight. He guessed Quick would be heading for an airport on the mainland, from there to somewhere the UK government would find it hard to extradite him.

Holly, then Sabri, climbed on board. Cheryl froze on the pontoon.

'I can't,' she said. The life jacket was strained around her girth. 'I can't do it again.'

'Course you can.' Robin held on to her hand. 'This thing will fly over the water. We'll be in St Mary's in time for breakfast. Aren't you starving? I know I am.'

Tara climbed in ahead of Cheryl and then she and Robin coaxed the terrified woman aboard. They settled her near the bow and then Robin leaned out to untie the line and release them. Once he'd done that, he took hold of Cheryl's hand again.

'He didn't ruin my life.' For once, Cheryl spoke loud enough to be heard clearly, even above the engine noise. 'He gave me friends.'

Chapter 89

Tara watched Tug steer them away from the pontoon. She wanted to ask how he knew which way to go, but the engine was loud and already they were bouncing uncomfortably on the waves. Out of the protection of the harbour, the sea had grown big again.

St Helen's, she knew, was one of the most northerly of the Isles of Scilly and so she guessed he'd be taking them in a southerly direction, but the other islands were nothing more than low, hazy shapes on the horizon. Somehow, though, she wasn't afraid. She trusted Tug to get them home safely. It was as simple as that.

Another sound, louder than their engines, drew all their attention. She looked back, sensing the others do the same, and saw the white helicopter rise over St Helen's.

The chopper turned north-east and vanished into the cloud.

Chapter 90

Logan Quick caught sight of the RIB with its seven passengers a second before he entered the low cloud cover. It would be at St Mary's long before he reached Exeter, but he figured it would take time for them to share their stories with officialdom, for the authorities at St Mary's to run the various checks and counterchecks and consult their superiors on the mainland. The chances were slim of there being anything to hold him up at Exeter Airport, to prevent his chartered flight to the Channel Islands taking off. From Jersey he planned to fly to Switzerland where he hoped Lauren would join him. He was leaving her more than enough money to divorce Thomas.

He had lawyers waiting for him in Switzerland, as well as one of the best private clinics in Europe. The events of the last few days had entailed keeping a clear head, but now he could look forward to the morphine again. He'd spend his last months in the foothills of the alps alongside the woman with whom he'd found solace over the course of the past year.

Logan had loved one woman in his life, and she'd been lost to him many years before. Shelley. He didn't expect to see her again, he'd never believed in an afterlife, but the thought that death would no longer separate them was comforting in its way.

He wondered, for a moment, whether Thomas might become a problem. When he learned his wife was leaving him, that she and his best friend had been having an affair for months, he'd be pissed off. But there was nothing he could say without incriminating himself, and he too was being left enough money to soften the blow.

His kids, he was sure, would adopt Cobalt.

Through occasional breaks in the cloud, Logan could see the ocean, steel grey and choppy beneath him. The wind was picking up but that would work in his favour. He'd be at Exeter in no time.

The next day, he would issue the necessary instructions that left the bulk of his estate to the eleven weird and wonderful good causes he'd found on an idle internet search. The 501st Legion was his favourite, a charity that brought together *Star Wars* enthusiasts to participate in costume-based local fundraising, but he also had a soft spot for Be a Dear and Donate a Brassiere, an organisation that distributed bras to women who were homeless or living in poverty. None of the charities he'd name could even begin to cope with the money he was leaving them, of course. More chaos left in his wake.

The Critter Connection, that was another. For fuck's sake, who'd set up a charity for neglected or abandoned guinea pigs? These people deserved to be messed with. He was laughing as he adjusted course ten degrees to the east.

It happened in an instant.

First, the engine sound changed from a loud, steady roar to that of metal parts clanging together. Then he began to spin. And fall.

Logan recognised the problem at the same moment he realised it wasn't merely mechanical failure. His tail rotor had been deliberately sabotaged. *How?* was his last thought. *How the hell had they done it?*

The ocean opened its mouth and swallowed him whole.

Chapter 91

Sabri spent the ferry crossing on deck. She'd seen more than enough of the sea to last a lifetime, but she didn't want to delay a second in spotting her family, waiting on the dock. Tara, bless her heart and rich husband, had bought a phone at St Mary's and passed it around the group. Jason and the kids had been worried to death about her after so many hours of radio silence, but they were absolutely fine and would meet her at Plymouth. They didn't give a toss that she'd given the token back, all they wanted was her home again. They wanted to go back to normal.

Sabri felt a hand on her shoulder and turned to see Robin. His hair blew in the wind and he smelled of the sea, but she imagined they all did. Around his neck hung the black binoculars she remembered from the yacht.

'Finished eating?' she asked.

He grinned. 'Charlie and Cheryl were making their way through the dessert menu when I left. The others are on their way up.'

He passed her the binoculars.

'Did you nick them?' Sabri asked.

'Bastard owes us something.' Robin blinked in the sunshine. 'Even if it is just an early glimpse of some friendly faces.'

Sabri fixed the binoculars on the distant land, but it was still too far away to see anything much.

'They're going to get away with it, aren't they?' she said. 'Quick, Thomas, that woman, what was her name?'

'Lauren,' Robin reminded her. 'And probably.'

After their uneventful arrival at St Mary's the group had attempted to contact the local police. It had taken a while: the police station was only open for a couple of hours every morning and the telephone number took them straight to a voice message. Eventually, though, they'd given their story to a bemused young constable.

Sceptical at first, especially as he'd never heard of the personal locator beacons Tug told him could have enabled both Quick and Thomas to be picked up out of the water, even in a storm, he'd finally been sufficiently convinced to take statements and pass them on to his superiors on the mainland. Someone, he'd told them, would be in touch.

'What I don't get,' he'd kept repeating, 'is why? Why would Logan Quick leave you these tokens, only to lure you out here and try to kill you all? It makes no sense.'

Acting on Holly's advice, they'd said nothing about the accident thirty years ago. All had insisted they had no idea why Quick had singled them out in the way he had.

'Quick will be miles away by now,' Robin said. 'As for the other two, we don't even know if Thomas and Lauren were their real names.'

Movement behind Sabri told her the others had arrived. They spread out around her, all leaning against the rail. Charlie climbed up onto the first rung and was quickly pulled back down by his mother and Tug.

'Can you see anything?' Charlie asked her.

Sabri scanned the railings surrounding the waiting area on the dock. There they were. The kids all intent on their phones, of course, but Jason staring out at the white ship heading his way. He couldn't see her, it wasn't possible at that distance, but she lifted her hand all the same.

'I think your mum's on the dock,' she told Cheryl, before handing over the binoculars. She'd caught a glimpse of a large woman in her seventies standing at Jason's side.

'Yes, I can see her.' Cheryl didn't sound overly keen on the idea of meeting her mum. 'She's talking to a woman in black leather.'

'What?' Robin grabbed the binoculars from Cheryl. 'Bloody hell,' he muttered under his breath.

'What is it, a reception party?' Tug was standing directly behind Sabri, tall enough to see even over her shoulder. 'You expecting anyone?' he went on, and Sabri glanced back to see Tara at his side.

'Not unless they're psychic,' she replied, and the two of them stepped a little apart, intent only on each other.

'Can I have a look? Robin, can I see, please?'

Reluctantly, it seemed, Robin handed the binoculars to Charlie.

The boy focused the glasses. Then, 'It's Coffie. Mum, Coffie's come to meet us.'

'I don't think so, sweetheart.' Holly looked oddly sad. 'He wouldn't even know we're coming back.'

'He does. I called him. Tara let me use her phone. I told him everything.'

'Is Coffie a very tall, good-looking Black guy in a sharp suit?' Sabri asked.

The younger woman's face transformed. 'I guess,' she replied.

Charlie was waving frantically. 'It is him.' He passed the binoculars to his mum. 'Isn't it?' he pressed her. 'Isn't that Coffie?'

Holly held the binoculars up to her face. For a second or two, she stood as still as stone. Then, Sabri saw a tear appear from under the black plastic rim and roll slowly down her face.

Chapter 92

The Guardian, 30 October
Sally Grant writes: Lay Off Holly Baker

The hounding of personal injury barrister and single mum Holly Baker, possible beneficiary of Logan Quick's controversial will, has gone too far. What has this young woman done, for heaven's sake? Put herself through university? Chosen a professional field that will help others rather than be financially rewarding for herself? Support, entirely alone, a young son with autism and a seriously ill father? When the household budget didn't add up (spoiler, it was never going to) she used her natural beauty and sensuality to provide an entirely legal service to consenting adults. Her clients were more than happy (I've heard of no complaints) and she paid her bills. Where's the harm?

How much of the bile thrown her way in the last week, on mainstream as well as social media, reflects the sanctimonious smugness of those who've never faced the struggles she has; or ill-concealed envy that no one would pay good money to see us naked?

Rumours abound that Ms Baker was being blackmailed by an old friend (who needs enemies?) and that her refusal to pay up led to her public outing. Devon and Cornwall Police have declined to comment on an open case and Ms Baker herself is staying tight-lipped. But if any good is to come of this mess, let it be a warning to potential blackmailers: other people's secrets, however salacious, are not your cash cows.

Shining a possible light on Holly's horizon, her local MP, Sarah Leaming, believes social services should be able to pick up some of the bills for her father's care going forward. So, even if Logan Quick's controversial will brings no financial gain to Ms Baker and her fellow token recipients (she and they are still insisting they gave the tokens back), things might be looking a little easier in the Baker household in future.

Chapter 93

The Telegraph, 17 November.

Speculation is rife today, as solicitors acting for the late billionaire Logan Quick are preparing to read his last will and testament at their offices in Exeter. Reclusive businessman Quick, who had been suffering from terminal cancer, died last month in a helicopter crash off the coast of Cornwall. He was alone on board.

Weeks before his death, in a move that made headlines around the world, Quick announced that he was leaving the bulk of his fortune to seven people from the southwest, all of whom had been sent what was described as a token. Shortly afterwards, the seven were named as Trevor Winter, fifty-five, a retired seaman; Tara Webb, fifty-five, a former nurse; wedding planner Robin Knight, fifty-two; Craig Lewis, fifty-four, a retired fireman; ambulance driver Sabri Carter, fifty-four; Cheryl Young, fifty-one, a carer, and personal injury barrister Holly Baker, thirty. All seven token recipients have denied any previous relationship with Logan Quick.

The cause of Logan Quick's helicopter crash remains a mystery. While Quick's body was quickly recovered from the sea, it is believed the wreckage is unlikely ever to be found. As conditions on the day were more than suitable for the short flight, most commentators have assumed either pilot error (most likely, given Mr Quick's state of health) or mechanical failure.

Amanda Quick, Logan Quick's ex-wife and his two children, Ludo and Coco, are not expected to attend today's reading. A source, who asked not to be named, informed the Telegraph that Quick previously set up trust funds for his children along with similar funds for several valued staff members, and that they are not will beneficiaries.

In spite of six of the recipients insisting that the tokens were voluntarily returned to Mr Quick and that they no longer consider themselves beneficiaries, all are expected to attend the offices of Barker, Momen and Dodds today. The whereabouts of the seventh, Craig Lewis, are presently unknown and all attempts by the Telegraph to trace him have failed.

The reading will take place at 11 a.m.

Chapter 94

Holly looked in dismay at the media scrum surrounding the entrance of Barker, Momen and Dodds. Many of them were familiar faces; these last couple of weeks she'd felt she was almost on first-name terms with half the world's paparazzi.

Shortly after arriving home from the Isles of Scilly, she'd come clean about her escort work to her head of chambers and to Charlie's father. After allowing themselves several days to mull it over, chambers had decided to be supportive. She'd avoid court appearances for the foreseeable future, confining her work to behind-the-scenes support for her colleagues and allow time for any fuss to die down. There'd be some impact on her income, but all things considered it could have been a lot worse. Nor did it seem there was anything to fear from Tim. Belinda was pregnant, it turned out, with IVF-conceived twins, and both she and Tim had made it clear they'd neither of them welcome a challenging ten-year-old into the family. Conscious that he might not come out of the whole business well, Tim had even offered to start regular maintenance payments.

The two worst threats dealt with, Holly and Coffie had met with Chris, telling him in no uncertain terms that no more money would be forthcoming and that if he did betray her, they'd get the police involved. News had leaked, days later, but so far the internet website that had run the story was declining to name their source. Privately, the police weren't confident about a successful prosecution.

Outside the offices, an attempt had been made, by means of rope and a chain of black-clad security guards, to create a clear walkway to the doors, but zoom lenses and mics on long poles leered into the space like raptors ready for a feeding frenzy.

'Turn round,' Holly told Coffie. 'Drive us home. Better still, take Charlie to school. I should never have agreed to this.'

'No way.' Charlie started banging on the car window. 'Tug's here. Look, in that black car. It's Tug.'

Entrance to the car park was being carefully controlled. A man in a high-viz jacket exchanged a few words with Coffie and they were allowed through. Charlie was still trying to attract Tug's attention.

'You've got competition in the hero-worship department,' Holly muttered.

Coffie lifted his sunglasses a fraction so that he could peer at her beneath them. 'With Charlie or both of you? Because one I can cope with. The other, not so much.'

Holly looked away before he could see her blushing. 'You two look like extras from *Men in Black*,' she grumbled.

Charlie, who would have been out of the car already had it not been for Coffie's child locks, was dressed, like his hero, in a three-piece suit with black sunglasses. She couldn't afford it, but he'd begged and begged and in the end she'd thought, sod it. Her son had to start taking priority over her parents. It was that simple.

'They won't let either of you in the meeting,' she warned, as Coffie parked the car. 'Token recipients only.'

'We're your bodyguards,' Charlie said. 'In case those punks try anything again. Coffie, will you let me out already?'

The child locks were released, and they all climbed out. Cameras started clicking and the mass of onlookers surged forward.

'Step aside,' Coffie drawled, as he and Charlie took up their positions on either side of Holly. Seriously, had the bozos rehearsed this?

'Let the men come through,' Charlie growled.

Better get it over with. Holly, and the two men she loved, set off across the car park.

'Never a dull moment,' Tug said, as he and Tara walked past security. A lot of security.

'I quite liked my dull life,' Tara replied. 'Well, some of it.'

'We'll get it back.' Tug took her hand as they made for the stairs.

The night before, she'd amazed him by saying she'd decided to sell her house.

'I've been clinging on to my old life.' She'd waited for the ad break before dropping her bombshell. 'It's time to build a new one.'

With me? He'd wanted to ask it, hadn't quite had the nerve.

'Something smaller will be much easier,' she went on. 'A spare bedroom for when the boys want to stay and a garage or something I can use as a studio. A bit of a garden might be nice.'

'Got anywhere in mind?' he asked, conscious that his heart was beating painfully hard.

'Actually,' she'd said, 'I was thinking of Dittisham.'

'I can't believe you gave that token back,' Sheila grumbled, as the car pulled up outside the solicitors' offices. 'What possessed you to do such a thing? Very nice car, though. I could get used to this.'

'I don't advise it,' Cheryl said, as an engine roared loud and insistent behind them and she turned to see Robin and his biker girlfriend glide into the car park. 'It's gone, Mum. We won't inherit anything.'

'So why are we here? Why did they insist we come?'

'They didn't insist you came.' Cheryl smiled to herself. 'Only me.'

Her mother grunted.

'Holly thinks it's about closing the case,' Cheryl went on. 'Confirming that we no longer have the tokens, so the money will go elsewhere. They may ask us to sign something saying we accept we're no longer beneficiaries. Then they'll make a public announcement. It will all be over soon.'

Their driver got out and walked round to open Sheila's door. 'Do you need a hand, Mrs Young?' Cheryl heard him say, as Robin and Jax made their way over.

Robin had got even better looking these last few weeks, Cheryl reflected. He'd grown a short beard and his hair was longer, making him look even more like the pirate Tug insisted on calling him. So glamorous, these new friends of hers.

But Cheryl was feeling better about herself too. She'd lost four pounds and Sabri and her daughters were teaching her the art of charity-shop dressing. It was amazing the bargains you could pick up, especially when you were a bit of a plus size. Not that she intended to be that for much longer. A pound a week, Sabri had told her, that was sensible, sustainable weight loss.

The driver opened Cheryl's door.

Smoothing down her new dress, originally from Hobbs in a dark cherry red, a fraction of the price second hand, Cheryl got to her feet. If this was to be her last taste of the highlife, she was going to enjoy it.

'Thank you all for coming,' Joe Caiger began.

Robin winked at Cheryl, who turned as red as her dress. She has a crush on you, Jax had warned him the night before, but the truth was, Cheryl had a crush on all of them, even little Charlie and the Carter kids. She'd lived with no company but her mother for far too long.

The tables in the firm's conference room had been arranged in a square. Robin and Cheryl were sitting directly opposite Caiger. Sabri and Holly were to their left, Tara and Tug on their right.

As they'd been warned, only the six of them had been allowed into the conference room; Jax and the others were waiting outside. There were gaps visible through the blinds, though, and more than once, Robin had caught sight of eyes, at roughly the height of a ten-year-old boy, peering in at them.

There were a lot of security guards present; almost as though Logan Quick's entire fortune was somewhere in the building.

Caiger, at the front of the room, was flanked by four of his colleagues, three of them male, the other a woman. All looked older than Caiger, maybe senior partners in the firm, but Robin guessed he shouldn't be surprised by the formalities. Logan Quick's will would have been a big deal, even if it hadn't been quite so eccentric. On the table, directly in front of the man to Caiger's left, sat a slim, black briefcase.

'I appreciate these last few weeks have been difficult,' Caiger went on.

'No shit, Sherlock,' Tug muttered, earning himself a frown from Tara.

'So, I'm sure you'll all appreciate the chance to put the speculation to an end and move on with your lives,' Caiger said.

'Actually, we've already done that,' Tug said.

Robin had known the big guy wouldn't be able to keep his trap shut. Say nothing we don't have to, Holly had repeated, when they'd all got together earlier in the week. And certainly nothing about the accident thirty years ago.

As they'd expected, the police had been unable to find either Thomas or Lauren and the boat, *Gemini*, had vanished completely; joined the hundreds of other wrecked ships around the Scillies, had been Tug's guess.

After a slight frown of disapproval at Tug's interruptions, Caiger cleared his throat. 'Mr Quick's will is very short and very clear. Having previously made generous financial arrangements for his ex-wife, his children and his staff, his entire remaining fortune is to be shared between the seven individuals who are currently in possession of the tokens. For the avoidance of doubt, these are the same tokens that were previously sent to Mr Trevor Winter, Mr Robin Knight, Mr Craig Lewis, Mrs Tara Webb, Mrs Sabri Carter, Miss Cheryl Young and Miss Holly Baker. They are of a unique construction, built by a process that has never been made public, and their authenticity can be easily verified.'

Tug gave an ostentatious yawn.

'Mr Quick's residual fortune, after the various trusts for the benefit of family members, inheritance tax and our own fees, will be in the region of four billion pounds. You'll all shortly be very wealthy people. My congratulations.'

'Before you get carried away, mate,' Tug said. 'You should know we were telling the truth when we said we no longer have the tokens. We gave them back. You'll probably find them somewhere in his house on St Helen's. Maybe you can claim the money.'

Caiger paused for a moment.

'We anticipated this,' he said, and looked to the man at his left. 'Because there's been a development.'

A development?

The man on Caiger's left was unlocking the briefcase. Sabri watched him open it and take out a short stack of cream-coloured envelopes. They'd been tied together with a narrow red ribbon, and they looked identical to the one she'd received just a few weeks ago. When all this had started.

Untying the ribbon, the man got to his feet and proceeded to walk around the room, stopping first behind Tara and placing one of the envelopes on the table directly in front of her. Tara stared at it, almost as if she expected it to move by itself. Tug received the next envelope and then the man moved around the table corner to place envelopes in front of Robin and Cheryl.

Sabri smelled his aftershave, a strong combination of pine and citrus, as he leaned over Holly's shoulder.

'Please, nobody touch them,' Holly called out.

Nobody did.

Sabri's own envelope, one that had her name handwritten in capital letters, the address care of Barker, Momen and Dodds, appeared in front of her and then the lawyer moved back to his original seat. Apart from Holly's interruption, the sequence had taken place in complete silence.

'I want confirmation of what they are, first,' Holly went on. 'Mr Caiger, what are these and what are we expected to do with them?'

'As you will see, they are unopened,' Caiger replied. 'So, we can't say for certain what they contain. But they came by registered post, with a covering note, explaining that they appertain to Mr Quick's will and that they should be handed out at the reading.'

'I want to consult my colleague,' Holly said, giving a quick glance around. 'I want to ask Coffie's advice. Are you happy for me to do that?'

One by one, the others nodded their agreement and Holly left the room.

'Why doesn't she want us to touch them?' Cheryl had pushed her chair away from the table and was staring at her own envelope as though it might bite her.

'She's worried we might compromise ourselves,' Sabri replied, although she really hadn't any idea.

'I was given a summons once,' Robin added. 'Once I'd touched it, it was deemed to be in my possession.'

Sabri looked towards the five lawyers at the head of the room. None of them were showing any sign of hearing the discussion taking place in front of them.

The door opened and Holly came back in.

'Coffie says it's a bit irregular, but then everything about this whole business is. He thinks that as we've all renounced our interest in Logan Quick's will, he can't see any way we can be harmed by this. He thinks we might as well open them.'

'If it explodes, I'm suing,' Tug announced, before sliding his finger beneath the envelope flap and ripping it open.

As Sabri's eyes fell to her own envelope, as she reached out to lift it up, she heard the soft clang of something metal landing on the tabletop.

'How did this happen?' she heard Tug say.

Sabri pulled out a sheet of A4-size paper before upturning the envelope. A token fell out.

'Mine's the same,' she heard Tara say. 'Number five. This is my token.'

'Mine too,' Cheryl replied. 'Number six.'

Sabri opened the letter. The wording was all too familiar. *This is your token . . .*

It wasn't quite the same, though, not as pristine as the original letter, and it hadn't been signed.

'What does this mean?' Cheryl asked.

'It means if Quick didn't have time to change his will, we inherit after all,' Tug replied.

'Jesus,' Sabri heard Robin say.

'We can't,' Holly jumped in. 'I don't want anyone getting carried away. We had to have been in possession of the tokens when Logan Quick died. We weren't. He died the day we all went to St Helen's. After we'd given them back.'

'That may or may not be the case,' Caiger replied. 'But his death was only officially declared four days later when his body was found. By that time, the envelopes had already arrived and been registered here. So, even though none of you were aware of it, they were returned to your possession then.'

'We've discussed this at length.' Finally, one of Caiger's colleagues, the same man who'd handed around the envelopes, spoke. 'And consulted legal counsel. There is no doubt in any of our minds that the will stands. And that the six of you are the beneficiaries. Once again, congratulations.'

Sabri wondered if she was going to be sick. Out of the corner of her eye she saw Cheryl clasp her hands to her face.

'There were seven tokens,' Tug pointed out. 'One of them was sent to Craig Lewis, also known as Logan Quick himself. Who's got the seventh?'

The men at the front exchanged glances.

'The current holder of token number three has been in contact with us,' Caiger explained. 'He preferred not to attend this meeting, but he does intend to claim his seventh share of the inheritance.'

'We appreciate that this news will come as something of a shock,' his colleague said. 'And while none of you are our clients, we think it not remiss of us to give you some very general advice. Do nothing in a hurry. Take some time. Miss Jennings and Mr Bridgman are our trusted financial advisors and are willing to give you immediate financial advice should you need it. They can be at your disposal over the next few days.'

The woman and her colleague gave unsmiling but not entirely unfriendly nods around the room.

'We've also taken the liberty of booking a private house on the edge of the national park,' Caiger said. 'We recommend that you all stay there for the next few days. Take some time, get used to the idea, consult our advisors. We can arrange for any family members to join you by the end of the day.'

He glanced left and right, and then all five of the lawyers got to their feet.

'We'll give you some time,' the senior partner said.

Tara and Tug were the last to leave the offices of Barker, Momen and Dodds. As they waited in the reception area for their car to arrive, she was conscious of all eyes around watching them: the security guards, still in their flanking positions; the receptionists behind the front desk; the staff members in the main work area beyond the glass walls. All were trying to be discreet, but Tara could feel their collective gazes burning into her shoulders. She moved a little closer to Tug, as though his bulk could shelter her from them.

This was how her life was going to be from now on. Always the object of curiosity. Public property.

Outside, the last car pulled up and the security guard in charge nodded to Tug. Time to go.

Taking advice from Holly and her boyfriend, the six of them had agreed to spend the next few days in the hideaway the firm were providing for them. The Carter family would be driven over that evening. They needed time, Coffie argued, to take everything in; to think through the implications of what the sudden influx of money would mean. Above all, they needed to be together.

'It couldn't have been Quick himself,' she said, as Tug joined her on the back seat and the car doors closed. 'He left the house before we did. We saw his helicopter take off.'

'That git would never have sent them,' Tug replied, as the car started to move, and Tara turned away to avoid the flash of camera lenses. 'The last thing he wanted was his six arch enemies benefiting from his will. All he ever wanted was to fuck us up.'

'Maybe he has,' Tara said. Four billion pounds. It was untold wealth.

'Resisting the temptation of Scotch at five hundred quid a bottle won't be any harder than saying no to Asda vodka,' Tug replied. 'I've bigger problems than Logan Quick's billions to worry about.'

He reached out and took hold of her hand. 'And there are things I want that money can't buy.'

Tara let herself lean against him. 'I guess we'll cope,' she said.

Chapter 95

From the top of the stairs overlooking the main entrance of Barker, Momen and Dodds, Thomas watched Tara and Tug leave the building.

He'd been sorely tempted to keep all six tokens, the morning his so-called best mate had left his home on St Helen's, and his time on earth, for good. And when the seventh and last had arrived, FedExed over by Robin Knight, it had seemed fate was taking a hand.

But Lauren had argued that one would be more than enough, especially given the settlements Logan had already made to them both. More to the point, she'd been spot on when she said the two of them would find it much easier to stay under the radar if all attention remained on the six people who'd already become overnight media stars. The whole world was talking about Tug, Tara, Robin and the others; few people had even heard of Thomas and Lauren. She was right. She was always right.

Sometimes Lauren scared him. Her willingness to go along with killing six people, not to mention abducting a kid, had unnerved him. She'd been the one to investigate how helicopters could most easily be sabotaged. And then there'd been her ability to wrap Logan entirely around her finger. Much of what had been done the last few weeks of his life had been her idea, rather than his. And Logan had had no idea that, throughout, her loyalty had remained with her husband.

At least, he hoped it had.

Epilogue

Sabri resigned from her job as a paramedic. She and her husband now run the Carter Trust, providing funds for young women of colour and those from a disadvantaged or immigrant background to train as doctors. Their eldest daughter, Maddy, is applying to medical school. They don't expect her to be offered a place, she's simply not as bright as her mother, but her fifth choice is to study nursing at Birmingham. Sabri thinks Maddy will make an excellent nurse.

Cheryl and Sheila are in the process of booking their next cruise. Sheila likes the idea of the British Virgin Islands, but Cheryl's preference is for the Far East. The ultimate decision will be Cheryl's of course, her mum perfectly understands that, but Cheryl suspects she'll probably opt for the Caribbean. Her mum won't be around for that much longer and letting her have her own way isn't such a big deal anymore.

Tara and Tug moved to Dittisham. When they're not swimming or sailing, Tara is preparing for her first exhibition and Tug spends his time hunting down former servicemen who've fallen on hard times. He and Charlie devise ever more devious ways of transferring much-needed funds without the recipients having any idea who their benefactors are.

Charlie started his new secondary school a few weeks ago and has more friends than he knows what to do with. Holly worries that the half who aren't motivated by his mother's money are intrigued by her reputation as a former call girl. Hormones are pumping in boys of eleven rising twelve and she's unnerved by some of the glances she gets when Charlie's friends come to the house. Coffie, ever unflappable, tells her to chill. When it comes to friends, Charlie is more than capable of sorting the wheat from the chaff, and at least now he has a big enough pool to fish in.

Coffie and Holly plan to get married in the spring. They're hoping Robin will officiate, but as he and Jax haven't been heard of for some months – the last communication came from somewhere in the Pakistan mountains, she isn't sure he'll be back in time.

Thomas and Lauren's whereabouts are unknown.

Acknowledgements

First and foremost, my sincere and heartfelt thanks to my wonderful editor, Sam Eades. Over the course of eight books, she has been at my side, guiding my steps and cheering me on. She has been insightful, diligent and always diplomatic; her advice has kept me on the straight and narrow more than once and I will miss her more than words can say.

Next, I guess, is my equally great agent, Anne Marie Doulton of the Ampersand Agency. If I ever lose her, I'll try to wax just as lyrical; frankly though, if that were to happen, I'm not sure I could go on.

Andy Burtenshaw and Paul Barker have been invaluable in making sure the nautical detail in *The Token* is as correct as the demands of a thriller can allow it to be. Any mistakes are a) mine and b) deliberate.

Thanks also to Charlotte Mursell, Leodora Darlington, Aoife Datta, Lucy Cameron, Paul Stark and Anshuman Yadav at Orion Fiction and to Rosie and Jessica Buckman at the Buckman Agency.

Credits

Sharon Bolton and Orion Fiction would like to thank everyone at Orion who worked on the publication of *The Token* in the UK.

Editorial
Sam Eades
Charlotte Mursell
Leodora Darlington

Copy editor
Francine Brody

Proofreader
Holly Kyte

Audio
Paul Stark
Louise Richardson
Georgina Cutler-Ross

Contracts
Rachel Monte
Ellie Bowker
Tabitha Gresty

Design
Charlotte Abrams-Simpson
Nick Shah

Deborah Francois
Helen Ewing

Editorial Management
Anshuman Yadav
Charlie Panayiotou
Jane Hughes
Bartley Shaw

Finance
Jasdip Nandra
Nick Gibson
Sue Baker
Tom Costello

Marketing
Lucy Cameron

Production
Ruth Sharvell
Katie Horrocks

Publicity
Aoife Datta

Sales
Dave Murphy
Esther Waters
Victoria Laws
Group Sales teams across
Digital, Field, International and
Non-Trade

Operations
Group Sales Operations team

Rights
Rebecca Folland
Tara Hiatt
Ben Fowler
Maddie Stephens
Ruth Blakemore
Marie Henckel

Dear Reader,

We'd love your attention for one more page to tell you about the crisis in children's reading, and what we can all do.

Studies have shown that reading for fun is the **single biggest predictor of a child's future life chances** – more than family circumstance, parents' educational background or income. It improves academic results, mental health, wealth, communication skills, ambition and happiness.[1]

The number of children reading for fun is in rapid decline. Young people have a lot of competition for their time. In 2024, 1 in 10 children and young people in the UK aged 5 to 18 did not own a single book at home.[2]

Hachette works extensively with schools, libraries and literacy charities, but here are some ways we can all raise more readers:

- Reading to children for just 10 minutes a day makes a difference
- Don't give up if children aren't regular readers – there will be books for them!
- Visit bookshops and libraries to get recommendations
- Encourage them to listen to audiobooks
- Support school libraries
- Give books as gifts

There's a lot more information about how to encourage children to read on our website: **www.RaisingReaders.co.uk**

Thank you for reading.

---

[1] National Literacy Trust, Book Ownership in 2024, November 2024
https://nlt.cdn.ngo/media/documents/Book_ownership_in_2024

[2] OECD. 2021. 21st-century readers: developing literacy skills in a digital world. Paris, France: OECD Publishing.
https://www.oecd.org/en/publications/21st-century-readers_a83d84cb-en.html